Angie
&
Debra

Part two of the Lyndford story

Angie
&
Debra

Part two of the Lyndford story

Francis John Simcock

Autumn and summer
Are gone long ago
Earth is dry at the centre.
But spring a new comer,
A spring rich and strange
Shall make the winds blow.

Alfred Lord Tennyson – Nothing will die

YouCaxton Publications

24 High Street, Bishop's Castle, Shropshire. SY3 8JX
www.youCaxton.co.uk

Published in Great Britain by
Francis John Simcock

ISBN 978-1-909644-02-1

Cover Montage by YouCaxton from original artwork by Betty James

Set in Adobe Garamond Pro.

Printed and bound in Great Britain.

Introduction

This story was inspired by an event in a family well known to the writer. However, the characters and happenings in the book and others in the Lyndford series are completely fictional. Anyone kind enough to read it, and anxious to relate its locations to places on the ground or the map will not need to be a genius, if he or she has any knowledge of Shropshire and the Welsh Marches, to identify "The Junction" and "Bishops Keep." But Lyndford itself, like its inhabitants, exists only in the imagination of

Francis John Simcock   2011

One

The girl in the lane

At first I thought it was a deer, or a calf, perhaps even a big dog, lying on the side of the lane and picked out vaguely by my car's ancient headlights. But as I slowed down, I saw two human feet just off the tarmac. I stopped the car, left the lights on and the engine running. The unshod feet were on the ends of a pair of denim-clad legs belonging to a not very big human being, apparently female, whose head was a foot lower, in the ditch. I got the impression I was looking at a corpse, until I heard a faint moan. I squatted down to take a closer look and saw a cut, still bleeding, reaching from ear to chin on a sepia-toned face. I fetched a rug from the car, to put round the woman, girl or whatever she was, for it was a cold October night and her clothing seemed pretty unsubstantial.

She was warm, and I could feel her heart beating. But I also saw more. She was bleeding through her thin button-down shirt, all she seemed to have on above the waist. And I thought I saw heavy bruising, on her face, round her neck and down her side as I undid the shirt to examine the wound. It was ghastly – a raw gash, 12 inches long, all along her ribs. She was obviously urgently in need of medical attention. I spoke to her, softly, but there was no response. Could I get her into the car without exacerbating the damage, I wondered. Should I leave her there while I went for help, found a phone and sent for an ambulance? I knelt down beside her, trying to ascertain how strong her breathing and pulse were.

Then I saw headlights coming along the lane, quite quickly. But the car or whatever it was stopped a hundred and fifty yards away, no doubt when the driver saw my own rear lights. Almost immediately, it started to back away, and I heard it reverse into a field gateway and go off again, the driver's foot hard on the accelerator, it seemed to me. What on earth was that all about? The only houses along the lane, barely wide enough for one vehicle and with "tarmac" not much more than a courtesy description for the surface, were my cottage, its empty neighbour and the farm, a quarter-mile further on, before it threaded through the forest via a roughish track. Could the car be anything to do with the girl? My neighbours at the farm were away, and anyway they wouldn't have behaved like that. More likely poachers or even a courting couple looking for a remote spot, but still, you never knew. I decided I must get her away from where she was.

The obvious right thing to do was to get her straight to a doctor. The local cottage hospital was only two miles away. Or I could take her with me until I found a phone and summoned expert help. And that was the course I decided upon – either phone or hospital, whichever showed up first.

I opened a back door of my 15-year-old Austin, for once pleased with its age which meant easy access and a big back seat. I picked up the girl - she was light enough - and lifted her as gently as I could through the door, the rug still round her. But she screamed - a cry of panic, or pain, or terror - and as I laid her on the seat she tried to hit me, and the scream turned to sobbing words .

"No, no, no..." I heard, before she passed out again.

I started to drive on towards the town, but I'd not gone more than two hundred yards when I heard and felt her moving about. I got out and opened the rear door. She was clawing desperately at the back of the seat, as though she was trying to fight her way out. As she saw me, she screamed again and shouted.

"No, no, never, can't make me," I think was what I heard. And: "Oh, Mama, Mama." Before she seemed to lose consciousness again.

The way she had been throwing herself about made me decide I had to change my plan. Even the perfunctory look I'd given her injuries made it obvious she must not be allowed to carry on in that way. I acted quickly, while she was still quiet. I was going to take her to my cottage.

I turned round in another gateway, and at the cottage, I left her in the car while I unlocked the door. It was quite dark, so I quickly lit the kitchen lamp – electricity was still months, years away – and carried her in from the car. She moaned and struggled weakly, but I was able to take her through the kitchen and into the other downstairs room, which I used as my bedroom. I laid her on the bed and pulled the eiderdown over her. My mother had insisted on providing a couple of hot water bottles when I first took occupation, and I filled them from the kettle which was simmering on the hob of the kitchen range, and put them alongside her, before filling the kettle again.

I hardly knew what to do next. I must get that medical attention to her as quickly as possible. But by now I thought she was not in danger of dying, immediately, and if I could I should get her to a state where I could persuade her I was trying to help her, and to that end she must keep quiet and still. I could then resume my intention of taking her to hospital or the doctor.

I decided, rightly or wrongly, that I should try to get some liquid into her, and the best thing would be warm, sweet, tea. In the old adventure books, it was always whisky or brandy, but I'd read or been told somewhere that alcohol should not be used in this kind of circumstance. As soon as the kettle boiled, I made a pot, poured a cup, added sugar and milk, and with a teaspoon, tried to get some between her lips. I was pleased that she actually swallowed some, although with no other sign of returning to full consciousness.

I was about to turn my attention to looking at the wounds, when I thought the car outside would be better out of sight, just in case. The girl's outburst, her injuries, and the appearance and disappearance of the other car, had left me with the strong feeling that something nasty was going on. There was a track into the wood opposite, which would offer a degree of concealment, at night anyway, and I thought my motor would be better there. First though I decided I should have a weapon of some kind, so taking the only torch I had I went out, locking the door, and into the outhouse at the back, where there were some lengths of wood, waiting to be sawn into logs. I chose one and sawed a three-foot length from it, to make in effect a two-inch thick cudgel. Better than nothing, I thought, and thus armed took the motor off the road, using no lights and listening carefully as I returned to the house. But I heard nothing.

I had a small bottle of antiseptic, my mother's provision again and I put a measure into a big basin of hot water, found a clean face flannel, not too easy in my establishment, and returned to the bedroom, to set about cleaning the cuts, but as I wiped her face I noticed blood oozing through her short, curly, black hair, then bruises and swelling round her neck, under her jaw, and at the top of her chest. As I was swabbing the wound in her side my impression of more heavy bruising was confirmed, all down her body, and an ugly abrasion with blood seeping from it. I tried to roll her over, gently as I could, to see if there was more damage - there was, more bruising - and she screamed, and cried out: "No, Jerry, no, no..."

I thought: "You've got a broken rib, my girl, unless I'm mistaken." She moaned miserably as I turned her back again but I persisted, always trying to handle her gently. I found a sheet in my chest of drawers, old but perfectly clean, and tore a strip from it to make a bandage which I bound round her before buttoning the shirt again and undoing the top button of her jeans.

I had some canned soup in the kitchen, and I heated a tin, partly for myself and partly for the girl if she recovered enough to take it. I kept looking at her, and thought she was stirring slightly, and moaning, so I gave her another sip or two of tea, and this time, as she swallowed it, her eyes opened, wide, and she looked at me with something like horror.

I said: "It's alright, you're safe, nobody's going to hurt you. Just lie still. You're alright here...."

Her mouth opened as though she was trying to say something, but I tried again: "Don't try to talk. Just lie still and drink some more of this." I put the cup to her lips this time and she took some of it in.

I left her a moment while I dealt with the soup, some of which I put into a bowl and took to her, to see if she would take some. I put another pillow under her head, spoke to her and offered her a spoonful. She took it and tried to sit up, but sank back with another moan.

I said: "Don't try to get up. I can give you this where you are." Which I did, and eventually she took nearly half the soup, which I thought was a good sign. But it seemed to exhaust her, and I sat down beside the bed while I drank the rest of the soup myself, with a piece of bread and a cup of tea, in lieu of the pie and pint I'd been on my way for.

I stayed there for about half an hour, checking to make sure she was still breathing. I was still wondering what I ought to do about her, but I was reluctant to make any moves towards getting her into the car again before I was sure she knew what was happening, and would co-operate.

She showed no signs of returning to a normal waking state, but her breathing was stronger and more regular. I felt her heartbeat and that too seemed regular, and she felt warm. I again decided the best thing was to leave her be, so I put out the light in the kitchen and went outside as quietly as I could, locking the door as I went and listening for any untoward sounds, for five minutes or so. I heard nothing, the same when I edged round the corners of the house, and I went back in, leaving the kitchen still dark.

In the bedroom, she had started to moan again. I made more tea and as I put it to her lips she opened her eyes and looked straight at me.

"Thanks, man," she husked.

I said again: "Don't talk. Just stay quiet." But she showed increasing signs of becoming aware of what was around her. Her big brown eyes, full of sadness as well as pain, I thought, were roaming round the room, resting on me from time to time.

In another few minutes, she said: "Me side hurts. Did he cut it?"

"Somebody did, and I think you've got a broken rib," I said. "Do you know who it was?"

"'Course, it was one o' them two. An' that Jos, he hit me an' kicked me. Have you seen 'em?"

"No. They're not here, anyway. There's only me. Don't worry, I'll look after you."

"Thanks, man," she whispered again, but again, the few words seemed to have exhausted her and she lapsed back into silence and semi-consciousness, for best part of half an hour, during which I had taken another look and listen outside.

By now I'd come to the conclusion that she was in no immediate danger of dying, although certainly in urgent need of that medical attention.

I should get her to hospital, which would of course bring in the police. There had been a little fear in my mind that they would connect me, being me, with whatever crime had been committed against the girl but that was something I would have to deal with if it happened. The fear was in any case growing less as she talked, and accused "Jerry," whoever he was. I thought she would be alright where she was until morning, when perhaps she would be fit to travel. A questionable decision, no doubt, but I became pleased, later, that I made it.

It was by now ten o'clock. I went outside, to look and listen again, but heard nothing. It had started to rain, and felt colder. I put more wood on the fire, and tried to make myself a bed of sorts on the old wooden settle, in the kitchen, but first went to take another look at her – and was shocked to find the double bed empty. It was almost against the wall on the one side, and she was down behind it, moaning and sobbing.

"What are you doing there?" I asked, as I pulled the foot of the bed round so I could get at her. But she just squeezed further into the corner I created. I said: "Let me help you back on the bed." She sobbed: "Them's here. I heard 'em. Outside, man. Them'll get me. An' kill me this time, sure."

"They're not there," I said. "I've just been outside, and there's nobody there. Perhaps it was me you heard. Come and lie down on the bed. Look, I'll stay close to you. I won't go away. I won't let anyone touch you. Come on, please."

I must have given her a bit of confidence, for she allowed me to lift her - I tried to be as gentle as I could, but she winced and sobbed at every touch. I pulled the clothes over her and said: "Just lie still."

She sighed, obviously in pain. I asked : "How does your side feel?"

"Hurts, man," she said.

I said: "Yes, I bet it does. You can breathe alright, though, can't you? Take a deep breath and tell me where it hurts."

She did, and gasped.

"There, man," she said, pointing to her side.

I said: "I'm pretty sure there's a rib broken, or at least cracked, as well as that cut. You must just lie still and keep warm."

I had no medication of any kind, apart from some very mild pain killers. I gave her a couple, with another sip or two of tea. Otherwise all I could do was to add a blanket I'd taken from the bed upstairs to the quilt and refill the water bottles from the kettle I'd left simmering.

Taking my cudgel, I went outside again to take another look. I turned out both lamps to give the impression, I hoped, of going to bed, and waited a few moments before unlocking the door and easing back the bolts - I was glad I'd oiled them - and slipping outside. It had stopped raining, and I stayed perfectly still for minutes, but could not see, hear, feel or smell anything apart from the hoot of an owl and the fluttering of the bats which had come out from their home in the cottage's tiny cockloft.

Back inside, I relit a lamp. She was still tucked up in the bed, but moaning and sobbing.

I said: "Can you hear me?"

"Yes, man."

"I've been outside again and I can't hear a thing. I don't think there's anyone about. Do you want another drink, or some more soup?"

"Oh yes please. Tea. An' soup."

Whatever terrors were threatening her mentally, physically she was obviously better than she had been. I took the lamp into the kitchen and set about the food and drink. I propped her up a little which made her wince and cry out gently, but she took both liquids gratefully.

I said: "Now lie down again and sleep."

She said: "Don' go 'way, please."

"Don't worry, I won't," I assured her.

Poor little thing, wherever she was from, whoever she was, she didn't deserve to be treated the way she clearly had been. I sat down on the chair, by the bed, trying to work out possibilities. I still knew that the need for medical treatment was urgent. I started to try to talk to her about getting her to hospital, but she had taken me at my word and gone off to sleep – perhaps the painkillers were helping, mild as they were. Her sleeping made me start to wonder again whether I could get her to hospital. But it would mean retrieving the car from its woodland hideaway, and although I had not been able to detect anyone outside, I was by now so sure that she was the victim of some terrible foul play that despite having told her there was no-one around I could not feel 100 per cent certain that I was right. If there was anyone, they must see and hear me bringing the car to the gate, and transferring the girl to it would be the perfect opportunity for them to get at her. I decided to leave any action until morning, and continued to sit by the bed.

A couple of hours later, I'd nodded off, but woke to find myself cold and aching all over. She seemed to be sleeping. I decided there would be no harm in lying down on the old settle in the kitchen - it was after all no more than ten feet away. There was an old air force sleeping bag in the wardrobe, which I took out as quietly as I could and tried to make myself comfortable on the hard, narrow bench. But before I could get to sleep there was a scream from the bedroom.

I struggled out of the sleeping bag, grabbed my torch and the improvised cudgel and dashed into the bedroom. She was trying to sit up, her eyes wide, arms thrust out in front as though trying to fend someone off. I caught her hands, pushed her down as gently as I could.

"Ssh, ssh, it's alright, there's nobody here to hurt you. I won't let anyone hurt you," I said.

"Said you wouldn' go 'way," she accused me.

"I was only in the kitchen. I had to find somewhere to lie down."

"Stay here. So I feel safe. Can't you lie down here? Hold me hand, man."

I was touched by the way she seemed to have invested her confidence in me. The proprieties of lying on the bed beside her did not worry me, but there was not much spare room. I might hurt her if I started to thrash about, which I did at night sometimes. However, if it made her happier, that was how it should be. I fetched the sleeping bag, put the torch on the bedside table and leaned the stick against it, and climbed partly into the bag keeping one arm out so I could, as she asked, keep hold of her hand.

I didn't sleep for some time, but she seemed to go off immediately. As usual at the end of a semi-sleepless night, I dozed heavily near morning, waking as the dawn started to appear, about half-past six, it would be. I woke quickly, though, put my feet on the floor, still in the bag, shrugging them out to look at the girl. She was awake, but crying, softly.

"Does it hurt?" I asked.

"Yes. Sorry, man. Didn' wanna wake you."

"You didn't. But how do you feel? Where's it hurt most?"

"Me side. An' me neck hurts."

"Yes, well, we must get something done about all that, quickly. Would you like some breakfast, though, first? Could you eat something?"

"I don' know. But, er, mister, I need somethin' else. I s'pose you've got one, somewhere."

"Yes, but it's a bit primitive, and it's outside, down the garden. I don't think you should go outside, until I've done a bit of scouting round. There's a toilet bucket upstairs. I think it would be better if you used that. I'll fetch it down. But do you think you can get out of bed? You must be careful with that side."

"Guess so. P'raps you could help me."

I fetched the lidded pail downstairs and gave it a good wash at the kitchen tap - a decent cold water supply was about the only amenity the cottage possessed, at that stage. I took it into the bedroom, with a toilet roll, and a shirt of my own, much too big of course but hers was torn and bloody, and she made to get out of bed. I helped her, half lifting her, but with a few winces and gasps, she seemed to be able to stand.

"Shout if you need any more help," I said. I was pretty desperate for the same kind of thing, myself, but I didn't want to go outside until I'd told her what I was doing. I busied myself clearing out the fireplace, and lighting a new fire, and as I finished she shouted: "Mister!" I went in to find her sitting on the bed, panting and gasping. She'd put the lid on the bucket and I took it away and put it in the back kitchen, for the time being.

When I got back to her she said: "Please, d'you think I could wash me a bit?"

"Of course. It'll have to be in a bowl, I'm afraid. Wait five minutes and I'll have some hot water. But look, I'm going to go outside and have a look round, while it heats up. I shall go through this door and lock it after me. You stay there, or lie down. I won't be more than a couple of minutes."

I picked up my cudgel and went out, locking the door as I said. I first of all went down the garden to the privy, across the road to check on the car, which appeared in order, then all round the cottages, which took very little time. I could see nothing whatever to cause alarm. I went back in, prepared hot water, soap, facecloth and towel, took it into the bedroom and put it in front of her on the bedside table, while I took the opportunity to give myself a cold swill in the kitchen. Shaving would have to wait, for the time being

To my surprise, she appeared in the doorway, looking pretty groggy and leaning against the door jamb, and still wearing her own, damaged shirt.

"You shouldn't try to walk," I said. "Did you manage?"

"Yes. Thanks. Couldn' carry the water though. An' I can't get me shirt off."

"Do you want me to help you?"

"Yes, please, mister."

I eased the garment, gently as I could, over her head. She had nothing underneath it, not even a bra, a fact that would provide certain lawyers with ammunition in the future. But although her firm young breasts would have excited almost anyone in different circumstances, I was too concerned with her immediate well-being to be affected in that kind of way. I helped her into a polo shirt of my own.

"Lie down again. I'll see to those things."

"Couldn' I stay here. I can sit in that chair."

I helped her to the upright fireside chair, the only comfortable seat in the house, but it seemed to please her.

"What can you eat? I've got cereal, and eggs, and bacon."

"Have you got a banana?"

"I have. But look, I shall do three eggs, and plenty of bacon, so if you want any when you've eaten your banana there'll be some for you."

While I was preparing the food, I thought it was time a few formalities were established. I said: "We ought to know each other's names. Mine's Alastair - Alastair Jameson. Will you tell me yours?"

She hesitated. "Don' think I should. Might get you inter trouble."

"Look, we're going to a hospital, and they'll need to know your name. And we'll have to tell the police..."

I might have hit her across the face. She screamed : "Oh no, man, no, you can't tell them. You mus'n, you mus'n..."

I gave her time to calm down, then said: "Look, my dear, you need medical attention. That cut needs stitches, for a start, and if infection sets in it could kill you. And you must have an ex-ray, to make sure nothing's been damaged inside. And that cut on your face needs more attention than I can give it."

She stared at me pitifully: "Mister, I can't go to the police. You don't know..."

I said nothing. This was bloody awful, to say the least. I could not just do nothing about her injuries. But her protests had given me an idea. First, though, we should have something to eat. It would only take minutes, and we both needed it.

"Here's your banana. Would you like some cornflakes? Or anything else?"

"No thanks, man," she said, quiet again now. But as I finished cooking my eggs and bacon, I saw she was crying again.

I said, gently: "Won't you tell me your name, please. It can't do any harm for me to know that."

"Alright. It's Debra. Mister, don' tell the police. They'll send me back, an' I'll get killed, sure."

Two

Flight

Before we go any further, I think I should put myself into the picture, explain perhaps how I came to be living in a primitive country cottage in Shropshire. But it isn't any kind of idyllic scene I'll be painting.

My great grandfather on my father's side - his mother's father - was an aristocrat, a baronet; but about as useless and feckless a specimen of the breed as you could find in a year's search of Debretts and the society drinking dens of London and the South of France. My mother started life as kitchen maid to his daughter, my grandmother. They were wonderful women, both of them. My second and third cousins, Grandfather Rogerson's grandchildren, are still pretty useless. My father's father was a landowning squire, one of a long line, but most of those thousands of acres have gone.

He, my grandfather, must have been a strange individual. He hung himself after my father and mother were married - seems that although he was otherwise a good bloke he couldn't take his son and heir marrying a servant girl. My dad ended up with a very good job, however, and my brother and I both went to a posh public school. At the time I'm telling about, he, my brother, was on his way to a good level of business as a land and estate agent, making as much of a success of his life as I had made a mess of mine so far.

When I left school, we - Britain - were in the run-up to the war. Chamberlain was in the middle of his ineffectual attempts to stop Hitler having his evil way with the rest of Europe and everyone was hoping the war wouldn't happen. My father never had any illusions, though. He had gone all through the first war, and been badly wounded, and had watched the sting of defeat feeding the Nazis' ambitions.

There was some talk that I might go to Oxford. I'd done reasonably well in my matriculations, high grades in maths and English, and been quite decent at sport, and in those days you more or less walked into university with good results from a public school like Shrewsbury. But apart from anything else, I'd had enough of book study. I decided to join the RAF, not so much because the war was coming but because I wanted to learn to fly.

Dad agreed without too much demur – he'd done pretty well the same thing before the first war – although Mother was not too happy. I went to the recruiting office at Leicester, which was where we lived. Dad had charge of a big estate. I was assured that with my educational background I could soon make my way into the air however I joined, so to cut out delay and paperwork, I enlisted in the ranks. My uncle Giles started in the army that way and became something of a hero, like my dad. And believe it or not, in spite of my background, I was already somewhat at odds with being a member of the officer-cum-aristocracy class.

Square-bashing at Filey in Yorkshire was a bit hard-going, especially as we had a bloody-minded flight-sergeant who found I was from a public school and made me equal top target for his wit with a poor little sod who hardly knew his left from his right - goodness knows how he got into the RAF at all. But I got through it, and on passing-out day the flight-sergeant even shook my hand and said: "You done well, boy." Perhaps he wasn't quite so bloody-minded after all, although I've sometimes wondered what happened to the poor little sod.

I'd already applied to be considered for aircrew, and to train as a pilot if possible, and I was accepted. But my hope of becoming a fighter pilot was dashed because I was good at maths and came top of the navigation class in my pilot's exams, and I was more or less dragooned into the RAF college at Cranage as a flying navigational instructor. It left me a bit disappointed - although the pay was good - but probably saved my life during the war that was by then going full blast.

You see, I did so much flying that piloting a plane became second nature, which made all the difference when I eventually went operational, on bombing raids over Germany. So many of the poor kids had had only a few hours flying experience and had to concentrate so hard on piloting the thing, and finding their way, that they could not keep a proper lookout for enemy fighters or anti-aircraft fire. I had one or two narrow squeaks but only once did I think I and my crew were not going to make it, when one of our Whitley's engines was hit and caught fire. We were lucky, though. The whirring propellor put the fire out and we were able to limp home.

But I was also pressured into taking a commision, which marked the beginning of a downward slide. The warrant officers were a more sober lot, many of them a bit older, but the commissioned officers were around my own age, and lived it up pretty riotously, a natural reaction I suppose to the way they put their lives on the line every night or two. I joined in the high life, centred on the pubs round our Lincolnshire base, and kept it up for longer than a lot of them - they didn't survive as long as I did, poor devils.

I became pretty matey with a bloke called Steve Parrimore, who'd come into the bomber brigade with a reputation as a daredevil, in and out of the air. He'd been a Hurricane pilot in the Battle of Britain, shot down God knows how many Germans, but had transferred to Bomber Command because, he said, that was where the action was, in the later years of the war. He was a squadron leader, which you'd think would have meant he carried a degree of responsibility, but although he was a good organiser and the blokes thought the sun shone from his you-know-where, I think he'd almost got a screw loose, because he seemed to want to court danger, in and out of the air, and in and out of the air force, as I was to find out. But like me, he came through the hostilities unscathed, and we were demobbed together in the summer of 1946.

I went home to my parents for a few days, joining my younger brother Peter who'd also been in the RAF, and distinguished himself, ending up as a squadron leader at 24. There was a lot of discussion about what we were going to do. Dad wanted us both to qualify as land agents and surveyors and start a business, which he'd finance. Peter was all for it, but frankly I didn't want to know about studying and qualifying, or for that matter being stuck in some stuffy old office in a country town like Shrewsbury, which was where they had in mind. But before I had come to a decision, Steve rang from London, and said he'd like to talk to me about a proposition he'd got for me. I told Dad and Peter to count me out of their plan, and took off for the smoke.

I found Steve ensconced comfortably in a Notting Hill flat, in the company of a personable young lady who he introduced as Julia. He packed her off to "go and find us all some food, darling, and don't forget a bottle."

"She's a good kid, but she doesn't know anything about what I'm going to tell you, and it's better that she doesn't. Girls talk to other girls, and God knows where it goes from there," he said.

"It sounds very mysterious," I said.

"I think it's better that we keep it to ourselves. You'll see why in a minute."

"Go on."

"I'm on to a good thing, Ally, but I need help with it. No, not money" - seeing alarm bells ringing behind my eyes - "practical help.

"I know a chap who's bought a lot of war surplus stuff, for practically nothing, and he's taken me in on the deal. It's everything from electrical goods and clothing to radios and saucepans and even guns and ammo. He got it cheap because it's a bit - shall we say warm. Between ourselves, and this must be strictly between ourselves, it got 'lost' when our lot got out of Burma.

"My chap happened to be able to move it off quickly, in a ship he'd got an interest in, which was why he got it so cheap. The trouble was, the ship's captain was told he had to make space for some other cargo, so our stuff had to be unloaded, in Egypt, where it is now. It's quite safe, but not for too long - as soon as the wily wogs get wind of it, it'll start to disappear. We want to move it to this country, pronto, which is where you come in."

"Jimmy's got hold of a couple of Dakotas – another of his fiddles, I expect. I'm going to fly one, but we need another man with good flying experience, and preferably a good navigator. It's got to be someone who can be trusted so I thought of you."

I goggled: "Two Dakotas - however much stuff is there, for goodness sake?"

"Well, he tells me there's a couple of tons altogether, and some of it's pretty bulky. Jimmy says it's got to be moved in one go and one plane certainly won't take it all. The Dakotas are at an airfield in Norfolk that's not being used now. The idea is we pick them up there, fly out to Egypt and bring the stuff back to another airfield that's not operational, in Shropshire. We'll have to help do all the loading and unloading,and you and I will have to take the Daks back on our own."

I goggled some more. "Who the hell is this bloke, Steve? Is he British?"

"Sort of. He's Irish, and he can fly himself. And that's as much as I can tell you about him, Ally. Now, are you interested? The fee is five hundred quid, all in cash, although some of it might be dollars."

I sat up and took notice. That was real money.

"It sounds a bit iffy, but yes, I'm interested. What else can you tell me?"

"I'm not going to tell you much more. Jimmy bought the stuff legally, he assures me, and he's got a receipt and an invoice. But he's got no import and export papers, or anything like that, and some of the stuff like the arms wouldn't be welcomed in this country, which is why it's all got to be kept a bit QT. But you needn't worry about that - all you're being asked to do is to fly a plane."

"What do you know about the kites? Are they airworthy?

"Christ, Ally, you know Dakotas, they go on for ever, don't they? But I did ask him about that and he assures me they're fully fit for service. I don't know whether he actually owns them, in fact I don't care, and neither should you."

"It's a hell of a long way to fly a plane on your own, and navigate."

"Jimmy's got another bloke who can fly. He's a bit of a thug, I reckon, but he was a sergeant in the Raf and skippered a Halifax or something. Jimmy assures me he's a competent pilot. My idea is he'd come with you and Jimmy with me. But you'd have to be in charge of navigation, Ally - that's one reason we want you. I bet there aren't many bods in the whole of the Raf who've clocked up more flying hours than you, and you were especially good because of your job. You didn't only have to navigate and more or less fly the thing, you had to teach the young bugger in the other seat, as well. Have you ever flown a Dakota? If you have, you'll know how simple they are, and reliable."

"I've never piloted one, but I've travelled in them. Yes, I know they're OK. But what about arrangements for taking off and landing? Are there radios? And we'd have to refuel halfway, wouldn't we?"

"Yes, and Jimmy's got that in hand. Somewhere not far from Rome. Guy who owes him a favour runs a little airport, perfectly OK for planes like these. The refuelling stop will be properly organised. I don't know details about Suez or Shropshire, yet. But radios - no there aren't any.

"Now, are you in? I need to know right away - we've got to be off by the end of the week."

I was excited, but worried. I'd have liked to have known more about the whole thing. I had the impression there was a lot Steve wasn't telling me.

For a start, paying five hundred quid for three or four days work started one or two alarm bells ringing. Then, the idea of all this stuff coming from a battle zone in the far east wasn't very convincing. Could there be enough profit in it to transport it these huge distances? This Irish guy Jimmy who could fly about in his own plane and lay on these arrangements all round the globe, "on the QT," was a bit mysterious, not to say mind-boggling. And having to move it in one go?

Excitement and doubt briefly tussled in the A.C.G. Jameson grey matter. But it was no contest, really. "OK, Steve, count me in," I said.

*****

Actually, it went pretty well, as far as I was concerned. I stayed in Steve's flat for a couple of days - he and the girl Julia slept in the bedroom and I had a put-you-up in the living room. He told her to escort me, or be escorted by me, round London while he "got on with his work." Really he was getting me out of the way, didn't want me to know any more about it all than I had to. Later I found there was not only a lot he was not telling me, but a lot of what he did tell me was just not true. He was a complex character, Steve.

In the war he'd been something of a hero, dedicated and loyal to country, cause and comrades, despite an apparent personal recklessness that none of the rest of us could have got away with. I was pretty careful when it came to flying; he seemed to approach it all with a kind of gay abandon. An air vice marshal once told a group of us, and I always remembered it: "There are plenty of bold pilots, and plenty of old pilots - but there are not too many old, bold pilots." But even the top brass seemed to accept a devil-may-care approach from Steve without batting an eyelid.

On the third day, he asked me to stay in the flat and pack my bag because we'd be off to Norfolk later on. And sure enough, in the afternoon he rolled up in his MG and we were off, Steve driving the way he flew. We were there - a hundred and twenty miles, and no motorways in those days - in two and a quarter hours.

Boss Jimmy was at the airfield. Somehow, I'd expected him to be big and beefy, with a cigar permanently in his mouth. He was five foot six or thereabouts, weighed no more than eight stone, clean shaven except for a pencil moustache, with short, neat dark hair, spoke with only a faint Irish accent, his face broke easily into a smile, and he greeted me with a handshake as Steve introduced me. I immediately liked him, although I couldn't say quite the same for the chap with him, who was big if not beefy, who never smiled at all and who I immediately classified as Jimmy's minder and strong arm man, who should not be tangled with, and who answered, if he ever did, to the name of Dermot. I could see why Steve thought he was a bit of a thug.

The airfield looked tidy enough, and the Dakotas were being fuelled up as we got there. But we were not leaving until early next day, because even Steve was not prepared to fly best part of 1,500 miles at night with no navigation system except eyesight. He was quite prepared though to climb into his plane and take off with only a perfunctory warm-up, while I insisted on doing a proper pre-flight check. It was all AI however - the Dakota appeared to be in excellent order, as Jimmy had promised, and check over completed we went off to the local pub, where he had arranged accommodation for the whole party.

Because of my supposed navigational skills, I was to lead the way, but when I asked Jimmy for some kind of directional guide, he said: "Oh, just make for Rome." And Steve quickly added: "When you see me peel off, follow me. We'll probably have to circle the field a couple of times to make sure it's OK for us to go in, but Jimmy's got the signals arranged. You just follow."

"What if we hit bad weather, either on the way or when we want to land?"

"We won't. The weather forecasts are perfect, all the way." And that was about as much as I could get out of him, except a sharp glance that implied: "Don't be a bloody old woman, Ally."

I studied the maps carefully, making sure there were as many landmarks I could recognise as possible. Apart from reservations about Steve's happy-go-lucky weather forecast, though, I was not too worried about the flight. I knew I could recognise Paris, Mont Blanc and the Matterhorn, which were directly on the route I could follow simply from compass bearings. Then the Italian coast would soon be visible, and you only had to follow it until you reached Rome. Always provided it stayed fine with the cloud high enough to fly under so you could see the ground.

Cloud proved to be no problem, however. There was hardly any, most of the way. As soon as we got a bit of height I asked Dermot to take over while I looked at the maps - it was really for me to make sure he was indeed competent, which he appeared to be. By four o'clock in the afternoon we passed the "island" of Orbitello which meant Rome was only about 60 miles away. Soon after, Steve, who'd maintained station 200 or 300 yards away and slightly behind my port wing, peeled off as he'd promised, and I followed him. God, I hope Jimmy knows what he's looking for, I thought, because apart from a lake called Bracciano, there did not seem to be much in the way of landmarks. The lake must have been his clue, though, for we flew directly over it, Steve almost immediately began to descend, and I saw why. There was an airfield straight ahead and we were pointing directly towards the runway. I couldn't see any signals, but he went straight in. I did a little loop round and followed. All hunky dory. And the props had hardly come to rest before a tractor came and towed the planes back to the airfield buildings for refuelling and Jimmy took all of us to a small local hostelry.

Next day we set a compass course for Suez and when we saw the North African coast Steve again peeled off, apparently to pick up some pre-arranged signals at the airport, where we landed without incident. Once again Jimmy's organisation worked well, for the runway was all clear. We couldn't be hustled off to our accomodation, however, for almost as we arrived, so did two biggish, canvas-hooded trucks which had to be unloaded immediately, into the planes. There was a lot of stuff, but all of it was boxed or crated, some of the packages big and heavy, others quite small. We were pretty tired by the time Jimmy led us all off to our accommodation for the night, which was fine with a good meal laid on, and we didn't talk much, though I was becoming increasingly worried about the whole business - not about the flying or the planes, which were excellent, but what this was all about. Too late to back out now, though, and my thoughts didn't keep me awake.

The Dakotas were both loaded, fuelled and ready for take-off at dawn, Jimmy seeing to the airfield formalities, whatever they were. The load made the planes slightly more sluggish, but they were after all transport aircraft, and we were only a few knots slower. I had familiarised myself with the layout of the Italian coast and the "toe," Naples and Rome were again easy to recognise, Steve peeled off as before - he'd been on my starboard side this time - and we landed normally in Italy. We ate and slept at the same inn, and left for Shropshire halfway through the morning. I wondered why we did not start earlier, but Steve said the rendezvous time at Heath Field, north of Shrewsbury, was not until 8pm. Near dark, I thought, but didn't say so.

I knew this part of the country quite well, from my school days and holidays spent with my grandmother and my uncle, and Heath Field was easy to recognise, coming soon after Roden Hill which was still actively operational, and between two converging trunk roads. Again Steve peeled off and landed first and this time I recognised the identification he and Jimmy had looked for - a single light at the start of the runway and three in a triangle at the far end. We were no sooner both down than another couple of trucks complete with hoods appeared and before you could say Jack Robinson we were switching the cargo on to them and they were heading north up the main roads, this time with Jimmy and Dermot aboard.

"What now?" I asked Steve.

"Now we take these kites back to Watton."

"Not in the dark, for Christ's sake," I said. "Can't we stay here and go first thing in the morning?"

"No, Ally, we can't. We've got to be there by 10 o'clock. There'll be a special signal that I'll recognise very easily and they're putting out runway lights. There'll be no problem."

He was right, of course. Our wartime experience made navigating to Norfolk easy enough, and the arranged signals meant there was no problem with landing. Steve had the cash to pay me - I found more than half of it was in dollars, which in fact meant a bonus, and although we were pretty cream-crackered by then, he insisted on driving back to London immediately.

Next morning, I supposed I would go to Netherton - my parents' home - but Steve said there was surely no hurry, why not spend a few days with him, and we'd enjoy ourselves a bit. Besides, he had some more interesting projects coming up, that I might be able to help with. So weenjoyed ourselves within the limits of the austerity - it was not two years since the war had finished, remember - that cramped the style of anyone aiming to light up the town.

I tried, quite gently, to wrest from him some information about Jimmy and the operation we'd been involved in, but Steve wasn't having any. However lighthearted and carefree he had seemed in the airforce, and since for that matter, he knew how to keep his mouth shut, which he'd obviously been told to do. I soon gave up trying.

Three

Angie

Among the delights we sampled over those next days was the company of a bevy of young ladies - the girl Julia had disappeared, I never knew why or where – who swarmed round Steve like bees and the proverbial. I never knew where they originated – I think perhaps one or two were ex-WAAF acquaintances of his. Most of the girls were in their twenties, I thought, and fitted the description of dizzy blonde, whatever the colour of their hair, and were not really my cup of tea. But one, whose name I gathered was Angela – they called her Angie - was a bit younger, I guessed 19 or 20, and quite different from the others, quieter and apparently more serious. I wondered rather what made her go round with that giddy gang, but I took to her immediately. She was a pretty little brunette, with dark wavy hair, big brown eyes that smiled easily, and a shapely, full mouth under a retrousse nose. She seemed to like me, usually came to sit near me, wherever we were.

It soon became apparent that another of the girls, Josie, had attached herself to Steve, or him to her. Anyway, they were an item, and in a very few days she had replaced the missing Julia, in the flat and in Steve's bed. He said there was no problem for me, the bed-settee was still there and I was welcome to it, but I found the situation uncomfortable and decided I must find myself another pad, or go home to Leicestershire.

This seemed to alarm Steve. "Look, Ally, I don't want to lose touch with you. I'm pretty sure I'll want your help again. There'll be more lucrative jobs coming along, for both of us. Stay around."

I was still not wildly happy about the job I'd done with him but I agreed to "stay around." I was well in funds so I took a room in an hotel just down the road, and continued to see Steve daily, usually over a lunchtime pint. The rest of the time I spent wandering round London, watching repair work start on the devastation of the blitz, meeting up with Steve and the bevy in the evenings, usually at one pub or another. Angie was still among them, and as I said, she seemed to like my company, and I certainly liked hers, although I had no designs of "that" kind on her – she did not seem "that" kind of girl, despite the company she was keeping. In fact I thought she seemed a bit down, not happy about something. But I talked quite a lot to her, and it did not take long for me to find that she was well up to, indeed beyond, my own intellectual level, which at that stage could only be described as mediocre. Years in the RAF had driven much of what I'd imbibed at a very good school into the dungeons of the mind.

Much of our talk ranged round our likes and dislikes in the fields of music, films and other entertainment, and I discovered there were one or two pre-war pictures she would have liked to see, because her mother had told her about them. One was *Stella Dallas*, and I discovered it was being shown at a film club Steve had told me about, in the West End. It was a club where the movies were often the kind you'd never take anyone like Angie to, but on this occasion there was nothing on the bill to worry about, and I asked her along. The picture was about a working class girl who married an upper-crust man, both found she could not come up to his expectations, and she turned her affection and hopes to her daughter only to find the daughter leaving her for the high society of her former husband's family. It ends with Stella watching the daughter's wedding through a huge window and the daughter suddenly realising, too late, that her own mother had not been invited.

Although it was obviously a masterpiece of its day and genre, it did not particularly enthrall me, and I asked Angie afterwards if she had enjoyed it.

"I don't know whether I could say I 'enjoyed' it," she said. "It made me sad. And made me think. Didn't it you? My mother told me about it. She said it was the best film she ever saw. I'm glad I've seen it. Thank you very much for asking me to go, Alastair."

"What did it make you think?"

"Oh, it doesn't matter. Just about family, and things."

I could see she did not want to talk more, but the outing led to other evenings alone together. I asked her if she would like to go to another cinema, and we arranged to meet at a little cafe near my hotel, from where we went to see another film, a sequence that was repeated two or three times during the ten days or so following the flying trip.I soon began to see that she was a quite special young woman, and I believe now that it must have been during that period that I fell in love with her, althoughI did not fully realise it at the time, and there was almost no physical contact between us, even in the darkness of the picture house. We just watched the film, and afterwards went for a cup of coffee, and discussed what we had seen. Some of it was pretty rubbishy stuff, and I found she was ready to say what she thought of it, although somewhat apologetically, I suppose because I had taken her there. But there was one film of a higher stamp, like that first one, and it was discussing it – and for that matter the rubbish – that led me to further appreciate her intellectual calibre. The "good" film was *Wuthering Heights*, again at that club, and we were in the cafe, afterwards.

"I can't understand why they changed it so much from the book," she said. "Heathcliff was a lot more sombre, and darker, and more powerful, than Laurence Olivier made him. And Cathy was wilder, I think. I don't think the film did anything like justice to the book. They seemed to be keener on showing off the stars than in reflecting it as Emily Bronte wrote it. And why did they have to change the story at the end? There was much more to it, after she died."

I'd never read *Wuthering Heights*, or indeed other fiction at that level, except the few works we'd had thrust upon us at school, and this was another indication that her intellectual capacity and perception was way above mine. Apart from that, I knew little about her, and she knew even less about me. She had never minded showing she liked my company, but nothing more. We'd said little to each other about our backgrounds. I didn't even know what she did for a living, for instance. But this particular conversation led directly into that unexplored territory.

"You've read quite a lot, haven't you," I said.

"Yes, I love reading. Don't you?"

"You make me ashamed of myself. I've read very little."

"I don't suppose you had much time for it, in the war."

"There was plenty of time, only we didn't use it for reading, or anything like that. We just used to buzz off to the pub or something."

"Did you drink a lot?"

"No, not really. At least, some did, but not most of us. It was more that we just wanted to live it up. I suppose it was a natural reaction to the kind of thing we were doing the rest of the time."

She wanted to know more about life in the air force, and I told her – some of it, at least. And that led to asking about me, where I came from, family, what I was going to do. I told her the facts about my life to date, including, very sketchily, the flying I'd recently done with Steve, but about the future I could tell her nothing, because I didn't know. Nothing had appealed to me, up to then, which I suppose was why I had joined up with Steve.

I was happy though to tell her about my mother and father, and grandmother, and my Aunt Billie, who'd been a suffragette. Although I had made it clear, through declining my father's invitation to join him and Peter in the estate business, and buzzing off to London to join my wild friend, that I was somewhat at odds with them, I really admired them and knew I ought to try to be more like them. Talking to a person like Angie, two or three levels above me intellectually and perhaps morally, no doubt helped bring the feeling nearer the fore. Guilt, I suppose it was. I know I was quiet for quite a time after I had told her all this.

She said: "You've gone very quiet. Is there something the matter?"

"No, nothing special. But tell me a bit about you."

It was her turn to go quiet. For a moment I thought she was even going to cry.

She said: "My dad's in the merchant navy – a captain. He was torpedoed. And his ship was bombed. My mother's from Scotland – she's there now, looking after my gran."

I asked if she had any brothers or sisters.

She seemed to hesitate.

"My brother's doing his national service."

"No sisters?"

She was quiet, almost tearful again. I waited a few moments.

"Only Josie."

"Is that... the Josie I know?"

"Yes." I saw she was crying. And I began to understand. I found my handkerchief - luckily it was clean - and wiped her eyes.

"Don't cry - I'm sure there was nothing you could do about it. I don't think any harm will come to her. Steve's not a bad bloke, you know."

"He doesn't want to marry her though, does he?"

"I don't know," I lied.

"Does your mother know about it?"

"No. I told you, she's not here. I daren't tell her."

"So you and Josie are living together, just the two of you?"

"Yes. Well, we were. There's only me now."

"When are your parents coming back?"

"Dad's only been gone a fortnight. I think he'll be away another month, this trip. Mum - I don't know. Gran can't be left alone, and there's nobody else. I don't think she'll be back for a long time, until Gran..." She wept again.

"Come on, sweetheart, I'm taking you home."

I already knew that she lived in St Johns Wood, only a mile or so away, and we started to walk.

The house turned out to be a solid-looking detached villa. I went in with her to find a comfortable middle-class family home; hats and coats and a telephone in the hall; some old but elegantly "good" furniture in the living room, and photographs of Josie and Angie as schoolgirls, and a young boy.

"Would you like a cup of tea or coffee?" she asked, and went into what I assumed was the kitchen to make it.

Sitting over the coffee, I started to talk about Josie. This was not the kind of background I'd expect a fast and loose girl to come from. I asked whether she had had any other boy-friends.

"She had one for a long time. It started before she left school, but he went in the army, and got killed when the second front started. She was very upset – ill, almost, for months. Then she got in with that crowd, not long ago. Dad didn't like them, but she kept on going about with them. And he had to go away, with his ship, and Mum had to go to Scotland to look after Gran. They were so worried about her, Alastair."

"Why did you get mixed up with them?"

"I know it sounds silly, but I could see she was – oh, likely to go off the rails or something. I thought if I went out with her, with them, it might stop her doing anything terrible. I mean, having a young sister around her it might – I don't know, make her more responsible or something."

"How did she come to be involved with those girls? I wouldn't have thought they were her type - I'm sure they're not your type, are they?"

"No, they're not. Two of them work with her, at least for the same firm. She's got a pretty good job for somebody her age. I think perhaps it was all to do with losing Derek. She'd always seemed quite serious and steady before that."

"How old is she?" And the answer surprised me. She was 21. How old did that make Angie, for goodness sake? She looked years younger than her sister. I had to ask.

"Seventeen. Last month," she said.

I said: "I thought she was older than that." But I was quiet for a few moments, digesting my surprise. As was she, who was the first to speak.

"Does that mean you don't want to see me any more, Alastair? Do you think I'm just a child?" And I could see she was near to tears again.

"No, it doesn't mean that," I said. "I think you're very mature for a girl of your age. You leave me well behind in many ways. But I am a lot older than you, in years, aren't I? Eight years older, and I've knocked around a bit. I bet you're still at school."

"Yes."

"Sixth form?"

"Yes, I've just started my last year."

"But - you don't seem to have been there much, this last week or two."

"No. I think I'm going to leave."

"Why? Are you unhappy there?"

"No, it isn't that. I've enjoyed school, on the whole, and I've done alright. It's... all this other. I know I'm younger than her, but somehow I feel responsible."

Seventeen, and feeling responsible for an older sister. If I hadn't seen it before, this would have made me realise that here was a very special young lady. Her anxiety about Josie should not let her abandon her own education, though, and after a moment's thought I said so.

"Angie, I'm no person to preach to you; but how would abandoning your education help the situation with your sister? It wouldn't, would it? What would your father and mother say? If they're going to be upset about Josie, more than upset I expect, what would it do to them if you gave up school?"

"Yes, I know. But I can't work, I can't concentrate. I'm thinking all the time about... that, and her, and what will happen when they find out, and everything."

"What are you doing at school? I suppose it's for Higher School Certificate, is it?"

"Yes, I'm doing English, and biology, and chemistry."

"How did you do in School Certificate?"

"Four distinctions and the rest credits."

"Golly, that's terrific. You certainly mustn't give it up. Have you any idea about what you want to do, afterwards?"

"Dad wants me to be a doctor. That's what..."

"What?"

"I'd like that, as well. At least..."

"At least what, Angie?"

"Oh, I don't know what I want, now. How can I set myself up to be something like a doctor when I've got a sister who..." And the tears flowed once more. I caught her hand and put my arm round her shoulder.

"Angie, Angie, you can't let what's happened to her ruin your life.

You must keep up your studies and make the most of yourself."

"And then there's ..."

"What?"

She wouldn't go any further. Instead, she asked: "What school did you go to?" "Oh, a boarding school. Public school - Shrewsbury. My family had gone there for generations."

"Did you – were you happy there?"

"Yes, I suppose so. I liked the sport, and I had one or two good friends. But I know now that I didn't make the most of it, although my exam results at the end weren't bad."

"But the war came, didn't it? You went into the air force. You couldn't have done anything better than that. You were a bomber pilot, weren't you?"

"Yes, but never mind about that. It's not important. Tell me about how you're managing, on your own. Are you alright for money? And what about ration cards and everything? Can you deal with that?"

"Yes. My dad left us some money, and the ration books just stay at the shop."

She was silent for a while. Then: "I wish I could do something about Josie. I wish I could get her to come back. I can't bear the thought of what will happen when Dad and Mum come home."

I said: "Would you like me to talk to her?"

"But what could you say? She hardly knows you, and she doesn't know that I've been talking to you about her. I think she'd just think you were being a busybody, or a goody-goody. She's old enough to make up her own mind about all this, she'd say – and she is, isn't she? I think she's still in a terrible state of mind, though. I don't think I'd mind if I thought it was serious between her and Steve, but it's not, is it? I think she's just another girl, for him... oh, Alastair, what can I do?"

I said: "I'm going to talk to Steve. I won't say anything to Josie, but I'm going to tell him what I think."

She was silent for another few minutes. My arm stayed round her shoulder. Then she said: "And it's so horribly lonely. Alastair, couldn't you come and stay here with me? So I'd not feel so awfully alone?"

*****

She was not inviting me into her bed. I'd already learned enough about her to know that. But I could see that there was more to it than loneliness. She had fallen for me, as I knew by now I'd fallen for her. I'd never been in love, but I certainly was now. It was not lust, far deeper than that. There no words of love between us, no embrace beyond my arm round her shoulder, and her hand in mine. But I knew. And I knew that although I'd never even kissed her, what must inevitably happen if I agreed to stay in her house. More, even if we managed to keep relations on a non-carnal basis – what would happen when her father or mother returned and found a 25-year-old male living there?

I'd been no Don Juan up to now, and sexual encounters could be counted on very few fingers, but they had existed, and I'd felt no guilt about them. The other parties had been more than willing, and young men in their twenties do not turn down that kind of invitation. Angie though was not "one of them." As much as I had seen of her up to then had left me, must have left anybody, in no doubt that she was anything but a good, caring, highly intelligent girl who must not be hurt. I think that must have been the point when I began to realise I must do something about myself, pull myself together, stop thinking – as much as I thought at all – only about Alastair C. G. Jameson.

I told her I could not possibly stay in the house with her, but I would be there as much as I could. She accepted it all, albeit reluctantly. Then we had another talk, about her, when she accepted my urgent demand that she must go back to school, and work hard again.

Next day I carried out my intention of talking to Steve about him and Josie. At least I could tell him about the kind of distress that it was causing Angie. I also decided I would tell him I wanted no more to do with Jimmy and Co's operations. The fears that had been nagging away about earning that kind of fee, from whatever kind of business that paid it, had grown. I must take steps towards getting myself some kind of proper job, even though I still didn't know what I really wanted to do.

At our lunchtime meeting he greeted me with: "I've got something to tell you about," and went off to get a couple of pints. When he came back, I said: "Steve, there's something I want to say to you. It's a bit difficult, but I've got to say it. You know I'm seeing a bit of Josie's sister, don't you?"

"Yes, and good luck to you, old boy. But take care - you wouldn't want the sea captain to come home a bit suddenly, would you? You know how old she is, I take it."

"There's nothing like that, Steve, and there won't be."

"Ho, ho. I've heard that before. What about that pretty little thing you went missing with at Lincoln? I wouldn't mind betting she wasn't a day over15."

"That was then, Steve, and this is different. And anyway I know she was 17. But that's not what I want to talk about. I just have to tell you about Angie now."

"What about her?"

"She's very upset about you and Josie. I've found her crying, and she's saying she means to leave school, because she can't cope with the worry."

He looked at me over his glass. "So what do you want me to do about it? Smack Josie on the bottom and tell her to go back home like a good little girl?"

"I'm not suggesting what you should do. I just wanted to tell you how upset Angie is."

"Ally, if you and me hadn't been pals for so long, I could be getting very angry. Josie's a big girl now, you know, and I'm not going to upset my sex life because you've had an attack of the goody-goodies. I'll tell you what you should do for little sister. You should give her a bloody good rogering - it's obviously what she wants, and what she needs, mate. It's what they all want. That'd stop her being upset."

I don't know about Steve being angry with me - I don't think he was capable of being really angry with anyone, because he was almost amoral. Almost but not quite, as will appear. But I think that was the beginning of the end of my friendship with him. Whatever the state of my own feelings for Angie, and hers for me, I knew her concern for Josie was real. The thought of her sister hopping into bed with someone she hardly knew, the grief it would cause her parents, was heartbreaking for her. I said no more, however, and Steve dropped the subject.

"Anyway, let's talk about something more important," he said. "I told you there could be another well-paid job or two about. Well, Jimmy phoned last night. He wants us to fetch some stuff from Holland. We'd use his plane, and it would just be the two of us. It wouldn't be more than a few hours work and there'd be a couple of hundred smackers for you. Are you on?"

Why on earth I didn't turn him down there and then, I don't know.

Not that it would have made much difference in the long run. Events outside my control but that would shape the future course of my life were already well under way, I know now. I knew I was getting myself mixed up in something ropey. No normal business could pay £200 for half a day's flying. I suppose I was still under Steve's charismatic influence. Perhaps it was the money. So much has happened since then, I find it impossible to remember the way I thought. So, I said yes, I was on, and simply asked for when and where.

"Monday, from Amsterdam to Watton," he said. "We go in the morning and you come back in the afternoon. I've got to stop in Holland to see to some other business. There'll be no problem at Watton, same arrangements as before, and you can bring my car back here."

I arranged to meet him on Monday morning. This was Friday and I went to Angie's about five o'clock. She opened the door.

"Hello. I was just starting my prep - I've got an essay to finish. But it can wait - I've got the weekend. I thought I'd get it done so I'd have the time free."

She was quite different from the evening before; bright, matter of fact; greeting me almost as though we'd known each other for years. School, homework, essays had never been mentioned until then. I wondered if something had happened, on the Josie front, to cheer her up. But I only said: "No, I think you should get on with it, Angie. How long will it take you?"

"Oh, perhaps an hour and a half – less perhaps."

"Have you got any food in the house?"

"Yes, plenty."

"Could I make a suggestion, then? If you show me where everything is, I could perhaps cook a meal while you do your work - unless you'd rather not risk my cooking and I'll take you out afterwards."

"I'd much rather stay here."

It was a pretty mundane meal - just a couple of not very big lamb chops, with potatoes and carrots, and Angie found a tin of peaches for dessert. No wine or anything like that. We ate at the kitchen table, and talked about her work at school, and her friends. She made me tell her about flying, and those nights over Germany, and asked whether I'd had many girl friends, which I could truthfully answer in the negative, for the couple of young ladies who'd shared in my "experiences" certainly could not be called friends. And she made coffee, and we washed up. She washed and I dried.

Why on earth I had to choose that moment, in the middle of one of the most prosaic jobs on earth, to declare my love to Angie, I'll never know. Perhaps it was because washing up is a domestic chore often shared by a married couple, or "partners" as we must now have it. I don't know. But it happened – I knew I'd found something precious. A person I wanted to spend the rest of my life with, and care for, and make myself worthy of. I'd only known her for a month or less, but I knew.

Hands in the sink, she turned her head and laughed at me: "I don't suppose you've done this many times, Alastair - or cooked a meal?"

I put down the tea towel over my arm and caught her hands, suds and all.

"No. But I'd like to do it every day of my life, if I could do it with you."

She looked up at me. "You mean you want to spend your life washing up?"

"You know what I mean, Angie. I want to spend my life with you. I love you."

She took her hands out of mine, dried them quite calmly, on the tea towel that was still over my arm, put her arms around my neck. It was almost as though, 17 years old or not, she'd known this was coming

"I love you. I knew I was going to love you the first time I saw you, even when... I'll always love you... always... Alastair..." And she kissed me, sealing the love that had invaded our beings without a single embrace, hardly a physical contact, and taken root there. But then I kissed her again and again, wrapped my arms round her, revelled in the warmth of her. And she whispered: "Alastair, my darling. Don't ever leave me..."

*****

But of course, precious things are so often fragile. Our new found joy suffered what turned out to be its first blow even as we recovered from our euphoria to finish at the sink. The phone rang.

"That was my mother," Angie said a few minutes later. "Gran's died."

"Oh, my sweetheart, I am sorry."

"It's not so awful for me. I hardly knew her, and she was very ill, in a lot of pain. It's good that mum was there. She had no-one else."

"Will your mother be coming home?"

"She thinks she'll have to stay for the funeral, and see the lawyer and so on. But she'll be coming home then. Oh, Alastair, she'll find out about Josie. Whatever shall I do?"

I knew what I must do, or try to. In spite of the frosty reception I'd had from Steve, I must help her get Josie back home. She must not sink back into the state she was when I first knew her.

I did not tell her how Steve had met my approach. It would only have made matters worse. But I thought I knew what she must do. She must seek out her sister and ask her to come home, or if she would not, tell their mother herself what the situation was. I said so, but I also warned her of the kind of reception I thought she'd get from Steve, if he was in on the meeting.

We talked about it all evening. I tried to ease her distress, not terribly successfully, because the situation was, well, what the situation was. Unless Josie would come home and put it all behind her there was going to be a family row. And Angie somehow thought she was to blame for it all, or anyway believed she would be held to blame. I tried to tell her that she was in no way responsible for her older sister's behaviour, and no-one would think otherwise,

---

but I couldn't quite convince her. She was so worried.

"Mum'll say I should have told her. But I couldn't. And I kept hoping she'd see sense. She's not like that really, Alastair. Really, she isn't."

We talked round it for half an hour and more, and I came up with an idea we could at least try. I told her I would go with her to Steve's flat next morning and get him to come out with me for our usual lunchtime sandwich, pint and chat, while she talked to Josie.

I was sitting on the couch, she on a chair close by. She sank to her knees in front of me, caught my hands and burst into tears.

"Oh, Alastair, I love you, I love you," she sobbed. "You are so good. Whatever could I do without you? Hold me, please. Don't leave me."

I pulled her up onto my lap, and once again dried her eyes, and kissed away the tears.

"I'm not good, my little sweetheart, but I'll try to be, for you. And I'm not going to leave you."

We stayed like that for perhaps an hour. She actually went to sleep, her head on my shoulder. I became quite uncomfortable, but I think I'd rather have died than disturb her. In spite of the worry about Josie, which I was now understanding and sharing, I was indescribably happy. Life, through this little schoolgirl, had suddenly become full of meaning, deep, mysterious, right, all-consuming, all the adjectives you could think of to describe the surge of emotion that welled up as I kissed her hair and forehead again and again, as she slept.

She woke, opened her eyes and looked at me. "I've just been dreaming," she said. "I dreamt I was somewhere that I thought was heaven. And it was. It was being with you."

I held her closer. "Angie..."

"Yes?"

"One day, when you've become a doctor or whatever it is you want, and I've made something better of myself, would you marry me?"

"Oh, Alastair, my darling Alastair, of course I'll marry you. Only I don't want to wait that long."

"We'll see. But I won't let you marry me until I'm worth marrying."

"You're worth marrying now." And she kissed me again.

After another few minutes, she whispered: "Don't go away. Stay here tonight."

"My darling, I mustn't."

"Yes, please. Just tonight. I just want you near. I feel safer. You can sleep in Mum and Dad's room and I can find you some pyjamas."

"Suppose someone sees me here, and tells your mother and father?"

"I don't care. It'll be alright when I tell them all about us."

"After Josie?"

"I'm not Josie."

In the end I agreed, and we stayed where we were, apart from making tea and nibbling biscuits, until after midnight. She showed me the bedroom and the bathroom and I was soon in bed, doubting whether I should sleep. But I did, quickly and for hours, until it was daylight and a knock on the door woke me. It was Angie, fully dressed in a skirt and jumper and carrying a tray with two mugs of tea. She put it on the bedside table and sat down on the side of the bed.

"Did you sleep well?"

"Like a log. It's a very comfortable bed. Have you been up long?"

"About two hours. I've been doing some school work."

"I thought you'd only got that essay."

"I've been looking up some biology stuff. I lost a lot of ground when I was chasing around after Josie, and..."

"Going around with me?"

"No, I wasn't going to say that. It's just that... I want to do it again, now."

"Sweetheart, I'm very pleased. Keep it up, won't you?"

She was quiet for a few moments.

"It's you,. You made me see I ought to. I think some girls would say 'oh it doesn't matter, I'll be married soon' but I don't think you'd like that, would you?"

I thought a while.

"I certainly think girls, women, ought to make the most of any talents they have, not just think of themselves as houswives or men's playthings, not that being a wife and mother isn't important. P'raps it's the most important thing of all. But you could be that as well as being a doctor, I'm sure."

I was amazing myself. I hadn't known I thought that way. But I was quite sincere.

We were drinking the tea as we talked. She said: "I think you should get up now. There's a spare razor and stuff in the bathroom."

"Yes, miss. On one condition. You give me a kiss first."

I'd have loved to pull her down on that bed with me. And she'd have come,

I know. But it must not be. Not for years, until I had at least started to make something worthwhile of myself. And for now, we must try to solve the problem of Josie.

She had breakfast ready by the time I was downstairs, and afterwards we set out for Notting Hill, opting to walk - on air, as far as I was concerned - on a very pleasant late October morning. It was after midday when we got there, and I suggested she should wait in a churchyard while I went to dig out Steve and make sure Josie was in. If I wasn't back in twenty minutes it meant the coast was clear for her to see her sister.

It worked out. Steve and I went to our usual lunchtime watering hole. I thought he seemed a bit quieter than usual, but we talked about the Dutch trip and finalised the arrangements.

"What sort of plane is it?" I asked.

"It's a Piper Cub, high wing, not very old. Two-seater, but there's a bit of room for luggage. The stuff you've got to bring back doesn't amount to much, bulk-wise. A couple of chaps will meet you at Watton and take it off to Jimmy."

"What is it?"

"Look, Ally, you don't need to know that, in fact I don't know myself, in detail. If anyone asks you, it's just a couple of parcels and you're simply flying the plane. Got it?"

"Yes, Steve, I've got it. But I also want to tell you that this will be the last job I'll be doing with you. It's pretty obvious it's not quite all above board. I'm not criticising you, you do what you want, and I promise I won't talk about it to anyone. But I'd rather not be involved, if you don't mind."

"Well, I do mind, because you're someone I can trust, and guys like that don't grow on trees. But of course it's up to you. I must warn you though. Don't talk to anyone about it. The consequences could be unpleasant. OK?"

"Yes, Steve. I've already said I won't talk about it, and I mean it."

He fetched another two pints, and we sat and drank, in silence, before Steve started to talk again.

"Ally, there's just something I want to tell you. It's about Josie. I'm sending her off home, tomorrow. I've got things to do today, but I'll tell her in the morning. I never thought I'd hear myself saying this kind of thing - you must have touched a bit of a nerve the other day when you talked about little sister being upset. I don't think Josie's quite the kind of girl I thought she was. She'll be better away from blokes like me. I don't think I could ever settle down into some steady job, or something. It'd send me off my rocker."

I was moved, a bit. I'd certainly never expected to hear anything like this, from him. I saw that he was indeed not quite amoral. I said simply: "Thanks, Steve."

I didn't go back to the flat with him - I thought it might be embarrassing all round. I just went to the churchyard where I'd left Angie, and found her already there.

I said: "How did it go?"

"Oh, Alastair, it was awful. When I told her about Gran she didn't seem to care. I said Mum would be coming back very soon, but it made no impression. I begged her to change her mind, and told her how upset Mum and Dad would be, but it didn't seem to make any difference. I don't think she'll come back home."

After a few minutes on the verge of tears, I said: "Steve's just told me something. He says he's going to tell her to go home, tomorrow. What I said to him the other day seems to have made an impression on him."

"Oh, Alastair, that's wonderful, if he does. Do you think he meant it?"

"Yes, I do. But what you've just told me about Josie leaves me a bit worried. After being like that with you, I wonder whether she'll just come back with her tail between her legs. Might she be so ashamed she'll head off in another direction and perhaps go even further off the rails?"

"I don't know. But I see what you mean. But what can I do?"

"It's what can we do, my darling. I'm in this with you, you know." I knew however that somehow we had to talk to Josie and try to persuade her to return home.

There was a cafe almost opposite the flat, and we went there for something to eat. Angie asked if I'd please come back and stay with her. I said I would, but only for that night, Saturday. I told her I'd agreed to go to Holland with Steve on Monday, and would have to be back at the hotel on Sunday night. She could telephone me there. But that set me thinking.

At first, I wondered about trying to phone Josie at the flat, if we could find the number. Then I realised that would be no good, because Steve would be there. Anyway, talking on the phone would probably do as much harm as good. The only way was to see her face to face. I said all this to Angie.

"Look, do you know what I think is the only thing we can do? I think we should stay around here all day tomorrow and try to catch her as she leaves. Then we might be able to do some good. Steve will have just told her to go home, I reckon, and we'd catch her while her nerves were raw. It won't be the

Francis John Simcock

pleasantest thing in the world, hanging around like a pair of private eyes, but I think it's the best hope."

"I'll do anything, if it will get her back."

We decided we'd stay in the cafe as long as possible, just in case we saw Josie then, and were able to talk to her. But after more cups of coffee than either of us wanted, we felt we had to leave. We went to my hotel to grab some clothes for me, and made our way back to St Johns Wood. We didn't enjoy quite the euphoric evening of the night before. Angie was too stressed out by her fears over her sister, and I was worried about it, too.

One thing I wanted to say to her though, and did: "Dearest Angie, I want you to promise me something. Whatever happens, however things turn out, you will keep on with your studies, and do your very best at them. For as long as it takes."

She promised, and sealed it with another long, loving kiss. I slept well again, after half an hour of pondering about Josie, hoping we were doing the right thing, and that it would work out.

*****

Next morning, we equipped ourselves with a large umbrella, for rain was threatening, and again set off, after an early cornflake breakfast, for Notting Hill. We took a bus part of the way, and by ten o'clock we were at the churchyard, from where we could see the front door of the house containing Steve's flat. We said we'd give ourselves an hour there, then move to the cafe, where we could have something to supplement the cornflakes, and the inevitable cups of coffee. There was no sign of Josie and just after midday we went back to the churchyard seat.

We nearly missed her then. There was a bus stop almost outside the door, and she came out, carrying a holdall, behind a double-decker. But Angie spotted her and we set off in pursuit. Her heavy bag slowed her and we walked quickly, and we caught up with her in a couple of hundred yards. Angie touched her arm and said: "Josie, please stop a minute."

"What do you want?" she asked.

"We want to talk to you. Please."

She looked at us. I said: "Please, Josie."

We all stood there, Josie stony-faced, Angie silently imploring.

I said: "Come and have a cup of coffee, or something, Josie, please."

Angie caught her hand, and started to lead her towards the cafe. I said: "Let me carry that bag," and she released it. I think I knew then that we were going to win.

In the cafe, I ordered coffee and asked Josie whether she would like something to eat. She said not, but would not look at either of us, only down at the table mat and the coffee when it came. Then I saw she was weeping. Angie, who'd been sitting next to me, moved round and put her arm round her sister.

"Josie, it's alright, it's alright. It's alright, Josie."

We let her cry, but when I said: "Please drink your coffee," she did.

Angie said in another few minutes: "Will you come home with us, please?"

She did not reply, but started to cry again, quietly. I decided the two should be left alone, and went to organise a taxi to take us to St Johns Wood. She came with us without argument, took out her own key to the house. I paid the taxi driver and followed, with her bag. Josie went straight upstairs, Angie clung to me in the hall and her own tears flowed.

"Oh, Alastair, how wonderful. Isn't it? Thank you, thank you."

We started to get some lunch, and talked about what to do next. I said I did not think we should say much about Angie and me. If we displayed too much happiness it might depress someone who'd just gone through a period of upset like Josie's, starting with her own loss, then the distress she had caused for Angie and eventually would have caused for their parents. If Josie asked questions, that was the time to tell her how things were between us.

Angie went to ask her sister to have some lunch. Slightly to my surprise, she came down with her, and sat down with us at the kitchen table. I kept very quiet, left any talking to Angie, but she restricted it to asking Josie about her food. However, as the meal came to an end, and we were drinking our tea and coffee, Josie started to speak, to me.

"I suppose you think I'm just about the biggest fool in the world," she said.

"I know about your terrible tragedy, Josie," I said, hoping that was answer enough.

"We were so happy, you see. But I know I shouldn't have let myself get mixed up with that lot. That wouldn't bring him back."

We were all quiet for a few minutes, before Josie spoke again.

"Are you and Angie ... together?"

Angie answered: "Yes. I love him, Josie. And he loves me. He's been wonderful."

I felt myself blushing. I said: "I've done nothing wonderful, Josie, only tried to pick Angie up a bit."

She said, almost weeping again: "I'm terribly sorry. But I'm very grateful, Alastair. I think what you said to him made all the difference. I think he'd have just gone on until he got fed up with me, if it hadn't been for that."

Angie looked at me quizically. She didn't know about my chat with Steve. But she didn't say anything, then.

Josie asked: "Are you still living at the hotel, Alastair?"

"Yes. But I should tell you, before you hear it from anywhere else, I've stayed here the last two nights."

"He slept in mum and dad's room," Angie said very quickly.

"Yes, well, I wouldn't have expected anything else, from you," Josie said. "Nor from Alastair, now."

Angie coloured to the roots of her hair. Me too, but I managed to mumble something deprecatory.

We were all quiet for a while, and through the washing up. Josie started to talk.

"You haven't heard any more from Mum? About the funeral and what she's going to do?"

I answered for Angie: "These things can take time, Josie. Your mother will have a number of things to do up there. She told Angie she'd let her know as soon as she could."

Angie said: "I haven't told her anything about... you not being at home. I'm not going to, and I don't think you should."

Josie looked as though she was going to cry again, but she didn't. Instead, after a moment, she asked: "Do you know whether she's been able to let Dad know about Gran?"

"I don't know for sure, but I expect she's been able to get something to him through the owners," Angie said. "He'll be in India or somewhere now. I don't think Mum would want him to try to get back."

I wondered about Josie's job, at a big stockbroker's in the city. I didn't suppose she had been going to it.

"No."

"Have you spoken to them at all?"

Angie interjected. "They rang to ask about you, the second day you weren't there," she said. "I told them you were ill, with 'flu. I know it was wrong, but I had to say something. They asked me to let them know how you got on, and when you were likely to be back. That would be ten days ago now."

"I'll ring them tomorrow and tell them I should be back on Tuesday. I just hope it'll be alright."

Josie suggested that Angie and I should go for a walk. I think she thought we would like to be alone.

"Will you be alright, Josie?" I asked.

She looked at me, smiling a little quizically. "If you mean will I do something silly, or run off or something – no, Alastair, I won't. That won't happen again, I promise. And again, thank you very much. I think you and Angie are going to be very happy."

"I've made her promise that she'll keep up her studies," I said. "I want to marry Dr Royston. I don't mind waiting."

Regent's Park was not the warmest place on that October morning, and although we did more walking than sitting, I wanted to talk about the future, mine in particular.

"The trouble is, I don't really know what I want to do," I said. "My father would like me to train as a land agent and surveyor, then join him and Peter in a business. Even now I've met you, I don't really think that would be right for me. I think I'd get fed up with it."

"What about flying? You're doing some now - isn't there more of that?"

"Look, sweetheart, I mustn't say much, and you mustn't repeat what I do say. I'm not happy about these jobs with Steve. I've told him I won't do any more after tomorrow."

"What do you mean, you're not happy about them?"

"I 'm not sure there isn't something... not quite right. Don't ask me to say anything more, though. I've promised I won't."

She was quiet, and we walked on another hundred yards.

I said: "Pilots are ten a penny at present, with all of us coming out of the air force. I might be able to get a job with an airline, but to tell the truth, I don't really think I want to. I've had enough of aeroplanes, I reckon, and day to day flying is pretty dull, you know. I joined the RAF because I wanted excitement, and I got it, in the end, but I've had enough of that, too."

We walked another spell.

"What I want is something new, something I've got to learn but that will lead to a worthwhile occupation in the end. As I said before, though, I don't know what. Unless..."

"Unless what?"

"You may think this is silly, but I've a funny idea I wouldn't mind being a farmer."

"Well, why not? My grandfather - mother's father - was a farmer, and from what I've heard from her, he was always happy, although he never made much money."

"You know, as I told you, our family's always lived by the land, one way or another. But as to farming myself, I know so little about it. Only what I picked up from my dad's work, in the school holidays, and you can imagine that wasn't much."

"Couldn't you learn? There are agricultural colleges, aren't there?"

"Yes, but I don't know how useful they are to a practical farmer. And again, I haven't got the kind of money it takes to set up in farming."

"Wouldn't your father help? You said he wanted to set up a business for you and your brother."

"I don't know. But I shall talk to him about it."

After another few minutes of walking, her hand delightfully in mine, her head now and then leaning against my shoulder, she started to talk.

"Alastair, why don't you come back to us, after you've done your flight tomorrow? There'd be nothing... improper... about it with Josie home as well."

"I had thought about it, sweetheart, but I really think it would be better if I didn't. Your mother is likely to be back before long, and I'm looking forward to meeting her, and your father, but I don't think they'd appreciate finding me already living in your house. No, I think I'd be better staying at the Royal, for the time being. I think I'll go home to Netherton, for a few days, to talk to Dad. Do you have a half term holiday?"

"Yes, next month."

"How long?"

"A week - well, four days."

"I'd like to take you there. Would you come?"

"Oh, Alastair, I'd love to. But don't you think your parents would think I was too young for you?"

"My mother was hardly any older than you when they were married. And Dad was about my age."

"Half term would have to depend on it not being just as my dad got back. But I think he would have been here for a few days, by then."

Another little walk, before she asked: "How do you think Josie is?" "Well, I think she's taking it all very well - surprisingly well. Don't you? You know her best?"

"Yes. I just hope she doesn't have some kind of a breakdown, or something."

"I fancy you won't say anything about... her... what happened... to your mother?"

"No, unless I'm asked, and that would only be if Josie told her first, wouldn't it? And I don't think she will. I hope not."

It was growing dark when we got back to 55 Wood Road, and I was alarmed when the house appeared to be in darkness. But I needn't have worried. We soon saw the kitchen light was on, and found Josie completing preparations for Sunday afternoon tea. At eight o'clock I left for the Royal Hotel, Notting Hill.

Four

"I promise"

Next day the Dutch trip was completed without incident. The Piper was already fuelled up when we got to Watton after another ride in the Parrimore hotmobile. The flight to a little airfield just south of Amsterdam took an hour and a half, I was there for only as long as it took to refuel, and I was back in Norfolk before it was completely dark. Not to my surprise, Dermot was there and took the single parcel - only about as big as a small tea chest - out of the plane, handed me an envelope which turned out to contain 40 five pound notes, and departed without uttering more than a dozen words.

Steve's MG was in the hangar, complete with keys and a full tank - petrol rationing never seemed to cramp his motoring style - and I drove back to London, stopping at a roadside cafe for something to eat. I thought of going first to St Johns Wood, but it would have been very late, so contented myself with phoning from the cafe's call box. I told Angie about my trip, and she gave me the good news that Josie had contacted her boss, all was OK there, and she was going to work next day. Josie herself seemed fine, just subdued, she said. I told her what I was doing and said I'd see her next evening, at home. I drove on to Notting Hill, put the car in Steve's lock-up just round the corner, and dropped the keys through his flat's letter-box, all as per instructions. And went to my hotel, for the last comfortable night I'd have for a long time.

After breakfast next morning, I went back to my room and started to try to work out what I should do next. I was still firm in my intention to have no more to do with Steve and his companions, and as I'd told Angie, the idea of farming now attracted me. But how to go about it was another matter. I'd very little money, not a great deal more than the £700 I'd been paid by Jimmy and Co, and I was quite sure that would not be enough to set me up. I was in the middle of wondering whether my father would help when the phone rang. It was the hotel receptionist to say there were two gentlemen to see me, would I come down to the lounge.

One said: "Mr Jameson? Alastair Jameson?"

"Yes."

"We're Metropolitan Police officers. I'm Detective Chief Inspector Woods and this is Detective Sergeant Mallory. We want to talk to you. Come with us, please."

My stomach churned. I knew at once it was about Steve and his friends.

I said. "What do you want to talk about?"

The chief inspector said: "I don't think I can say, here. We can talk at the station."

There were two or three other hotel guests in the room, and I could see their ears were cocked - the two were fairly obvious policemen, even though the chief inspector had kept his voice low.

I said: "I'll get my coat."

"Alright. Sergeant Mallory will come with you."

This was awful. It was clear they didn't mean to let me out of their sight. But there was nothing I could do about it, except go along. I fetched my coat, with Mallory, who I thought took a hard look round my room, locked the door and gave the key to the receptionist, as usual.

The police station was as they said, only round the corner, not more than 200 yards away. The two were completely silent all the way, and when we got there Chief Inspector Woods told the sergeant at the desk: "This is Alastair Jameson. We're talking to him in my office. Let Mr Cockram know, please."

This was all doing nothing for my peace of mind. It looked like serious stuff. My fears were proving well-founded, I was thinking. I'd promised Steve I'd keep my mouth shut, but would I be able to. And how and where would I come out of it?

In the chief inspector's office, the sergeant put a chair in front of the desk, Woods sat in his own chair, but Mallory remained standing. Worse and worse, I thought gloomily.

The chief inspector said: "Now. Is your name Alastair Charles George Jameson?"

"Yes."

"Do you know a Stephen John Parrimore?"

"Yes."

"And a James Patrick Shaunessy?"

I thought briefly. This was obviously Jimmy.

"The name is unknown to me."

"I hope you're not going to try to be clever, Jameson. We think you do know him."

"I assure you I have never heard that name before now."

"Didn't you fly to Italy with him, very recently?"

"Oh, that must be Jimmy. That was the only time I met him, and I never heard his full name."

"What were you doing with him?"

"I was flying one of two aeroplanes."

"Who flew the other?"

"Steve Parrimore."

"What were you doing with the aeroplanes?"

"We collected a cargo to bring back to England."

"Collected it from where?"

"Suez."

"And what was the cargo."

"I understood it was war surplus, from Burma."

"What kind of war surplus?"

"I don't know the details. I was never told."

"Where did you bring it to?"

"An airfield in Shropshire – Heath Field."

"How much were you paid for flying your aeroplane?"

I thought for a moment. I knew where the mention of £500 would take them.

"Is that important?"

"I warned you not to try to be clever, Jameson. It won't do you or anyone else any good, you know. I ask you again - how much were you paid?"

"Five hundred pounds - about. Some of it was dollars."

"I should have thought that was at least twice the going rate, perhaps three times. Isn't that right?"

"It was good pay."

"Tell me a few more details. Where did you take off from?"

"It was an old airfield in Norfolk."

"Watton?

"Yes."

"Where did you fly to?"

"Italy first, then on to Suez."

"And where was your stop in Italy?"

"I don't know the airfield's name. It was near Lake Bracciano, north of Rome."

"Another more or less disused airfield, isn't it? And when you came back, where did you land?

"Heath Field, in Shropshire."

"Disused again. All a bit cloak and dagger, wasn't it?"

I didn't answer.

"I'll ask you again. What did the so-called 'war surplus' consist of? Why couldn't it be brought in by the usual channels? Why these special flights and highly-paid pilots?"

"I don't know. I was asked to fly a plane, for a fee."

"Why you? Who engaged you?"

"Steve Parrimore. We'd been in the RAF together and he knew I had a reputation as a good navigator."

"Yes, Flight Lieutenant Jameson, we know about your war record, and his. My job is not to have opinions, only to find the facts, but I must say I think it is a great pity that two people with such records should be mixed up in this kind of thing."

He paused as the door opened and another, slightly older man came in. Woods immediately got up and went outside with him. They came back in a few minutes and the sergeant found the new man a chair, near to Woods, who said: "Jameson, this is Chief Superintendent Cockram, who is leading this investigation. I've told him about our conversation so far, and that I believe you have told me the truth, as far as it goes, up to now. But I think there is more, probably a great deal more, that you can tell us.

"Now, this 'war surplus cargo.' What was really in it?"

I thought, wondered how much I could say, bearing in mind Steve's warning that consequences of talking could be "unpleasant." I was sure he meant I would be visited by Jimmy's heavies, if I said much. But as I knew so little, I decided, very quickly, that honesty was the best policy.

"Well?" Woods asked.

"They assured me it was properly bought and paid for and they had the documents to prove it. The only things they hadn't got were export and import licences, and that was why it couldn't come in through the normal channels."

"And why hadn't they got the licences? Plenty of war surplus material has been brought in, perfectly legally."

"I think there might have been some arms and ammunition in it."

"Might have been, Jameson? There was, wasn't there, and you know it."

"Yes."

"How much?"

"I don't know. I was only told there was some."

"And what else?"

"Electrical goods and radios were mentioned."

"And…?"

"Sorry, chief inspector, I don't know what you mean."

"What else?"

"I don't know of anything else."

"Drugs, for example?"

I started, looked sharply at him. So that was it. And they were on to it.

"If there was, I knew nothing about it. I really didn't."

They both looked hard at me, obviously trying to decide whether or not they believed me.

The chief superintendent spoke next: "Where were you yesterday, Mr Jameson?"

Again I decided on honesty.

"I flew to Holland, with Steve Parrimore, and brought the plane back myself."

"What for?"

"I don't know why Steve stayed in Holland. I brought a parcel back."

"A parcel of what?"

"I don't know. Someone took it off the plane when we landed. I brought Steve's car back here."

"Someone? Who was that?"

"Dermot somebody. I don't know his other name."

The two officers glanced at each other, before the chief inspector said:"Now, Jameson, we think you're being reasonably straight with us, and I'm going to be straight with you. That cargo you brought from Suez included a large consignment of raw opium, many hundreds of thousands of pounds worth. And the rest was almost entirely made up of guns and ammunition. Shaunessy, Jimmy as you know him, is one of the people behind the trade, and he's already in custody. Your friend Parrimore will also be in the care of our colleagues in Holland before too long, I believe. We have the evidence to charge them, Shaunessy in particular, with very serious crimes which I hope will put him behind bars for a long time.

"It's fairly clear to me, not only from this interview but from other things we know, that you were not directly involved in the drugs business. You might even want to help us. Perhaps to stop this material, or some of it, getting out on the streets or wherever they peddle it. You see, it won't be there yet because, being raw opium, it will take time to process etc. Would you be prepared to help?"

"I don't like the idea of drugs, but I don't see how I can help you. I've told you all I know."

"Perhaps. Who took the cargo off you in Shropshire?"

"Two chaps brought lorries and it was loaded into them."

"Would you recognise them again?"

"I don't think so, not to be certain. It was quite dark and we didn't have much in the way of lights."

"What about the other places? Suez?"

"I think it was four men who brought it in lorries. I helped load it into the planes, so I saw a bit of them, but they didn't really register. I think they were locals - Arabs, anyway."

"What about the people at the airfields, Watton and Bracciano? You'd see a bit of them, surely. Do you know their names?"

"The chap in charge at Watton – I think he's the owner – was called Doug. I don't know his other name."

"Would you recognise him if you saw him again?"

"Yes."

"And Bracciano?"

"Yes, I think so."

"And you're sure you don't know anything about where the drugs and the other cargo was going, from Heath Field?"

"No, they just went off towards the road."

"Very well. Now, are you sure there isn't anything else you can tell us about where this 'cargo' was coming from or going to?"

"I don't think so."

"What about the parcel from Amsterdam?"

"It was just a parcel. Steve gave it to me at Amsterdam and the chap Dermot took it off me at Heath Field."

"Right. Well, Jameson, I'm prepared to accept that you're being straightforward about your part in this. It will stand you in good stead in what is bound to happen to you, although I must warn you that if we find you've been trying to pull any fast ones on us, you are likely to wish you hadn't."

It sounded like an echo of Steve's "unpleasant consequences."

I asked: "I've not tried to deceive you, and I won't. What happens now, chief inspector?"

"You will be arrested and charged with aiding and abetting the illegal import of drugs and arms."

"Oh, my God." My head went down between my knees.

The superintendent said sternly: "We've no option, my lad - you did just that. You knew you were involved in something that wasn't above board, didn't you, and you're going to have to take the consequences."

I just crouched there, head still down, and they let me. I know I should have expected this, but when they started to talk about helping them my hopes had risen. Perhaps I'd "got away with it." After a few minutes I pulled myself together enough to sit up straight, to ask: "What must I do now?"

"You should make a written statement saying in effect what you have told us, and you will be held here for tonight. Tomorrow you will go before a magistrate. We shall ask for you to be remanded in custody for some time. At the end of that time you will appear before the magistrate again. At that stage, if you wish to apply for release on bail, pending the case being heard by a higher court, we shall probably not oppose it, depending on what has happened in our inquiries into the whole matter. Now, have you a solicitor you want to contact? Or anyone else?"

Oh, God, Angie, I thought, my beautiful little girl. And my parents. What would it do to them all?

"Would it be possible for me to make a phone call? Just to tell someone I won't get to see them tonight?"

The chief inspector said: "We'll have to monitor the call. But yes, I think we can allow that. Do you want to make it now?"

"No, later on, please – about five o'clock. The person won't be home much before that."

"Yes, alright. What about a solicitor. If you haven't got one, there's a duty rota. One of them will help."

I thought a moment. What was the good, I thought in my ignorance. He could do me no good at all. I was obviously going to prison.

"No, it doesn't matter," I said.

*****

They duly went through the arrest and charging procedure, including taking my fingerprints, and I was shut into a miserable cell with no furniture, only a hard bench with an apology for a mattress. Later they brought me blankets and some food, at lunch time.

"You're lucky – it's Maggie's head girl in the canteen today," said the constable who delivered it. "Cup of tea just now?"

I wondered whether he and his jovial mates ever spared a thought for the agony some of the poor devils in those cells were going through. Not that most of them deserved to have a thought bestowed on them, no doubt. But I ate the meal of meat balls and veg, apple pie and custard, and it wasn't bad, although I hadn't much appetite . The mug of tea was pretty good, too, and as I drank it I pondered over what I could do now, assuming I had the right or power to do anything.

At first, Angie occupied all my thoughts. How good everything looked two days ago. I was almost a hero in her eyes, coming to the rescue like the white knight, sorting out the problem of Josie, making me almost believe it myself. Certainly it had helped make me determined to pull myself together, to earn a proper place in the world through my own efforts, so I could marry her with something worthwhile to offer for her future and mine. Now I was going to have to tell her to forget me. Oh, my darling little Angie, what am I doing to you? Will you keep up your work, as you promised? And then I thought of what must follow - she'd meet someone else and forget all about me.

I drifted on to think about my father and mother. There had been I, about to ask my dad for advice on my future. Now all I could do was tell him I was almost certainly going to prison. Not for being bad, just weak and reluctant to buckle down to some real work, because I didn't want to be bored. Some white knight! But I knew that my father, and even more my mother, would never wash their hands off me. They would want to help me in any way they could. I wondered whether the police here, who seemed a pretty decent lot, would allow me to write to them. I knocked hard on the cell door. A constable pushed aside the window grill.

"Would it be possible for me to write to someone - my father?"

"I'll ask."

A few minutes later: "The chief inspector wants to see you again. Come with me," and he escorted me to his chief's office.

"You want to write to your father, Jameson?"

"Yes, please. To my father and mother. I want to tell them about this now. I don't want them to hear about it any other way."

"Yes, that'll be alright. We'll find you the necessary. But I must see what you write. You can do it now, and then you can make that statement.

Sergeant Mallory will take it down to your dictation."

"You haven't forgotten about the phone call I asked if I could make, have you, Inspector"

"No, I hadn't forgotten. Later on, I think you said."

"Yes, about five oclock. Please. When sh – the person – is home."

"A young lady?"

"Yes," I said, feeling myself redden.

"What does she know about this?"

"Nothing at all, except that I've been on a couple of flying trips. And she wasn't going to know. I told Steve Parrimore before Monday that I wouldn't be having any more to do with him. Now I shall have to tell her what's happened. I expect that will be the end."

"Look, lad, you did a very silly thing, and as the chief said, you're going to have to take your medicine, even if you were only a pawn in the game. But you've got a long life ahead of you and I know you come from a very good family. I hope you'll sort it out. I'll tell the desk sergeant to let you make that phone call. He or someone else will have to listen in, but unless you say something you shouldn't it won't go any further."

I was almost weeping, and he could see it. I said: "Thank you very much. Thank you."

As we went past the desk sergeant, the chief inspector said: "Let Mr Jameson have some writing paper and an envelope, sergeant - and something to write on, there's nothing in the cell. He's writing a letter that I must see before the envelope is sealed. Then he'll be making a statement with Sergeant Mallory. And I've given him permission to make a phone call, which you will monitor and report to me. About five o'clock, Jameson?"

"Thank you," I said, and was left in charge of the constable who took me back to the cell.

Moments later, the sergeant appeared with a writing pad, envelope and ball-point pen - and a small folding table.

"My Gawd, young feller, you've made some kind of impression on the guv'nors," he said. "The occupants of these little palaces don't usually get this kind of treatment. That's his own biro that I happen to know his missus gave him. Shout as soon as you've finished your letter - don't seal it, mind - and I or someone will take it to him. And I'll fetch you for that phone call at five o'clock."

"Or just before, if you can, sergeant. Thank you."

That letter was easily the hardest I had ever written. It was good that they'd given me a whole pad of paper, for it took several attempts before I could get going. In the end I said they would be shocked and distressed at what I had to tell them, but then I more or less recounted what had happened, starting with Steve contacting me, which they knew about, going through the whole trip, and the Dutch one, and ending with my arrest. I also told them I knew nothing about any drugs being involved until I was told about it by the police, although I knew the cargo included arms. I said I should almost certainly go to prison, and that I was bitterly ashamed of it all, and that I should have known all along that it was shady business. I did not say anything about Angie. I thought she would probably disappear from my life - I wouldn't even see her again.

I let the custody officer know the letter was finished, and he took me with it to the chief inspector.

"While I'm looking at this, you can do that statement, with the sergeant," he said. "He's next door. You can go through."

Sergeant Mallory said: "You can write this yourself if you wish, but we usually find it more satisfactory to do it with you. But I shall write only what you tell me, you can correct it as we go along, and at the end you add a short statement in your own writing, and sign it. All clear?"

It was, and when we finished, I was quite happy, if that's a word you could use with reference to me on that day, to sign it as "my own statement, made of my own free will."

By then, it was nearly five o'clock. I asked if I could make that phone call. I was shaking like a leaf as the sergeant dialled the Royston's number. Angie answered - Josie would not yet be home from her first day back at work.

"Hello," she said.

"Angie, it's me, Alastair." I was almost breaking down.

"Alastair, whatever's the matter? You sound awful."

"Angie, I won't get to see you tonight. I'm sorry."

"Why? What's happened? What is it?"

"I can't tell you much. I'm at a police station."

"Where? Oh, Alastair, have you had an accident? Are you alright?"

"No, I've not had an accident."

"What are you doing at a police station?"

"I've been arrested" - I heard her gasp, almost scream. "It's to do with Steve and those flights I did. I can't tell you any more."

"But you didn't do anything wrong, did you?"

"They say I did. I should have known it was wrong, anyway."

"Oh, Alastair. Can I see you? What police station is it?"

"I'm not sure I'm allowed to tell you that... hold on a minute while I ask." I looked at the chief inspector, who had joined us and was obviously listening, although only the sergeant could hear Angie.

"She wants to know where I am and if she can see me."

"Yes to both. I shall want to see her sometime, anyway."

I spoke to Angie again. "The station's at Notting Hill. The chief inspector says you can see me, but he'll want to talk to you."

"I'm coming right away. I'll leave a note for Josie and get a taxi."

They took me back to the cell. I sat and wept, without tears. Not for myself, but for what I had already decided I must do. Even at that stage, I knew I must break off from Angie, not allow her young life, so full of promise, to be blighted by being tied to someone whose disgrace must reflect on her as well. I knew that she would not part willingly. She was as deeply and truly in love with me as any 17-year-old could be. If this had not happened we could have spent our whole lives together, in great happiness. But it had happened. When I thought of what her father and mother, and her brother, who had not even met me, would think and say when they learned about me, my stomach turned over. No, it was the only thing to do, the right thing for her, in the long run.

I 've wondered many times since, at various intervals, whether I was right. Was not the truth that I was wallowing in self-indulgent self pity, and making myself believe I was "doing the right thing?" Would she not have coped with the disaster hitting her newly found love? Our few weeks acquaintance had left me with the feeling that she was destined to do great things with her life. Would she not have revelled, almost, in triumphing over the adversity. Seventeen years old or not, would she not have emerged, bringing me with her, from the gloom of that October evening to a bright dawn? But then, in that miserable little cell, I was proud of my decision, and I have never really thought since, at various times of more mature consideration, that I was truly wrong.

It must have been an hour and a half later when I was taken out of the cell to the chief inspector's office, and found Angie there. She flew into my arms, despite Sergeant Mallory's protests - waved away by the chief inspector, who however told us both to sit down.

"Miss Royston has been singing your praises, Jameson," he said. "How you rescued her sister from the clutches of a certain gentleman you know, and how you couldn't possibly do anything wrong. I've tried to disillusion her, but she won't have it." He did not smile, but I'm sure there was a twinkle round his eyes.

Angie said: "Could I possibly see Alastair alone, for a few minutes, Inspector?"

"That is against regulations, I'm afraid. But, if you would consent to being searched - by a woman officer - and be under observation from someone who could see but not hear you, I will agree to it, for ten minutes. It will have to be in the cell, though."

I was taken away, but five minutes later Angie was shown into the cell, the door locked but with an officer standing outside looking in through its window. We sat down on the "bed" and she took my hands.

"Oh, Alastair, my Alastair, whatever is going to happen to you?"

"I shall go to prison, there's no doubt about that."

"But you did nothing wrong, really."

"How much have you been told?"

"Only that you've been charged with aiding and abetting - oh what was it - the illegal import of drugs and arms. Was that what they were doing? You didn't know, though, did you?"

"I knew there were some guns and ammunition in the stuff. And I should have guessed there was more to it. I should have had nothing to do with it."

"Oh, Alastair. Alastair." She looked into my eyes.

"What's going to happen now?"

"They're going to take me to a magistrate tomorrow, and ask for me to be 'remanded in custody' I think they call it. That will probably mean I'll be kept in a prison somewhere for some time, I don't know how long. The inspector says I might be allowed out on bail after that, until the full court hearing. The judge will decide what's happening to me then, but I'm sure I'll be sent to gaol."

She clasped my hands tighter.

"Alastair, my love, I shall be waiting for you, however long it is. You're good, not bad. I want to marry you."

The full strength of my resolve had to be called up, before I could say: "Please listen carefully to this, Angie, my dear, dear little Angie. I don't want to say this, but I must. I must."

She looked at me with tears welling. I think she knew what was coming.

"I want you to go away tonight and never think of seeing me again..."

"No, no," she almost shouted.

"You must, my love. You must follow the course that's right for you – finish your schooling and go to university, and become a doctor – a famous doctor, probably. You can't do that if you're tied to a jailbird."

Francis John Simcock

"No, Alastair, no. I won't. You can't make me. You're not a jailbird, you're a dear, good man. You've already saved me, and Josie, from some awful things. Whatever happens, I'll be waiting for you..."

"I've been weak and foolish, Angie. I'm not good enough for you. You must not, must not allow your life to be ruined through being weighed down by someone like me..."

There came a loud knock on the door.

"Angie, my darling, you're going to have to go. Just make me a promise, or rather repeat one you've already made. Whatever happens to me, will you promise to do what I said - work hard to finish your school, go to university. Promise, Angie - whatever happens."

The door opened.

"Promise, Angie?"

She wept bitterly. "I promise, I promise," she sobbed, and was led through the door.

Five

The Message

I passed a pretty awful night, not from physical discomfort, although there was some of that, but agonising over Angie and my parents. At about eight o'clock they let me out to go to the lavatory and wash - nothing was said about shaving - and afterwards I was brought a pretty decent breakfast of a bacon sandwich, toast and tea. About ten o'clock a sergeant came for me with the words: "Come on, lad, you're going to court," and produced handcuffs which he put on my wrists. I was taken outside to a car, with a driver and two other officers, and we drove round the streets for five or ten minutes, to arrive at the court.

They took the handcuffs off and I was sat with the two constables in the well of the court while a case of dangerous driving was continued. I thought the driver, who narrowly escaped killing an elderly woman, deserved all he got - a heavy fine and a year's driving ban. Then it was me.

Chief Inspector Woods was there and told the magistrate, after I'd been asked to confirm my details: "The prisoner, Alastair Charles George Jameson has been arrested and charged with aiding and abetting the illegal import of drugs, arms and ammunition, your worship. We believe he helped the import by flying one of two aircraft involved, and that he knew the activity was illegal.

"This is part of an ongoing investigation into a very serious crime, in fact a number of crimes, involving a number of people. We have many more enquiries to make, and we are asking that this person be remanded in custody for an initial period of 14 days."

The magistrate leaned over and talked to the clerk, for a few minutes. Then he said: "I shall grant your application, Chief Inspector."

To me, he said: "You will be remanded in the custody of His Majesty's Prison Service for 14 days, and will then be brought back to this court. Do you understand.?"

I said: "Yes, your worship," and they took me away and back to the police station.

There, they told me I could if I wished be taken to the hotel to collect clothes and other items.

"If you don't, you'll have to wear prison clothes," the sergeant who now appeared to be in charge of me said.

I said: "Yes, please, and I'd like to pay my bill. But they've taken my wallet."

"I've got it, and your watch and your other things. Yes, you can do that."

It was not pleasant, going into the hotel in the obvious charge of two uniformed policemen, although they'd removed the handcuffs. But it was achieved, and with my small suitcase we were soon back in the car and on the way to what I later found was Brixton Prison.

Everything except a couple of Penguins I'd already read was taken from me, I was made to take a bath, given some of my own clean clothes and escorted along noisy galleries to the cell where I was to spend most of the next fortnight. It was slightly superior to the one at the police station. The bed was reasonably comfortable, there was a chair, a small table with drawers and a toilet bucket for furniture. The green and cream paint was reasonably fresh, and the graffiti was just about as boring as you could expect, although there was one witty poem about a golfer who allowed his wife to be made free with by a tiny chap who was supposed to have been a genie, cooped up in a glass bottle for a thousand years.

My life through those two weeks was pretty miserable, as you can imagine. The couple of dozen "remands" spent several hours of each day, morning and afternoon, doing sewing repairs to mailbags, sitting on hard chairs, with no tables or benches, on the ground floor of the huge hall round which were three storeys of galleries and cells. The work sessions were broken up by the dinner break and morning and afternoon exercise sessions, when we trailed in twos on a marked path round one of the outside "yards." I found myself more often than not in the company of a lad of seventeen or eighteen, more or less the duplicate of the "poor little sod" I remembered from my square-bashing days at Filey. He was there on a burglary charge, and when I asked him whether he had done it, he said: "Cor, 'course I did." And gradually he told me how he'd been caught - he'd taken some of the jewellery he'd stolen to a pawnshop - the very next day.

I asked: "What made you do it? Haven't you got a job?"

"'Ad one or two, but they was never any good. They all fort because I was not very big they could make me do all the fings nobody else wanted to. S'pose I should've put up wiv it, until I could get somefin better, but some of 'em got right up my nose. I was on to somefin better a coupla times but the blokes I was wiv – builders, they was – wouldn't give me a reference. I wuz a runner for a bookie before I copped this lot - that's 'ow I come to do the job, see. One o' the punters told me abaht this 'ouse, reckoned it were easy as fallin' off a log, an' so it was, until 'uncle' told the rozzers abaht the stuff I'd sold 'im."

"I suppose you think you'll go to prison," I said.

"Yah, year stretch, I reckon."

"And what about after that?"

"Dunno, mate. 'Ave to see what comes along. Tell yer, mate, I wish I could get out o' this, though. Ain't no life for a dog."

I thought again, poor little sod.

The third day I was at Brixton, my own routine was broken when one of the warders - officers to themselves, screws to the inmates - came to the sewing group and shouted: "Jameson!"

"Yes, sir," I responded - you were told you must always call them "sir."

"You've got a visitor. Come with me."

"I asked: "Who is it?"

"Young lady, name of Royston."

I stopped. "I don't want to see her - sir."

"An' suppose I tell you you've got to see her, Jameson?"

"Please don't. It's for her sake."

He was a middle-aged man, with a not-unkindly look about him. And he looked hard at me then.

"Have you got her in trouble?" he asked.

"No, sir. But I think it's better if she goes away and forgets about me. I've already told her so, but I suppose she hasn't accepted it."

"I'm going to see if the governor can see you," he said. "Go back to your place for a minute or two."

Ten minutes later he returned and spoke to the officer in charge of us, who beckoned me out.

The middle-aged officer, who I found later was a senior man, I forget the title they gave him - said: "The governor wants to see you. Come along," and I was taken to the governor's office.

He was a sober-looking, also middle-aged chap, who said immediately: "Mr Johnson says you don't want to see your visitor. Why not?"

"Sir, she is very young, in fact still at school. I have only known her for a few weeks, but she is very fond of me, in fact we have both said we would like to be married. But that was before all this. She is a very bright girl, and wants to be a doctor. I think I would be a millstone round her neck, sir. I've already asked her to please go away and forget me, and get on with her work and career."

The governor looked hard at me, as the officer had.

"You mean you want to get rid of her."

"No, sir. I want her to get rid of me, because that's what would be best for her. She shouldn't be mixed up with... somebody in prison."

He looked hard at me again.

"If most of the men in here came to me with that kind of story I wouldn't believe them, Jameson. I'd think they were trying to be clever. But for some reason I think you're being honest. In any case, I can't force you to see her, so I won't try. Go back to your place."

I asked quickly, before Mr Johnson could lead me away: "Could I possibly ask if Ang - Miss Royston - could be given a message, sir?"

"I'm not sure I can do that. What's the message?"

"As I said, I've already asked her to go away and forget me, and I got her to promise that whatever happened she would keep up her studies, and university, and medical school or whatever you have to do to become a doctor. Could she be reminded of that promise, when she's told I don't want to see her? Please."

Again he studied me.

"I shall tell her myself," he said.

*****

I was never told how Angie responded to my refusal to see her, or to my message. But next day I was again summoned to see visitors, two of them this time. It was my mother and father.

They were waiting in a quite comfortable room reserved for remand prisoners' visitors. My mother burst into tears as I was seated down opposite them across a table, with an officer standing a few feet away. I said: "Please don't cry, mother. It's not the end of the world."

We all sat there, before my father asked: "Are you alright, Alastair?"

I assured him I was perfectly OK, which I was, physically. But I added: "Dad, I'm so sorry."

He grasped my hand across the table, and squeezed. The officer looked as though he was about to tell us "no touching," or whatever they were supposed to say, and I gently took my hand away.

Dad said: "I've been told what you're supposed to have done. The chief inspector told me. But I'd like to hear it from you. However did all this come about? What did you do?"

I told him exactly what had happened, from start to finish. And at the end, I said: "I knew there was something fishy about it, Dad. But I did not know drugs were involved. I promise you I did not know. It came as a surprise to me. But I should have known it was something nasty, by the secrecy and the amount they were paying me. I should have had nothing to do with it, I know now."

"Oh, why did you, Alastair," my mother sighed. "You only had to ask us if you needed money."

"It wasn't that. I didn't need money."

"Why, then?"

"Oh, I don't know. You know I didn't like the thought of the land agent thing, and I guessed Steve would have something more interesting in view - more exciting, I suppose I mean. I was a fool. When I found out what it was I should have told him I wanted nothing to do with it. But it's too late now."

My father, who I'm sure never did a really foolish thing in his life, said: "Everyone makes mistakes, son. But it's never too late to put your house in order."

Mother, again near to tears, burst in: "Darling, you know we'll never stop loving you, whatever happens. Whatever happens. And we'll always stand by you - always."

"Always, Alastair. But I think you know that," my father said..

I was almost crying myself. I said: "Yes, I know. Of course I know.

And I know how badly I've let you down. But I promise you nothing like this will ever happen again. Whatever I have to do, if I have to labour down a coalmine, I'll never do anything like this again."

"No, I'm sure you won't," Dad said. "But the important thing now is to decide what we have to do."

"There's nothing we can do," I said. "Only wait. I did it, and I'm going to suffer for it."

"Yes, I'm afraid you are," Dad said. "But there are things we can do to try to make sure your suffering isn't any worse than it has to be. The first is to get a good lawyer, one who can put your case over properly. I've not done anything about it yet, because I wanted to talk to you first. But I shall start on it tomorrow.

"We had a long talk this morning with Chief Inspector Woods. He was very straight with us, Alastair, and told us as much as he could about the case. What he said corroborates what you've told us, pretty well exactly. I don't think you have anything to fear from the police - they won't try to make things any harder for you than they can help. He told us that at the moment they are minded not to oppose your temporary release on bail when you go before the magistrate again, although he did warn us that circumstances may change that. He didn't say what he meant by 'circumstances.'

"One thing he told us though - there's a young lady on the scene. Are you going to tell us about that?"

"There was a young lady, father. Not any more."

"Go on."

"I've told her I don't want to see her any more. She must go away and forget me."

"Oh, Alastair," my mother said. "Do you really mean it? Was it just a casual - thing?"

"No. I loved her. Still do. And she loves me."

"Well, won't she stand by you then?"

"I'm sure she would. But I don't think it would be right, for her. You see..." And I told them all about Angie, and Josie, everything, including that her parents were both away and did not know anything about me.

"She's not much more than a child, mother. What are they going to think when they come back and find she's tied up with a criminal, because that's how everyone will see me? And she's got a fine future ahead of her, if she sticks to her work. I've made her promise that she will, and I think she'll keep it. But I don't want her tainted, and pulled down, by being tied to somebody in gaol, which we all know is where I'm going to be for God knows how many years."

My mother once again, almost sobbing: "Oh, Alastair, please, don't say things like that. If she really loves you, and you love her, she won't want to leave you. I wasn't much more than a child – hardly as old as her when I found I loved your father. All of us, your grandmother and all, went through the most terrible time because your grandfather didn't want him to marry me, but we've never regretted it. Never. Please don't be too hasty, if you really love her. Think again about it."

I could see the officer looking at the clock. We'd already had well over the permitted visiting time.

I said: "Our time's up, Mother. I'll think hard about what you've just said."

Dad said, as he got up to leave: "We'll see you again as soon as possible, dear lad. Is there anything you need? How's the food?"

"I wouldn't mind a couple of books, and some more underclothes and shirts.

Otherwise I'm fine. The food's not too bad - as good as in the Raf, anyway."

The visit over, it was back to the dreary prison routine. Seeing and talking to my parents though had a dual effect. On the one hand I was cheered up. To know, or rather to have re-emphasised that your mother and father think the world of you, and are there for you in spite of what you've done, is wonderful. On the other, the shame that had been growing in me even before the arrest was multiplied by seeing the love pour out of them, in circumstances which they could never have imagined. The only time my dad had come within a million miles of prisons, or even courts, was when he'd had to speak to police or magistrates about some estate employee who'd gone off the rails. The idea that he'd have to visit one of his own sons in an intellect-sapping, dolorous institution like HM Prison, Brixton, especially as it must have appeared to him from the outside, would never have occurred to him. Or to my mother, whose world had been filled with love and more love, above all for and from my father, and us, her children; and my grandmother - who occasionally, when she was recalling the past, she still slipped into calling "the mistress", to my father's amusement

As I promised my mother, I thought hard, agonised, about Angie, going deeper through the instinctive reasoning that had made me tell her she must go away and forget me. Knowing that she could be there for me, staying by me, waiting for me, believing in me, was a potential stimulant to my spirits as powerful as my parents' solicitude. But what would it all do for her? I knew that I cared deeply for her, and that if these horrors had not come upon us I would have delighted in watching her develop her obvious potential, getting to know her father, mother and brother, seeing Josie put the unfortunate blip in her life behind her. But how different it was now.

I could not but think of meeting her parents as another horror. Then I tried to put myself into their position, and beyond them the position of people with whom she had to have important and life-forming contacts.

How would it affect relationships with her teachers, for example her stiff, spinster headmistress (I did not actually know whether she was either stiff or unmarried, but I could not imagine the headmistress of a slightly upper-crust girls' school being anything else). Interviewed by Oxford or Cambridge admission boards, would they ask her if she had a "young man" and what did he do? If any of these real or imagined situations blocked the path to her career, how could I live with myself?

My mother's reply to that may well have been: "None of it is as important as real love, Alastair. Ask your father, or your Aunt Billie. They looked as though they might have to sacrifice everything for love. But they never hesitated."

I re-made my decision without giving mother a chance to preach her gospel. I decided I must stick to it. I was surer than ever that I'd come to the right conclusion. I determined however to contact her just one more time. I would write to her.

I wrote: "My dearest Angie, I am not going to say anything to you that I have not said before. But I hope I can get more over to you this way than in the few brief words that were possible at the police station.

"I love you, my darling Angie. I would like more than anything in the world to be married to you and to live with you all my life. But we must both forget all that, because of what is happening to me. I think to be attached to someone in prison, perhaps for many years, can only drag you down, and stop you realising the potential that I know you have.

"It may possibly help to know this. The days leading up to that weekend when we brought Josie home, when I first realised how much I loved you, had a tremendous effect on me. It made me see that I must change my approach to my own life, stop simply looking for things that excite me, or interest me and me alone. And it is you who have done it. I don't know how. But you did it. And I will stick to it.

"Please, please do not try to contact me again. Try to forget me. You will in time. And above all remember your promise to keep up your studies, work hard, and come out of them as the valuable member of society that I know you want to be."

The senior "screw" who had the censoring of the letter called me before him and said: "Cleverdick, aren't yer, Jameson?"

I said: "I wouldn't be here if I was - Sir. The letter is to her, not you, and I don't think she will think that."

He looked nastily at me, as though I was some small vermin that he'd like to crush under his boot, but said only: "No more insolence, or you'll be sorry, Mister Jameson." He reminded me of the drill sergeant at Filey. Thank God not many prison officers are like him. It will perhaps be noted that he is the only one, so far, that I've labelled "screw."

Six

Agony: *Angie*

When I received Alastair's letter, do you know what it made me want to do? It made me want to find Steve Parrimore and murder him. I could only see him as a worthless, mindless shit. He came near to ruining the life of my sister, and he parted me from the man I loved the first time I saw him, and who I wanted to spend my life with. And that is the only time I shall use that kind of language. And I don't really mean it, about murdering him, I mean. I could not kill anyone, even him or any of that rotten, conscienceless crowd who didn't care how many lives they ruined in satisfying their own greed. I know I would never have met Alastair if it had not been for Steve. I know he, Steve, had a terrific war record. And I know now that he was a long way from being the top man in the organisation. I still hated him. I don't any more, because I've grown out of it, and I know a little more about him. But I still think he is, or certainly was then, that worthless and mindless you-know-what.

The governor of Brixton Prison was a really nice man. He said Alastair had asked him to talk to me, and he'd said he would, which was very unusual. He said that although he could rarely say it of people who came into his prison, he thought Alastair was anything but a bad man, essentially, and his guess was that he'd eventually come through his troubles and do something worthwhile. Then he gave me Alastair's message.

I was crying, and the governor actually came to me with his handkerchief. I was too upset to take in everything he said, but I know he told me he had a daughter my age, and very like me. He said only I could decide whether to cast off from Alastair, and he wouldn't presume to offer his advice on such a close personal matter. But he wished us both the best of good fortune, wherever our paths took us.

The next few weeks were probably the most difficult period in my life, even harder than when Josie got mixed up with Steve Parrimore. I'd given my promise to Alastair, but I was far from sure, at that stage, that I would keep it. I would give up school, go and work in a shop or a factory, anything, just to be around when his ordeal was over. I'd be there for him, help him work that farm or whatever it was he decided to do. And oh, my darling, have your children, and bring them up, and be grandmother to their children.

Then I would think again about the promise, and the agony that I could see in his face and voice in that police cell, and in the words he had written. And I knew that behind the agony there was a greatness in him, that made him put me before himself. He could see what it would do to my parents, for instance, if I took a course that would distress them even more than they would have been distressed to come back and find Josie living the fast and loose life from which Alastair had rescued her. And after a while these were the thoughts that won out. I would have to keep my promises.

So I kept up my hard work at school, as I'd promised. In fact I gave up hockey to make more time for study, although I'd been made captain of the first eleven. Josie told me not to overdo it, on the basis of all work and no play being certain to make Jill a dull girl. But I was determined to keep my promise, whatever happened. I had to tell her about Alastair - it was impossible not to, when he didn't appear. But she had had a glimpse of what he was really like, and knew that he was, in the prison governor's words, anything but a bad man. What an understatement, I thought.

We had to decide how much to tell Mother, who had phoned to say she should be home in about another week. She wanted to know whether we were going to Gran's funeral, but both Josie and I thought we would not. It would have meant three days off work and school, and Josie did not think she should take that time off bearing in mind what had just happened. I did not want to miss three days, just because I didn't want to miss three days schoolwork. Both of us, me in particular, hardly knew Gran, who was an odd character. She had hated the thought of our mother marrying an Englishman, my father especially, and that plus the war had kept us apart. I remember going to stay with her when I was about five, and hating it.

Josie and I both agreed we should tell Mother nothing about either Steve or Alastair, unless she picked up something elsewhere, which we thought was unlikely. It was most improbable that anything would come from Josie's firm, and although I'd had a dodgy spell at school, when she first went to Steve's, it was only for a very short time, and since then I'd been going like a train, so it was not likely my parents would pick up anything from that source.

I heard nothing more from Alastair, but towards the end of his second week in prison, before my mother got home, we had a phone call from his mother. She said she and Mr Jameson would like to meet me. I didn't quite know what to say. I told her Alastair had told me I must forget all about him, but she said she knew that, and she didn't want to interfere, but she - they - would still like to see me. She was so insistent, and sounded so nice, that I agreed. They asked if they could come to my home, the next evening, and I agreed to that, as well. I was pretty uncertain as to whether I should have, but when I told Josie, she thought it could do no harm.

They were the nicest people, outside my family, that I have ever met. Mr Jameson came from a family of landowners, Alastair's mother was his mother's kitchen maid, at least that's how she started. They were so genuine, and caring, you knew no son of theirs could be truly bad, even if you did not know it for yourself. They told me quite a lot about their family, and a bit about how they fell in love - you could see they still were - and I soon knew

I would have loved being welcomed into their family, as I was certain I would have been. But I told them again that I had promised Alastair I would not try to contact him, and would work hard at my own career. And as Mr Jameson was talking to Josie, just before they left, I told Mrs Jameson something I had already decided in my own mind, however. I could not forget him, I would always love him, and when I had fulfilled my promise about working towards a career, I meant to break the other part of it. I would try to contact him.

She said: "Oh, my dear..." and I could see she was almost crying. She put her arms round me. What a lovely lady. But I didn't see them again. I guessed they told Alastair about seeing me and he'd persuaded them not to repeat it.

Mother came home, and there were of course plenty of tears then. She'd been away for nearly two months, and it had been an enormous strain for her, being away from us and seeing her own mother suffer and die. But she was very pleased with how we'd managed, kept the house going and everything, and that Josie's job and my school work were going well.

"Och, ma wee bairns, ye've done sae weel," she said - I don't think her Scots accent had even begun to moderate despite 25 years in the south of England. Some of my teachers had difficulty in understanding her, and even my father had occasionally to ask her to repeat something.

She soon settled down into running the house, and her daughters, as before, and I was not sorry to be relieved of some of the chores, although both Josie and I made sure we still did as many of them as she would allow. Dad came home quite soon after her, which meant that apart from my brother Stewart, who didn't get home very often, because he'd elected to do his NS with a Scottish regiment, keeping up some family associations, we were again a normal household. He, my dad, was soon due to retire from the merchant service, probably after another couple of voyages, which meant he would be home a great deal more by the time I went away to college, if I did.

As we hoped, Mother did not pick up anything about what had happened to Josie and me during her absence, and we were most careful not to let anything slip out. I continued to work very hard, to the extent that our parents also told me not to overdo it. I wanted a university scholarship if possible, to ease the financial burden on them. But my main incentive was my promise to Alastair. I was determined that if and when I was able to contact him again, it would be as "Dr Royston," so he'd know I'd kept it. "Overdoing it" was not on the cards. I needed to work. It was a way of saying "I love you." I didn't cry, very often. But at weekends, when I would make the beds for mother, the tears could not always be kept back as I smoothed the pillows and quilts in my parents' room, where he had slept those two nights.

Christmas came, and the school holidays, and Stewart was home for nearly a fortnight. As he went back Dad, who'd been working at his firm's docks at Tilbury for some weeks, again went to sea, and was gone for most of my next term. During the Easter holidays I worked even harder, revising for the exams in June. Mother said I looked ill, but I felt fine, I was eating normally, and I made a point of walking for an hour every day, even when it was raining, usually in the park where I had spent afternoons with Alastair. Once, I saw a man walking in front of me who looked just like him from the back, and my heart did a dozen somersaults. But it wasn't him, of course, and that much misnamed organ resumed its place in the empty pit of my stomach.

My Higher School Certificate exams came and went, and the scholarship exams for Oxford, Cambridge and London. I thought I'd done badly in everything, and I spent the rest of the middle summer months resigning myself to failure, or at least to less success than I needed to achieve what I wanted. I got a temporary job with Josie's firm, as a messenger ferrying notes, stationery and everything else that need carting round the big and complex offices. I was though given one or two little jobs to do which involved transcribing information from newspapers and other sources into shorter versions, and one day a departmental head had me called to his office where he asked me what I was planning to do for permanent work. I told him and he said the firm would be prepared to consider me for a position, which however I declined. I was still determined to study medicine and become a doctor, even if I had to focus my sights a little lower initially.

When the exam results came out in August I found to my delight that I had made top grades in all three of my subjects. I'd been told that the medical school at London was as good as they came, so my mother and I decided that was the one to go for, as I could then live at home, although a different decision might be called for if I was found to have won either an Oxford or Cambridge scholarship but not one for London. That did not happen, though. I was awarded all three, so London it was. I took up my place at the end of September.

Living at home, undergraduate life for me was not the great social adventure that it is for most. I was still in the frame of mind that I was doing it for Alastair, although as time went on I became engrossed in my work, enjoyed it for its own sake and began to look forward to the end result. But I didn't ignore the social life completely. I became friendly with a girl who came from the same part of the world as his grandparents, which gave me a rather strange, vicarious sense of connection although I did not tell her anything about my relationship with Alastair.

*****

Although I obeyed Alastair's wish that I should not try to get in touch with him, I scanned the newspapers every day, the Evening Standard in particular, and half way through my first year at university I found the headline I had been looking for, and dreading. It said: "Long sentences for drug and arms traffickers," and "Big international gang broken up." Apart from the report which filled most of the front page, there was a feature article inside which told how a huge police operation had finally brought those concerned to court.

I looked desperately for any mention of Alastair, but found his name only at the end.

"Another former RAF pilot, Alastair Charles George Jameson, 26, pleaded guilty to aiding and abetting part of the gang's multi-million dollar operations, and was sentenced to five years, reduced to three years and five months because of the time he had already spent in prison."

I'd heard nothing from him, or his mother and father. I didn't know whether he had been kept in prison right up to the trial, although that was implied by the Press report. There was no further mention of him anywhere in the paper.

Steve Parrimore however earned plenty of words and comment, much of it about his war record, although it was clear he was nowhere near the top of the operation. That honour seemed to lie with American, Dutch and Irish individuals, including one James Patrick Shaunessy, who I thought was probably the "Jimmy" I'd heard mentioned. He'd been sentenced to 18 years. I read all that was in the Standard, and bought another couple of papers, including The Times, which said more or less the same things in slightly more sober language. But no mention of Alastair either, apart from a bald statement of his crime and sentence.

I toyed with the idea of trying to see him again, and went to the Notting Hill police station to see if Chief Inspector Woods could help me - I wasn't even sure that he was still at Brixton, for I had an idea he would be sent somewhere else to serve his sentence. The chief inspector was quite kind, but he couldn't help immediately. Alastair had been at Brixton all the time since his arrest, and Mr Woods had seen him there, said he seemed well enough, although rather depressed. But he did not think he would still be there.

"If you really want to see him, I'll find out where he's been sent," he said. "But that's as far as I can go – you'll have to contact the prison authorities yourself if you want to visit him. But as you're not directly related to him I doubt whether they'll allow it. Of course, you know, he'll be out in a little over two years, as long as he behaves himself ."

I asked whether his parents had been to see him again, and he said they had, many times.

"They're very good people, Miss Royston. I'm sure they'll help him get on his feet when he comes out. He's lucky to have such a family behind him. His father offered to stand surety for him, if he could have bail, but we daren't agree to that, at that stage. He was a potential witness, and we were afraid he might be got at if he was out of custody - his life might even have been in danger. In fact we've asked the people at Brixton to keep a special eye on him.

"I shouldn't really be talking to you or anyone like this, because I'm a policeman and my job is to catch criminals, and I'm glad to do it, because I don't like them. But I don't think he's what I would call a criminal, even if he has committed a crime, and he's had to be punished for it, if only as an example to others. But we should all be pleased that he didn't get in any deeper. This was a very nasty gang he was mixed up with, you know."

I liked Mr Woods, and I was grateful to him for talking to me, just a schoolgirl, more or less, the way that he did. And although I wanted to see Alastair more than anything in the world, I decided I would not try, for the present. Instead I would write, as soon as I knew where he was.

The chief inspector kept his word and within a week the station phoned to say he wanted to speak to me. I called back and he told me Alastair was at Lewes prison, where he thought he was likely to remain. He even gave me the telephone number and address.

I telephoned Lewes, they told me what I had to do about writing, warning me that of course all mail was examined before prisoners could have it, and that they were only allowed a limited number of letters.

But I wrote one, telling Alastair how much I loved him, that I was waiting for him, that my work was going well, a bit about Josie, Stewart and our parents, and that I'd seen his, which however I was pretty sure he would know already. But the letter, which I thought so optimistically would restore our love to its rightful course, in spite of my breaking my promise, was never posted.

I put it into the small attache case I used for my papers, and next morning, after breakfast, went to fetch the case from my bedroom. Hurrying because I had not much time to catch my train, I tripped on the carpet at the top of the stairs, and went crashing to the very bottom. I was knocked about a bit, although without any serious injuries like broken bones. Dad was home, as it happened, and he and my mother picked me up, made sure I was not seriously hurt, and took me to sit down. A short while later, he came into the sitting room with a letter in his hand. It was the one I'd written to

Alastair. The case had burst open, scattering the contents, and he had found the envelope, addressed to Alastair at HM Prison, Lewes.

"What's this, Angela?" - he was one of the few who didn't shorten my name.

"It... it's... Oh, Dad..."

"Is it your letter?"

For an instant, I thought of saying I'd been asked to post it. But I dropped the idea immediately. I'd never lied to my dad since I was a small child.

"Yes, Dad."

"It's to someone... in prison!"

"Yes."

"How come, Angela?"

"Dad, it's alright. Please, he's not... like that. He's not a criminal, Dad, he's not... really..."

"What's he doing in prison, then, Angela?"

I just cried. I couldn't do anything else. The fall had knocked me for six, for a start. Now this. I cried and cried.

Mother came in with the drink she'd been making for me.

"Does it hurt sae sore, ma baby?"

"No, Mum, it's alright. I'm alright," I managed.

Dad ushered her out of the room, the letter in its envelope still in his hand. They came back in a few minutes, by when I'd managed to more or less stop sobbing.

Mother said: "Oh, dear, baby. What's all this?"

By now I'd recovered enough to start to think coherently. If I told them everything, Josie's part in it would come out. That would leave them as devastated as learning that I was involved with a criminal. Perhaps more devastated. But how else could I convince them what Alastair really was – a good man, not some kind of crook?

My parents were both old-fashionedly straight-laced, when it came to morals, sexual or otherwise. Dad, as a seaman all his life, knew a great deal about the seamier channels frequented by so many of his shipmates and crew members – ports with a wife in each, and all that. He never talked about it to us, but he didn't have to for us all to know where he stood in such matters, and to know, through instinct and such hard facts about him as came through from various sources, that he had never navigated such waters himself. Honesty was one of his watchwords, keeping promises and vows another. He never laid a hand on any of the three of us, but I remember shivering with fright, or perhaps in awe, when Stewart, aged about seven, had to admit not only that he had "taken" - the word stolen was never actually used - a ball from a neighbour's garden, but had then broken his promise to my mother that he would take it back and admit his "crime." Even today, whenever I hear a reference to "the day of judgement," it is the vision of my father's face on that day, never the face of a high court judge in his robes and wig, or of the Almighty on his heavenly throne, that flashes through my mind.

My mother's Presbyterian upbringing had resulted in an approach to life not so much similar as parallel. Honesty and keeping promises ranked just as high in her scale of essentials, but alongside was another: love, and love that must be shown, especially to children, and very especially to her own children. Given a situation like Stewart and the neighbour's ball, she would gather him to her, her own eyes full of tears, and reduce him to at least the same degree of penitence as did the awful sternness of my father.

For either parent, though, the knowledge that their daughter had hopped into bed with someone like Steve - or with anyone, for that matter - without a second thought and with no care for the consequences, would be a terrible blow, that would shatter their lives. At least, that is what I thought, which was what mattered for me on that day. (I know now of course that lives are not blown apart so readily, especially the lives of people as strong as my parents.)

The upshot of my rapid thinking, however, was that I must say nothing about Alastair, except to admit that I loved him, wanted to marry him one day, and to implore them to believe that he was not "bad," but was in prison because he had agreed to help an old RAF colleague and fellow pilot. I could not even reveal, to them, the facts of how I came to know him, without involving Josie, I feared. Therefore I must keep everything I said to the absolute minimum. Even something like his extracting my promise to work and qualify would bring an inevitable: "But why would he need to do that?"

So of course what I could and did say cut no ice at all with my father, and not much with my mother.

Dad listened, asked a few questions, the worst of which was: "Does Josie know about this?"

I almost said: "No." But instead I masked it with: "Dad, please don't tell her. Please." The lie was implied of course, but at least I hadn't spoken it. I was desperately afraid that if Mum and Dad talked to her about it, her part in it would come out, because she too believed in Alastair. She would want to defend him and me.

Another question from Dad, and I could guess how hard it was to ask: "This... love affair, I suppose I must call it... hasn't gone too far, has it?"

"No, Dad, and if you knew... Alastair... you wouldn't ask."

"Oh, ma bairn," my mother sobbed.

"And is that all you're going to tell us?" Dad asked. "There must be more you can say. Where does this Alastair come from? What was it he did - you say to help his friend - that landed him in gaol? How old is he? Has he got parents? Do you know them?"

"He was a pilot in the RAF in the war and his friend asked him to fly a plane to Egypt and back. It turned out it was carrying drugs, and guns. Alastair didn't know that.

"He comes from Leicestershire. His father manages a big estate for a lord. Yes, I've met his parents, and I think they're wonderful, and you'd say the same. He'll be 26 now."

Dad said: "That's all very well. But what are the people you have to deal with if you're going to get on with your career going to say if they know you're tied up with a... someone in prison?"

"He's told me to go away and forget him. That's why."

Dad looked at me. "You've been to see him, in prison?"

And my mother said, tearfully: "Oh, no, Angie..."

"No, I tried to, but he wouldn't see me. I saw him when he was arrested. He made me promise that I'd keep up my studies. And when he wouldn't see me at the prison, he asked the prison governor to remind me about it."

"It sounds to me as though he just wants rid of you, Angela," Dad said. And he added, quite harshly, for him: "I don't like you being mixed up with somebody so much older, let alone somebody in prison. I think there's more to this than you've told us. And I will say now, you will not pursue this foolish affair, with my approval. We can't have a jailbird in the family."

I suppose that realistically I should not have expected any different kind of reaction from my father. I'd been hoping that if I had managed to keep my secret from him and mother, they would see Alastair in a different light when they got to know him face to face, and met his mother and father, and saw that he was pursuing his life, and some worthwhile work, whatever it turned out to be, in a very different way from the past. And I'm afraid Dad was right to be concerned about what people I had to impress would say, especially those in the medical hierarchies.

I still determined to write to him, however, and I did, pretty well on the lines of the letter Dad found, which incidentally he never gave back to me. I don't suppose he and Mum read it, because I think they'd have told me if they had, and I never asked. But very foolishly I told Alastair about the incident, and Dad's reaction. I suppose I wanted to open the way to telling him how in spite of it I would be waiting for him.

Seven

In Brixton Gaol: *Alastair*

My mother and father came to see me again during my second week in Brixton. They brought the things I'd asked for, which reached me through the official channels, and told me they had arranged for a highly recommended local solicitor who would in turn brief a barrister. My father didn't say so, but I'm sure it was a case of "no expense is to be spared."

There was also a much less welcome visitor: Chief Inspector Woods. Not unwelcome personally, for I had grown to rather like him, but because of the news he brought.

He told me: "I'm afraid I have to tell you something you won't like, Jameson," he said. "But it's unavoidable. We will be opposing bail for you on Monday" - the day I was to go before the magistrate again. It was a shock - I'd been hoping, almost expecting, that I could go home to Netherton.

"Can you tell me why?" I asked.

"I can tell you some of it. We shall want to be talking to you again, because there may well be things you can tell us that will help in our investigations. That means we want you to be at hand. But more important than that, if they - the people at the top of this gang - know you are helping us by supplying information, they may well try to get at you, to stop you."

Steve's warning about "unpleasant consequences" came back. But I only said: "As I told you before, I don't think I've more information to give you. I don't know any more."

"I'm not saying you've held anything back, not deliberately, anyway. I don't think you have. But even if you can tell us absolutely nothing, the others may think you can. We'd rather have you under our eyes. Have you had any approaches while you've been here? Has anyone been paying particular attention to you?"

"Not that I'm aware of, chief inspector. One or two have asked what I'm here for, but only like they seem to ask anybody new."

"Good. If there was anything, ask to see the governor, and mention my name. I hope you won't be here too long, but I can't guarantee anything.

And you know, any time you spend in custody is normally taken into account in any prison sentence you get."

It was obvious he could not tell me any more. But the message coming through was that they, the police, were worried about my safety, as well as concerned that they might lose some evidence. You bastard, Parrimore, I thought. You were supposed to be a friend.

Anyway, Monday came, and I was taken to court, where almost the first person I saw was my father who introduced the solicitor who would be looking after my interests, James Southernwood.

He told me: "I've been briefed by the police, and your father has confirmed everyting they've said. The chief inspector seems to be taking a very decent view of it, I must say. But I'm afraid it's a waste of time asking for bail. The police would oppose it, and I understand they have good grounds for doing so. I will come to see you very soon wherever you are. But I must warn you, I think it is going to be some time before it all comes to trial."

I told him I had already gathered that, from the police.

A very brief procedure saw Chief Inspector Woods asking for a further remand in custody.

"This is a complex matter, and we have many more inquiries to make," he told the magistrate, who agreed to his request without asking any questions, except to Mr Southernwood , whether he wished to say anything.

The solicitor said only: "Thank you, your honour. My client's father is prepared to offer whatever sum is required as surety if bail is allowed. However, we are not asking for that at the moment."

I was allowed a very few minutes with my father, who could not say much, only: "Try to stay cheerful, my boy. Your mother, and Peter, and Kathleen all send their love. We'll see you as often as we can."

At Brixton, I was returned to my old cell, and in the afternoon joined the happy band of mailbag repairers, and in the exercise yard my friend the poor little sod, whose name it appeared was 'Erbie, and who I had grown to rather like. He was much more intelligent than he seemed at first sight, and later on we had some interesting conversations, which were among the few diversions to help alleviate the dreary misery of the year and more I spent in Brixton, awaiting trial.

I can truthfully say that that year was the unhappiest of my whole life. Worst of all, of course, was the loss of Angie - for I was determined to stick to my decision to break off from her. Whenever I thought of her, which was many times every day, at first, the thought of never seeing her again brought that feeling, a very physical feeling, of desolate emptiness in the pit of the stomach. As time went on - and on, and on - thoughts of her returned less often. Other matters usurped her place. It's like that with men, some of the great philosophers have told us. Women, some of them anyway, love to the exclusion of almost everything else. If love for their man fades, love for their children takes over. A man, though he may feel for his mate as powerfully as she for him, will pigeonhole his love within the cabinet of his life, where it lives alongside his work, politics, religion, sport, all else that makes him tick. I know that my father loved my mother beyond words, but he also loved his work and his country in equal measure, and she was the gainer for it. My love for Angie was as real, and as deep, as love by one person for another can ever be. But, as I just said, it could not oust all else from my mind. And I hope any woman who reads this will not immediately consign the words to the fire or the dustbin.

Apart from the loss of Angie, I was dropping into a deeper and deeper depression engendered by the miserable state of regard I had for myself, almost a feeling of contempt. The regular visits of my parents, although greatly looked forward to, left me sinking deeper into its morass, for many months, each time after they had gone. And when my brother Peter and sister Kathleen came in their place, it was even worse. There were they, obviously on their way to worthwhile and responsible places in society and the world, coming to see their elder brother whose thoughtless adventure had landed him in gaol. The only other person in our family who had seen the inside of a cell was my Aunt Billie, and her very brief sojourn there had been in a great cause. But I was pleased that she never came, although my mother and father told me she had offered to, and she sent her best wishes, which I knew were sincere. I expect my parents had told her it had all been a piece of stupid thoughtlessness, nothing worse.

Then there was Brixton Prison itself. Not just the building, although that, even the physical nature of it, was enough to send anyone but the most insensitive moron round the bend. And if it didn't, the utter pointlessness of the mind-numbing, morale-sapping routine, the slopping-out, the baths and showers supervised by officers who in a few cases were on a lower intellectual - and moral, for that matter - level than some of the prisoners, would complete the job. Nowadays, we are told that hordes of prisoners have mental problems. What a surprise! If they didn't when they went in, they'd certainly acquire them by the time they came out. Remand prisoners were not forced to work, but the only alternative was to be "banged up" in the cell for the duration of the work sessions; and the only work available, for them, was on the mailbags - seated on half a dozen rows of hard chairs, three or four feet apart, with no work table, under the eye of an officer seated at the front on a high chair, and not allowed to talk. The eight-hour day was broken by a lunch-hour back in the cells, and by the exercise periods when you walked round and round a yard in twos. You were allowed to talk there, however, which was when I had my conversations with Erbie.

Adding to the pressures on my own sanity was the apparently unremitting uncertainty about when it would all end. Would my trial be this month or next; this year or next? Southernwood the solicitor came to see me not long after my second court appearance, but he could tell me little or nothing more than I already knew from the police. He endorsed Woods' admission that I was being detained essentially to make sure I was not "got at", but had no information at all about whether the police had anything else they wanted me to "help" with. He said there was no point in further visits, or involving a barrister, until there were positive developments, and of course I had to agree.

One of the chats with Erbie I remember was about politics, and the new Labour government. He started it with: "Bet you're a true-blue, ain't yer, Ally, wiv your grandad, or great-grandad or somefink bein' a lord."

"Not a lord - a baronet - a 'sir'. That's a step below a lord. And he was a pretty useless individual, from all I've gathered - I'm not proud of being his great-grandson. And as a matter of fact, Herbie, I'm not a true-blue at all. I voted Labour in the election."

"Cor, I bet yer folks didn't like that. Why did yer?"

"I think I was just swimming with the tide, really. Most of the blokes I knew in the air force thought we should have a change."

"D'yer fink they wuz right?"

"I don't know. Too soon to say. What do you think?"

"I don't fink any of 'em 'ave any idea of what poor buggers like me really need. If they did, they'd make sure we got a job, so's we didn't end up in places like this all the time."

Another time, after he'd been unusually quiet for a few minutes: "D'yew believe in God, Ally?"

I was taken aback. Religion was about the last thing I'd have expected Erbie to talk about.

I said, feeling my way: "I don't know. I don't believe the way they seem to think we should. I don't believe there's an old man with a beard, sitting on a throne up there, with his beady eye on us all the time; or that if we're good we'll go to heaven, and the other place if we're bad. I believe in good and evil, I think. I'm prepared to believe that there's some force out there that's behind the world, and the universe, but not that God made the world just as it is now. Nor in all the mumbo-jumbo that goes on in the churches. What do you think?"

"Dunno, mate. P'raps wot you just said. What do you fink abaht Jesus Christ savin' the world an' all that, then?"

"I don't know, Herbie. I'm inclined to think he was just a very good man. But you're taking me out of my depth, you know. What's made you want to talk about it?"

"Oh, it's just that me muvver's gone all religious. She's got this bloke, see, an' 'e's converted 'er, or somefink. I fink 'e's just aht fer all 'e can get. But it's made me fink abaht it." And we went on discussing his "forts," and some of mine, for the rest of the session.

Again, when he had asked me about where my home was, and it led to my telling him a bit about Lyndford and the Welsh Marches, where my father and mother came from, he said: "Cor, wish I lived in the country."

"Yes, well, I think I want to go back there, when all this business is out of the way." And I told him of the idea that had been forming, that I would like to be a farmer, like my uncle.

"Gosh, Ally, that 'ud be great. I couldn't never be a farmer, course, 'cos I'd never 'ave the money. But I'd like to work with animals, an' on the land, an' that. When we wuz kids, before the war, me dad used to take us 'op pickin', dahn in Kent. That were smashin'. We used to 'ave to work like niggers, but it were smashin', reelly smashin'." His pinched face beamed, and his five foot four frame seemed to expand to fill a prison suit about three sizes too big. It was a conversation that stuck in my mind for a long time, and led to a bit of good I was able to do, years on.

I asked him what made him do the burglary, apart from being told about it by one of the bookie's punters. I said I didn't think he was really a criminal type.

He said: "I just couldn't get a job, Ally. I was livin' off me muvver, an' I 'adn't even got enough money to buy 'er a birthday present. An' this 'ouse I done belonged to a bloke I knew was nuffin' more 'n a villain 'imself, an' I didn't see as robbin' 'im was much of a crime. I can tell you I shan't do anyfink like it again, though."

Erbie was taken for trial soon after Christmas, and sentenced to a year, as he'd expected, which meant that with remission and his time on remand he was sent out into his wretched little outside world while I was still some time away from my own high court appearance, although I didn't know it then.

*****

I was hauled before the magistrate at regular intervals all through the spring and summer of that year. Each time James Southernwood was at the court but could give me no more information as to when my trial was likely to be. I was almost beginning to feel as though I was in some kind of Kafka-esque situation from which I would never emerge.

Remand prisoners were always kept one to a cell, about which I was pleased. By carefully timing a "fall out, sir?" request to the officer in charge of the mail-baggers, and by having a strong bladder and a regular digestive system I was able, more often than not, to avoid one of the most unpleasant aspects of prison life in those days, "slopping out", when you carried your own body waste in chamber pot or bucket to the disposal point. It also meant a sweeter atmosphere in the cell.

I have never smoked since being made violently sick by the weed in the usual place at school, behind the bike sheds. I therefore never became involved in dealing in "snout", the universal currency among prisoners at the time I was there. But my abstinence also took me out of the contact with others that the snout trade involved. I don't to this day know how it was all managed, but I could see enough to know that managed it was, even among "remands".

Chief Inspector Woods, with his sergeant, Mallory, in tow, came three times at various stages of my remand, and I have to say gave me a pretty hard grilling, although he was never personally unpleasant. On his first visit, he questioned me at length about the Dakotas, obviously seeking information about who they were provided by and on what terms. All I could tell him was about Steve's remark, and it was no more than that, that they were probably "one of Jimmy's fiddles." He also asked about the Piper I had flown to and from Holland, who I had seen on that trip, but every bit of my knowledge on that score amounted to just about zilch. I had to admit, as I had previously, that Steve had positively declined to give me anything but the information needed for me to fulfil my role in the affair, a point which must weigh against me, for it clearly showed he had something to hide.

He also showed me a number of photographs, asking me if I knew any of the individuals on them. I expected some of them to be of the airfield people, and perhaps they were, but I didn't recognise any. Except one, which took me by surprise, because I thought he was already in custody. It was Dermot, the "thug." I told him I knew him only as Dermot. I thought he smiled faintly, but he said nothing more.

Second time he came, he asked me only for a few details about the times of our departures and arrivals, and loading and unloading the cargo, all of which I told him as well as I could remember. Both times I asked him of course if he could tell me anything about the trial date, but all he would, I think could say was that the enquiry was progressing.

The third time however he was able to tell me, after more questions, that he had every expectation of the case being heard early in the new year. His questions however were quite different from prevous visits. He asked me very pointedly if anyone in the prison had approached me about the issue. I told him they had not, he looked at me very hard and repeated the question, or rather: "Are you sure?" But I was sure and said so. I did quite a lot of hard thinking afterwards, but I still could not recall anything that might have been construed as such an approach. I'd talked to a number of different men in the exercise yard, after Erbie left, but the conversations had never amounted to more than the prison equivalent of mess-room small talk; and as far as I could recall, I'd never spoken to anyone in the main body of the gaol, except officers. A man I walked with two or three times did say to me of an officer who supervised us one day: "Don't ever talk to 'im. 'E's a nark;" but that officer never spoke to me as an individual.

Just after Christmas however James Southernwood came to see me with some very interesting news.

"I'm pleased to be able to tell you, Alastair, that the trial is to start at the beginning of February, probably the first Monday in the month. There will be at least seven men on trial, including yourself, Stephen Parrimore and James Shaunessy. One of the others is from Holland and one is American, which is partly why the investigation has taken so long."

I asked him if he knew any other of the people charged and what the charges were.

"James Shaunessy is charged with illegally importing proscribed drugs, and arms, and importing other goods without a licence; your friend Parrimore is charged with knowingly helping those illegal activities. I haven't been told this officially, but I know they believe they belong to a big international cartel, part of which is involved in supplying arms to the IRA - the Irish Republican Army

- which is beginning to build up again in Northern Ireland. You didn't know anything about this, I hope."

"I certainly did not," I said. But I shuddered. God, this could take me away for years.

Southernwood arranged to visit me again as soon as the trial date was confirmed, when we would go through my involvement in detail. He also told me he had briefed a barrister, a rising young man, who would want to spend some time with me.

"Your father told me to spare no expense. I think he would have gone for a KC, even, but I'm inclined to think that would give the wrong impression - the impression that you were more deeply involved than you were in fact. This was just a foolish mistake on your part, wasn't it, and that is what we must get over."

Time started to go a little less drearily after that. In fact, only a week later Southernwood came again, when as he had said we would, we went through everything, starting with my family background, school at Shrewsbury and my RAF experience. My dealings with Steve, the trips to Suez and then to Holland were all noted in precise detail. A few times he questioned me as closely as had Inspector Woods. Angie was never mentioned, nor Steve's involvement with her sister.

Another week on, only a few days before the trial, the exercise was repeated with the barrister, Rupert Maconachie, a younger brother of whom, it turned out, I had known slightly in the RAF. I must say his personality did not impress me greatly, although he appeared to be extremely thorough, going deep into detail, as I told my father when he asked me what I thought of him. But he said: "Southernwood thinks very highly of him, Alastair, and I think highly of Southernwood." Which was good enough for me. And Maconachie proved to be a most effective advocate in court.

The trial was confirmed as starting on February 2nd, at the Old Bailey and was expected to last at least a week. I would be there throughout, Mr Southernwood told me, reminding me of something I had only just begun to think about - how would Steve and co look on me? Would I be a "grass" in their eyes, spilling everything I knew to the police?

Eight

The Old Bailey

I'd never seen the inside of a judge's court before, and I found the atmosphere of the Old Bailey awesome, dusty and dreary all at the same time. How many villains, not to mention a sizeable tally of innocent men, and women, had heard that bewigged, red-robed judge, or one of his generations of predecessors, pronounce their doom under a square of black cloth, from that same bench high above the well of the court, I could not help wondering at various stages of the proceedings, when no doubt my mind should have been on more important things. But before my thoughts reached that point, I studied the judge's face. What kind of man was he, under all that regalia? Would I be just another of those villains, in his eyes? Was there any room in his legal agenda or moral philosophy for making allowances for a stupid mistake?

The cells under the court were my first experience of the building. Steve, Jimmy, Dermot and their cohorts were there as well, I did not doubt, although I did not see them until I was taken up. Apart from officers, Rupert Maconachie and James Southernwood were the only people I saw, and that only for ten minutes, in the cell. The barrister asked if I had anything else to tell him, I said not, and he told me only to be absolutely straightforward in answering any questions, either from him or anyone else.

"I am quite sure that is our best line of defence," he said. "To get over the message that you are a basically honest person who got caught up - very foolishly caught up, and you ought to have known better - in the machinations of these people, who are admitting some serious crimes which I am quite sure will see them sent to prison for a long time."

I assured him I had no intention of being anything but straightforward. He said: "No, I think not. But you may be asked some questions that you find hard to answer simply."

When I was taken into the court, the others, six of them, were already lined up in the dock. But my first thought was to scan the public galleries, and I saw my mother, father and Peter. They all smiled encouragingly.

The preliminary proceedings, which took a surprisingly long time, ended with all the six being identically charged with the import of illegal drugs, in the form of raw opium. Jimmy and Steve were also charged separately with importing classified goods, including arms and ammunition, without an import licence. The charge against me was aiding and abetting all the illegal imports. All seven of us pleaded guilty. Then there was an adjournment, for which I did not understand the reason, at the time, although later I guessed and much later, years later, I was told I had guessed correctly. We the prisoners were all taken back to the cells. I came face to face with Steve and Jimmy, both of whom only acknowledged me with a nod, although there was no sign of any malevolence towards me. I did not recognise any of the other four, and it barely registered that one of those who had featured prominently in the operations I was concerned with - Dermot - was not there.

Next day, the nitty-gritty of the case was embarked upon. I did not understand why it all had to take so long when everyone was pleading guilty. But I gradually came to realise that there were undercurrents which the prosecution wanted to bring to the surface. Three of the six's other four were non-British, one American, one Dutch, the other Irish, and the leading barrister for the Crown spent all day outlining the international nature of the drugs side of their organisation, for that is what it turned out to be. The sixth was the owner or whatever of the Watton airfield and, it appeared, the procurer of the Dakota aircraft. This case was only directly concerned with the operations in which I had been involved, but the prosecution, despite some opposition from the defendants' barristers, wanted to bring out just how big the whole thing was. Millions of pounds worth of opium, most of which was for conversion into heroin with an illegal value of many times more millions, was involved in a worldwide organisation, they said.

I never fully understood the complexities of it all, legal or otherwise, but, less than two years later, when the Irish republicans had restarted activities in earnest, after the wartime lull, I came to the conclusion that the IRA was involved and that the whole thing was, perhaps still is, a fund-raising effort for that campaign of terror. In fact this was more or less confirmed by a prisoner with whom I came into contact just before my release at the end of my sentence. He also helped confirm another conclusion I'd reached, that Dermot, the "thug," was an undercover police agent - and obviously a very good one if he had been able to reach the height of minder and apparent right hand man to Jimmy Shaunessy, who I gathered was not far from the top of the set-up. This man, Irish himself, but not an IRA sympathiser, reckoned the six at the Old Bailey had pleaded guilty to avoid bringing many more into the prosecution net. I still have no idea how Steve Parrimore came to be involved, whether he was a republican supporter or whether he was just in it for the kicks and the money. I think mostly for the kicks, probably.

At the start of the fourth day, my barrister, Maconachie, put in a plea that the case against me should be adjourned until those against the others had been concluded. Again there was an adjournment, not for long this time, but when we were brought back the judge said he had accepted the plea, and I would be dealt with later. I was however allowed to stay in court, and was glad I had, for I heard something that went a long way towards restoring my faith in Steve as a half-decent guy. His barrister made a great deal of his war record - called him a hero of the Battle of Britain - and when, before sentence, the judge asked him whether he had anything to say, he said he had been no hero, but was just doing what dozens of other people in the forces were doing. He drew the line, sensibly I thought, at using the expression "only doing his duty," but he said he had realised that being involved in the drugs trade was utterly wrong. How much Steve might have been trying to save his own skin I don't know, but I do know that he had no need to say what came next.

"Your honour," he said to the judge: "I would like to say something about Alastair Jameson, if I may."

His lordship said brusquely: "You may not, at this stage. But if when I deal with him you wish to say something in evidence, I will allow it, if his counsel agrees."

He went on to sentence the six, of whom only Steve opted to make any personal statement. He sent Jimmy Shaunessy away for 18 years, four of the others to 15, and Steve to 10.

When he uttered the usual "take them down," he added. "Parrimore is to remain in the court precinct, and be brought up if required to give evidence."

There was another short adjournment, during which Maconachie asked whether I wished Steve to testify. He did not advise it, because we did not know what he would say. But I had been impressed by what he had said to the judge, and I decided the risk was worth taking.

"As you wish," the barrister said. "We'll call him. And perhaps you're right."

The indictment against me had already been stated, I had pleaded guilty, and the proceedings were therefore quite swift. Prosecuting counsel told the judge that there was no question about the facts of the case - I had agreed to pilot one of the aircraft on the Suez drugs run, also to fly another aeroplane to Holland and back, for a total remuneration of £700, a figure far above the "going rate," indicating that I knew it was an illegal or at least questionable operation.

Maconachie then had to call Steve, before his final plea on my behalf.

He asked him: "Have you something to say about my client, the defendant Jameson?"

Steve, who had been reminded that he was still on oath, said: "I want to make it clear that to the best of my knowledge Alastair Jameson had no knowledge that the cargo he was being engaged to help transport contained opium or any other drugs. He asked a few questions about it and I told him it was war surplus material which included some guns and ammunition, which was why it was being brought here without an import licence.

"I would also like to say something about what happened afterwards, before the Dutch trip. I had become involved with a young lady, who was under stress because her fiance had died. Alastair persuaded me that I was doing wrong by her. He is a good man, your honour, and I would beg you to deal with him as leniently as possible."

I saw my mother weeping into her handkerchief, my father's arm around her. And I thought: "Thank you Steve. I'm sorry I thought quite so harshly about you."

I have not seen or heard of him since that day. I can only hope that after he served his sentence – he'd be in prison for six or seven years, at least – he would surrender to the better sides of his nature and stay away from villains like Jimmy and the others.

Any doubts I might have had about Maconachie's personality were sent flying by his address to the judge on my behalf. He hit exactly the right note, I am certain, inciting but not overdoing my own war record; the love and confidence my mother and father had for me and in me; and my own sincere regret for my part in the nefarious enterprise.

He concluded: "You have heard what the witness Parrimore said, m'lud. I can say also, and not just because I am his counsel, that I had formed exactly the same opinion myself. I can also say that I believe him to be absolutely genuine when he says he is deeply ashamed of what has happened. He admits he should have known that there was something very questionable about this offer of such a substantial reward for a piloting operation - in fact he knew it must be illegal. But if he had dreamed that drugs were involved he would not have touched it. I believe him, m'lud, and I would ask you to believe him also, and to allow him to pick up the pieces of his life, which he is desperate to do, as soon as possible. Thank you m'lud."

The judge asked me if I had anything to say before he passed sentence.

I said: "Only to repeat what Mr Maconachie said, Your Honour. And to thank everybody who is standing by me, especially my father and my mother; and to promise that nothing like this will ever happen again."

The judge looked at his notes, but I could see he was not reading them, just giving himself a little time.

He said: "Alastair Charles George Jameson: you come from a background of which you should be very proud, and to which you have brought disgrace of which you should be ashamed, as indeed your counsel believes you are. And I listened carefully to what the witness Parrimore said.

"I accept that what you did was foolish, or perhaps foolish and weak, rather than deliberately wicked, and I am taking your excellent war record into account. However, the menace of illegal drugs, which can cause untold misery to countless people, has to be fought by those with responsibilities for the public good, with whom intelligent people like you should align yourselves, not with those of the kind who are just beginning long periods away from society. I would therefore be failing in my duty if I did not punish you for this crime, for that is what it is. I sentence you to imprisonment for five years."

It was no more, perhaps less, than I had expected. I gathered I could positively hope for a third of the sentence to be remitted, "for good behaviour," which I was determined to earn, and which would reduce the term to three years and four months. Then the time I had been on remand would be taken off, taking it down to only a little over two years from that point. To someone who had already been more than a year in gaol, it could have been much worse.

Nine

Letters

I was sent back to Brixton initially, and told I would be sharing a cell with a man of my own age. But two days later I was told I was going to Lewes, because it was "more suitable" and Brixton was overcrowded. I thought nothing could be worse than Brixton, so was not too upset, except that it would be further for my parents and my brother to travel, on visits. I was wrong. Lewes was much worse than Brixton, in terms of the place itself. The only good thing was that I had a cell to myself, for most of the time I was there. But it was an awful chamber. It stank, and was cold, and the decor, what you could see of it through the graffiti, might have been calculated to depress the most optimistic of temperaments.

Only two visits a month were allowed, I found, and prisoners and visitors had to jump through a number of hoops to get those authorised. On the positive side however, the officers I first encountered, through the registration procedure, seemed a pretty human lot. I had brought some books with me among my personal property and when I asked if I could keep them the officer in charge said: "You can have 'em back when we've checked 'em to make sure there aren't any files or ladies' automatics hidden in 'em, son." Prison humour, but at least I wasn't called a cleverdick because I could read and write and express myself reasonably coherently.

I was soon asked whether I had any preferences about the type of work I would do. They'd been told I was not a violent type, apparently, so could be allowed to work with other prisoners at cleaning, in the kitchens, or the gardens - the last however only after a month of behaving myself in the cleaning department, in other words trying to make the lavatories slightly less insanitary, mostly. I had no hesitation in opting for the gardens, even though it was a bitterly cold February. At least spring and summer must follow.

I had started to work in the gardens before my mother and father were able to visit for the first time. Although they were desperately anxious to see me, it was difficult for Dad to get away, because he was up to his neck in organising the wind-up and sale of his employer Lord Netherwood's vast estate. The "old" lord had died and his son, a big man in business, did not want to be encumbered with country property, and had agreed with my father that it should be sold, where possible, to existing tenants.

Dad and Mother however were pleased to see that I seemed in better spirits than at Brixton. Indeed I was, I think because the uncertainty had been removed, and I could start to work, in my mind and indeed in practical ways if possible, towards a future. Even on this first visit, I broached the idea of farming to my father, an idea which became increasingly attractive to me the more I thought about it, although the practical difficulties were formidable. Just for a start, I knew so little about it. Faced with a tractor and a plough, I'd be completely at sea, and if I managed to use them to produce a ploughed field, I'd have no idea about what to sow on it. Set me to buy a cow or a ewe and I'd probably end up with a bullock and a ram. Then, I had very little money. The few hundred pounds I still had in my bank account would not go far towards setting me up in agriculture.

Dad did not pour cold water on the idea, though. In fact he was pleased, and said so. But he warned me of the problems and urged me to think hard and be sure that was what I really wanted. And I did think, but came back to the same conclusion. I could think of nothing else that would bring some solidity and satisfaction into my life.

Now in all the words that the reader has been asked to plough through, covering the previous year and more, he, or perhaps more especially she, will have noted only the briefest of references to Angie. Had she been dismissed so easily from my thoughts? Was the love that had hit me in that St Johns Wood kitchen so shallow? No, it was not.

And in spite of what I said a little while back, about men pigeonholing their love's love, and all that, I don't think there was a single day when I did not wonder what she was doing, whether she still thought about me. Was she keeping her promise to work hard at her career - although I had no real doubts about the answer to that one. Would she forget me, as I had asked?

I had been at Lewes for only a few weeks when I was given the answer. I had a letter from her.

"My darling Alastair," she began. "I have only just found out where you are, and for how long. My love, I hope it is not too terrible. I wish I could see you, but I am told it would probably not be allowed, and anyway you would probably refuse to see me, like that other time.

"My darling, I am keeping my promise to you and working very hard. I got very good HSC results, and scholarships were offered at three universities, including Oxford and Cambridge. But I went for London because I've been told their medical school is the best. I am now nearly at the end of my first term and enjoying it very much, as much as I can enjoy anything, without you there.

"I am keeping that promise, my dearest, but I cannot obey your order to forget you. I will never do that as long as I live. And some day I want us to be together again. Please, Alastair, do not say that can never be. You are not a criminal, in spite of what has happened, which was only because that awful Steve talked you into it.

"I have to tell you though that something pretty dreadful has happened. My dad found out about your trial and everything. I tried to tell him what you are really like, but I could not say as much as I wanted to or he would have found out about Josie. Oh, Alastair, he told me I was to have nothing to do with you because of the effect it might have on my career. I wanted to say I did not care, because you are more important to me than any career, but I know you will think the same way as he does. The trouble is, too, that he could just be right, because the medical people are a stuffy old lot. But once I have qualified, it will not matter. And I know that as soon as Mum and Dad meet you and get to know you they will love you just as I already love your mother and father.

"Please, my darling, keep cheerful and look forward to that time, when we can be together for always. I love you, love you, love you."

You can imagine how that hit me. I'm not ashamed to say that I cried as I read it. I began to think along the same lines - in two years I would be out of here and able to see her, hold her, care for her again. Except of course that I would be the one who had to be cared for. Then the arithmetic of time entered the euphoric equation. She would not have qualified when I was released. She would still need to be making good impressions on the "stuffy old lot" in the medical hierarchy, with whom she would only have barely come into contact by that time. And she would need to keep her nose clean, as it were, for many more years, if she was to make the kind of progress of which all around her knew she was capable. Her father was dead right, as I had been when I told her to go away and forget me. It was one of the few good things I had done in my life, I thought, in a resurgence of stupid pride.

But whether it was stupid pride or not, I knew I had no alternative. I must tell Angie that I could never be for her. I must get the message over so that she could start on her life - she was still only 19, for goodness sake - unencumbered by someone who, whatever she said, was a criminal in the eyes of most of the world. I used my first permitted letter to write to her.

"My dearest little girl," I wrote. "I hate to say it, but this is the last time I shall write to you, and you are right, if you came here I would refuse to see you. Not because I do not love you, but because you MUST break off any ties to me, as I told you before. Your father is quite right, association with someone who can only be looked on as a criminal by almost everyone would be disastrous for you, for many years to come. If we got together when I come out of prison, it would have to be kept secret, and sooner or later it would leak out. Please, please, try to clear me from your mind, and concentrate on becoming the great doctor I know you will be.

"Just one other thing. I don't suppose it was reported in the papers, and if it was I know you have not read it, otherwise I think you might not have thought Steve was quite so 'awful.' He spoke up for me at the trial, andtold the judge I did not know drugs were involved, and about the business with Josie - not mentioning her by name, of course. And he asked him to deal with me as leniently as possible. There was nothing in it for him, he had already been sentenced, and I really think that he, and my counsel, influenced the judge.

"Goodbye, my darling. Please remember your promises to me, as I am sure you will. And one day, marry someone who is truly worthy of you."

You can also imagine what it cost me to write that.

*****

I don't think there is any need to dwell at length on the details of those two years at Lewes. I kept myself to myself as much as possible. Prison is not a place where friendships can be formed, on the whole, and to be brutally honest, most of the blokes there were not types with whom I had anything in common. Not they were all bad people, by any means – inadequate, rather, unable to cope with the world as they came up against it. There were a few out-and-out baddies, of course. A couple who had been there all through the war were pointed out to me as leaders of the Brighton racetrack gangs and, I was told, should on no account be tangled with. Yet they seemed to be the ones on the best terms with the officers, or at least some of the officers. There was a chap who, I was told, had killed his wife. He seemed to me, from the little I saw of him, to be the most harmless, self-effacing little guy you could imagine. I saw him on a couple of occasions at visiting times, with two daughters who clearly adored him. I wonder what his story was.

I spent little time, in fact none, doing a philosophic ponder about the rights, wrongs and common sense of locking up the kind of men making up the prison population as observed from my limited perspective. Only later have I come to wish we could do something more constructive. But it was clear in pre-1950 days that prisons were universities of crime, on the one hand, and instruments for driving the desperately inadequate into even deeper sloughs of despair, on the other. The idea of prison as a deterrent is positively laughable. It might make people like me say "I'm not going through that again," but people like me would have said it anyway, for other reasons. The inadequate cannot help re-offending, by their very nature. The bad guys simply think they won't be caught again, and prison helps them to avoid being caught.

Far more important to me, then, was the fact that my father and mother came to see me regularly, my Aunt Billie and her husband Peter Hood a couple of times, likewise my own brother and sister. Uncle Peter was my dad's sergeant in the first war, they were badly wounded at the same time, and have been close friends ever since.

When Dad came on his second visit, he asked if I was still serious about wanting to be involved in farming, which I certainly was, and he brought me a couple of books, which I was allowed to keep after they had been vetted, and several copies of The Farmers Weekly, which he rightly said would bring me up to date with the agricultural world. On his third visit, he repeated the question again - was I still keen? And being assured that I was, he promised to give me all the help he could, as long as I realised that I was starting on a tough road, along which I would inevitably encounter a great deal of hard work and many problems and worries. I did not know it at the time, but he had come out of his stewardship of the Netherwood estates as a quite wealthy man, absolutely legitimately of course, and he would   use some of his money to help me into farming.

His encouragement made me an avid reader of the books he brought me, although I was not stupid enough to think they alone would make me a farmer or a stockman. They did however encourage me to the extent that I began to dream of myself as successful and well-off, and that fantasy went hand in hand with another - to then being able to seek out Angie again, find her still free and able to marry me. For despite my resolve to make her cast herself off from me, she was still there, night after night. Foolish wraiths indeed, but as long as they remained only that, I could see no harm in dreaming myself to sleep on them. And indeed there was not, I'm sure. They did not begin to make me veer from my resolve.

They were very different from another series of dreams, nightmares, that began to visit me during the second year, triggered I think by reading some correspondence in one of the newspapers Dad was allowed to leave for me. They were the precursors of a debate, often a quite bitter debate, still going on today, about whether the campaigns to blanket bomb and firestorm bomb German cities, in particular Hamburg and Dresden, could be justified, for it was almost admitted that they were basically terror campaigns. But under the influence of what I read, I began to dream of screaming women and children fleeing from the devastation of our bombing. I saw them jumping into canals and rivers and suffocating in their own or communal cellars, which actually happened, I know now, because the massive fires above, deliberately caused by our incendiaries, sucked out all the air.

Now, I realise that what seemed then to be one long horrific dream only came to me on a handful of occasions, although when it did, it took me days to get away from its effects. I won't pretend that it suddenly made me turn pacifist, or believe that what I had been part of was no better than the atrocities committed by the other side. Hitler and his cronies, and some of their followers were pure evil, there was no other way to describe them. Belsen, Auschwitz, Dachau and the other horror camps should have left nobody in any doubt about that.

We were never told in the air force that our "good work" had such inhuman results. If we had, I don't suppose more than a tiny handful of us would have given it a second thought, even if we knew we were dropping our bombs mainly on innocent women and children. We believed, no doubt rightly, that our nightly missions - from which so many did not return, for the Germans were still blasting us heavily with increasingly accurate anti-aircraft fire, and putting even more fighters into the air - were hastening the end of the war and the Nazi regime.

If I'd been halfway near religious, I would no doubt have sought out the chaplain. But as I think anyone reading this will have realised, I did not have, still do not have, any religious beliefs of the conventional kind. Especially do I not believe in God who is almighty and creator of heaven – whatever that is – and earth, or in a Messiah who was his son. Or in the infallibility of the prophet Mohammed, or the Buddha, or coming back to a second life as a cat or a dog or a lion. There may be a God, or rather a force for Good. I hope so. I believe in good people. But as I told Erbie at Brixton, I had no time for the mumbo-jumbo of church services and ceremonies. If there was an omnipotent Master, would he have allowed the Germans to slaughter Jews in gas chambers, or us to bomb all those women and children, then go on boozing sprees as soon as we got home? And above all, has not religion, at least the extremists and bigots in it, caused more evil than anything else in the world, except perhaps greed?

But bringing myself down to earth, and particularly the earth in the Lewes Prison gardens, and to an encounter that was to have some effect on my later life. By the time I was in my second year there, beginning to count the days, or anyway the months, to my release, I had established myself as a prisoner who was interested in the work and could be relied on to do a decent job. I was not a "trusty" – a status accorded to men serving long terms, trusted to take charge of tools, rotas and even keys of outside buildings – but I was often given charge, on an informal basis, of small groups doing specific jobs, always under the overall supervision of an officer. So I was not surprised to hear him say to a newcomer one day: "Jameson'll show you what to do, son." But I was surprised to see this particular newcomer. It was Erbie.

Talking, unless about matters directly concerned with the job, was still not allowed, so I had to wait for an "association" period to ask him what he was there for.

"I thought you were going to go straight," I said. "What have you done this time?"

"Grievous, Ally. A year."

"What do you mean, grievous?"

"Grievous bodily 'arm. I put a bloke in 'orspital. An' I'm bloody glad, Ally. 'E deserved it."

I was astounded. Apart from anything else, the idea of little Erbie duffing up anyone to the extent of causing grievous bodily harm was remarkable. I had to ask what it was all about.

"D'yew remember I told yer abaht that geezer who'd got me muvver goin' all religious? Well, d'yer know what 'e really was, Ally? 'E was a pimp - a bleedin' pimp. 'E was tryin' to get me muvver to go on the game. Me muvver, Ally, me own muvver!"

"What happened?"

"Well, after I got aht o' Brixton I got a job wiv an old mate o' me dad's, helpin' 'im on an 'ot dog stall 'e 'ad at the football grahnds an' the dog tracks an' that, so I was often aht late at nights, an' didn't see much o' mum. The bloke, Marvin 'is name was, used to come rahnd regular, an' 'e didn't seem too bad, but after a time 'e stopped comin', and me mum seemed to go very miserable, so I started to ask 'er what was the matter, as if I didn't know, or so I fort. But I wasn't very 'appy wiv what she told me. I said, like, was it Marvin, but she seemed to want to put me off. 'Oh, it's nuffin,' she said. 'Nuffin' you can 'elp wiv. I'll sort it out.' An' fings like that. Yer see, Ally, I fort praps e'd got 'er in the family way an' then buggered off. She's not very old, yer know - she was only 15 when she 'ad me, an' she's pretty good lookin'. It was a bit awkward, asking me own mum abaht that kind o' fing, but I did, an' that's when she told me, one afternoon when I wasn't workin' 'cos the 'ot dog stand was bein' painted up. 'E told 'er what 'e wanted 'er to do. It was, yer know, a bit 'igh class. She was to 'ave a flat, or a room or somefink an 'e'd send in the fellers. It was awful, Ally. Anyway, she'd told 'im what to do wiv 'is flat, an' 'e turned nasty. Said 'e was givin' 'er a week ter fink it over, an' if she didn't agree to it she needn't fink abaht any boy friends in future, 'cos 'er face wouldn't stand lookin' at. I told 'er I'd get a couple o' me mates an' we'd sort 'im out, but she said I mustn't, 'cos she fort 'e was part of a gang of pimps who ran all that part of London, an' we'd all end up in the river, in concrete overcoats.

"Anyway, almost as soon as she'd finished tellin' me all this, we was in the kitchen, who should come in but Marvin 'imself. Just walked in, bold as brass. 'E was a bit put aht ter see me. 'E just said: 'You cut along, little man, me and your ma 'ave got some bizness to talk about.' I was dead scared, Ally, but I wasn't goin' ter just let 'im beat 'er up wivout doin' anyfink, was I. I said: 'She's not goin' to 'ave anyfink ter do wiv your kind of bizness, mate. Just leave 'er alone.'

"'E wasn't a pertickler nasty looking bloke, Ally, but there came a look on his face that yer could only call evil. 'E said: 'I've got somefink in my pocket that'll leave yer wivout yer ears and yer nose if I use it on yer. Nah yer ma wouldn't like that, would she? Just scoot.'

"I acted scared, which wasn't 'ard, I can tell yer, 'cos I was terrified. I said: 'Alright, alright, it's between you an' 'er. I'm goin' out. I'll get me coat.' An' I opened the door under the stairs. There was a couple of real 'eavy Indian clubs there that I used for a bit of a workout sometimes. I grabbed one and swung it 'ard as I could into 'is knees, before 'e could realise what I was up to. There was an 'orrible crack, Ally, an' 'e went straight down, an' Mum screamed. I 'it 'im again, on 'is arm, an' I fort I broke it, an' that time it was 'im who screamed. I didn't 'it 'im again, only kicked 'im in the ribs, an' 'e screamed again.

"Mum yelled: 'Erbert, no more. You'll kill 'im.' I said: 'One rat less in London won't matter, will it?' But I didn't 'it 'im again. 'E was blubberin' on the floor. 'E said: 'Yer've broke me arm, yer little bastard. Get a doctor.'

"Mum went to the phone box an' rang for an ambulance. The driver asked a few questions but they took 'im away. Turned aht 'is kneecap was smashed but 'is arm wasn't broke. Next mornin' the cops came an' took me an' I was charged. I told 'em what it was abaht, but it didn't seem to make no difference. So 'ere I am. Twelve munfs. You'll be goin' out just before me, I reckon, Ally."

I asked: "I know he got what he deserved from you, but didn't the police charge him with anything?"

"Nah, I told yer, it didn't seem to make no difference, what 'e'd done. Me uncle reckons there's some 'igh-ups in the cops as are in the gang's pocket. 'E's probably right. I know it does 'appen."

"What about your mother? Do you think they'll get at her again?"

"She's given up the 'ouse an' gone up to Derby, to 'er sister. That's where they come from. I fink she'll be alright there."

"And what about you? Will they want to pay you back for it? And your job - will it still be there?"

"The job's alright. Me uncle - I call 'im that but reely 'e was just a mate o' me dad's - says 'is missis can fill in. Don't want to lose me, 'e says."

"Do you think they'll leave you alone? Where will you live?"

"Uncle reckons 'e can find me a pad, and I can stay wiv 'im for a bit."

"And the other?"

"Yer mean, will they want to do me? P'raps. I'll just 'ave to watch me back."

"Would you still like to live in the country, and perhaps work on a farm or something?"

"You bet I would, Ally. But I can't see 'ow I'm goin' ter do it. No farmer 'ud give me a job, would 'e? An' there's somefink else - I've got a girl. We want ter be married, as soon as we can afford it. She's a smasher, Ally, works in a lawyer's office. She's too good for me, I say, but she tells me I'm talkin' rubbish. It makes movin' away 'arder, though, although she reckons she'd like ter get aht o' London, as well."

I told him he must keep in touch. I'd had the glimmering of an idea.

Ten

Back to Shropshire

When I was released, I went "home" to my parents. Not to Leicestershire, for my father had by then more or less completed his winding up of the Netherfield estate and moved back to Shropshire, where he was helping my brother establish his land agent's business. He and Mother said I must stay with them for as long as I wanted, while I got the whole grisly affair out of my system.

Dad and Peter also repeated the offer of a slot in the new firm, but although I was grateful for their generosity, after I had previously turned them down in order to go off on a disastrous wild goose chase, I again declined. I felt I must do something on my own, as much as possible, and prove that I was more than just a giddy-minded lightweight. I said as much to Dad.

"My boy, if you ever were a lightweight, or giddy-minded, I'm sure you're not now," he said. And he repeated his offer to help me into farming, as he was helping Peter into his enterprise. I said I would of course accept his offer, but his financial contribution must not mean he and Mother suffered. He said they could manage what he thought was necessary without any problems, and we discussed ways and means.

Dad said I needed at least a year's practical experience, as a pupil or worker, before I could take on a farm of my own. I had to agree, of course. As I said before, my knowledge of practical farming was almost nil. He thought I might go to Uncle Giles, on the old Lyndford Home Farm, which was now a 700-acre mixed holding where I would experience almost every branch of agriculture except large-scale arable. I was not immediately overwhelmed by the idea, because I wanted to stand on my own feet as soon as possible, but I soon saw that this was probably as quick a road to that end as I was likely to find.

Dad and Mother were now living at Lyndford Manor, the old family home. Uncle Giles had persuaded them to return there because he and Aunt Elizabeth, marrying late in life, wanted somewhere new to both of them, and opted for Home Farm, which made sense all round because it was the centre of his farming operations. Aunt Elizabeth, the widow of a former tenant farmer, had helped my grandmother run the manor as a hostel for land army girls and was worried that people would think she only married my uncle as a means of getting hold of it for herself. Uncle Giles had to work hard to persuade my parents to go there for Mother was worried that she would be tarred with the same brush, having started life as the kitchen maid there. But by the time I returned they had settled down quite happily and saw a great deal of Uncle Giles and Aunt Elizabeth.

So I accepted my uncle's offer of pupilage, and was grateful that he paid me normal farm wages, which as my mother would not accept any financial contribution from me meant I built up a useful addition to my limited capital. Every day I rose at the crack of dawn, not literally although much earlier sometimes, in the winter months, to help milk cows, or shepherd sheep, feed pigs, ride a corn drill, hump bales of hay and straw, and eventually work horses, drive tractors and various machines. I was taught to plough and sow, and reap and mow, and do, or at least familiarise myself with, the accounts, the milk records, the pedigree society and agriculture ministry requirements. Aunt Elizabeth, led the way in explaining the office work, of which there is a great deal more, on the farm, than city or industrial folk have any idea of.

The graft on the Lyndford farm left me physically exhausted and should, I suppose, have driven Angie out of my consciousness. But she stayed there, and my mother, inspired no doubt by her immoveable belief that love was the be-all of existence, helped kill off any chance that she might not.

"Alastair," she began one evening when we happened to be alone: "Have you heard anything recently about – Angie?"

My insides took the kind of leap they always did if she was brought to their attention, but I said, quite quietly: "No, Mother, and I don't expect to."

She waited a few moments, then resumed: "Are you still of the same mind, then?"

I said Angie would never be out of my mind. I had not previously told her about her father finding her letter to me, and his subsequent attitude, but I did so now and added that I thought he was right in his opinion of the effect an association with me would have on her career.

She looked at me sadly: "Yes, I suppose so." The "but" was unspoken, and Angie's name was not spoken again, for some time.

After I'd been at Lyndford about a year, I wondered whether I might be able to progress further. I had kept up my reading of farming books and periodicals – being as much puzzled as enlightened by some of them but I think managing to sort out the valuable grain from the theoretical chaff, with the help of Dad and Uncle Giles. So that my father, who knew pretty well as much about farming as his brother, thought it was feasible, with him to keep an eye on me at first, which ideally meant any farm I bought or rented ought not to be too far away. He joined me in looking and listening for anything that might be suitable, but it was my Aunt Billie, who farmed with her husband Peter in the north-eastern corner of Shropshire, who came up with the one we eventually went for. It was about 200 acres, mixed beef and arable, about 10 miles from Lyndford. She and Peter were friendly with the owner, who was something of an eccentric, planning to retire when he would sell or rent the holding – but not to anyone who wanted it for anything but farming, she said.

"He's a rum old boy, but absolutely genuine. He's a bit like your grandfather, Alastair, thinks the world, or his bit of it, should stay just as it is, which of course we all know it can't. I think he'd rather like your story, though, and if he liked you he'd sell to you at a reasonable price, as long as he thought you genuinely wanted to farm it."

With Dad listening in, I immediately phoned Mr Arkinstall and said I understood he was thinking of selling the farm.

"I met be," he said. "Who wants to know?"

I said I was Mrs Billie Hood's nephew, I'd been in the air force in the war and I wanted to set up in farming.

"Who's your father, then," he asked.

"His name's Charles Jameson, Mr Arkinstall. I'm Alastair."

"You mun be grandson to old Squire Jameson, then - him as hung himself when yer dad married the maid, daft old bugger. I know your uncle, Giles, a bit. He was chairman of the war ag in the war."

"Yes, sir. I'm working for Uncle Giles now, until I can find a farm of my own. I'll remember you to him."

"Ar, well don't remind him about the time I threatened to throw him off the farm when he told me I'd got to grub up my old orchard and plough it. But we were good friends enough after - I was goin' to plough it anyroad. An' he was only trying to get us all to do our bit for the war."

"Can I come to see you, sir?"

"Yes, lad, an' bring your cheque book, if it'll stand it."

"I don't know about that, Mr Arkinstall, but I'll bring my father, if I may." And we arranged to go in a week's time. I'd have liked to belt off that minute, but Dad said it didn't do to seem too eager, even if he was a good old lad, as Aunt Billie said.

The farm turned out to be about two miles from Cravenbury Junction, only about 10 miles from Lyndford, and at the end of a long lane on which it and its two cottages were the only buildings. Beyond, the lane deteriorated into a track leading into hundreds of acres of forest, I learned later. The farm itself gave us a bit of a shock. The house seemed quite well looked after, but the buildings appeared run down. Doors were unpainted, one of the two dutch barns had sheets of its corrugated iron roof missing, one cowshed at least had a couple of broken windows, we could see as we drove up and on to a rough stone yard around which the house and some of the buildings were grouped. Two dogs lay outside the back door, one on each side, and bared their teeth as we approached. They did not however move as we knocked on the door. A lady, quite well dressed and of a pleasant appearance, opened it.

Dad said: "Mrs Arkinstall?"

"Not quite, but it'll do," she answered. "You're Mr Jameson - and son, I presume. Come in. Ben's expecting you."

She led the way through what at a glance looked a well-ordered kitchen and into a comfortable sitting room where a gentleman was sitting before a log fire.

"Mr Jameson and - Mr Jameson," she said.

"Thank you, my dear." And to us: "Will you have something to drink? Tea, coffee, somethin' else?"

"Coffee would be very nice for both of us, I think," Dad said.

Mr Arkinstall said: "I hope you don't mind if I don't get up. I'm afeard sittin' down's about all I can do nowadays, wi'out help. Please sit yourselves down."

When we had, he said: "Now, you've heard I met be wantin' to sell up, have yer?"

Dad said: "That's right, through my sister, Billie Hood."

"An' met you be interested in buyin', Mester Jameson?"

Dad looked at me as if to say I should do the talking. I said: "It's for me actually, Mr Arkinstall. I want a farm, although my father would be providing the finance, or most of it."

"An' what d'you want it for, young man?"

"Why, I want it to farm, and make a living at it."

"What are you doin' now?"

"As I told you on the phone, I'm working for my uncle, at Lyndford. I was in the airforce in the war."

"An' what have you been doin' since then?"

I looked at my father. His look seemed to say: "Tell him. It will be alright."

I said: "I've been in prison, Mr Arkinstall"

"Go on. Tell me about it." So I did, in outline anyway. At the end he said: "An' I reckon you've learned a lot, eh, lad?"

"Yes, sir. A very great deal."

"An' now you want to go farmin'. Why?"

"I suppose it's because our family has always lived by the land, one way or another. Obviously it's about the most important job there is. And I want to make something of myself."

He looked at me speculatively: "It's a good job you've told me all that, Alastair. Yer see, I knew all about it. Yer aunt told me. If you'd tried to cover it up I'd have shown you the door. Now I reckon we can talk business."

By now, "not quite Mrs Arkinstall" had brought four mugs of coffee, with milk, cream and sugar, and taken a seat herself.

Mr Arkinstall resumed: "I should have introduced you to Nina. Mrs Morrison, my housekeeper. We're going to be married next month." We both stood up and my father said: "Very pleased to meet you."

The old farmer resumed: "Now, I'll tell ye the position. I've bin here all my life. I was born here and my father was born here, when it was on the old earl's estate. I had a son but he died in the war – he were a pilot, like you, and he got shot down over Germany – else I reckon he'd 'a bin runnin' the place now. Nina's got a daughter, but she's in America, married a chap she met in the war, and they're doin' very well. So you see we've nobody to pass it on to.

"I got hurt about five years ago. Horse kicked me. I can just about walk, with a crutch or that frame there, but I canna drive or do anythin' to speak of in the way o' work. I've only got one chap now - the others I 'ad were no good wi'out somebody standin' over 'em all the time, an' the whole place 'as gone downhill, as I daresay you can see. Nina drives me about in the jeep, but it doesna amount to much in the way o' work.

"Now, I reckon I feel a bit the same about this place as your father did about your Lyndford, Mester Jameson. I don't mind a bit o' change, but I dunna want all this ground to go under a lot o' houses, or factories, or holiday camps or summat. I want it to grow bullocks, and sheep, and a bit o' corn. It's not doin' much o' that now, I know, but that's because I'm knocked up, and I canna do anythin' myself, or even see to it bein' done. Nina and your sister - your aunt, young feller - they've been good friends for a long time, and when I talked to her about it was when she told me about you.

"Now then, I'll be straight with you. I amna goin' to sell this place to anybody who isna goin' to make a proper job o' farmin' it. I don't mean they've got to farm it exactly like I have - they can grow wheat or summat on most of it if they want to, although they'd soon find it's not the place for that. But they mun farm it. I'll have a - what d'ye call it Mester Jameson? - a bit put in the sale agreement" - "a covenant?," my father interjected - "Ar, that's right, a covenant, I'll have that put in, that they munna sell it for anythin' other than farmin.' I know that'll knock the price down, but I don't care. As long as I can get enough from it to buy us a decent cottage and give us a pound or two to keep us, that's all I want. An' if I canna find somebody who I think wants to look after it properly, I shallna sell. Not for any price."

I liked old Arkinstall, and so did my father. And it seemed that we might be able to get a farm, from him, at a better price than from most other people, and one that I could get stuck into and make something of. I had no objection to his proposed covenant, although Dad warned me that I could not possibly know how circumstances would pan out for me and for agriculture, over the years. Anyway, we pursued the idea, starting with a good look round the two hundred and twenty acres and its buildings, driven by Nina in the "jeep" which was actually one of the new Land Rovers. Although its hedges were badly overgrown, gates and some of the fences much in need of attention, and parts of the buildings called for repair, the farm as a whole did not look unproductive, even in its present state.

I had come to the conclusion, and my father emphasised through our many discussions, that milk production was almost an essential for someone without much capital, because of the guaranteed market and the monthly cheque it brought. He was therefore disappointed that although the farm had one cowshed where milking had been done at some time, and there was an old dairy, the farm as it stood contained no provision for dairy cows, although he cannily spotted a possibility for doing something about it. There was a covered yard, used for housing beef cattle, and a building adjoining which could easily be adapted to make one of the "milking parlours" that were then beginning to come into vogue, and are now almost universal.

I had all along told Dad that I wanted him to provide as little cash as possible. Most of the purchase of the farm, and the capital to run it, would have to be borrowed, and paid back through my own efforts. That was the way I wanted it, and although he was sceptical, he accepted it. I imagine his thinking was that he and Mother could always bail me out if the worst came to the worst. We had agreed however on what we could run to and entered into negotiations with Mr Arkinstall, on that basis. He told us what he wanted, and we agreed to it immediately. The figure was low, not ridiculously so for a farm that would need a great deal of work, but low enough to make it a definite economic proposition for us.

In the course of our discussions, we got to know Benjamin and Nina Arkinstall, as I thought of them all along, pretty well. He told us how he, or rather Nina first, had got to know Aunt Billie. It was through my sister Kathleen. Nina was involved with a women's organisation, Kathleen had interviewed her for her paper, a friendship developed, and led on to Aunt Billie who in her young days was a militant campaigner for women's votes.

" 'Er told us about how 'er come to marry Peter, an' that led to talkin' about you and your missis," he told Dad. "But of course the whole county knew what happened to Squire Jameson. Poor old gentleman, even if I did call him a daft bugger. He musta bin in a terrible state."

"What about you, Alastair?" he asked. "I hope you've got a young lady somewhere. You need a wife if you're goin' to be a farmer, you know. You canna be out all hours, and come in cold an wet sometimes, then have to start on the housework."

I told him I did not have a young lady, nor was I likely to have, for the foreseeable future. I would employ a housekeeper sooner or later, I said.

Mr Arkinstall knew nothing about Angie, but his question was another knife twisting in the wound. I had tried, and was still trying, not to forget her, that would never happen, but to keep myself on terms with the decision I had made nearly four years before. I was going to say I still agonised for her, night after night, but it was not like that. She was just there, would not go away, not that I wanted her to. I never dreamt about her, but many times I woke from a dreamless sleep, or one where I wrestled with the practical problems I was now beginning to encounter, to find her on my waking mind. And then I would wonder, as I wondered many other times, where she was, what she was doing. Would she have qualified by now, I pondered, not knowing how the medical system worked. If I made a success out of my farming, and expunged my criminal record from the public mind, could I seek her out? In ten years, she would still be only in her early thirties. But again I managed to conclude, not only that my decision had been right, but I must enforce it on myself as well as on her. I must, now and later, concentrate on the practicalities of the moment.

Dad put up enough cash for a 25 per cent deposit on the farm, also guaranteeing the Agricultural Mortgage Corporation loan on the rest, as well as giving me another amount to augment my working capital. The terms we agreed with Mr Arkinstall gave me immediate possession, as long as he was allowed to stay in the house until he had found a new home for himself and Nina, who was by then the actual rather than "not quite" Mrs Arkinstall. They said I could live in the house with them, but I was not enamoured of the idea. As I said, I liked them, but I felt, probably wrongly, that it would be too near to having Ben looking over my shoulder. Besides, I had a notion of my own.

I had all along meant to contact my prison friend Erbie and offer him employment, which I was sure he would jump at. I had no phone number for him, but I had the address where he was staying with his "uncle" so wrote to him and asked him to call me, reversing the charges. I told him what I had in mind, asking also if he was married yet. He was about to be, he said. It was perfect timing, for what I had in mind.

The two cottages, semi-detached, were about 400 yards from the farm itself. My idea, endorsed by my father, was that if Erbie and his bride would come to live in one, I would live in the other, while the Arkinstalls were still in the farmhouse, and Mrs Erbie would "housekeep" for me for the year or so I expected to be in the cottage. Afterwards I expected to employ another man, who would take over "my" cottage. I had already agreed to continue to employ Mike, Mr Arkinstall's man, on his strong recommendation, but he cycled daily from "The Junction" and did not need accommodation.

Erbie was immediately enthusiastic about my idea, although there were a few questions to be answered before we could finalise it all. There would be a delay while Connie, his girl-friend, worked out her notice at her employer's. I told him she would of course be paid for her housekeeping role, but he wondered whether there would be work for her afterwards. I said the farmhouse would certainly need housekeeping, more than the cottage, and provided we all got on with each other, as I was sure we would, that job could be hers. He was a little concerned also about leaving, letting down his "uncle."

"'E's been bloody good to me, Ally. You know I said I'd 'ave to watch me back from those pimpin' bastards. Well 'e's been watchin' it for me, won't let me leave 'is sight, 'ardly. 'An I know they was arter me one day, only they saw they'd 'ave 'im to contend with if they tried anyfink. Still, I reckon 'e'd fink it was best if I got right away."

Two days later, he called again. He and Connie would gladly accept my plan, but it would be a month before she could leave her employment. They would have liked to go for "a bit of an 'oneymoon" as well but that would have to wait. They would need all their cash to furnish their home, he said. But Connie was as keen on getting out of her office and the threat of Erbie being "got at." It all seemed to be coming together quite well. I was looking forward eagerly to getting to grips with the farm.

The cottages were nothing to shout about as living quarters, although in good repair structurally. They each had three bedrooms and downstairs a living kitchen and "back kitchen" or scullery, plus a sitting room, larder and outside coal and wood sheds, and a piped water supply from the farm's own borehole. But neither had either electricity or a hot water system, much less a bathroom, and toilet facilities were earth closets at the bottom of the gardens. I told Erbie all this, but that improvements would be a priority, and he said: "Well, it can't be worse than chokey, can it?"

"But what will Connie think?

"Leave Connie ter me, Ally - or should I call yer 'sir' if yer goin' ter be my boss!"

I told him the day he called me sir would be the day he left my employment. But I also warned him that of course he would have to be on agricultural wages, although living would be much cheaper than in London - no rent, and free milk, for a start. (Although the farm now had no dairy facilities, I had already determined to try to get back the previously-existing milk producers licence, and in the meantime to continue Mr Arkinstall's practice of keeping at least one "house cow.")

I duly took possession on the first of May, 1952, and with the help of an old pre-war Austin, my father, and of course my mother, moved into the cottage the next day. I bought enough second hand furniture to make lifebearable, and made the sitting room my bedroom for the time being.

Mother went to town on providing the extras. For the next year or two also she drove over at least twice a week bringing all the goodies she could lay her hands on – eggs, cream, pastries she or her cook-girl had made, garden produce of every kind, even pork, ham and bacon when a pig was killed on the Lyndford farm. Erbie and Connie, when they eventually moved in, also came in for a share of her largesse, and she rarely failed to visit the farm for a chat with the Arkinstalls, while they were still there, and later at the house they bought on the outskirts of The Junction.

Connie turned out to be a gem of a girl. Not terribly good-looking, but intelligent and with lots of charm, she was quieter than her extrovert husband, who she clearly worshipped, prison record or not. She took to country life

Francis John Simcock

like the proverbial duck to water. Unlike so many townsfolk who enjoy the country for a short time, then long for the bright lights again, she seemed to revel in rustic surroundings, and coping with the problems and even hardships, like tripping down the garden to the loo in the pouring rain, cooking on an old-fashioned kitchen range or paraffin stove, washing clothes in the sink and "dolly tub," ironing them with primitive flat irons heated on the fire.

The man Mike also proved to be a fine acquisition. Like the two cockneys, as they were immediately called by the locals, he was not bred to farm work. He was a former bricklayer and jobbing builder who had lost his wife and two children through a hit-and-run car accident that sent the driver to gaol and left him unable to cope with life and work as it had been. Benjamin Arkinstall had found him in the lane, surrounded by empty beer bottles, and while he had no time for drunkards, could not leave the man there to die perhaps in the freezing cold. He got him into his car, took him home where then housekeeper Nina helped care for him, eventually installing him in a snug outhouse where he stayed for years. At first, he was completely apathetic, but over the weeks he started to take an interest in the workings of the farm, and to do jobs that were put his way. Then Arkinstall's accident seemed to galvanise him into action and he became a devoted and valuable employee, picking up farm skills readily and using his own builder's expertise when it was called for. A few months before I came along, on one of his occasional nights out, he had met a lady of his own age who he eventually married and went to live with in her own house. But he never wanted to go back to his old work.

I'm getting ahead of myself though, by some distance. Before Erbie and Connie arrived, events occurred that were to take my life along another track, one I'd never dreamed of.

Eleven

Debra

That day, I'd been working since dawn, with Mike, repairing fences and cutting a hedge, and the work had left me tired out, to the extent that when I'd lit a fire in my cottage, despite being hungry I flopped down in the fireside chair and went to sleep for more than an hour. It was by then nearly eight o'clock and I decided a pie and a pint at the Junction pub was a more attractive proposition than peeling potatoes and cooking a meal. Which was how I came to find Debra.

I was greatly concerned that next morning when she objected so strongly to her plight becoming known to the authorities, the police in particular. It might rebound on me after all if she was in trouble herself. I did not feel I could bulldoze her into hospital. She would have to be persuaded, which meant I must know more about what had happened. At the same time she was urgently in need of medical treatment. All of which brought me to my Aunt Billie.

She was not a doctor, and it was many years since she had worked as a nurse. But she was a lady of such resource and understanding that I was sure she would be able to help. Anyway, it was better than doing nothing. The first problem though was how to get in touch with her. There was no phone in the cottage, at that date, but I had a key to the farmhouse and there would be no difficulty about calling from there, although the Arkinstalls were away. The problem was what to do with the girl. I dare not leave her in the cottage and I was reluctant to take her even the quarter mile to the farm, in the car. I told her my plan, and though reluctant to bring anyone else in on her situation, she agreed to it when I said I would take her to hospital if she did not.

Keeping my cudgel with me all the time, for I was still afraid the girl had been the victim of foul play, which might well be ongoing, I backed the car out of the wood, and tried to make sure there was no-one else around. I concluded there was not although in the light of subsequent events I'm not sure I was right. I put my heavy woollen dressing gown on Debra and carried her to the motor. I locked up and we were at the farm in two or three minutes. There was no-one around, the Arkinstalls being away, and Mike was not there, and I sat Debra down in a semi-easy chair in the kitchen while I phoned my aunt. It was

Peter who answered but I asked to speak to her.

"Alastair - to what do we owe this unexpected honour? Is everything alright?"

"I'm fine, thanks, Aunt Billie, but I have a problem I hope you can

help me with. Can I tell you about it, but in the strictest confidence? Don't tell anybody, please - except Uncle Peter, of course."

"You sound very mysterious, my dear. Of course I won't say anything to anybody. I hope it's nothing to do with your other troubles, though."

"Oh, no, it's nothing to do with that. But - oh, Auntie, I'll tell you." And I told her, about finding the girl, and her injuries, and her reluctance, in fact refusal, to go to hospital because it would involve the police.

I said: "Aunt Billie, she'll have to go to hospital, and that means the police will be brought in, doesn't it, but I really would like to persuade her that that's the right thing to do. Right now she goes up the wall if I mention hospital or police. But I've got absolutely nothing here in the first aid line, not even any strong pain killer. I'm very worried about that wound - not that it's very deep or anything, but I'm sure it ought to have something to stop it going septic, and I've got nothing only Dettol. And I think she ought to have an x-ray, in case she's got internal injuries. Do you think you could come over and have a look at her, and bring all the stuff you can that might help? And I think you being here would help convince her."

"It's a long time since I did anything medical, Alastair, except on animals, but I can tell you're worried and I'll come, as soon as I can get a few things together. I keep a pretty full medicine chest, thank goodness."

While I was waiting for her, I did the milking, telling Debra exactly what I was doing and where I was, and locking the farmhouse door while I was outside. I'd have got Mike to milk the cow but he was having the morning off to go to the dentist. There was no heating in the house - there was an Aga in the kitchen but the Arkinstalls had allowed it to go out while they were away - so I took the liberty of taking an eiderdown off a bed and putting it round her. I put the milk away in the cool room and washed the pail, then sat down with the girl to wait for Aunt Billie. She had to come about 30 miles so would be an hour or more. I wondered whether I ought to have called my mother, who would have come much more quickly, but I just did not want to involve any more people than I had to, for the time being.

Not surprisingly, Debra looked haggard and drawn, but when I asked her how she felt she said only: "Hurts, man, hurts." I thought there could be no harm in giving her something for the pain, if I could find it, but a hunt through the kitchen cupboards revealed only aspirin. I dissolved a couple in water and gave it to her. Perhaps it did some good for after a little while it was she who started to talk.

"D'you live here?" she asked.

"No, not yet. It belongs to me but the people I've bought it from are still living here while they find a new house. They're nice folk - they won't mind us being here."

"It's a farm, isn't it?"

"Yes, it's how I'm making my living."

"What d'you grow? Cabbages an' taters an' that?"

"No, it's a stock farm, mostly. Beef cattle and sheep, and pigs. I'm going to keep poultry, and grow some corn. And I'm hoping to have cows, for milk."

"Thought you'd brung that milk from your cows."

"There's only one, what we call a house cow. I want to have 30 or 40."

"Golly, man, that's a lot o' cows. Take you all day to milk them."

"No, because I'll have a milking machine. It will take about two hours in the morning and the same at night."

"My folks got three goats. An' they grow corn, an' banana, an' they keeps chickens, but we don' often have eggs because they have to kill the chickens for us to eat."

I'd have liked to have let her talk of her "folks" lead into all the questions I was dying to ask, but I thought she had talked enough for the time being.

I said: "Debra, I think you shouldn't talk any more. Just keep quiet until my aunt arrives."

She said: "Alright, Mister Alastair - is that right?"

"Yes, that's right."

"Just hold me hand, please. Makes me feel better."

I moved my chair closer and took her hand. Poor little thing, I thought. How come you're so far away from home, and what evil sod has done all that to you?

She seemed to doze, and we stayed like that for quarter of an hour or so until there came a knock on the door. I went to it and asked, without opening it: "Is that you, Aunt Billie?"

"Yes." I opened the door and she came in, carrying a small holdall.

"This is my Aunt Billie, Debra. She's a nurse and she's going to have a look at you. That's alright, isn't it"

"Yes. Thanks."

My aunt said: "Is there anywhere we could lay her down?"

I looked in the sitting room. There was a chaisse-longue which looked ideal, and I went in search of a bath towel to go under her. We took off the dressing gown and helped her on to the couch.

Aunt Billie looked first at the cut in her side, then felt gently where I thought the rib might be cracked, and asked her to breathe deeply, as I had, finally at the bloody lump on her head. She took me back into the kitchen.

"You really must get a doctor to see her, Alastair. She's pretty badly injured, you know. I can put some antiseptic ointment on that cut, and dress it again, and give her a bit more pain killer, but apart from that, I can't do any more than you've already done. What's wrong with taking her to hospital or getting a doctor here?"

"They'd have to tell the police, wouldn't they, and any mention of them really distresses her. I don't know why."

"What do you know?"

"Not much more than I told you on the phone. I found her on the side of the road, just the other side the cottages. She was unconscious then, in fact at first I thought she was dead. But she recovered when I got some tea, and some soup, down her. But she's terrified of something, or someone. She wouldn't tell me her name, only Debra, and when I said she'd have to go to hospital and they'd want it, and they'd have to tell the police, she went crazy.

"Oh, and there was a car came down the lane when I was picking her up, from this direction, and when it came near my car it turned round and went off, past the farm here and I suppose up through the woods - there's nowhere else it could have gone. It might have been nothing to do with her, but I can't help feeling mighty suspicious, Aunt Billie.

"Look, do you think you could talk to her? See if you could find out a bit more?"

She looked hard at me, and said: "Alright. First though I'm going to do what I can with those wounds. I don't think we need to be too worried about the possible broken or cracked rib - she's breathing pretty normally - but that cut really does need stitching. And she must have an ex-ray, to see if there are any internal injuries. That's why I think she should go to hospital, as a matter of urgency.

"Before I talk to her, though, I want you to give me more details of how you found her, and what she's said to you - everything since you picked her up. And while I'm seeing to her, see if you can light that cooker, and make us all a cup of tea. I need some hot water, anyway."

Actually, the water in the taps was still quite hot - the Aga had only been out for two days. And I found a Primus stove under the sink which quickly provided the tea. By the time I'd also lit the Aga, Aunt Billie had finished her ministrations to the girl, and joined me in the kitchen.

"Now, tell me absolutely everything you can, from the beginning. What she's said, and everything." Which I did, including her asking "Jerry" to stop hurting her, and that her "folks" grew bananas, and maize, and kept goats and chickens.

My aunt asked: "She hasn't actually said where she comes from?"

"No, but it's obviously the West Indies. And I think her family are pretty poor."

We went through to Debra and my aunt started to talk to her.

"Are you feeling any easier, my dear?"

"Yes, thank you, ma'am. A lot."

"Debra, I want you to listen very carefully to what I'm going to say first of all. You have some injuries that could be very serious. You might even die from them, if they're not properly looked after. Most important, you need to have an ex-ray, to see how badly you are hurt inside. You know what an ex-ray is, don't you?"

"Yes" - in a whisper.

"Also, that bad cut needs far more treatment than I can give it. Not to mention that knock on your head. First, can you tell me when all this happened?

"Yesterday – afternoon, I think."

"Alastair tells me you don't want to go to hospital. Why is that, my dear? It really is where you should be, you know."

"Him says them'd tell the police."

"Yes, they're obliged to, by law. What's wrong with that? Whoever did all this to you should be caught, and punished, shouldn't they?"

"Reckon so, but ..."

"But what, dear?"

"They'd send me back. An' then they'd get me. Oh, miss, don't let 'em get me again. I'd sooner die here. Mister Alastair, hold me hand, please - don't let 'em get me..."

"Debra, they won't get you. I won't let them, I promise."

Aunt Billie and I retired to the kitchen. I said: "You see what I mean."

"Yes. Poor little thing. But it doesn't change the facts, Alastair - she needs to go to hospital. But I've had an idea. You see, I'm not at all sure that she's right when she says they'd send her back, to Jamaica or wherever it is. Unless that is they want her there for some crime she's either committed or she's involved in - in which case I'm afraid there's nothing we can do.

"Assuming that's not the case, and she's done nothing of that kind, I really don't think they would. You know, people in the West Indies are told they must think of Britain as the mother country, their second home. Now, I know the chief constable quite well, through some work I'm involved in. I suggest that if we can get Debra to tell us all about what has happened, and if it is nothing very reprehensible on her part, I talk to Duggie Hammond and get his opinion on it. I think I can do that confidentially. At the worst, it might help us to persuade her.

"There's just one other point we should not lose sight of, as well. You, and I, could both be in trouble if anything happened to her as a result of those injuries. I 'm not saying we should just hawk her off to hospital and the police, willy-nilly, but I think we should be aware of it."

"Aunt Billie, I'd already thought of it. I'm terribly sorry. I shouldn't have got you involved," I said.

"Don't talk rubbish, boy. What are aunts for? Now, let us talk to Debra again. We must move quickly. I'd like to see her in that hospital today, and it's nearly eleven o'clock now."

Debra had gone off to sleep under the influence of the pain-killers, but we decided we must wake her.

"Debra," I said as soon as she was compos mentis, "We must talk to you. You must tell us more about yourself, and how you come to be in this terrible situation."

And as she flinched and turned her head away, I added: "My dear, I promise you that not a word of it will go beyond Aunt Billie and me unless you give us permission. She knows someone who may be able to help, but first we have to know everything - everything."

The girl turned away - I thought she was crying - but after a few minutes she looked at Aunt Billie and said: "Are you fright'nd you'll be in trouble if I die on you, Miss?"

"Yes, child, we might be in trouble. But it's more important than that. We just don't want you to die. You've been treated very badly and we want to help you get over it. Won't you tell us what we need to know so we can do that?"

And as Debra again turned away, my aunt added: "Look, Debra, I'll make you another promise. Neither Alastair nor I will breathe a word to anyone about what you tell us if you say we mustn't. Unless - oh, child, it's hard to say - unless you die. Then we'll have to tell people, or we shall indeed be in trouble. We could even go to prison."

Debra was quiet for another few minutes, then: "Alright, miss. I'll tell you. Can I have a drink of water, please?"

I fetched it and she drank, mouthfuls. I said: "Before you start, can you just tell us your name, and how old you are, and where your home is?"

She said: "It's Edworth - Debra Edworth. I'm 17 years old and I come from Masterman Creek, Jamaica - him's about 15 miles from Kingston."

"Is your father a farmer, Debra?"

"Don' know whether you'd call him that, but him has three or four bits of land, an' grows corn, an' banana, an' has chickens, an' goats for milk."

"What did you do when you were at home? Did you have a job?"

"No, there weren't no jobs. I could've got a job in Kingston but me mama an' papa wouldn' let me go there. They said I'd get into trouble. 'Spect they were right - there's terrible things happens in Kingston. I worked at our school a bit, cleanin' and sometimes lookin' after children, an' they paid me, but only a dollar or two."

"So what happened? How did you come to Britain?"

She seemed to gather herself, then started to talk.

"There was this feller. Him come round lookin' for girls to work in England. Said his organisation, he called it, would pay for us to go. It was about thirty pounds. Then they'd pay for us to stop at a special place they'd got, an hostel or somethin', and we'd be given a job, either workin' as a servant in a big house or cleanin' offices. Him said we'd be paid at least five pounds a week, which we'd keep for ourselves apart from a small amount - he said – that'd go to the hostel for rent. Me father asked 'what about the thirty pounds' and he said folk in England was so desperate for girls like us to work in their houses that they paid 'my organisation' to find them, and the passage money come out o' that. Him showed us letters from ladies who'd employed girls he'd found, an' were very pleased with them, an' some more papers that him said were guarantees that we'd have jobs. The papers had big headings at the top - the Anglo-Caribbean Employment Society I think it was - an I read them. Papa doesn' read much. Anyway, him said we should think it over for a day or two an' him went away. Mama and Papa didn' want me to go, but I thought it was too good a chance to miss. I wasn' goin' to do any good at Masterman Creek, was I? There wasn' no young men to marry me - them'd all gone away to Kingston, or America. I'd jus' grow into a poor old woman like me Aunt Mima who lives in a little hut on the sea shore an' collects things that's washed up, an' sells 'em."

She stopped, clearly tired, and after a moment asked whether she might have another drink. Aunt Billie asked whether she'd like tea, and she said oh yes please. My aunt went to make it, and I told Debra to have a rest for a minute. Apart from her obviously needing it, I thought it was essential that both of us should hear everything she said.

The tea brought, however, she resumed. She now seemed to want to talk.

"Anyway, I got me mother and father to say I could go, on a ship that went from Kingston in two weeks. When the man come back, we all signed a paper to say I agreed to 'the terms,' him called 'em, and him said I mus' be at the port office at a certain time. They said I must have some more clothes if I was goin' to England, which was always cold, they said, and they went with me on the bus that picked up every day at The Creek to buy 'em. I think Papa borrowed the money, because him had never bought me or me little brothers such clo's before. I had three lots of underthings, an two pairs o' jeans, an' shoes, an' shirts, an' warm jumpers. an' a coat, an' a hat, an' a suitcase to put them in. I kissed him, an' Mama, an' cried as they saw me up the gangway on to the ship. But I was very excited. I was goin' to England, an' I'd soon be rich, an' be able to pay to go back an' see them.

"I was a bit disappointed when I found I wouldn' have a cabin of me own on the ship, and I'd have to sleepin a big room with about twenty other people, some of them girls like me. Still, it was only for four days. I got talking to two of the girls an' they tol' me they'd signed up with that society too an' were bein' met at Liverpool, like me. They said some of the others had, as well.

"There were three women waitin' for us at Liverpool, a bit older than me an' the others, but dark-coloured like us. They split us up into twos and threes. Me an' two others went with a woman who said we should call her Martha, an' she took us to a car outside the docks. 'Just do 'xactly what I tell you and you'll be alright,' she said. I didn' like her. The car driver was a big white man she called Jerry. I didn' like him, either. At least, I didn' like the look of him, because he never said anything to us in the back, all the way to where we were goin' which I found out later was a city called Birmingham, that I'd heard about, at school.

"It was dark when we got there. Martha said: 'This is where you get out, ladies,' and she got out o' the car. I started to get out as well, but she said: 'Not you, darlin. You're goin' somewhere else. Stay here with Jerry.' I sat back and in a few minutes a man come, a black man this one, an' got in the car beside me, on the back seat. Him said: 'OK, bud,' and Jerry drove off. I asked where we were going?' and the black man said: 'We'se gwine to

Wolverhampton, honey. We'se got a nice little place for you, there.' I thought he sounded like an American. I didn' like him, either.

"When we stopped, they took me into a house and showed me into a little room with a bed but not much else. Jerry said: 'Bet you're hungry, girl.' I said I was but what I wanted most was a lavatory. Him showed me to a bathroom, it wasn' very clean but it'd got what I needed. He was waitin' outside the door when I'd finished. It was like I was a prisoner. Him said: 'Stay in there,' - the bedroom, he meant - 'an we'll bring you somethin' to eat.'

"They brought a plate o' beans, 'n toast, with an egg, and a cup o' coffee. It didn' look too good, but I was awful hungry, an' I ate it, an' drank the coffee, while the man watched me, all the time. Him took the plate an' things away an' said: 'You go to sleep, now, honey." I said could I go an' wash in that bathroom, but he tol' me no, I could wash in the mornin.' I thought I could slip out an' wash when he went, but the door was locked.

"I was frightened. I'd heard about girls gettin' taken away an' then made go with men, in Kingston, but I didn' think that kind o' thing went on in England. It's the mother country, where they look after you. That's what we've always been taught. But this didn' seem right, nohow.

"I still got me suitcase, but I didn't get undressed, an' I didn' sleep much, although the bed was comfor'ble. Them lights in the street outside kept me awake, as well, 'cos the curtains to the winder was thin and didn' keep much of it out. Anyway, it came daylight and sometime after the man Jerry opened the door with some breakfast, some kind o' corn stuff and a mug o'coffee.

"I said I needed the lavatory an he said alright, an' took me into a bathroom. They was soap and a towel in there so I had a wash as well. After a while he shouted me to hurry up. Like the other feller the night before, him stopped while I ate the breakfast, watchin' me all the time, but him didn' say anythin'. Then him went out and I heard him lock the door. I was more frightend'n ever, Miss Billie. I knew there was no nice job an' five pound a week for me, whatever they was thinkin' o' doin' with me. I thought I should just get away. I looked out the window but there wasn't no hope that way - it was high an' got bars across."

She stopped, and I thought she was going to cry. She certainly looked near to flaked out. Aunt Billie said: "Take your time, Debra, take your time, my dear."

"Could you help me sit up a bit, please?" We did, one on each side, very carefully.

I said: "Would it help if we asked you questions rather than making you tell it all yourself?"

"Pr'aps," she said.

I asked: "How long did they leave you there?"

"Hours and hours - leastways, it seemed like that. But it was still daylight when they come again. An' this time there was a woman with 'em. Jerry said her name was Marigold an' she was goin' to talk to me, an' they went out.

"This Marigold, she says to me: 'If you behave yourself, Debra, an' you're nice to people, you're goin' to make a lot o' money. First though - have you ever been with a man?'

"I just stared at her, Miss Billie. I knew then, dead sure, what they wanted me for. I shouted at her and tol' her I wasn' goin' to do it – never. But her jus' laughed an' asked what I thought 'em brought me over for.

"I told her what the man in Jamaica told me, and about the papers him showed me, an' the job him said I'd get. Her laughed again and said that was just to put me mother's mind at rest. An' her said I needn' think I could get out of it. One or two had tried but... an' her didn't say what.

"I said they could kill me if they wanted, but I wasn' goin' to do that - not for money. I couldn't never look me mama in the eye again if I did."

"Her said I'd better forget me mama. An' if I didn' play poker, her called it, what I'd get'd be worse'n bein' killed, an' I'd still do it, in the end.

"An' another thing her said: if I got back to Jamaica, I wouldn't last a week there. 'Our friends in Kingston,' her called 'em, would have me in a wooden box before I could tell me mama what had happened."

She looked near to collapsing again, and this time the tears did flow. She asked: "Can I have a drink, please?"

My aunt said: "Of course, my dear. What would you like - tea, or water, or there's some milk."

"Oh yes, please, milk. I haven' had milk since I left..." and this time the tears did flow.

I went into the kitchen with my aunt. I said: "Have we heard enough, Aunt Billie. Can we try to contact your friend the chief constable?"

"Yes, I think we can. Although, to tell you the truth, I think it's hardly necessary. No court would send her back to Jamaica if they heard what she's just told us. One thing, though. It might insult her, but I think we should just make sure she's done nothing the police there could possibly want her for. And then we should tell her what we propose doing, and get her to that hospital as quick as we can."

Aunt Billie took the milk to Debra, and said: "My dear, I think you've told us enough, for the time being. You've had enough. Now I am just about certain there's no chance that anyone will try to send you back to Jamaica, if you don't want to go. But I have a friend who can tell me for sure whether I'm right. Just one thing though - you've never been in trouble with the police at home, have you? He'll want to know that."

"Oh, no miss. I never been in no trouble. Not never."

I also had one more question for her: "Can you just tell us - was it those men, the one you called Jerry, and the other one, who caused all these injuries, hitting you and cutting you?"

"It was Jerry hit me, mostly. It was another one had the knife thing - cut me."

"The black one - the American?"

"No, not him, him didn't do nothin' like that. It was another one, when 'em took me an'...

"Look, leave it for now," I said. "You can tell us another time."

*****

My aunt went to the phone. She must have had the number with her, for I immediately heard her talking, and the name Dougie mentioned. I stayed with Debra, who reached out and caught my hand. You poor little thing, I thought. Do you think I can protect you? And I more or less resolved there and then that I must do my best to do just that, above all not let those bloody awful thugs get at her. I just sat there, holding her hand, and she seemed to go to sleep.

After a few minutes, Aunt Billie opened the door and beckoned me through to the hall, where the phone was. She said: "Well, he says he can't be certain what will happen without knowing absolutely all the facts, more than I could tell him just then, but he's sure as he can be she won't be sent back to Jamaica, if she doesn't want to go. He agrees with me, we should get her to hospital right away. Get an ambulance, he says. In fact he says he'll lay that on, if we agree - if the hospital people and the police know he's referred her to them, it'll probably help. Shall I ring him back and ask him to do that?"

"Do you think it's best?"

"I don't think it can possibly do any harm for them to know there's a bit of brass involved. Now, is the address here Forest Farm?

"Yes, Forest Farm, Cravenbury - the lane's called Forest Road where it goes into Cravenbury.

She went off to call her top brass friend. I sat down again, by Debra, who gave a little murmur as I picked up her hand. Gosh, I thought, I hope your confidence in me isn't misplaced. I'm not some kind of superman. But of course it all had the inevitable result. I was right away back to thinking again about that other little girl, and wondering where she was and what she was doing, and whether my heart, stomach, limbs and everything else about me would ever stop pounding, floundering, whenever I thought about her.

Aunt Billie reappeared and brought me back to earth.

"It's done," she said. "He thinks the ambulance will be here in quarter of an hour or even less. Do you know, Alastair, he even offered to come over himself, if we thought that would help, but I told him I thought the fewer people she saw the better, at the moment. I think we should just let her sleep 'til they come, don't you?"

She sat down herself. "She seems to have taken a shine to you, doesn't she," she said, noting Debra's hand in mine.

"I think I'm probably the Caribbean equivalent of a knight in shining armour, come to her rescue," I said. "I just hope she doesn't get disillusioned until she's a lot better. Do you think she will get better, Aunt Billie?"

"Oh, I think so, now we're getting her some proper treatment. But what on earth is she going to do? She can't go back, that's clear, and she can't be turned loose here. You know what everyone thinks about coloured people. She and her family must have been pretty naive to think she'd walk into a job, even as a servant.

"I expect they're so poor they're ready to grab at anything that seems to offer the prospect of something better," I said.

We sat silently again, until I said: "I wonder what happened after... they took her away. I think she was going to tell us. I want to know, sometime, Aunt Billie..."

"So do I..." as there came a loud knock on the door. It was two men, in peaked caps and white coats, one white and one black.

The white one asked: "You've got a young woman got to go to hospital?"

I said: "Yes. But you'll need a stretcher. She can't walk."

"Oh, we can manage her, mate" he said. They almost pushed past me into the kitchen.

Aunt Billie came out of the sitting room. She smelt the rat quicker than I did. These were no ambulance men.

"Where is she?" the one asked.

"She's upstairs, in bed," my aunt said. "Down there and up the stairs and it's the first room."

They went off.

"Quick, in here," Aunt Billie said, pulling me into the sitting room.

"Pull those chairs across."

We both heaved at two big easy chairs and bunged them against the door. She said: "And the sideboard."

It was all we could do to to move it, but we did, and added it to the chairs, as we heard the two come back down the wooden stairs and try the door.

"That'll hold 'em back for a bit," my aunt said. "But I bet they'll soon be round to the window."

But she was wrong. We never saw them again, and in a few moments we found out why. The real ambulance had arrived.

It took us a few minutes to realise what had happened. We heard a loud knocking on the kitchen door but nothing more on the door we had blocked up. Then we heard a shout: "Anybody in? Ambulance! Anybody in?"

Aunt Billy said: "It's the real one, I'm sure. I think they've frightened those two away. Come on, let us get out."

We wrestled the sideboard and the two chairs out of the way enough for us to open the door. I looked out, and could see no sign of the two bogus ambulance men. But I met the newcomers coming in through the door.

"Are we at the right place? This is Forest Farm? And Mrs Hood?"

"Yes, you're right. I'm her nephew, Alastair Jameson."

"Oh, yes, your name was mentioned. We've come for a young lady, quite badly hurt, we're told."

"Yes, she's through there. But you'll need a stretcher. She can't walk."

"Fetch a stretcher, Alan," said the first man.

I led him into the sitting room and to Debra. Aunt Billie had wrestled the chairs to one side, although the sideboard was only marginally out of the way.

"Let's have a look at you, love," the man said - I took him to be the driver.

Aunt Billie said: "She's got a bad cut on her side, and I think she might have a cracked rib. You can see all that bruising, and that big contusion, and there's one on her head."

"She's been dealt with well, at any rate," the driver said. "Are you a doctor?"

"No, but I was a nurse."

"Right, let's have you, darlin'" the driver said. And he and his mate lifted her ever so gently – I wondered at how such burly and tough-looking men, who looked as though they might have been more at home in a rugby scrum, could be so wonderfully careful – and onto the stretcher. We went outside with them as they loaded her into the vehicle.

"Are you coming with her, Mrs Hood?"

"If it's alright, I think she would be happier if my nephew came. He found her and she seems to like him near her," my aunt said. "I'll follow in the car, then I can bring him back. You're taking her to Shrewsbury, I suppose?"

"Yes, to the emergency department. Do you know where it is, in case you lose us?"

"Yes, I know it. I'll be a little while - I need to phone my husband to tell him what's happening."

I got into the ambulance and sat opposite her. She stretched out her hand, and the ambulance man said.: "There's a stool here, Mr Jameson. I think she'd like you to be a bit nearer."

Twelve

"Better you die, girl"

When we reached the hospital, a doctor met us immediately and Debra was wheeled into a side room. I stayed in the reception area, and the receptionist asked me for details, first about me, then her. All I was able to tell her was her name and age. She said she assumed I was not a relative, but asked where she came from, and I told her somewhere near Kingston, Jamaica, and she had only been in Britain for a few days, at the most.

She said: "I imagine you know, Mr Jameson, that we have to inform the police about anyone who comes in with injuries that appear to have been the result of violence of any kind. Is there anything you want to tell us before we do so?"

I said: "I would prefer to talk only to the police, if you don't mind."

"That's alright. Do you want to tell me what her connection with you is?"

"I found her on the side of the road, near my house. Now unless you need anything else for your records, I really would prefer to talk only to the police."

I sat down and waited. My aunt came in and told the receptionist she was with Debra who had been brought in, badly injured.

"Where is she?" she asked.

"The doctor's examining her," the receptionist said, and asked for Aunt Billie's details.

My aunt, who had not noticed me, sitting just out of her eyeline, gave them to her and said: "My nephew was with her. Where is he?"

"Right behind you, Mrs Hood," the receptionist said. We sat down together, and my aunt said: "You've seen nobody yet, of course."

I said no, they'd told me they'd have to tell the police, and I was wondering whether we ought to speak to them soon, bearing in mind the appearance of the bogus ambulance men, at the farm.

"I'm worried," I said. "They're obviously a pretty desperate lot. They might try to get at her here."

"I think that might be overdoing it a bit," Aunt Billie said: "But I'll have another word with Doug Hammond and tell him what's happened."

She asked if she could use a phone. The receptionist was reluctant, but when my aunt told her the call was to the chief constable and was about Debra, she agreed. "Use the one in there," she said, pointing to a small room. "That's where the police go if they have to interview anybody in private."

My aunt beckoned me, and I joined her. She got Mr Hammond immediately, and told him all that had happened, including the appearance of the fake ambulance men.

"I think they mean mischief, Dougie," she said. "Could you not get your local people to send someone along - someone senior, I should say. And tell them to talk to me, and Alastair - they'll probably frighten the girl and won't get anything out of her. She's pretty ill, anyway."

After another brief exchange, she put the phone down and said to me: "I think someone will be here soon. I hope they'll see it our way."

In reception, a doctor was waiting for us. He said: "Mrs Hood, Mr Jameson - my colleague is carrying on with the examination of the young lady. It's a nasty business. What do you know about it - about the young woman?"

I told him we knew very little about her except that I'd found her in the road near my house.

"When was this?" he asked.

"Last night - about eight o'clock."

"Why didn't you get her here then? You could see she was badly injured, surely."

I explained my difficulties, not wanting to leave her while I found a phone, reluctant to take her any distance in my car, how she had thrashed about in the car leading to my decision to take her to my house, and her reaction when hospital and police were mentioned.

"Did you bandage her - whoever it was made a very good job of it?"

"No, that was Mrs Hood, my aunt. She used to be a nurse."

"Do you know how she came by her injuries?"

Aunt Billie took over: "Not the full story. She told us enough to allow us to persuade her she must come here. But there's more to it, we're sure. We stopped her talking because it was exhausting her. But look, doctor, we don't mind telling you anything you need to know, but the police will be here shortly. It will be a senior officer, I believe, and we'll have to go through it all with him."

And as she finished speaking, two policemen came through the door.

One said: "Good afternoon, Dr Clarkson." And to us: "Mrs Hood and Mr Jameson?"

We acquiesed. He went on: "I'm Chief Inspector Allinson, Shropshire

Constabulary, and this is Sergeant Peacock. I understand you've brought in a young woman, with some bad injuries."

"That's right, chief inspector," my aunt said.

To the doctor: "Can I see her?"

"Yes, but you can't talk to her - at least, she can't talk to you. She's not well, at all, and she's under sedation."

He went to the door of the room where Debra was, and asked: "Alright for the police officers to come in?" And to them: "Go in, Mr Allinson."

The sergeant followed his chief, but the doctor stayed with us.

I asked: "How is she?"

He said: "As long as we don't find any serious internal injuries, and no infections develop, I don't think her life's in danger. The delay in getting her here didn't help, of course. But she'll need a lot of care, for quite a time. What do you know about her?"

"Only that she comes from Jamaica and according to her she's been brought over here on the pretext that she'd be found work. But it seems they really wanted to make her into a prostitute. I don't think she knows anyone in this country, apart from the people who did that to her if you can call that knowing them."

"Do you know what sort of a life she had in Jamaica?"

"Only what she's told us, which pointed to their being very poor. Her father is some kind of very small farmer. She thinks he had to borrow money to kit her out for this country."

"She doesn't appear to be undernourished, at least."

"She ate a good breakfast this morning," I said. "A banana and some cornflakes."

The two police officers returned. "Alright if we use the usual room?" the chief inspector asked. And he ushered us all onto chairs round the table.

"Now, what is all this about?" he asked. "Tell me what you know. Sergeant Peacock will be taking some notes."

I told him, the lot, starting with how I came to be living in the cottage, had fallen asleep after a hard day's work in the open air and decidedto go for something to eat at the pub. How I'd found the girl, seen her injuries, put her in the car, the mystery car in the lane, decided she was not fit to take anywhere because she was thrashing about, my efforts to make her as comfortable as I could, her terrified flight behind the bed because she thought "they" were outside, how she eventually went to sleep, breakfast next morning and her horrified reaction when I said she should go to hospital and the police informed.

"Why was she so frightened of the police?" he asked. "Was she in trouble back at home?"

Aunt Billie chimed in: "We asked her that, and she said she was not, most emphatically. I'm sure she was telling the truth. As I'm sure Alastair will tell you, she was threatened by the men here."

"It was a woman, actually. She told her if she didn't play ball they'd do all kinds of awful things to her, and if by any chance she succeeded in getting back to Jamaica their friends there would 'have her in a wooden box' - those were the words she used, Debra said - before she knew what was happening."

"Go on," the officer said.

I told him about deciding to take her to the farmhouse, where there was a telephone, and my idea of contacting my aunt, who used to be a nurse and how when she came she insisted Debra must go to hospital right away, and how she contacted someone for advice about whether she was likely to be sent back. I did not mention who it was, but Aunt Billie again chimed in.

"It was the chief constable, Mr Hammond. I know him well. But please don't think I was trying to pull strings, chief inspector. We just needed advice, and he gave it."

"When my superintendent told me to come here, he said it was on an order - a 'most urgent request' he called it - from someone in high places and I had an idea who it was," Allison said. "We're not too keen on jumping when people in other kinds of high places tell us to."

"Yes, well, that was after the fake ambulance men turned up. I was a bit desperate by then, so perhaps I was trying to work a string or two."

"'Fake' ambulance men?" the officer said, almost incredulously.

"Yes," I said. "Your chief rang for the ambulance and we were waiting for it. Debra had gone to sleep - she was absolutely shattered by the talking and my aunt had given her some painkillers - and we were waiting for it to come and these two men in white coats knocked on the door."

I told him how Aunt Billie sussed the bogus crew, sent them off to a wrong room, about the hasty barricade and how the real ambulance had arrived just at the right time.

"Would you recognise these men if you saw them again?" he asked.

"To tell the truth, all I saw were two white coats and peaked caps. Except that one was black and the other white, no, I don't think I would know them. Sorry."

"How did they know she was there, do you think? You said you hadn't seen anything of them when you looked around from your house."

"I can only think that I was wrong, and they were watching all the time, somehow. There are a lot of places round the cottages where they could hide and watch."

"Has the girl told you anything about what happened to her after she landed in this country - at Liverpool, I presume?"

"Yes, she told us in some detail." And I recounted most of it, starting with how she had been "recruited" in Jamaica with the promise of a job in this country and how she had been rapidly disillusioned after being taken first to Birmingham with two other girls, then to Wolverhampton on her own.

"We thought we must stop her talking at that stage because she was very clearly tired out and still in pain, in spite of my tablets," my aunt said.

"So you haven't been told the details of the assault?"

"No, we've been told nothing of that, except when I picked her up she screamed at 'Jerry,' who as I told you drove the car that picked up her and the two others at the docks. I think we'd have soon got to that if we hadn't stopped her."

Allinson said: "Yes, well, I think it's going to be a day or two before we can talk to her, isn't it, doctor?" - to Clarkson, who had sat in throughout the interview.

"Yes," he said.

"I hope it will be as soon as possible. We need to get after these villains and the girl's information will be essential."

My aunt said: "Chief inspector, I think it would be in everyone's best interest if my nephew was with Debra when you talk to her. She seems to regard him as her protector, her saviour even, and I'm certain she would talk more readily if he was there. Even if I was there – but he'd be best."

"Would it not be better if she had a solicitor present?"

"Good heavens no. That would put her off, not help her to talk. She's not a criminal, chief inspector, as I'm sure you will see very quickly when you talk to her. I did think of suggesting you wore plain clothes when you see her, but on reflection I think a kind man in uniform would be more reassuring."

Allinson laughed. "I'll try to be kind, ma'am. Please don't note that, sergeant - it might not do my credibility any good."

Aunt Billie had not quite finished with him though. She said: "As I'm sure you will have seen even without talking to her, this is a pretty ruthless and resourceful gang. The ambulance episode shows that, doesn't it? Do you not think she ought to have some protection, even in here?"

"You may have a point," he said. "My problem will be finding officers to do it. To put someone here for 24 hours a day means taking three men off the beat every day, or away from other duties."

"Would it help if my nephew and I spent as much time here as we could?"

"It sounds as though the young woman would welcome that. But no, Mrs Hood, from the protection point of view there can be no substitute for an officer on the spot. I'll talk to my superintendent and see what we can do."

*****

That was on the Tuesday. It was Thursday before the doctors would allow the police to see her, interrogate her I suppose you'd call it. For although the chief inspector was very pleasant with both of us, accepted what we told him and there was never a mention of my record, which the most basic of routine checks must have thrown up, I had a feeling he was not quite convinced that Debra was a totally innocent party. Or anyway that there was not some more to it than we had been told so far. And as it turned out, he was right, in that.

Both my aunt and I went to see her twice on Wednesday. She came in the morning and we went into the farm house to put things to rights before the Arkinstalls returned. She also came to inspect the cottages, and was slightly alarmed, as my mother had been, to note the lack of amenities.

"It's not much better that the one your uncle and I lived in when we were first married, but that was thirty years ago," she said. "Are you going to do something about it?"

I was, of course. I could manage to rough it for a few months, but Erbie and Connie would be coming inside a month, and I wanted the other to be in decent shape for, eventually, the herdsman I hoped I'd need to look after the dairy side. To get a good man I would need to be able to offer him a decent house. My plan was to put in a hot water system and a bathroom in each, just as soon as I could get the work done. But money was tight, and although I meant to do as much of the work as possible myself, with Erbie, and Mike's help and supervision, it would still be costly. And farm work must not be neglected.

But, back to Debra. We phoned on Wednesday morning but were told only that she was "reasonably comfortable." My aunt asked if we could see her, they wanted to know whether she was a relative, Aunt Billie said she was the nearest thing she had to one, and they said yes, but you won't be able to talk to her.

I talked to Mike, told him a little about it all, and asked him to look after everything at the farm if I was missing - a pretty superfluous request, actually. We went to the hospital in the afternoon and although we were pleased with one thing we saw - a police constable stationed outside her door - we were alarmed when we saw Debra. She looked far worse than at any time since I had picked her up in the lane 40-odd hours before, and did not open her eyes when we went in to the little room. My aunt asked if we could see Dr Clarkson, who as it turned out had just come in.

"Don't worry too much," he said. "She's as well as can be expected. We've stitched that wound, and so far there's no sign of serious infection. She has a cracked rib, but that's nothing to cause concern, and there's a fair amount of internal bruising. The delay, and throwing herself out of bed and so on won't have done her any good, and the emotional strain she's obviously been under is taking its toll now. But I've told Chief Inspector Allinson there can be no question of her being able to talk to him until tomorrow at least - probably not until Wednesday. She must not be agitated - her most urgent need is for rest and quiet. But you are welcome to sit with her if you wish. I have an idea that if she sees you when she wakes up, it will be good for her."

We took him at his word, and sat down, one each side of her bed. And after a few minutes she did open her eyes, looking in my direction. You couldn't say she smiled, but it was the nearest thing to it, and her big brown eyes beamed. She reached out her hand, and I took it. "Oh, man," she said.

I said: "Aunt Billie's here as well." She turned her head a few degrees. "Hello, Miss Billie," she said.

My aunt told her: "You mustn't talk, Debra. Just be quiet. We're here."

We stayed like that for an hour or more. She opened her eyes a couple of times, looked at us and there came that little half smile of satisfaction. It was almost as though she was saying: "It's alright now, I'll come to no harm, now."

Nurses came in and checked her pulse, took her temperature, adjusted the drip on the stand at the side of the bed, looked at the dressing on her middle.

Aunt Billie asked: "Everything alright?"

"Fine," the senior one said.

My aunt wanted to do some shopping in the town, so we decided we'd not go back to the farm, but would have something to eat there and see Debra again in the evening.

Over the meal, for which Aunt Billie insisted on paying, she asked about my farming plans. I told her I was hoping to get back into milk production and people from the agriculture ministry were coming to see me, that week, to discuss the feasibility. I also told her of my plans for the cottages, and the strain all the work would put on my financial resources, and she made several suggestions for some short term projects to bring in cash relatively quickly, like selling grass "keep" in the spring, letting out shooting rights, even stocking up the farm's two decent size pools and selling the fishing, all ideas that over the years would become common practice. I said I'd consider them all, but I didn't want to upset Ben Arkinstall who'd sold me the farm on the understanding that it would be farmed.

"Let me talk to him," she said. "I don't think there'll be any problem."

We went back to the hospital and found Debra much the same - perhaps a little brighter - and the same policeman on duty. Again she wanted me to hold her hand, with a result similar to the afternoon's. As we drove home, I said: "Assuming the police don't have any claims on her, what do you think she'll do when she's fit enough to come out of hospital, Aunt Billie? From what we've heard, it doesn't sound as though going back to Jamaica's much of a prospect. And there isn't much of a prospect here, for coloured folk, is there?"

"You're right there, my boy. But I don't think we can just wash our hands off her, can we?"

"No, we can't. But it's no use even talking about it at the moment, is it, much less trying to make plans for her. We must wait and see what happens."

Next day Aunt Billie went to see her, straight from her own home, and I went in the evening. I found her visibly, although not massively improved. She wanted to talk, as well as have me hold her hand.

"Are you feeling any better?" I asked.

"Oh, yes, man," she said. "It don't hurt so bad, now. Yes'day, I thought I gonna die."

"No, no, Debra, you're not going to die. You'll soon be well and strong again."

She relapsed into silence, a thinking kind of silence, however. I said nothing - it was better she was not encouraged to talk too much.

Suddenly she said: "I think a police man is comin' to see me tomorrow. Him won't take me away, will him?"

"No, my dear, he certainly won't take you away. He'll want you to tell him all that happened, though, and they'll try to catch those people who did all this to you, and punish them. They're bad people, aren't they? But I don't think you need be afraid of this policeman - Chief Inspector Allinson is his name. Aunt Billie and I both thought he seemed a good man. But he'll want to know everything that happened, and he'll ask you some questions about yourself and your life in Jamaica. Just answer everything truthfully and you'll have nothing to worry about."

I did not say anything about my possibly being there when Allinson came to see her, because although he had not seemed totally opposed to the idea when we broached it, neither had he approved it. But next morning, when I was working with Mike, still on the fencing and hedge cutting, along the lane, he turned up, with his sergeant and a man in plain clothes who I took to be a detective.

He said: "Good morning. Could we have a word?"

I said of course, and offered to take them into the farmhouse or my cottage, and make them a cup of tea or coffee. Allinson said: "I'd like you to take us first to the exact spot where you found the young woman."

We drove in their car to the "exact spot." As far as I could tell there was nothing to be seen of any significance, in fact I could not be certain that it was the exact spot, to within a few yards, but they spent best part of half an hour examining the ditch and the roadside. I thought I heard the plain clothes man say, quietly, "Nothing here, sir."

Allinson said: "Could we go back to your cottage, and have a look round - and we'll accept that cup of tea, if it's still on offer."

Inside, he said, as I busied myself with kettle, teapot and cups: "I'm going to talk to Debra this afternoon, but I wanted first of all to familiarise ourselves with the surroundings, and have another little chat with you.

"This is where you live, is it? Why not the farmhouse? That belongs to you, doesn't it?" I explained.

"Let's see. You carried her out of your car, you say, and in here. Where did you put her?"

I showed him, then the stairs and the room above; where I'd "hidden" the car; my improvised cudgel, everything. The sergeant and the detective appeared to be scruitinising it all carefully.

"Good," Allinson said. "Now I'm going to put something to you. You are the Alastair Charles George Jameson who was sentenced to five years imprisonment for aiding and abetting drug and arms smuggling, are you not?"

Oh, God, I thought. I wondered when it was coming. The other two officers were looking at me very hard.

I said: "Yes, I am. But I must repeat what I said at the time, and I've told everybody who matters, since, I didn't know drugs were involved. But I wondered when that was going to come into it."

"Well, you tell me how it comes into it."

"It has nothing whatever to do with it."

"Are you quite sure? Because we believe there is a drugs angle to this."

"Chief inspector, that doesn't surprise me totally. But I have told you absolutely everything that happened, and that Debra told me and my aunt, to the best of my recollection."

He looked hard at me, for several seconds. It reminded me of those other interviews, nearly five years before, also with a policeman I grew to like, even though I'm not wildly fond of police people, in general. But eventually: "I accept that. And I think I can tell you that I accept that you are an innocent party in all this."

"Thank you. Can I ask whether you have made inquiries about - Debra?"

"We have. They're not complete yet but up to now nothing untoward has shown up."

"I'm very pleased. But I'd be very surprised if there was anything."

"Now, you, or was it Mrs Hood, wondered whether you might sit in on my interview with her. It's quite irregular, but we've decided we can allow that. Your aunt believes your presence will give her confidence in telling us everything."

"I do believe it will. The poor little thing thinks I'm some kind of guardian angel or something."

And that was it. We all finished our tea and went to the farmhouse, where I showed him where Debra had lain on the chaise-longue, and how we had barricaded the door. He asked me for all I could tell him about the two fake ambulance men, which was not much, and whether I or Aunt Billie had seen a vehicle, which we had not.

*****

I took my own car - something else the other two officers had subjected to the scrutiny of their fine-tooth comb - to the hospital where we all had a bite to eat before the plain clothes man left us.

Debra looked another stage improved, propped up on pillows, as we were ushered in to her little room, after a warning from the sister-in-charge that she was not to be harrassed or excited - doctor's orders. I took it on myself to introduce the officers. I sat close to the bed on one side and she put out her hand for me to hold - it seemed almost an automatic reaction to my presence now. Allinson took off his cap and sat opposite, but also quite close.

"Hello, Debra," he said. "I have seen you before, but you were out to the world so you didn't see me. I want you to tell me all that happened, right from the start. Take your time. I may ask you some questions, if there's anything I don't understand, perhaps. And the sergeant here will take some notes."

She looked at me, as if to ask "is it alright?" I said: "Start right at the beginning, Debra - what happened in Jamaica."

With only a little prompting from Allinson, when he did not quite follow her, she went right through it all, from the approach by the man from "the Anglo-Caribbean Employment Society" to her experiences in the house at Wolverhampton, including how she finally knew she was brought over to be a prostitute, and there was no way she could get out of it. And was told that a "wooden box" at the hands of "our friends in Kingston" awaited her if she by any chance managed to get back to Jamaica.

This was a point where the chief inspector asked her a couple of questions. Was she absolutely sure she was being threatened with being killed, he asked.

"Oh, yes, Mister Police Man," she said. "Her meant that."

That was as far as Aunt Billie and I had allowed her to go, but now she seemed quite strong and ready to tell the chief inspector everything. I'm not putting it into her own words here - the combination of her semi-patois and the horrors she was describing make writing them down difficult, especially so far in the past as they now are.

That same afternoon, she was taken to another house, and "Marigold" told her that was where she was going to stay. It was quite a pleasant house, and Debra was shown into a comfortable if somewhat oriental bedroom - "all red paper an' mirrors an' things," she said - and the woman said two men would be coming to see her that evening.

"She give me some stuff I was to put on me, 'cos I'd never done it before, an' said the men'd give me five pounds each, that was just for me, 'cept a bit o' rent I'd have to pay. I told her I wasn' goin' to do it, but she said

I bloody well would, if I wanted to see me next birthday."

She said she looked at the window to see if it offered any hope of escape, but it was barred from top to bottom, and anyway it was too high up to jump. She tried the door, and to her surprise it was not locked, so she took her bag and walked out and down the stairs, only to see Jerry standing in the hallway.

"An' where d'yer think you're off to, girl?" he asked her - pleasantly enough, she said.

"Just gettin' out of here, man," she told him. He said: "No, you're not. Up them stairs. You got company comin'."

She tried to walk past, but he caught her arm, twisted it behind her and marched her up the stairs, telling her to "just stay there, baby."

After about an hour, it would be about eight o'clock, she thought, the door opened and Marigold showed in a big white man dressed in a white shirt, suit and tie.

"This is Debra," she said. "Gentle 'er, will yer - it's 'er first time."

The man said that was how he liked 'em - never wanted anything else. She was sitting on the bed and he sat beside her.

"You'll be alright with me, girl. I've had a lot of virgins."

She was shivering with fright, but he kept on talking as he started to take off his clothes. "Come on, Debra. Do your bit. Get 'em off," he said.

She begged: "Don't, please, mister. I told 'em I wasn' goin' to do it."

"You what! Oh God, don't say they've given me one of them as well as a bloody virgin. Come on, you little prick-teaser – I'm payin' good money for this. Here, I'll get 'em off you."

He grabbed at her, thrusting his hand up the skirt she'd been wearing since she got off the boat. She struggled, kicked out as hard as she could, lashed out with her fists, but he ripped off the skirt and then her knickers. She tried to get away, but he forced her down on the bed. She felt him entering her, and with a superhuman effort got her feet into his belly then, more by accident than design, a hard blow to his genitals. He screamed: "You black bitch! I hope they have your fucking guts, you stupid little cow!" But he rolled away, clutching himself and sobbing as he found his trousers, pulled them on and made for the door.

No more than a minute later, Jerry and Marigold burst in. He struck her a vicious blow to the head, and another to her ribs.

"That's for this one, madam," he said as she sunk almost senseless to the floor. "And it's nothing to what you'll get if you play this kind of fucking game again."

"I don't care," she cried as the tears streamed. "I'm not goin' to do it.

You can kill me if you like. I'd rather die."

"You won't die, baby - but you'll wish you fuckin' 'ad. Now, somebody else'll be up in a bit. Just you do what you're here for - savvy?"

"I won't, I won't," she screamed again.

The two went out. Debra collapsed on the bed, her head throbbing. After a while she started to think coherently. Was there nothing she could do to get away? She started to look round the room, seeking she hardly knew what - perhaps a weapon she might use to fend them off. She was by no means optimistic of being able to fight her way out - they'd probably kill her. But better if she went down fighting.

"Would it not have been better, Debra, to have given in to them and waited for a better chance to get away?" the chief inspector had asked at this point, as she paused, looking back on the horror of it.

She looked at him, almost pityingly. "Mr Police Man, if you knowed my mama, you wouldn' say that. She spend all her days workin', workin', workin'. When she wasn' workin', she was teachin' us. An' one o' the big things she tol' me was never to give meself to any man until him give me that gold ring. Never, never, never, she said. Better you die, girl, she said... An' I reckon I was thinkin' - 'yes, better you die, girl.'"

She went on to tell the tragic story, how she found her bag and took from it clean knickers and jeans, agonising as she did over what her mother would think if she knew what was happening. She looked in the wardrobe and in the dressing table's two drawers - nothing. Then as she straightened up she saw something protruding from the wardrobe's top. She took the room's only chair to stand on and found a walking stick. Better than nothing - she would go for it. But before she rushed for the front door, she decided to look round the rest of the house, in case there was a better possibility. She knew the room door was not locked, for she had heard or rather felt Jerry slam it and pace angrily away. Holding the stick like a club, she went out to the landing, this time turning the other way. Giggling voices sounded from one of the rooms. Others, looking to the back of the house, seemed unoccupied - no light showing under the doors. She tried one, went in, found the light switch and flicked it. It was almost exactly like "her" room - bed, red-shaded lights, dark decor, mirrors. She looked at the window. Bars there too - no escape this way. She switched off the light while she considered what to do, her head still throbbing but her brain clear enough.

Her best hope, she decided, would be to wait until they brought the other man they had promised, which might leave the front door unguarded, then make a dash while they were in the room, wondering where she had gone, perhaps going to search the room where she then was. She settled down to wait, standing in the dark with the door slightly open. Her head and side hurt, but she hung on, for an hour or so. Then sure enough she heard them coming up the stairs, three of them. Thank God, they were both coming up. She saw them open "her" door, and almost before they were through it, she was past and down the stairs. But Jerry was quick - probably spotted her flying past. He shouted: "Gil - stop her," and just as she opened the front door the black American appeared. She swung at his head with her stick, and made contact. But by then Jerry was downstairs. There was a short drive outside with two cars on it. She dashed past them on to the road, sprinting towards what she thought was a main road about two hundred yards away.

Jerry pounded after her, but despite her hurts, she outpaced him and reached two men walking towards her, well ahead of him. She gasped: "Please help me - them gonna kill me."

One of them laughed as he caught her. "Now who'd want to kill a pretty girl like you? Not you, would you, Jerry?"

They took her back to the house, but this time they thrust her down some steps into a cellar, lighted and clean enough but with only a wooden bench for furniture. The two newcomers, both black men, followed after a few minutes.

"You've not been behavin' yourself, missy, have you?" one said, as he started to undo his belt. "So we're gonna teach you a little lesson. First though you're gonna have to be shown that what you're here to do ain't so bad after all. Hold her, Jos - my turn first."

She struggled and kicked, this time aiming deliberately at the would-be rapist's vulnerable organs. But it was no use. "Jos" held her firmly against the wooden stairs while the other stripped off her jeans and pants and had his way with her, ignoring her screams and the sobs that followed.

"Your turn now," he said. But Jos took a look at the other's bloody parts and said: "No thanks, man, don't fancy her, not yet, anyhow." He gave her her knickers and jeans, told her to put them on.

As she struggled with the garments, still sobbing violently, he said: "Now, you fuckin' little whore. Are you goin' to play the game? Or do you want the biggest hidin' you've ever had in your life, an' then you'll still have to do it, if you have to be tied down. They's guys like it like that, you know."

She shouted: "Kill me, kill me! I won't do it! I'll never do it!"

"Oh yes you will" - and he turned round a ring on his hand and struck her a vicious blow to her face, raking his hand down her cheek. The blood welled up.

"What do you say now, bitch?" he asked, leering.

"I won't! Kill me!"

"Alright, if it come to that, we will. But try this first." He hit her in the mouth with the back of his hand, then took hold of her hair while he slapped her hard on alternate sides of her face.

"Well?"

"You'll never make me!"

The other one - she never learned his name, just called him the evil one - took over.

"Jerry says we can do what we like to you," he said. "He thinks you'se damaged goods, anyhow. I think you'se too good for that, though, even with that scar that'll come on yer cheek - it'll soon mend. Now, see sense. Praps they'll let you come home with me for a bit, an' I'll teach you the business, an' how to enjoy it. How about it?"

She spat in his face. He hit her, on the head, and she fell to the ground. He kicked her in the ribs, and stomach, several times. They might have killed her, then. But she got up, rushed almost blindly for the open stairs, actually making the first steps, and never saw the knife until it flashed for her midriff. But she was already falling, as the burst of energy, gathered in desperation from somewhere deep in her brave little psyche, succumbed to the effects of all she'd been through. And the fall saved her life. Instead of being buried in her stomach or her heart, the blade ripped along her ribs.

Thirteen

The end of a sickening story

She had difficulty getting the words out as she reached that part of the sickening story, through which we had all shuddered. Even the two policemen, presumably inured to all they encountered in the world of murder, rape and other villainy, appeared moved. I was shaking like a leaf. She never let go of my hand from start to finish, and towards the end I felt the dainty brown fingers convulse again and again.

As I said I would, I have set down this latter part of her grim experience in my own words. Trying to remember it all, so many years afterwards, will have meant a number of variations from her own, no doubt. But these last have been engraved on my memory, exactly as she spoke them, from that day to this.

"I ran fast up that street an' I thought I'd made it when I reached them two men in front of Jerry," she said. "Them was wicked men, Mister Police Man. Them was more wicked than Jerry or any of 'em, I think. They throwed me down some stairs into an underground sort o' place, an' a few minutes after they come down there as well.

"They said they was goin' to teach me a lesson, an' they hit me, an' kicked me. Then that one, him told the other one, him 'em called Jos, to hold me, an' he took me clothes off me, an'... an'... he did that..." and she sobbed, violent, retching, dry-eyed sobs. We all sat still, except Dr Clarkson - he had come in some time before, with the chief inspector's approval - who ministered to her as best he could.

He said: "I think we should give her a rest. She's had enough."

Allinson said: "I'm sure you're right, but if I could get just a bit more information from her it might help in locating these people. My guess is it's important to act quickly. Can we come back this evening and see how she is then? Say eight o'clock?"

"Of course," the doctor said. "I'm going to give her a mild sedative, but I think eight will be alright."

The officers left, but I stayed. I said: "Is it alright if I sit with her a little longer? She seems to like it."

"I'd be very pleased if you would. You are obviously good for her. I don't think you should try to get her to talk to you about this, though. She might want to, and we often find that people who have gone through this kind of awful experience benefit from talking. But she'll have to go through it all again to Chief Inspector Allinson."

I went back to her and told her I was going to get a cup of tea but would be back. She actually managed a smile, and whispered: "Yes, please, man."

I found a call box and rang Aunt Billie, who said: "I'm so glad you rang, Alastair. I was wondering how she was. I spoke to the hospital but all they would tell me was she was 'comfortable.'

"I think 'comfortable as can be expected' might be more accurate, Aunt Billie. She is improving, certainly, but this afternoon she had to go through telling it all to the police. At least, not quite all, because she broke down when she got to the nastiest part, and the doctor asked them to leave her for a while."

"Did they - were they - heavy on her?"

"Oh, no, nothing like that. Allinson was quiet and kind. It was what happened to her - it was awful."

"Will they let me see her if I come? Do you think I should?"

"I'd be very pleased if you would. I'm staying, probably until the police have talked to her again, this evening. I was there through it all, this afternoon, at their invitation. I'll tell you about it, if you come."

She came, within an hour. I was sitting with Debra by then, who was sleeping, apparently peacefully. I took my aunt into the waiting room, and told her all that the poor girl had related.

"I expect they'll want to know what happened after that. How she got from Wolverhampton to where I found her. It must be 30 miles, at least. Do you know what's just been going through my mind, though? I think they've either got some of their gang near us, and they were bringing her to them; or they thought they'd killed her, and they were going to dispose of her - bury her in the woods, perhaps. But how she came to be in our lane I don't know. I can't see them just dumping her there, not even if they thought she was dead."

"Perhaps they wanted to get her away from their brothel, then finish her off," my aunt said. "It's all conjecture, though. How does she seem, in herself?"

"I think she's improving all the time, physically - she's certainly much better than when you last saw her. But she is really distressed when she has to talk about... about... you know, you know, what happened. She was raped, horribly, Aunt Billie, among it all. I think it comes from her upbringing. The chief inspector asked her whether it would not have been best to go along with them and make her escape later, and she answered him quite sharply. Her mother told her she must never go with any man, unless she was married to him, she said.

"What kind of a home does she come from? Do you know?"

"It's very poor, I'm sure, from what she's said. And her parents, and for that matter Debra herself, must be pretty naive to fall for this kind of fiddle. But of course, if they were so very poor, they would grasp at anything that offered something better, wouldn't they? It sounds as though they might be religious, a bit like some of the American negroes. Very poor people often are, aren't they?"

We went out into the town for something to eat, which again my aunt insisted on paying for. Over the meal, we talked about my farming plans. I asked my aunt if she could go in to see Debra in the afternoon, the next couple of days, because I might be tied up with the agriculture ministry people, about the dairying.

When we returned to the hospital, we found Debra awake and very pleased to see us both. But we did not start talking about her ordeal because the police officers were due shortly. Aunt Billie left just before seven and I promised to let her know what I learned.

The chief inspector of course wanted to know what happened after the assault - as indeed did I.

"Are you ready to tell us some more, Debra?" he asked. "What happened after he took the knife to you?"

"I don't know. I didn't know nothin' 'til I felt 'em puttin' me in the car trunk" - she meant the boot. "I thought I was dyin'. I hurt so much. I come to a bit, then I went out again, then I come to again. The car was movin', fast, I thought. But I kep' seein' little bits o' light under the bottom of the lid. After a bit I realised why it was. It wasn' shut down proper. I began to think can I open it an' get out. I tried to reach where it was supposed to lock, but it hurt so much I went out black again. But it didn' last. I came awake again an' had another try, an' I found it. I worked the catch an' the lid come open a bit. I made up me mind I'd get out. Then the car stopped. It all looked dark outside, far as I could see, but I jus' kep' still, so them'd think I was dead.

But they didn' come to the trunk, and in a minute I heared one say: 'That's better,' an' him got back in the car, an' they started off. I acted very quick, then, mister. Before the car got goin' proper, I pushed the lid up an' managed to climb out."

"That must have hurt," Allinson said. "Where did you land? On the road?"

"Yes, mister. It hurted. I went out black again, an' sick, for a minute or two. Then I thought I gotta move from there, an' I tried to crawl off the road. But I couldn' get far. Me head went down in a hole" - it was the ditch, of course - "an' I had to stop. Me head was swimmin' round and I kep' going' black. Then I saw some lights an' I thought it was them comin' back for me, an' I went black again."

"It was in fact Mr Jameson?"

"Yes, mister."

"He took you to his house?"

"Yes."

"What happened there?"

"Him give me some tea, an' soup, an' looked after me, an' said I needn' worry, 'cause him wouldn' let nobody hurt me." And she clasped myhand a little closer, and a tear rolled.

Allinson was evidently satisfied to accept what my aunt and I had told him as to what happened next. He simply asked her: "Would you know these people who took you away, and those who assaulted you, if you saw them again, Debra?"

"Reckon so. Most of 'em, anyway."

"Good. Now, Sergeant Peacock has been taking notes of all you've told us. He'll put it down on paper and read it back to you, and ask you to sign it as your own statement. Or you can read it yourself, if you'd rather. If there's anything in it you don't think is quite right, it can be changed. We'll be back for you to do that, probably tomorrow. If you want to talk any more to me, before then or any time, tell the doctor or nurses here and they'll get in touch with me. In any case, I'm sure I shall need to talk to you again. Is that alright?"

"Yes, Mr Police Man."

"It's 'chief inspector', actually. Chief Inspector Allinson. Or you can just call me Mr Allinson, if you prefer."

"Thank you Mr... Allinson. Please..."

"Yes, Debra?"

"You isn' goin' to send me back, is you? Them'd kill me sure...."

"No, my dear. I think I can safely promise you that. You won't be sent back, until you want to go."

*****

Francis John Simcock

She was in hospital for a month. Before that I had told my mother and father all about it, everything that had happened, as far as we knew it. My mother was horrified, and took on her share, and more, of the visiting, sometimes with my father.

Mother had had little to do with people of different races, like most of the folk where she came from, but I never saw the least hint of the kind of revulsion that so many people appeared to feel at that time, and some still do. In fact, the opposite. If there was such a thing as love at first sight between non-lesbian women, it happened with these two. Debra said to me after Mother had visited her for the first time: "Oh, Mister Alastair, I does like your mama. Isn' her lovely?"- a sentiment with which I had no difficulty agreeing. And my mother said: "What kind of people are they who'd do such things to a sweet little mite like that? I do hope they catch them." And over the next two or three weeks, she talked to "the little mite," then read to her, and Debra took her hand, as she did mine and Aunt Billie's, and seemed to gather strength from the contact.

"What's going to happen to her when she comes out?" Mother asked, echoing the question Aunt Billie and I had already begun to pose. I had no doubt about one aspect of it. I was going to make sure she was adequately looked after, one way or another. But the means of doing it were not so clear. She could not come to stay with me, for obvious reasons, the most important being the "talk" that must follow.

It was easy to imagine. "'Ave yer seen that little black bit the new chap at The Forest's got livin' with 'im? 'Er inna very big, but I bet 'er's a goer - they all am, them blackies. An' they say 'er was a tart - that's why 'er was brought over." And so on. I was not terribly worried about the effect such talk would have on me, but my goodness it must not happen to Debra. If it did, I thought, I might almost as well have left her to die where I found her.

It was of course the eminently sensible, down to earth, yet imaginitive and inventive Aunt Billie who came up with what, with hindsight, was the obvious solution.

"She should go to your mother, Alastair. There's all the room in the world there, and plenty for her to do. And you can see how they get on. I think it would be the perfect solution. She'd be shown how we live here, and unless I'm mistaken, she'd learn very quickly. Shall we ask her?"

I called up the scenario I had imagined if she came to The Forest. "Just one thing," I said. "What do you think the people in the village would think, and especially the girls Mother employs?"

"Alastair, Alastair! What are you saying? You know how much your mother is liked and respected at Lyndford, and everywhere. If anyone can help Debra get over all she's been through, it's Dolly - your mother, I mean. In a different way, she's been there herself, you know. And I'll tell you what, my boy - if anybody tried the colour prejudice thing on, they'd get very short shrift from her."

My mother agreed to Aunt Billie's suggestion immediately. "I was going to suggest it myself," she said. "I can't think of anything better. Your aunt said she could go to her for a time, but I don't think that's half as good as coming to Lyndford.

"You know, Alastair, she's very bright. She has the makings of a strong personality, and I think I can help it develop. I've been reading to her quite a lot, and every time, before we start, she asks me questions about what we'd been reading the time before. She obviously thinks about it, and sometimes goes further than the book itself. I've been reading her The Golden Arrow, by Mary Webb - chose it really because it's about a girl called Deborah. She wanted to know all about the country, and if the Devil's Chair actually exists, and that led on to talking about religion, and old myths, and how John Arden and others like him made a living on their little sheep-walks. We even talked about class structures in Britain, and Jamaica, and I told her about how I'd been your grandmother's kitchen maid, and she cried when I told her about your grandfather. She's a good girl, Alastair. When I think about how she was treated by those awful men it makes my blood boil, and you know it takes a lot to make that happen."

It also took quite a lot to make mother indulge in a speech as long as that. Highly intelligent herself, she could usually make her point in comparatively few words. It showed, I thought, how Debra had made an impression on her.

Not long before she left hospital, my mind was eased about one aspect of the ghastly business that had been worrying me. Would it not be even worse if she turned out to be pregnant? But Mother revealed quite inadvertently that she was not, when I saw a packet of sanitary pads in her car, and as she saw my eyebrows go up, she said: "They're for Debra, thank God."

I told Debra about the plan for her to go to my mother's. I told her it was a big house, right in the country, which she already knew from her talks with Mother, that when she was well enough she would be expected to help run it, and that she would be welcomed in the village, we were very sure.

I was a little surprised therefore when she did not immediately welcome the idea as eagerly as I had expected. She sat still - she was by this time out of bed most of the time, usually wearing a gold-coloured dressing gown, and slippers, that Mother had brought her - and said nothing for a minute or so.

"Don't you think it's a good idea, Debra?" I asked. "It's beautiful at Lyndford and you get on well with my mother, don't you?"

"Oh, Mister Alastair, I love her. She's a beautiful lady. It isn't that..."

"What then, my dear?"

Her voice sank to a whisper: "It'll be a long way... from you... I wanted to come an' stay... with you..."

There. It was as good as out, I thought. The "little mite" had fallen for me, a man old enough to be her father, almost, and who, sorry as I felt for her, aroused no feelings of that kind in me. No-one else ever could.

I sat for as long as it took to recover some equanimity. "Debra, my dear, I will always care for you, and look after you, and I would love to have you stay with me so I could do that. But you cannot come to live with me. It's impossible."

"Why, Mister Alastair? Is it 'cause I'm... coloured?"

Again I had to think hard.

"Dear girl, I wouldn't care if you were sky blue pink, or sea green. But to be honest, the fact that you are... coloured... brown, a beautiful brown... would matter. People would think you were only there because you were something like those awful men wanted to make you."

I was floundering. I thought I had opened the pit of colour prejudice, that so far she had not encountered, hideous as her first experiences in Britain had been. I did not know that she had indeed already come up against it in hospital. Nothing open, but overheard remarks, sniggerings. And I had fallen into their trap.

I was wrong also in thinking she had fallen in love with me in the way I had fallen for Angie, and she for me. It was not like that, then. She was a curious mixture, at that time, of a naieve child from a primitive background and a young woman of intelligence and sensitivity who knew how the world of sex and the sexes operated. But my rescue of her, purely accidental as it was, had left her looking on me as a saviour and guardian angel, rather than as a potential mate. There was enormous, almost adoring, gratitude which was not the same as what we call being in love. But the perceptive sensitivity kicked in and rescued me from my mire of male egocentricity.

"Oh, Mister Alastair, of course I'd like to go stay with your mama. But you'll come and see me sometimes, won't you?"

"Debra, nobody could stop me," I said gratefully. And so she went to Lyndford, that haven, under my mother, of peace and tranquility.

Fourteen

Arrests: a farming year

Just after Christmas Chief Inspector Allinson, sergeant in tow, came to the farm again, with some good news.

"I expect you'll be pleased to know that our colleagues in Staffordshire have made some arrests," he said. "And we think there'll be more."

"The men who assaulted Debra?" I asked.

"Those, and some others connected with them. There's a lot more to it than the prostitution racket, although that's bad enough. The gang are running all kinds of illegal enterprises, we believe, including drugs. The Staffordshire force have had their eyes on that house for some time. It will be some time before we can get them into court, but I'm sure we shall, in the end."

"I also wanted to tell you that we don't think there's any need for round the clock protection for her, now. We shall need to keep in touch with her, but I don't imagine there'll be any difficulty about that, when she's with your mother - and incidentally, we think that's an ideal place for her to go. I know Mrs Jameson by reputation, and I've met her, and we're very happy for her to be in her care."

"So am I, chief inspector. So am I."

"We shall be asking her to identify those men, before long. How do you think she'll cope with that? And eventually, of course, with giving evidence in court."

"If you'd asked me a few weeks ago I'd have said she'd have been very distressed if she was brought face to face with them. But I've watched her getting stronger, and gaining confidence, and I think she'll cope. Even with giving evidence."

"Good. I have more news I expect you'll be glad to hear. There is absolutely nothing on her from the Jamaican police point of view. Her father and mother appear to be respected in their community, although they're very poor, as you suggested. I shall be telling her the outcome of our inquiries, and about the arrests, but I've no objection to your telling her."

"Thank you, chief inspector. I won't tell her unless it comes up through her, but thank you very much for telling me. I think it would be good for her to hear it from you, though."

"Just one other thing. Colleagues in the Met, as we call the London force, have told us that a certain Herbert Johnson, who is known to them, is moving here, to work for you. Is that correct?"

"Yes, he and his wife are going to live in the other cottage. They've only just got married."

"Would you like to tell me what you know about him? Unofficially."

"I don't mind telling you - unofficially or officially. But I would have thought he was too small game for police forces to be talking to each other about him. Asking you to keep an eye on him, is it?"

"Something like that. I will only say - unofficially - that I have very good reasons for asking you - reasons that I don't think either he or you need be worried about."

I had come to like Allinson. I thought he was not only a good and square copper, but one who could see into and through both good and bad people. I told him all I knew about Erbie. No doubt one bit of it helped make up the mesh of the anti-corruption net that tightened round some unsavoury parts of the Metropolitan Police a few years later.

*****

Before Erbie and Connie arrived, and just as Debra went to my mother's, I was given the go-ahead to restart milk production at the farm, subject of course to the usual provisos about satisfactory dairy arrangements, which were going to mean a great deal of work and the layout of more money than was readily available. I solved or at least eased the second problem by selling off the beef "stores" - cattle needing wintertime "finishing" - that had come as part of the farm purchase deal. It had been a good summer for grass and other harvested crops, which meant the animals fetched a decent price. Plans for a milking parlour and dairy were drawn up by the firm which would supply the equipment, as part of the deal, which did not have to be funded until it was delivered, the following year. I resolved that Mike and I, and, soon, Erbie, would do the bulk of the work. These financial machinations came out of my own head but were heartily approved by my father and uncles. I thought I was being no end clever until I was told it was all standard practice among the canny farming community. Still, I think they felt it showed I had the makings of a farmer.

Alongside this was the problem of the cottages, especially the one where

Erbie and his bride would be living. They would be with me in another week or two, and there was no prospect of getting the alterations done before then. I'd an idea though that they would take it in their stride, all part of migrating to the sticks, and would probably laugh when they saw the primitive loo at the end of the garden, and at having to take a bath in the kitchen. Which reminded me, I thought - I must acquire a tin bath and hang it on the wall outside, ready for them. They'd be better off than I was, for I had to travel the 10 miles to Lyndford for any serious ablutions. A bowl and face flannel on the kitchen table had to suffice the rest of the time, although I had no doubt the Arkinstalls would have allowed me the run of the farmhouse if I had asked.

One field of winter barley had been sown before I took over, and there was a good acreage of turnips on which the sheep, nearly all in-lamb ewes, could be folded through the rest of the winter, before they were brought indoors for lambing. Which of course turned out to be another chapter in the story of my agricultural indoctrination. However, after Christmas Uncle Giles very kindly offered the loan of one of his two shepherds, for as he and my father said, trying to tackle this job myself without expert help - Mike, top class aide that he was, was no sheep man - would be a route to certain disaster. My uncle would himself take his man's place with his own flock. But it meant he had to be found accommodation. I could not ask him to share mine, after the swish cottage he occupied at Lyndford. I found a place for him however, at "The Junction" as people still called Cravenbury from its railway town beginnings; paying the lodging charge myself - my uncle continued to pay his wages through the six weeks Bob was with me. But lambing is very hard work, as I found. Sometimes one or other of us never went to bed at all, shaking down in the ewes' shed as best we could. It was tough education - but do you know it was perhaps the most enjoyable education of my life, with the possible exception of learning to fly. And we had a very good season, with few losses and a high proportion of twin lambs.

Jumping ahead, I and my advisers decided a good acreage should be devoted to spring corn crops, which would bring income in the autumn, when the milk production project would be barely under way, if indeed it was by then, and would help pay for the cows I would have to buy. My father also had the idea that I might try a few acres of market garden crops - cabbage, brussels sprouts and runner beans - which although labour-intensive would find a ready cash sale in the local markets. I was sceptical, but Dad had never given bad advice in his life, so I did it.

All this of course implied cultivation. I could have brought in a contractor to do the ploughing, working down and sowing of the wheat and barley, but I had inherited, with the farm, two nearly new Ferguson tractors - those wonderful little machines which started the post-war revolution in farm mechanics, with their built-in hydraulic systems - and all the implements I needed. Mike may have been no shepherd, but in his few years with Ben Arkinstall he had become an excellent ploughman and indeed mechanic, and he taught Erbie, who through it all was like a dog with two tails, hard physically as he must have found much of the work. I had learned enough at Uncle Giles's to take my share of the work and he lent me - gave me, really, for it never went back - another "Fergie." It was a true delight to see all the little machines working in the same field.

Progress was made a little easier by a mutual decision on the cottages, actually Connie's suggestion. We would leave their renovation until the Arkinstalls moved out, when I could take over the farmhouse and she and Erbie could move into my cottage while theirs was being worked upon. The Arkinstalls actually left in the early spring, when I moved in to the farm house. I always kept in touch, though, and Ben would sometimes come along to run the rule over my farming efforts. He never bestowed plaudits on them, but Mike, who knew him well, said silence, from his old boss, could be taken as high praise. Mike was himself an example of this. He told me Mr Arkinstall never told him to his face how good a job he did - but the old man could not praise him highly enough, to me.

I knew I would like and get on with Erbie, and we proved that the old adage that you should never work for a friend could be wrong. Mike called me "gaffer" in our working relations, but I told Erbie to carry on calling me Ally, and it never seemed, in all the years we were together, to cause any problems or resentment between them. They knew I was the boss, but I never laid it on. Mike had his own ways, some of which would not have been mine, but I never tried to change them unless they made working together impossible, which happened rarely.

Connie, who I had never met until I collected the two of them from the station, was a charming girl, and turned out to be able and competent. They had intended to stay first for just a few days while they furnished the cottage, which was completely bare - Mike and I had however given it a wash and brush-up and laid in a supply of firewood - then go back to London. But they found a shop at The Junction which was able to supply most of their needs and deliver it next day, and they decided to move in with it. I never really had any fears that they would find their primitive home depressing, but I was agreeably surprised when they waxed almost lyrical about it.

"Gosh, Ally, from what you said I fort this was goin' ter be a terrible 'ole," Erbie said as I took them in. "It's good - we'll be fine 'ere. If we can take termorrer just to sort ourselves out, I can start work."

I'd taken the opportunity when they were doing their furniture shopping to buy a few bits and pieces for myself, to make the cottage a little more like home, especially as Connie was going to be looking after it, and me, for a time. We all took time out also for me to tell them about Debra.

They were horrified, but not completely surprised. They had some experience of that particular seamy side, themselves, as we know.

"'Ave the cops got anywhere wiv it, d'you know?" Erbie asked. "Assumin' of course they ain't bent like that lot dahn our way."

I told him I would stake my life on Allinson being anything but "bent," and in any case my aunt knew his boss, the chief constable, quite well. And I was able to tell him what the chief inspector had told me, that arrests had been made and the gang were a mob of real nasties. I did not tell him that Allinson had asked about himself. He would find out soon enough if my suspicions about the chief inspector's reasons for the inquiry, that a corruption investigation was under way, proved correct.

The housekeeping arrangements worked well. Connie soon transformed both cottages, and never gave any hint of missing the bright lights and modern conveniences of London. I toyed with the idea of installing a generator, but on being assured by the electricity board that their mains power was no more than a year away, and knowing there would be a sizeable bill from them at that stage, I dropped the thought.

Haymaking was the next big farm project, and as nearly always, proved the worst of my headaches to date, through a damp June and early July. Trying to get the grass cut when it stood best chance of avoiding the rain, getting it ready for the contractor's pick-up baler - which would usually turn up a day later than promised - was patience-taxing to say the least, to a newcomer to the game. Then lugging the bales to the Dutch barn by tractor, trailer and manpower - quite a lot of the latter when some of the bales had to be lifted many feet to the top of the barn - was hard work indeed for newcomers to the business like Erbie and me. Why on earth farmers persisted in making hay for so many decades after silage-making was proven to be a much more reliable way of conserving superior winter fodder has puzzled many better brains then mine. Nowadays most bales, when hay is made at all, are massive and are handled entirely by machinery.

Corn harvest - wheat and barley - started in early August and made up for the dodgy haymaking period with six weeks of almost unbroken fine weather. This was another job where we had to bring in a contractor with his "binder," the machine which cut the crop and threw it out in sheaves, which we then picked up two at a time and stood in six-strong "stooks" or "mows" as they were variously called in Shropshire before the combine harvester made them redundant. These were usually left for a week or two before also being carried, either into any remaining space in the barns or in temporary outdoor ricks, until threshing time. If the threshing was not going to be done until later in the winter the ricks would be thatched.

Threshing, or some aspects of it, was one of the most unpleasant farm jobs of the pre-combine harvester era. The contractor brought in the huge "threshing box" which separated the grain from the stalks, a baler or trusser to deal with the straw, and of course the big tractor to haul the equipment then to drive it via pulleys and huge belt. Before the war it was a steam engine providing the motive power, but by the time I am talking about the common power unit was the big single-cylinder Field Marshal tractor, which took so much starting that a cartridge looking like a 12-bore shotgun round had to be inserted. Threshing was often incredibly dusty, and some jobs could be dangerous. More than one man feeding the sheaves into the threshing cylinder, from the top of the box, lost an arm when he allowed himself to be pulled in. One or two were killed, even. And there were numerous accidents when people allowed themselves to tangle with the huge driving belts.

In between all this mainstream activity we tackled the market garden crops. Nobody among my immediate acquaintances knew much about the growing techniques for these, so I had to fall back on the national advisory service, whose people were very helpful, and on axioms that my parents' gardener came up with. One or other of them, or both, brought him over to spend two or three days at a time working with us, even lending a hand themselves, transplanting and hoeing cabbages and sprouts. Connie also worked in the fields at various times and would not have any extra pay - she said I was paying her amply for her domestic duties and it was in everyone's interest to make sure the farm became properly established.

We made a good start on the building of the milking parlour before the lambing. Mike brought in one or two of his old building industry friends, and the upshot of it all, including the granting of the milk production licence, was that I was in a position to buy my first cows, mostly in-calf second-calvers, in October. Their purchase was put out to a reputable dealer, recommended by Uncle Giles, and we bought Ayrshires for a start because although their milk yields were somewhat lower than Friesians, they were much cheaper. (We gradually changed over, however, because Ayshires are near to useless as beef animals whereas Friesian crosses are excellent for that purpose. Still are, although superseded by Charollais, Simmentals etc, etc.)

I advertised for a stockman, stressing the starting-up nature of the dairying enterprise and that general farm and other stock work would be involved, and although not exactly inundated with responses, there were enough to give me a reasonable choice. I did the selecting myself, preferring to rely more on my instincts than on references or high-flying technical qualifications. My choice was a young Irishman, Roger O'Connell, married with a young son and another on the way. I never regretted the choice, for he was a top-class stockman, even if a little hot-headed - we had a number of spats during the 15 years he was with me before he left to take over his father's farm in Ireland. Siobhan proved to be another Connie in being always ready to supplement the work force, when the demands of her family allowed it. Roger was there to see to the first calvings, nurse the querulous mums through the new parlour, and load the first churns of milk onto the collecting lorry. The first churn, indeed - there was only one for more than a week.

All of which I hope sums up my first year and a half of farming, on which I do not plan to use a great many more words in telling this story. It was an 18-month period that included another of the dramatic, indeed traumatic incidents in my life, and was filled with chronically hard work both by me and the others. But at the end I felt I was beginning to get somewhere, back with my roots and surrounded by a bunch of very good employees and friends.

Fifteen

A little poppet

It is a long time, or at any rate, many pages in my story, since I mentioned Angie. She was still there, though, invading my lonely nights, sometimes robbing them of the sleep that a hard-working life demanded. I continued to wonder exactly what she was doing, how she was progressing. Once I almost lost control of my resolve. What harm could there be in making some enquiries in that direction, just so that I would know something about her? I could tell the university I was an old friend, or even a relative, who was anxious to get in touch. But I soon saw where that would lead. She would be told about it, would immediately guess who the old friend was, and all the good work done by that heart-wrenching decision, to make her cast herself off from me, could be undone. I decided I must stick to my chosen path, including the hours without sleep.

No doubt the romantically inclined will have seized on the idea that Debra was going to take over, in my affections. She had indeed come to occupy a place there. I would have given almost anything to protect her from further evil of the kind she had already encountered, or any other kind. But my feelings for her were more like the love of a father for a precious daughter. No way could she supplant Angie.

After I took over the farm, I made a habit of going over to Lyndford for lunch each Sunday, when farm duties permitted. After we established the dairy herd - and he had made sure I was competent - Roger and I shared the Sunday milking and other stock duties and when it was my weekend "on" I could stay for no more than an hour after lunch. But that was some time ahead. The first time I went after Debra left hospital - it was now December - I found her lying, fast asleep, before a log fire, on a chaise-longue like the one she had occupied on that dramatic day in the Forest Farm house. My mother took me into the kitchen where we could talk without waking her. It was three days after she had arrived.

"How do you think she is?" I asked.

"Oh, I'm sure she's making progress. She isn't talking much, but she seems to be taking an interest in everything. Your Uncle Giles brought that little horse buggy round and we wrapped her up warm and took her out for an hour yesterday, which I'm sure she enjoyed. And this morning I walked over to the farm with her, and she met Elizabeth. But she soon gets tired, which I suppose is only to be expected. You go and sit with her - give her a surprise when she wakes up."

"What does Dad think about her, and you having to look after her?"

"Oh, he thinks she's a little poppet. And he knows I'm enjoying having her here. He's gone for a walk with his gun, and the dogs, but he'll be back soon - I told him lunch was at one o'clock."

"Does she need anything - clothes for example?"

"Well, she's certainly not got the most extensive wardrobe ever, but my things aren't completely out of place on her. She's wearing some of my underclothes now, and a jumper and skirt. But don't you worry about that, Alastair. I'll take her shopping when I think she's strong enough."

"Is she reading at all?"

"Yes. I've dug out a selection of books for her. I think she's quite bright, you know. Don't you?"

"She's certainly quick on the uptake. I think you'll be very good for her, Mother."

I took a newspaper and sat where she would see me when she awoke, which she did after quarter of an hour or so. I was directly in front of the big brown eyes and after only a couple of seconds her whole face beamed.

"Mister Alastair, Mister Alastair... oh, Mister Alastair..."

I got up and took her hand.

"Hello, Debra. My word, it's good to see you out of that hospital bed."

"Oh, them was good to me there, Mister Alastair. Everybody's good to me."

"You deserve to have people good to you, child, if only to show you there aren't many people like those awful men. But how do you like it here?"

"Oh, it's wonderful. Such a big house, an' nice things, an' Missis Jameson, an' Mister Jameson, an'... an' everything. Never seen anything like it. Aren't them awful rich, Mister Alastair?"

"They're not 'awful rich,' but they aren't poor, Debra. They've worked hard, all their lives, and they've earned everything they have, except this house. My father was born and brought up here but he didn't expect he'd ever live in it again. But shall I tell you something about him, and my mother?"

"It can't be anythin' bad. Her couldn' do anythin' bad."

"No, it's nothing bad. I think you're right, she couldn't do anything bad.

No, it's just that - she used to be the kitchen maid here, when she was younger than you. And my father fell in love with her when he was home from the army in the first war. She used to call my grandmother 'the mistress.' But they became very great friends. You'd have liked my grandmother, too."

She raised herself up, still keeping hold of my hand.

"Oh, I know about all that. An' your granpapa. She tol' me. I like all your folk. Is Miss Billie your mama's sister?"

"No, my father's. Yes, she's another good one. She was born here, like my father and Uncle Giles. When she was about your age she was a suffragette, then she was a nurse in that first war, and met Uncle Peter when he was wounded. My dad was an officer in the army and Uncle Peter was his sergeant."

"What's a – what you call it – sufferer somethin'?"

"Suffragette. It's what they called the women who were campaigning for women's suffrage – the right to vote. They did all kinds of things. One woman threw herself in front of the king's horse at a race track, and was killed. Some others tried to starve themselves to death, and they were forcibly fed, in prison. Aunt Billie went to prison, for a few days, because she wouldn't promise to give up demonstrating, or something. The war - the first war I mean – stopped their campaigns, but they won in the end – women got the vote."

"I think it must be awful to go to prison. Don' you think so, Mister Alastair?"

Fortunately, my father came in at that moment. I think I could not otherwise have avoided telling her about my own encounter with prison bars.

After lunch, when I noticed she ate well, I asked her whether she felt like taking a little walk. She accepted eagerly, and I took her to the church, and showed her the graves of my grandfather and grandmother, and many of the Jameson ancestors.

I asked her whether the chief inspector had been to see her. "Yes, him come yesterday. Tol' me them'd 'rested them men, an' I'd have to go an' 'dentify them."

"What do you think about that?"

"Don' want to. But I'll do it. Don' you think I should?"

"Yes, if you're up to it. What else did he tell you?"

"Said I'd be asked to give evidence in court, sometime. Don' want to do that, either, but if it means them men go to jail, I'll do that, too."

"Did he say anything about you – in Jamaica, I mean."

"Oh, yes, him said them'd made 'quiries 'bout me, with the police there."

"And? Did he say what the inquiries had found? Had the police in Jamaica got any reason for wanting you back there?"

"No, 'course not. I never done anythin' wrong, Mister Alastair. I tol' you an' Miss Billie that, didn' I?"

I could see that she was slightly hurt by the idea that we might have doubted her. I said: "Debra, we never doubted you for an instant. I just wanted to be sure Mr Allinson had told you himself."

"I don' wanna go back there. I don' think I'd feel safe, even if them men are all locked up."

"Nobody wants to make you go back, I promise you. We'll all help you do whatever you want. But what are you going to do about your parents? I don't suppose they've any idea what's happening to you. They must be very worried."

She was quiet for a time. By then, we were inside the church, which, I could see, she found awesome and beautiful, as indeed it was, even to a non-believer like me.

"Can I say me prayer, Mister Alastair?"

"Of course you can. Do you want to kneel down?"

"Yes, please."

I led her into a pew near the front, and put a hassock in front of her. She knelt, cupped her face in her hands, and I could hear her praying softly, for at least five minutes. I don't know what she was saying. Probably thanking God for her deliverance from evil. Also, praying for her mother and father, perhaps for my mother, and me. It affected me deeply, made me wish I could join her. But that would have been nothing more than sentimentality, hypocrisy. I had to sit there beside her, thankful at least that I had brought her to the solace I was sure she was finding.

In the porch as we went out, she sat down.

She said: "I started to write to mama and papa, before I come out of the hospital. But I couldn'. I felt so 'shamed. It made me think again - 'better you dead, girl'." And the tears coursed down her cheeks. I took her hand, as she always wanted.

"Will you write to them for me, please, Mister Alastair? An' tell them? An' tell them I'm safe now?"

I had to think for a moment. If some stranger wrote to them, after she had been away for nearly two months, would it not arouse as many fears as hearing nothing? But I quickly developed an idea about how it could be done. First, though.

"Did you not tell us that your father can't read, Debra? Would a letter have to be read to them by someone else?"

"Oh, him can read, but slow an' the big words make trouble for him. But mama, she can read fine."

"Right, I'll tell you what we can do. I'll write a letter, telling them what has happened, and who we are, and that you're staying with us, and you're getting better now. And you can write a bit yourself and tell them just as much as you like, without going into ... all that happened. How does that sound?"

"Oh, yes, please, Mister Alastair. Yes, please."

I said I could not do it that day, because I had to get back to milk and feed the cow, and some yearling cattle that had been too young to sell. But I would come to Lyndford again next day and leave those chores with Mike. In fact, I left everything with Mike next day, staying in to write the letter then take it to her.

Back at the house, my mother said: "My word, you're good for that girl, Alastair. She's as bright as a cricket today." And she looked at me quizzically. It was that romantic streak coming out.

I wrote my letter in the hope that the Jamaican police had not got round to telling her parents anything about her, in the course of their inquiries. I started by introducing myself and saying Debra had asked me to write, but this must not alarm them because she was well and happy, and would be writing her own letter to them. She had however had some unfortunate experiences which she found difficult to tell them about, herself, but had meant she spent a month in hospital. And I went through the whole sorry story, a summary, more or less, of what I've set down here, but leaving out the terrible part about the rape, saying only that it was because she would not agree to become a prostitute that she had been attacked and beaten. How I had found her near my farm, my aunt and I had looked after her, and she was now in the care of my mother and father.

I concluded: "The criminals responsible for Debra's injuries, and the swindle that persuaded you to send her over here, are now under arrest, at least those who are in this country. I hope the police over there will soon be on to their friends in Jamaica, also. As I write, she herself has been with my mother for four days, and is improving in health all the time. She wishes to stay in England, as no doubt she will tell you, and I and my family will do everything we can to make sure she is happy here. We like her very much."

Debra read the letter and wrote her own, first a psalm of regret that she had persuaded her parents to allow herself and them to be fooled the way they had; then a paean of praise for everyone who had helped her; finally an assurance that she was well and happy and that her ambition was to get herself a good job which would enable her to send money to them and eventually bring them to England.

*****

My brother Peter's land agency was going well, not well enough to put him in the tycoon class, but solidly. He had married a local girl who had joined him as his secretary, and they had a child on the way.

Kathleen, my sister, was now working on a national daily paper, and involved as much as her work allowed her in the new feminist movement getting under way in Britain. She had recently become involved with a London barrister, Michael Housman, and it looked as though they were on the way to making it permanent.

All of them were at Lyndford for Christmas, when I also spent as much time there as I could. None of them had met Debra before, but they immediately accepted her. My mother had two girls helping in the house - one was shared with Aunt Elizabeth - and the "live-in" one, who was from Sweden but engaged to an English boy, always had her meals with them, meaning there was no upstairs-downstairs atmosphere to cause potential difficulties with Deb. Peter, Aelwen, Kathleen and of course Michael only had the vaguest notion of what had brought her there, and I had to get them on one side and give them the outline, warning them not to quiz her about it – not that they needed the warning once they knew the story.

She continued to make good progress, and before Christmas was starting to do jobs about the house. She had even voiced little mutterings about her future, which amounted, although not in so many words, to the thought that she could not live indefinitely on my parents' largesse. Mother had pounced decisively on such ideas, she told me, telling her that the time for such thoughts, if it ever came, was many months away.

"I told her she was to look on herself as our daughter, until we felt she was properly able to fend for herself in a strange country," my mother said. "I was quite firm. I didn't tell her I loved having her here, which I do, but I think she knows that, by now."

True to her word, my mother took her shopping, to fit her out with all that a young Englishwoman needed, she said.

"She said she hadn't any money, but I said it was a Christmas present, and anyway I couldn't have my adopted daughter going about in my old clothes.

She said they weren't old, they were nearly new, but I told her they were too big for her and I wanted to hear no more about it," Mother said.

She certainly did a good kitting-out job. Debra looked like a young squiress when I saw her at Christmas, gracing my family's ancestral home in everything from jeans, slacks, check shirts, smart blouses and jumpers to frocks and coats, all in excellent taste and bang-on right for a girl of her age. I said as much to my mother.

"She chose almost everything herself," she said. "At first, she wanted to go for the cheapest, but I told her that was false economy. I don't think the result's too bad, is it, Alastair? And by the way, I'm giving her a small allowance, only two pounds a week. I don't think it's right that a girl of her age shouldn't have a shilling or two in her pocket, even if she doesn't go anywhere to spend it. She didn't want to take it, but I soon put her right about that."

"You know what she'll do with it, don't you?"

"Send it to her parents in Jamaica, I suppose. I know they're desperately poor. But I don't mind, Alastair. It's hers to do what she likes with."

I bought a little present for Deb, myself. Nothing much, just a small piece of jewellery in the shape of a sleigh and reindeer, purchased at The Junction, for I didn't want to spare the time to go further afield. When I gave it her, she burst into tears.

"There's no need for that, Debra," I said. "It's nothing much. Just a little present to mark your first Christmas here."

"Oh, Mister Alastair, it's just that you're so good to me. Can I kiss you, please?"

I put my head down and she planted a peck on my cheek.

"Will you do somethin' for me, please?"

"Of course I will, if I can."

"Would you buy me a little present to give your mama? I've got some money - she's givin' me some every week."

"Yes, I'll do that. But it will have to wait until the shops are open again. Do you know what you want to get?"

She shook her head. "Thought p'raps you'd know best."

I had an idea. "Do you do embroidery, Debra?"

"Don' know. What's 'broidery?"

"Oh, you know, stitching on things to decorate them. Like somebody's name on a handkerchief."

"Oh, yes, can do that."

Francis John Simcock

"Right, I'll get you something like a tray cloth, with a pattern on it that you have to embroider. She'd love that, if it's something you've done." And that's what happened, and she did love it.

No more was said, to me, about what was going to happen to Debra eventually until late in the summer. By then she was fully recovered and doing more or less a full day's work, helping my mother and father in whatever they were doing - cleaning, cooking, gardening, from time to time coming over to Forest Farm and joining in the work there. We did not allow her to do anything very heavy, but she joined me in some hand work in the hayfield, where the machines could not reach, and in hoeing the cabbages.

Later she joined in the "sticking up" as we called picking up the sheaves and setting them in stooks. She learned to drive the tractors and would ferry trailers about on demand, only once falling foul of a gatepost, thankfully with no resulting damage to speak of. She always wanted to be close to me, although she was as fond as ever of my mother. Erbie thought, like my father, that she was a poppet, and she got on well with Connie. Mike viewed her a little askance at first - "black" people were almost unkown in that kind of rural area - but soon became used to her, and fond of her.

Before this, in January, she had to suffer the ordeal of identifying some of the men, and women, in the "white slavery" gang. She had no hesitation in picking out "Jerry," the black American and the two who had eventually attacked her seriously, as well as the woman Marigold. Two of the Jamaican members of the gang had been caught on the hop in this country and she was able to identify the one who had recruited her. Allinson and his colleagues were delighted.

They were less pleased with Aunt Billie and I, when we failed to identify the two fake ambulance men - one of whom turned out to be Jerry. But Allinson wanted to have further talks with both Debra and me.

He said, in an interview room at Wolverhampton: "Do you have any idea where they were taking you that night, Debra? Had they said anything that could give you an idea?"

"No, sir," she said. "Only I thought they goin' kill me, sure."

"They never said anything about Cravenbury, or Buckley Forest?"

"No, sir. I never heard that."

To me: "You never heard anything, from those supposed ambulance men?"

"No, they didn't speak more than a dozen words, to me or in my hearing."

"You haven't heard, locally, of any curious goings-on up in the woods above you?"

"No. As you know, I've only been at the farm for a few months, and I've had very little to do with local people. I've been too busy. I've been to one of the pubs at Cravenbury a time or two, but I've never heard anything of that kind. I have to say, though, that I have wondered why they were taking her up our lane. It's a long way from Wolverhampton, and it goes nowhere, that I know of, except through the forest. It's an awful thought, but I wondered whether they were intending to... finish her off up there and...

"Tell you what, though, Chief Inspector. Why don't you have a word with my chap Mike Watkinson. He's a native - although, thinking about it, I suppose he'd have told me if he'd heard anything. He knows about Debra, at least he knows she was beaten up and fell out of a car."

"Thank you. We will have a word. Do you mind if we come to the farm?"

"Of course not. Have you any ideas of the kind I've just mentioned?"

"I can only say we think we may be – I emphasise, may be - conducting a murder inquiry. But I'd be grateful if you'd keep that to yourself for the time being. I think Debra can be considered a lucky young woman, though."

I felt sick at the thought. If what had happened to her could be considered good luck! But I asked only whether he had any idea when the case was likely to get to court.

"None whatever. To be honest, we're having to work hard to persuade the magistrates to allow us to keep this lot in custody. They've got some very good lawyers working for them. This identification evidence will help us, though."

I heard no more about the possible murder inquiry for many years, after incidents I shall set down in due course. I did learn however that not long after the court case, the course of which I shall also relate, there was quite a lot of police activity in the forest, along the track which was the continuation of our lane. They seemed to be giving the area a fairly intense scrutiny, according to my informant, a gamekeeper, and I was fairly sure it would be in connection with the possible disappearance of the other Jamaican girl. But neither he nor I learned of their finding anything of significance..

Sixteen

Ordeal by trial

Debra's progress continued through the year, physically and in other ways. Nobody ever tried to get her to drop her Jamaican way of speaking, but I noticed that some of it went, with time. She started to say "he" where it had previously been "him." The letter T began to appear on the end of words that had previously been without it. When I asked my mother whether she had been tutoring her, she said: "No, not at all. The only 'tutoring' I've done is in practical things. I told you she's a bright girl. She learns for herself."

This was at Christmas, the second since I'd been at the farm, and Debra at Lyndford. It led to the question, again: "What's going to happen to her?"

"Nothing need happen to her. Now Elsa's gone, she can stay and help me with the house for just as long as she likes. Your father and I really do enjoy having her here. She's got Elsa's room, for her own, and her own radio there. She doesn't spend a lot of time there but I know she appreciates having it.

"She asked me only the other day what I thought she should do, and I told her just the same as I told her a year ago - she was to look on herself as our adopted daughter. I'm going to step up her allowance - I won't call it wages, Alastair - and I shall tell her she can buy her own clothes and anything else she wants out of that. She's more than earning it. If she wasn't here I should have to have another girl. But I never say anything that could make her feel I look on her as a servant. But she needs something, now, to make her feel there's some purpose in her life. If I was younger I'd start something like fostering children, but... poor child, she deserves a better deal than she was going to get if you hadn't found her, doesn't she? It almost makes me ashamed of being British."

Another long speech for my mother. I thought the "but" related to her age, and was rather surprised, because she was only 55, and thought of herself, as indeed she was, in the prime of life. I should have known better.

Soon after that Christmas came the event that was to have another hugely traumatic effect on Debra - the trial of six of the gangsters for various offences ranging from abduction to rape and attempted murder - which however had to be reduced to causing grievous bodily harm. Four of them were also charged with keeping a brothel, and of possessing and selling illegal drugs. The murder inquiry was still ongoing, Allinson told us.

I also had to give evidence, and Aunt Billie, in a trial that eventually ran for four weeks, for all the accused pleaded not guilty. I was almost looking forward to it, although my role was comparatively minor, because I wanted to see the thugs punished. But I knew it would be an ordeal for Debra. Just how bad, and how serious an effect it would have on her, I only found at the time.

As Allinson had told me, the gang had some very capable, not to say sharp, lawyers at the solicitor end, and we prosecution witnesses were almost made to feel like criminals ourselves. My record was inevitably dragged up, in an attempt to discredit my evidence. I was virtually accused of taking Debra into my cottage for my own ends, and everything that happened there was subjected to intense scrutiny. I was completely open about it all, including how I had part undressed her, and spent the night lying beside her. Defending counsel's raised eyebrows were quite something to see.

I was quite able to cope with this kind of thing, and I think gave as good as I got, once or twice. But my heart bled for Debra. I had told her I was sure it would be an unpleasant experience, but I had no opportunity to warn her more specifically, and of the kind of slur that I could see coming, for she followed me in the witness box, and had been kept out of court during previous evidence.

Through the prosecution counsel, she told very straightforwardly of all that had happened, starting with the approach by the man from the so called Anglo-Caribbean Employment Society who had persuaded her to come to Britain; how she had been met at Liverpool, taken first to Birmingham then to Wolverhampton, where she had realised that they wanted her for a prostitute, had rebuffed her first would-be client, had tried to escape, been raped, beaten and wounded and finally managed to get out of the boot of the car. He voice sank almost to a whisper as she struggled through the most horrific parts of her ordeal, but apart from this and one or two minor misunderstandings because of her speech, you could say she sailed through it.

But cross examination by defence counsel was a different matter. Almost from the start, innuendo followed insinuation, hints preceded innuendo. The theme was that she was no better than she ought to be, that she knew all along what she was being brought to Britain for, but got cold feet at the last minute.

"Is it not the case, Miss Edworth, that you knew very well that girls like you were being regularly brought to England for the purposes of prostitution?"

She looked at him in wonder. The idea was completely foreign to her, then.

An objection by the prosecution was immediately upheld by the judge, and the question was withdrawn. But of course the point had been made, and that was only the start.

The sharp solicitors had done more than simply brief the barristers on the facts as we knew them. Their clients, dipping into money bags filled by girls like they wanted Debra to become, had dredged the alleys of

Kingston and found someone who was prepared to perjure himself by stating he knew of her by repute. This character would appear later in the trial, during the defence case, and be given the shortest of shrift by prosecution, judge and jury. But for the moment hay was being made even before the sun shone.

I should have warned her more specifically of what she was going to have to go through. We ought to have engaged a good lawyer to tell her about the twists and turns of the adversarial system. Despite what I thought had been my own brave show on the stand, I had behaved just as naively as had she and her parents back home. And although the police lawyer had gone through her evidence with her beforehand, and had even warned that the defence might try to bully her, she was totally unprepared for the way they tried to besmirch her.

Long before the end of her first afternoon in the witness box, she was reduced to a weeping travesty of the bright, attractive, intelligent girl we all knew. By questions like: "Come, come, Miss Edworth, surely you don't expect the jury to believe that a girl like you" - a little pause to allow the phrase to deliver the meaning wanted - "did not know what the man from the 'Anglo-Caribbean Employment Society' was really recruiting you for?"

Or: "Should you not have taken the opportunity to leave these people sooner, Miss Edworth, if you had changed your mind about going along with their plans?"

She just did not know how to answer questions of which the literal meanings were unclear, and after a while the judge seemed to have had enough. He halted proceedings and said to her: "I think it may be to the hearing's advantage if you took a break, Miss Edworth. We will resume at 10 o'clock tomorrow morning."

Outside the courtroom, Debra wept hysterically in my mother's arms, Dad and I standing helplessly by. We almost carried her out to Dad's car, where Mother continued to try to comfort her while we went back to try to get a word with the police and prosecution lawyers. There was plenty of sympathy for her, but only Allinson seemed to see through what was really the matter. Firstly that she did not understand why she was being asked questions that seemed to put her in the dock, rather than the villains who had assaulted her - hardly understood the words themselves, sometimes; and secondly that her questioners did not appear to believe her, when she eventually managed a coherent answer.

We had taken rooms in an hotel not far from the court. She had almost passed out when we got there, and it was all we could do to get her to stay on her feet, up the lift and into my parents' bedroom. She collapsed on the bed, still sobbing, great convulsive sighs that sometimes threatened to shake her to pieces. I took hold of her hand, a gesture that when she was ill from her injuries seemed to have an almost curative effect. But not now.

After a while she went quiet. "Debra, my dear," my mother said. But there was no answer. Tears were again soaking the bedclothes, and her feet and legs were quivering.

The rooms were quite warm, but my mother said: "I think we should try to get some hot water bottles and put them in her own bed. You go, darling" - to my father - "and see what you can do."

Dad was back in ten minutes, with the bottles and the hotel manager, who asked whether there was anything else he could do. Dad and Mother looked at each other. He said: "Do you have a doctor on call?"

"We do, and I can thoroughly recommend him. He's my own doctor, in fact. Would you like me to call him - he's probably just about finished his afternoon surgery, if he hasn't got any emergencies."

After the bottles had warmed her bed for a few minutes, I carried her into her own room and Mother put her under the clothes.

"I'll not try to undress her properly, just take this thick jumper off and loosen things a bit," she said. Debra was still sighing and sobbing, once or twice crying out, saying what we could not tell.

The doctor came in about half an hour. We explained what had happened in court while he examined her.

"Well, everything seems to be order," he said. "Her pulse is strong and her heartbeat's regular. And she's breathing quite normally, really, although it may not sound like it. That's a nasty cut but it's not recent, is it?"

My mother explained further, in fact Debra's whole story, in brief, and more on how she had been upset by the cross-questioning.

"The trouble is, she has to go back tomorrow, at ten o'clock," I chimed in. "And as you can imagine from what my mother's told you, she's a key witness. Do you think she ought to?"

"In her present state, no. But as I said, I can't find anything wrong with her physically. I think she's just very upset. I'll give her a sedative so that she gets a decent night's sleep. Call me in the morning about eight o'clock and tell me how she is. If necessary we'll have to ask the court if they'll allow her appearance to be postponed."

It was still only about six o'clock. The doctor's sedative seemed to do the trick and she slept for several hours. I stayed with her while my parents went for something to eat. Aunt Billie, who was due to give her evidence after Debra, had arrived by then, also staying at the hotel, and she joined me for my meal. We agreed that we should leave any action until next morning, after we had phoned the doctor with news of how she was.

Between us we stayed with her through the night. She half woke several times, but the sedative must have been pretty strong, for it was seven o'clock when she came fully to life. Both I and my mother were in the room. She looked from one to the other, as though wondering what it was all about.

"Hello, Debra," Mother said, with her beaming smile.

Almost in a whisper, but perfectly clearly, she responded: "Oh, Mama Dolly" - the name she had asked if she could use. And to me: "Oh, Mister Alastair - you watchin' over me bed again?"

She was obviously much recovered from the night before, and seemed to know what had happened, for she did not ask any questions, for example why she was still more or less fully dressed. We asked her how she felt, and she said only: "Better now, thank you, Mama Dolly." We asked whether she felt able to go downstairs for breakfast, and she said she would rather stay where she was, which suited me, because I wanted to have a good talk. It was not the kind of hotel where room service breakfast was normal, but Mother went down, and with a waitress, came back with trays, by when the rest of us, Debra included, had visited the bathrooms, washed, breakfasted and prepared for the day.

I had no option but to talk about the trial. I started: "Debra, I'm terribly sorry about what happened yesterday - "

"Not your fault, Mister Alastair. You didn't know..."

"I should have made sure you were better prepared. I didn't even tell you about how the system works in England. I should have. I was stupid."

"Never mind, it's over now."

I looked at her in surprise.

"Debra, you're due to go back on that witness stand again, in about two hours time. Didn't you realise?"

Her face dropped.

"I thought 'em finished," she said.

"I'm sorry, my dear. I think there's a lot more to come, I'm afraid. But we're wondering whether we can get your appearance postponed, perhaps until tomorrow."

She sat still, her breakfast only started. After a while, she said: "Have I gotta go there again?"

I said: "I don't know whether they can actually force you. But you are the most important witness on the prosecution side. It may be that the evidence you've already given may be invalidated – not counted – if you can't be cross-examined by the other side. I don't know that much about how the law works, but I have heard of trials having to be abandoned because some of the evidence has collapsed. But I think if we could get your appearance put off for a day, we could find out where you stand, more clearly."

My father had been in on most of the conversation, and he added: "I'm no legal expert either, Debra. I think Alastair has got it about right, though. We should try and get you out of the court for today, while we find out more."

She sat for another few minutes, picking at her breakfast.

"I think if I gotta go again, I should go today. You'll be there, won't you, an' Mama Dolly?"

"Of course we will," Dad and I answered almost in unison.

"Are you sure? Can you stand it?"

She took a deep breath. "Yes. I reckon."

I said: "Let me tell you how it works. It might make it a bit easier. You see, that man who said all those awful things to you has no power to accuse you of anything. You aren't on trial. He's trying to blacken your character so the jury won't believe your evidence. At least that's what he hopes. You did very well when you gave your main evidence, when the other counsel was asking the questions, and I'm sure that's what the jury will believe.

"What you've got to try to do is stay calm, remember this defence counsel is just 'trying it on' if you know what I mean. If you don't understand what he's asking, say so. Make him ask it again. He won't like that, probably. But answer truthfully, always. You have nothing whatever to hide, have you?"

"Should I have knowed what 'em really wanted me for?"

"Some girls would have known, but not you, Debra. Not you, my dear."

We called the doctor and told him the situation. I was almost alarmed by Debra's rapid recovery, and told him so. But he did not think there was any cause for alarm, it had just been hysteria brought on by her unpleasant experiences.

She was very quiet as ten o'clock approached. In court, I sat as near to her as possible, to give her comfort and encouragement. I don't know whether it was my little pep-talk, or my presence only ten feet away, or her own strength of character asserting itself, but she was quite different from the day before.

Today, the defence barristers seemed hardly able to faze her. Once or twice she even went on the attack, almost - asked one to "speak plain, please." And in one memorable little speech, that I could see made a huge impression on the jury, she asked: "Is you sayin' I was a loose woman, sir?"

Counsel countered with: "Well, since you use the words - were you?" And she drew herself up to her full five feet one and said, very firmly. "I tell you what me mama tol' me. She tol' me 'better you dead, girl - better you dead.' An' that's what I say, sir." Prosecution counsel, re-examining her in conclusion, asked her straightforwardly whether she had ever had sexual relations before coming to England, and she said, quietly but firmly: "No, sir, of course not." Afterwards Chief Inspector Allinson and the prosecution lawyers congratulated her warmly on the way she had given her evidence and stood up to the cross examination.

They never knew what it had taken out of her, though. That night she all but collapsed again. It was not quite as bad as the evening before, but she cried and sobbed, and did not want any dinner. My mother stayed with her all night, grabbing what sleep she had in an easy chair. We had intended to stay for another night in Worcester, until Aunt Billie had given her evidence, but because of the state she was in, Mother and Dad took Debra home while I stayed on to give moral support to my aunt, not that she needed it in the court. It would have taken more than an aggressive defence counsel to shake her. But afterwards I phoned home to ask about Debra.

"Oh, Alastair, I don't know what to make of her," my mother said. "She's just sitting about. She's hardly eaten anything today, and she doesn't seem to want to do anything. And she won't talk. When I ask what's the matter, she just starts crying and runs away."

"She's not - hysterical, like she was the other day?"

"No, not like that. But there's something the matter."

"What does Dad say?"

"He doesn't know what to say - except..."

"What?"

"She reminds him of your Uncle Giles, after the first war. He was suffering from shell-shock - and something else... a girl. She killed herself because of him. He says they used to call it 'black dog'."

"He got over it, though."

"Yes. He's very happy, as you know... Alastair... do you think you could come over? I think it would help. You're so good for her, you know."

So I went, only stopping long enough at the cottage to grab a morsel from the food Connie had left for me, and was at Lyndford soon after dark.

Debra was lying, fully clothed, on the bed in her own room, apparently asleep. But when Mother said, very softly: "Debra love, Alastair's here," she started to cry, and turned her face into the pillow, away from me.

I said: "Don't cry, Debra. Everything's alright." I took her hand, as she always seemed to want. But this time she took it away, and the sobs welled up.

I could do nothing only sit there. Gradually the sobs subsided. I took her hand again, and this time she did not remove it, although there was no answering pressure. I said: "Tell me what's the matter, Deb. What is it?"

This time she sat up, did look at me, but quickly turned away again.

She did not seem to want to meet my eyes, and the expression in her own, on the whole of her face, had become blank, lifeless.

My father joined us, and signalled me into another room.

I said: "Not good, is she?"

He answered: "Do you know what I think? I think she summoned up great reserves of strength to enable her to stand up to that cross-examination. Either out of loyalty to you – to us all – or because she desperately wants those men to get their deserts and she knew that her testimony was vital. Perhaps both. And I think it's drained her, mentally and perhaps physically."

"So what do you think we should do? Ought we to get the doctor?"

"I think we should if she doesn't improve quickly. But your mother's had an idea that might help. She thinks she should bring her over to you, and stay for a day or two. She loves the farm, you know, and..."

I knew what was in his mind, or rather mother's. I said: "We're about to start lambing. I'm going to be tied up day and night."

"How about if I come with them? Peter can manage without me, now, and there are plenty of things I can still do, about a farm."

I stayed at Lyndford until near bedtime. I persuaded Debra to leave her bedroom and sit with me in my parents' sitting room, and tried to get her to talk. All I could get from her were more sobs and tears, and I had no option but to leave her to Mother.

Quite early next morning, as I was finishing my breakfast after milking and washing down the parlour - it was Roger's day off - the three of them rolled up. Debra still looked drawn, and said nothing as she sat on a kitchen chair.

I said: "How are things?" - as if I could not see. Mother shook her head. Dad said: "No change."

I made them coffee, and Dad said: "Alastair, your mother has some urgent business in town, that she must attend to today. Could we leave Debra with you, for a few hours?"

I saw at once what the urgent business was - an excuse to leave Debra alone with me. Mother thought, and she was probably right, that I was the only one who could make any headway with her. I agreed, of course, and my parents left.

We went out to the farm buildings. I thought if anything could help, it would be the proximity of animals. And I was right, although not quite in such a broad way.

Erbie and Mike were just finishing their "yard" chores before leaving for the fields. They too tried to get her to talk but she remained dull and listless. It was Erbie who engineered a breakthrough when he whispered to me: "Why don't you take 'er to see the twins?" - twin calves born only that morning to one of the handful of Friesian cows in our still-small herd.

The little white-faces - their father by artificial insemination was a Hereford - were still tottery as they sought to suckle. But I saw immediately that they had got through to her. Her eyes came to life. She looked at the cow - second-calf heifer, actually - and the "cleansing" as we called the afterbirth still hanging from her down to the straw bedding, and she spoke.

"Is... that... alright, Mister Alastair? Is she alright?"

I mustn't show it, of course, but I was almost beside myself with pleasure, because she was taking interest. I said: "Yes, it's perfectly alright. It will come away in a day or so, all being well. And if it doesn't, Roger or the vet will take it away."

We stayed watching the trio for five or ten minutes. She never made any move to pet or fuss the calves, but I could see they had made an impact. Thank God, I thought. She's going to be alright.

I said: "Let's go and look at the sheep. They're going to have babies as well, in a few days."

The ewes, now many more than when I was initiated into lambing, were in a field adjoining the buildings. I told her how we would shortly be bringing some of them in to the lambing shed, where I would have to be with them most of the time, while they gave birth to their lambs, and I showed her the little cubicles made of straw bales.

"I'll have to stop with them all night, sometimes," I told her. "We have to make ourselves a bed, to get a bit of sleep."

"What do you have to do, Mister Alastair?"

"We have to make sure the lambs are born alright - sometimes the ewes can't manage on their own, especially if it's their first lambs. Then we have to watch them and sometimes help them to start suckling."

"Can I come an' help?"

"Yes, of course you can."

We stayed leaning on the shed gate, watching the ewes. I asked: "What's the matter, Deb? Did those men in the court upset you?"

The tears and sobs came again. I gave her my handkerchief, hoping it was clean, and she wiped her face.

"They didn' believe me, Mister Alastair. They thought I was like them... them bad women. I thought what will mama say if she knows what they're sayin' bout me. I felt sick."

"They didn't really think that, Debra. I told you, they were just 'trying it on.' The police know you've never done anything wrong. I think you did very well in court - and Mr Allinson thinks the same."

Silence apart from a sigh or two.

"Will you write to me folks again, please, Mister Alastair? They liked it that other time. You can tell them about the court better."

"Of course I will. When the case is over and those men are in gaol, as I'm sure they will be."

We watched the ewes for ten minutes or more, until she broke the silence.

"I wish I could see me mama and papa again, sometime," she said.

"Well of course. You will. You'll either go back home or they'll come here."

"I don't wanna go back. I'm frightened to go back."

"What, even if that gang have been caught and sent to gaol?"

"I think they've got folk there that'd kill me if I went back. An' 'sides, I wanna stay here, with Mama Dolly an'... an' you."

"Debra, you know you can stay here all your life, if you want to.

Mama Dolly as you call her says you're her adopted daughter, doesn't she?"

There was another silence, again broken by Debra.

"I love Mama Dolly, an' Mr Charles."

"They love you, Deb. ."

Then after another pause, out it came.

"I like livin' with them at Lyndford, Mister Alastair. It's lovely. I never knowed anythin' so good. But it's a long way from here." She put her head on her arms as she leaned on the gate.

"Couldn't I come an' live here, Mr Alastair? I c'd cook, an' clean, an' work on the farm, an'... an'..."

I said, gently: "I don't think it would be possible, Debra. And Connie looks after the house, already."

"Connie's nice, an' I like her, but..."

Another silence.

"Oh, Mister Alastair, it's not the same for her..."

I did not know what to say. I knew what was coming. A year before, when she had said something similar, I became convicted that it was saviour-worship, arising from gratitude for saving her from an awful fate. But now, and it was a feeling that had developed over the period, I was afraid it was more. She was a year older, a maturing young woman, and I did not know how to deal with it. Now here she was throwing herself, albeit throwing herself in the nicest, most restrained way, into my arms, or anyway into my house. As I've already said, I was very fond of her, I hated the thought of any further evil befalling her, I would have laid down my life to protect her. But so I would my mother, my sister, my daughter if I'd had one. In short, I did not love her, in that way. The way I still loved, longed for, yearned after that other, who I had not seen or made contact with for more than five years. Who I still had to forcibly push out of my thoughts when she invaded them, every time my concentration on cows, lambs, crops or keeping my financial head above water was allowed to relax.

Repeating myself again, I felt it would be impossible for Debra to come to live at Forest Farm as my housekeeper, maid, whatever. The gossip would be intolerable, especially in the aftermath of the court case which was already receiving considerable publicity. In spite of what I'd said to her about the groundless insinuations of the defence lawyers, some of the mud would stick in the minds of the "nigger hating" proportion of the British public.

How was I to deal with it, with her, already badly damaged by the treatment she had received at the hands of the villainous gang, and now by the subsequent events? Should I tell her about Angie, and that I could not ever love another woman? The thought of doing that horrified me. What would I be doing to her? I decided to consult that fount of all wisdom, my mother. Perhaps she would be able to get the message over without too much damage.

All this flashed through my mind in a few seconds, while I was still leaning on that gate, with Debra. But I had to say something there and then. I took her hand.

"Dear Debra," I said. "You know we all love you. We want you to be part of our family, all your life if you want to be. But as I told you a year ago, it would be impossible for you to live with me here. If I had a housekeeper, or a maid, she'd have to be old enough to be my mother, or be married, or something. People would say terrible things about you, and I couldn't have that. I don't care what they'd say about me, but not about you."

She sighed, a sigh of resignation, I thought. "Alright, Mister Alastair. I understand."

For a few days, I found no opportunity of talking to my mother as I wanted to. And the delight of being able to tell her and my father that Debra seemed to have come out of her silent dejection was much depleted by the knowledge of what I found impossible to tell them.

On Sunday however, after lunch, I managed to get Mother alone. I was very close to my father, but it was practical matters we talked about. Mother was the one with whom I clicked when it came to the emotions. This one was not easy, but I told her most of what had transpired. I said: "Couldn't you tell her how impossible it is? I mean could you not tell her about... Angie? So she knows that I can't possibly return her feelings."

Mother studied her sewing. "No, Alastair, I don't think I can. What makes you think it would hurt her less, coming from me? I think it might be worse, actually. She'd think you were afraid to tell her - you were being a coward."

I said nothing. She was right, of course.

A few minutes silence, and Mother put down her needle.

"Alastair, have you any idea where she... Angie... is, what she's doing now?"

"I'm sure she's doing what she promised - getting on with her career. She's probably qualified as a doctor by now."

"Then should you not try to find out where she is, and make contact with her? That way you would find out whether she still feels the same."

"I think I'd still be a millstone round her neck. She'd be 'the doctor who married that chap who went to gaol for drug-smuggling.' I told her she must cast herself off from me, Mother, and I still think that's the right thing for her."

"In that case, don't you think it's time to try to put her out of your mind?"

"Easier said than done, Mother. But I suppose you're right. I will try."

"And when you've succeeded, or even if you don't, you know what you should do, don't you?"

I knew what she was thinking.

"Mother, I'm nearly old enough to be her father."

"I don't think that's very relevant. I'm certain she'd make you a good wife.

She's a good girl. She's a hard worker, and she's bright. And quite apart from any romantic aspects of it, you need a wife, Alastair. Not just someone in your bed - a partner, a helpmate. Someone to talk to in the evening."

"You and Dad married because you were in love, though, didn't you?"

"Yes. We still are. But I've seen more than one so-called love marriage end up on the rocks. And I've seen one or two of the kind you might call marriages of convenience turn out to be very happy. My own Aunt Marjorie, for one. She married my uncle because he needed a wife, rather than for any romantic feeling between them. But in the end she'd have followed him to the end of the earth – in fact she did, pretty well, when they went to Australia."

I don't think my mother ever spoke words of unwisdom in her life. And I knew she was not breaking the habit then. But I could not quite accept what she was saying, applied to me. I wanted Angie for both reasons - because I loved her, passionately and deeply, wanted her in my bed and the other side the fireplace. But I also knew we could be partners in the way Mother was talking about. She would tell me about her problems and triumphs, failures and successes in the work in which I knew she would make a mark; and she would find the same kind of delight as Debra in the two white-faced calves, and the lambs still to come; and would understand financial and other problems besetting the farm, and help overcome them.

Still however I continued to believe that I was right in making Angie take her separate path. It would be many years before having an ex-felon as a husband or fiance ceased to be a stigma that could affect her career. At that stage I did not know how far she would go in her profession, but as I just said, I knew she could make some kind of a mark, and I must not get in her way.

There was another side, too, one that will put me in danger of being labelled prissy and perhaps hypocritical, but it was how I felt. Debra as a companion, the helpmate my mother thought I needed, I would welcome. But right then, the thought of sexual relations with her was actually distasteful to me. It would almost be incestuous. I liked her very much, loved her, but it was a protective kind of love, nothing like the desperate longing I had for Angie, her mere presence, in body and soul. Like I think most of the Jameson side of my ancestry, I was not and am not particularly highly sexed. We seem to have been less testosterone-charged than many men. In the air force, I'd had one or two experiences, but I think now that like the drinking, and the craving for excitement, they were part of the scene rather than indicative of the essential me. Unlike Steve Parrimore, for example, an absence of nubile young women eager to climb into bed, or more often the back of a car, with RAF officers, would have caused me no distress. The couple of girls to whom I lost my virginity left me somewhat ashamed, not for their sake, because they only got what they asked for and wanted, but on my own account. Although I was not brought up to believe in a male version of "better you dead, girl," indeed the facts of life were never a subject of discussion with either of my parents, there was always an implied philosophy that sex and love were inseparable. "Love and marriage – go together like a horse and carriage" as Mr Sinatra was to sing a year or two later.

None of this had anything to with her race or colour, or her looks in any way. Despite the scar on her face, which would be with her all her life to some degree, she was a very pretty girl. And in the respect that marriage between different races was acceptable, even welcome, I took after my mother, who was a lifetime ahead of most of her contemporaries in that respect. Far from feeling the disgust many British people professed if they saw a black man and a white woman together, or vice versa, I was happy to see racial differences eroded. I still am. It is a pleasure to know that we, many of us at least, are now putting behind us the prejudice that most people displayed when faced with the prospect of such unions, half a century ago.

I don't know what had happened in the Jameson family to change us from the conservative lot (very small "c", mind) we had been for generations. What mutation in the genes had made my father fall in love with the kitchen maid, Aunt Billie become a passionate suffragette, my Uncle Giles fall for a half-gipsy girl, after hundreds of years of family members loyally sticking to the principles of squirarchy? My own dislike of racialist ideas could have come from my mother, although I suspect her eagerness to see me marry Debra came more from kindness and pragmatism, and real affection for her, than from any particular principal. I have been told my great-grandfather hated slavery, and sided vehemently with the North in the American civil war. But I bet he would have stopped far short of accepting marriage to a black girl for one of his family.

There have been many arguments about the origin of racialism, especially between negro people and Anglo-Saxons. Why have the French not adopted the same attitude towards "black" folk that so many of we British have, and that we have passed on to many Americans? I suspect it is because the Anglo-Saxon or Teutonic people want someone to whom they can feel superior, or can blame for economic or other ills. They forget that we prospered by partly living off the backs of so-called inferiors, in India and Africa particularly, for many generations.

So, I wrestled with the problems. Or rather with the one, for despite my mother's urging, I never contemplated changing my mind about Angie. That was one of the few worthy decisions I made during that period more than five years before. But just then I could not think of Debra as wife or lover.

Seventeen

The lambing shed

My father and mother kept their word and came to stay, mother for the whole of the lambing period, Debra with her. Erbie and Connie had taken on the task of furnishing and otherwise bringing the farmhouse up a standard fit to accommodate them all, but that apart I did not want to take Erbie away from other work on the farm, like helping Mike repair fences, clean out ditches, and tackle the building repair and maintenance still waiting to be done. Roger was fully occupied with looking after the cattle, which meant I more or less had to take up residence in the lambing shed, for a month or more.

I found this no great hardship. I was warm and comfortable enough, I went to the house for my ablutions, and for my meals when they coincided with a lull in my duties as midwife, nursemaid and occasionally doctor to my woolly charges.

Debra had asked, that day when the two little calves had helped bring her back to normality after the harrowing experience in court, if she could come and help with the lambing. And right from the start of my month in lambing shed exile she spent most of her waking time there. She would bring me - and herself - a cup of tea as day was breaking, and delightedly examine any lambs born in the night. She carried messages between me and my mother and Connie who was still the nominal housekeeper, mostly about when I was likely to be in for meals etc. We were still awaiting our hook-up to mains electricity, meaning "Tilley" lamps were our main source of light, and Debra saw to their fuelling and maintenance. Fortunately, we had few orphans, or "cades" that year but she was the one to bottle feed them and arrange for their accommodation in tea chests and such like, in the house kitchen. But she also caught on quickly to the intricacies of delivering the little creatures, making sure their mother cleaned and dried them (or doing it herself with a handful of hay or straw) and getting them to suckle if necessary.

One night, about half way through the operation, new arrivals had been making their entrance one after another for forty-eight hours and more. About thirty ewes, nearly a third of the flock, had lambed during that period. I had been starved of sleep and was only able to leave the shed very briefly, and was frankly shattered. Debra appeared soon after midnight and announced she would be keeping watch while I grabbed a couple of hours sleep, and she would wake me if necessary. By then, I had complete confidence in her to know what "necessary" was, and I knew that a three-quarters-asleep shepherd was no good to his sheep, so I agreed, and was soon well away. I woke four hours later to find Debra missing - at the far end of the shed delivering the third of a ewe's triplets. Also her third midwifery operation while I was asleep. We dealt with this latest one, including persuading a ewe who only a few minutes before had had a single, to take one of the three, and she showed me the other newcomers, four lambs and their mothers, all doing well.

I said: "Why didn't you wake me? You said you would."

"I shouted at you but you wouldn' wake. You was right out. I thought of goin' for Mama Dolly, but I didn' think she'd know any more'n me, so I just did it. Then them was comin' so fast I couldn' stop to try to wake you again. Them... they... are alright, though, aren't they?"

"They're fine, girl. You've done a wonderful job."

After another couple of hours, during which only one ewe lambed, we thought there were no more imminent, and Debra said: "Why don' you go an' have a bath, an' change your clo's, an' have some breakfast, Mister Alastair, an' I'll watch here. I promise I'll come an' fetch you, if anythin' happens."

I took her at her word. After all, she had just proved her competence. I enjoyed the luxury of that bath, and the clean clothes, free from worry because I knew the sheep were in safe hands. And because I had made, or knew I was moving towards making, a decision.

I was never going to fall in love with her, our relationship would never be the inexplicable, once in a lifetime transport that had come to Angie and me. But all along I had felt the need to do everything I could to make her happy. It was very important to me that she should be happy.

Many young men, or women, who read this will no doubt have scoffed over my inhibitions about physical intimacy with Debra. I can imagine them saying to themselves, and perhaps to their friends: "Did you ever read such rubbish? He just didn't fancy it with a black 'un!" I repeat, it was nothing of the sort. Or if racial feelings were there, they were buried so deep in my psyche that I could not detect them. But, so help me, the idea that "relations" with Debra would almost be incestuous was there, and very real, even after I had come to the knowledge that hers for me were quite different. Why the feeling started to disappear I don't know. Perhaps the shared midwifery operations in the lambing shed had something to do with it. Then there were my mother's strictures about the need for a partner and helper, out of which more would grow. It had become clear to all who saw her at Forest Farm that Debra would make a partner par excellence for a young farmer. In any case, although I was not "in love" with her, I loved her, felt a real affection for her. And finally, I had come to accept that she really was in love with me. Perhaps it had grown out of gratitude for my rescue effort, the old white knight syndrome, but grown it had, and more than once she had been on the verge of saying so.

Then, Angie: If I was to keep to my resolution, and I was still determined to, I would probably never see her again. Although when that thought hit me, even in the middle of these musings, it was accompanied by another kick in the stomach.

The upshot of all this philosophical meandering and soul searching was a conclusion that I should pay heed to my mother and ask Debra to marry me. I am sorry, to anyone who reads this, that I have spent so much time, used so many words, in to-ing and fro-ing towards a decision that will no doubt have seemed inevitable. But it's how it was. And I'm afraid there is more of the same to come, for a time. Before I could take it any further, there was a lot I must tell her, about which she knew nothing.

While my mother was dishing up breakfast, and I was eating it, I told her what had happened, through the night.

"Alastair, Alastair, how many times must I tell you how good that girl is! Yes, she told me she was coming out to you, because you were so tired. But never mind that now - take her this tea and tell her to come for some breakfast, then she must have a bath and go to bed."

When I got back to the shed, with tea for both of us, I found she was already dozing, on my couch, with no signs of any imminent births. I sat down beside her, and took her hand, as so many times before. But this time, I said: "Debra, can I talk to you? If you're not too tired?"

"Oh, no, Mister Alastair, I'm never too tired to talk to you."

"I want to tell you things about me, that you don't know. And you might not like them."

"I don't believe there's anything bad to tell about you, Mister Alastair."

"Yes there is."

She looked at me, smiling, as much as to say "Don't believe you." But I ploughed on.

"You once said, when we were talking about Aunt Billie, that it must be

Francis John Simcock

awful to go to prison, Debra. Well, that's one of the things I've got to tell you. I've been in prison. I spent more than three years there. And I deserved it. It was because I'd committed a crime."

Her mouth dropped open, as she looked at me in shock and apparent disbelief. I waited.

She whispered: "Oh, no. No, Mister Alastair. You couldn't have. Not you..."

She took her hand from mine and put it with the other to her face. I said: "It's true, Debra. Can I tell you about it?"

"I don' know. I don' wanna know... yes I do... It wasn' anythin' awful, was it.... Please, tell me it wasn' anythin' awful..." She started to weep, and I took her handkerchief from her sleeve and dried the tears from her cheeks.

I asked again: "Please, can I tell you about it?"

"It wasn't somethin' awful, Mister Alastair, was it? Not somethin' to do with... women? Not like them...?"

"No, Debra, nothing like that. I just got involved in something bad that other people were doing. I'm very ashamed of it, though. I was very foolish and weak. Can I tell you about it? Please."

She said nothing, but nodded, slowly and still disbelievingly.

I said: "It was just after I came out of the air force..." and I went on to tell her about Steve, and how I thought he was offering me excitement rather than some mundane job; about the flights, and the drugs which I knew nothing about; and that I should have known it was illegal because of the amount I was being paid; and what the judge said when he sent me to prison. She listened to it all without saying a word, but most of the time looking into my face, as though searching for the man she knew, her saviour, rather than the weak fool I was telling her about. I said nothing about Angie. That was still to come.

At the end, I said: "The judge was right, Debra. I had to be punished to show how much society disapproved of such things."

I waited to see if she would say anything. After a few moments, she asked, quietly: "Was it awful in prison, Mister Alastair?"

"Pretty awful. But I tried to make the best of it. I studied farming, and I met Erbie there – but please don't think he was bad, because he wasn't really."

"Did Mama Dolly and Mr Charles know 'bout it?"

"Oh yes. And they were wonderful. They came to see me often, and then helped me get this farm – provided most of the money."

She was quiet again. Then she said: "I don't think you was bad, Mister Alastair. I don't think you could ever do something you knew was wrong."

It was my turn to want to cry. But I held back the tears and mumbled: "Thank, you, Debra. Thank you,my dear."

I was going to tell her about Angie. But right then I was too emotionally charged, and I think she was, to embark on that part of my story, and the rest of what I was going to say. I sent her back to the house to get some breakfast, and have a bath, and go to bed, as my mother had ordered. I saw to another ewe and the two lambs she produced without any help. About nine o'clock Erbie appeared to ask if I had any new orders for the day's work, which I had not, but I asked him to keep an eye on the ewes while I grabbed another hour or two's sleep.

About midday I woke to find Erbie gone and Debra perched on the end of my couch.

I said: "I thought you were going to bed."

"I did go, and went to sleep, but when I woke I couldn' go off again because I was thinkin' 'bout what you tol' me," she said. "Thought p'raps you'd be thinkin' I thought bad o' you."

"Deb, I could see you didn't. You said so."

She smiled, gratefully. But I made a snap decision.

"I didn't tell you everything I was going to, though." And when she looked at me in alarm, I added: "It's nothing like the other. It is connected though."

"Go on, Mister Alastair. I'm listenin'."

"Before I was arrested, after the flights I told you about, I met a girl, and we fell in love. Her name was Angie and she was still at school, about the same age as you were when... I found you. We fell very deeply in love, Debra. But when I was arrested, and it was obvious I was going to go to prison, I told her she must have nothing more to do with me. You see, she was a brilliant girl and was going to be a doctor. I knew that being attached to a convicted criminal would be very bad for her career. It might even stop her being a doctor at all."

She interrupted: "What did she say, Mister Alastair? Did she go away like you tol' her?" I could see she was ready to take the dimmest of views of a girl who could be brushed off like that.

"She tried very hard not to. She tried to see me in prison, when I was being kept there before the trial, but I refused to see her. She wrote to me, and said her career didn't matter, she was going to wait for me. But I'd made her promise, when she came to the police station after my arrest, that she'd keep up her work, and pursue her career, which I knew could be a brilliant one and she'd probably do a lot of good in the world, and I told her I wouldn't see her again, ever, and made her repeat her promise. In the end she accepted it, I think, but I've not seen her or heard of her again. I shall never try to contact her. She might meet someone else and marry him, and I mustn't do anything to upset that."

She had listened to the last part of all that in silence. Then after another silence, she said: "I knew you couldn' be bad, Mister Alastair. Only a very good man would do that."

"I don't know. My mother thought I was wrong, I think. She believes that love must rule everything, you know."

"Does her – she – know about this woman, then?

"Yes. She – they, my mother and my father – met her once."

"Does she still think you were wrong?"

"I think she has accepted that I meant what I said, and I still do."

We both sat on the couch. I heard a ewe bleating. We went over to seek her out. She was trying to give birth. Debra went to fetch a bucket of warm soapy water and antiseptic from the supply we always kept topped up, but there was no problem. The lamb was presented quite normally, I gave it one little pull and we left it for the ewe to lick and clean. We went back to the couch to wait a while until we were sure it was a single. I took Deb's hand again.

"I told you all that l because I wanted you to know about it before I asked you. If you would consider marrying me, in spite of it."

I expected tears, and they came. Again I took my nice clean handkerchief and wiped away the tears.

"Deb, if you say no, I'll understand. You won't want to marry someone with a past like mine, and another woman in the background... but I swear to you now that if you marry me I will stay faithful to you and only you. She's locked away..."

"No, Mister Alastair, you got it wrong. It isn't that. The prison thing doesn't matter. Nor the other girl. An' I know you would'n... go 'way from me. But you can't marry a girl like me. You got to marry some fine lady, not a poor girl from Jamaica, who's... I just want to come an' work for you, an' look after you... an' be near you... what would all your folks say if you was to marry me?... Mama Dolly, an' your brother, an' sister... an'... everybody..."

"Look, sweetheart, my mother would like me to marry you. She really does - she's said so. She terribly fond of you, you know, and she thinks you'd be good for me. And as for everybody else, as you put it - I don't know a single person who wouldn't be pleased if we were to be married. Either in the family or anywhere." Which might have been an exaggeration, because I'd never talked to anyone about it, but I knew everyone liked her.

"But you told me once that folk would talk, an' say bad things, an'..."

"That was if you came to live with me without being married. If we were, it would be very different. Look, my little Debra, tell me honestly - would you really like to be married to me? Just for me, and you, never mind anyone else?"

"I... mustn't, Mister Alastair. I'd pull you down. I can't even speak good English. I didn' have no schooling, to speak of. An' folk know all about... an' they think that's what I am..."

"Your English is getting better all the time – not that there was much wrong with it anyway. My mother didn't have much in the way of education, and look at her now. And you'll be the same, in time."

She sat without speaking, just looking round at the sheep. And I saw the tears start to run down her cheeks again - following the line of that scar, on one side. I took my handkerchief to them once more.

"If you mean by people thinking what you are - that they think you were a... a girl with no morals... you're wrong there, you know. That case was very widely reported, and nobody reading the reports could be in any doubt about what you're really like."

She still sat there.

I said: "Mother told me I was to send you in for your breakfast, and a bath, and some sleep. Won't you give me an answer, before you go?"

"No, Mister Alastair. I'm gonna talk to Mama Dolly."

It was a long time before I learned the details of that conversation, although it was obvious what its subject would be. But later in the day, things being quiet on the lambing front, I went in for lunch, with Mother. She had packed Debra off to bed again.

"She told me," she said. "Oh, Alastair, I'm so pleased."

I felt very sheepish.

"She didn't give you an answer, did she?"

"No, Mother. She thinks she's not good enough for me, or something."

"Ask her again, Alastair."

I did, that afternoon. She came out about five o'clock, when I was feeding and checking the ewes. No births were imminent. I said: "Let's have a look at those calves."

They were still in their loosebox, but their mother had been taken back into the herd. We leaned over the door, watching the little white-faces sleep.

I asked: "Well, Deb?"

"Oh, Mister Alastair...

"Are you sure, Mister Alastair? Are you sure you want to marry a poor girl from Jamaica who's been… used like I was. Won't you just wish it was that other one, who's… white… an' bin to college… an' can talk … 'bout anythin'… an'… never…"

"Deb, I thought I'd told you. I won't pretend I don't think of… Angie. I can't promise I won't think about her – sometimes – if I'm married to you. I will, I know. I'll wonder what's happening to her. But answer me this question, my little sweetheart. Do you love me? In spite of all I've told you? I think I know, but I want you to tell me."

She looked at me as though telling me not to be silly. But she whispered: "Yes. I love you more'n anythin' in the world."

"I'll tell you again. If you marry me, I will cherish you always, and look after you, like I know you'll look after me. Nothing or nobody will come between us. That's a solemn promise."

Another pause, and I asked again:"Debra, in spite of it all, will you marry me. Please say yes."

She said: "I was thinkin', before I come – came – out again, if it hadn' been for all that… that prison an' all, you'd never 've come to this farm. An' I'd've died that night. An' I'd never see them - those - calves, an' all the lambs, an' Mama Dolly… an'… an'… the best man in the world, who I love more'n anythin' an'…"An' tears, from two pairs of eyes. An' hugs, an' kisses. Ended only by the need to attend to another mother and baby. It was good that she was able to do most of what was necessary. I could barely concentrate as I framed a resolution parallel to the one I'd made five years before. Just as I'd cast off Angie, so she could not be dragged down by association with me, I resolved to do all in my power to make this brown-skinned child of the Caribbean, who I knew loved me with every part of her being, as happy and fulfilled as ever I could. Perhaps it would help in the balance of things.

*****

We were married in Lyndford Church, before all the family; Mother's brother George, his Staffordshire wife and their children and grandchildren; her sister Kate who was cook at the manor when Mother first went there; of course my own brother and sister and Aunt Billie and Uncle Peter, Uncle Giles and his wife Elizabeth. All my farm people, and the Arkinstalls, and a number of friends and neighbours. Left to my own selfish choice, I would have opted for a registry office marriage. But I never even mentioned it. I knew how much a "proper" wedding would mean to Debra, and to her mother and father, who were the very special guests. My mother had insisted that if it were possible they must come. Money was the only problem - it was still very tight with me and impossible for the Jamaicans - but Mother and Dad insisted on paying for transport and all other expenses, hosting them at the manor and showing them as much of Britain as they could. I know they had a wonderful time. Mother and Dad took them to London, and they actually saw the beautiful young queen and her handsome husband. There was a four-day trip to Scotland, day outings in Wales. Mr Edworth got on like a house on fire with my father, although when Dad told him to call him by his Christian name, he would never go further than "Mr Charles."

My mother also insisted that it must be a full-dress affair, and although that too would not have been my personal inclination, I could only agree with her when she said: "Alastair, it's got to be. For her sake. To help make up for the terrible things that happened to her. And for her mother and father. I expect they've felt horribly guilty."

Anyway, she looked delightfully pretty in her cream-coloured dress and veil. She would not have white, I didn't understand why and she wouldn't say, but my mother knew. Deb did not want a veil, either, no doubt for the same reason, but Mother persuaded her.

Besides family, there were a few more farmer-neighbours, and I overheard one of them say to Ben Arkinstall: "Wonder what owd squire would 'a made o' this, Ben." I did not hear the reply, but I know what Mr Arkinstall's view would be. I thought he himself risked causing an upset when he said: "I towld yer to get yerself a wife, young Alastair - but I didna think you'd have to import one." But the broad smile that went with it, and the warmth with which he greeted Debra - "I hear ye're no end of a good shepherd, missis" - put the remark in proper context. Mike said only: "Good work, gaffer." Erbie was almost crying with pleasure, and left it to Connie to wish us "all the happiness in the world, Mr Alastair."

Chief Inspector Allinson and his wife were there. I did not have much talk with him, but Aunt Billie did, and he updated her on the inquiries into the activities of the "white slaving" gang. Those we had given evidence against had been sentenced to long prison terms, which we already knew, of course, but he told my aunt as much as he could about the suspicions arising from their taking Debra down our lane.

"I don't think there's anything concrete yet," she told me some time later, and in strict confidence, for it had come from her friend the chief constable. "But the police still think there's more to it than has come out. Apparently there is at least one girl from Jamaica who has come over here and can't be traced. It doesn't bear thinking about, what they might have been planning to do with her, though. Oh, Alastair..."

I could not really spare the time for a holiday, and with Debra wanting to see as much as possible of her parents while they were in the country, we had decided to put off a honeymoon. So after the reception at the Manor, I took her off to the farm. It was by now, late April, daylight until well into the evening, and when we arrived, she said: "Can we go an' look at the sheep, Alastair man?" - I had only recently got her to drop the "Mister." We walked through and round them. The lambs were more than half grown, but she still recognised many of them and could remember their birthings. "Look, that's the one took us two days to get him to feed," she would say, or something similar of many others. Then we went to see the young beef cattle, including the two whitefaces that had played such a part in bringing her back from the abyss of depression after the trial. And as we made our way to the house, she stopped, and reached up to me. "I never thought I could be this happy," she whispered.

Indoors, I asked whether she wanted more to eat, a cup of tea? She said, softly: "No. Just love me, Mister Alastair."

If any fears about making love with her had remained, they would certainly have vanished right then. Or if she had given the impression of being afraid of sex, as she quoted the warnings of her mother, it was a completely false one. We climbed the stairs hand in hand, she threw off her clothes and was in bed - my bed - in seconds. And, barely nineteen years old, she taught me, whose sexual experience had amounted to two sordid, half drunken couplings, and hers to being violently raped, what it should really be about. Afterwards, as she lay in my arms, and murmured: "Oh, Mister Alastair, it was all worth it," I knew I would have no difficulty keeping my resolution.

Eighteen

A prospering farm, a body, but peace at last

Debra was well received in a neighbourhood where coloured people were almost unknown. The word quickly got round and was relayed to me, that "'er's damn good on the farm - as good wi' sheep an' everythin' as if 'er'd bin brought up to it." As soon as she had learned to drive, passing her test first time after little instruction, she did weekly shopping trips to The Junction and occasionally further afield, usually taking Connie, who continued to help in the house. I never heard of any unpleasantness arising from her colour, not that she would have told me about it anyway. But I think I'd have known, or heard it from elsewhere.

One little incident there was, I remember, but it caused only amusement. A few months after we were married, and in consultation with Connie, we decided we needed and could afford some new items of kitchen equipment. I told the suppliers the basics of what I wanted, but asked them to talk to my wife about the details. The rep duly phoned and arranged a time to call. Debra answered the door, and he said he had an appointment with Mrs Jameson. Deb, Jamaican accent and mannerisms still in evidence, as they were for all her life, said: "Yes, that is correct, sir, please come in," and stood waiting for him to start on his business. After a few moments, he said: "Could you tell her I'm here, please?" Quite amused, she said: "I do not think that will be necessary," and when he looked at her, added: "I am Mrs Jameson." The poor lad did not know where to put himself, but Deb was equal to the occasion and it all passed over without any ill-feeling. She was very good at dealing with incidents that might have caused embarrassment.

We never did have a honeymoon, because about four months after we were married, in the middle of our grain harvest, when she had been working as hard as any of us, we discovered I was going to be a daddy. Man-like, I immediately told her to get her feet up, but she told me not to be silly, and recounted her mother's experience when she was born - how she was cutting sugar cane when the pains started. Still, I made sure she kept her exertions to a sensible level. Connie had never stopped helping in the house, in line with my agreement with her and Erbie, which worked very well, for Deb was not mad keen on housework. She preferred being out on the farm, particularly with the animals.

It was a boy, who made his appearance with a minimum of fuss, not to say without the usual anxiety on his male parent's part. Deb wanted to call him Alastair, but Charles was my choice, after my father, and we settled for both, adding George for my maternal grandfather. He was quite dark, nearly as dark as Deb, but his features grew to be almost Greek god-like, resembling my Uncle Giles. Apart from the usual children's infections, and a broken arm at the age of six when he fell out of a tree, he was completely healthy, very athletic, more than moderately intelligent - and never wanted to be anything but a farmer.

The exercise was repeated just over two years later, but a girl this time. We had another argument because Deb wanted to call her Dolly after my mother. That was not on because Mother's name was not Dolly - it was Emily Jane, and she'd been called Dolly because as a toddler she was tiny. So we called her Emily Jane, which eventually became "Em" to almost everyone. She was somewhat sickly as an infant, but grew out of it and like her elder brother was very bright and sportingly athletic.

Number three was another boy, Edward, Deb's father's name, but about as unlike his maternal grandfather as possible. He was very light complexioned, for a start, with fair hair, a long, thin nose and blue eyes like my mother's. He was not as academically bright as his brother and sister, that is he did not do as well at school in subjects like history and geography, or even English. But in maths and the sciences, and all practical matters he could hold his own with them or anyone else and was most inventive. Before he was 14 he could strip down, rebuild and "tune" an engine, or any other piece of machinery. I don't quite know where it came from, but he developed a love of motorcycles and raced them at a high level in his early twenties. And the farm was dotted with modifications and improvements to machinery, and pure inventions like automatic feeders linked to an individual cow's dietary needs, that his active brain had come up with.

My father offered to pay for the boys to go to Shrewsbury School, where a succession of Jamesons had received most of their education. But I was not enthusiastic. I had nothing against Shrewsbury, but I did not want the boys to develop the feeling and attitude of superiority that I thought, rightly or wrongly, public schools engendered. At that time the eleven-plus was still in full swing in our area and all three were able to go to good grammar schools, although for Em it meant more travelling than we would have liked. We always made it clear though that distance must never prevent their taking part in after-school or weekend activities, which sometimes kept Debra buzzing about like the traditional blue-tailed fly.

Erbie and Connie also founded a family about this time, and with Roger and Siobhan's two, there was soon quite a community travelling down our lane to school.

Despite the agonies of parting with Angie, I was never anything but happy with Debra. Through the two-and-a-half decades we were together, though, my feeling for her remained one of warm, protective affection rather than the passionate love she had for me. We had few disagreements, fewer quarrels. The inhibitions I had agonised over vanished, and our sex life was just about perfect, unrestrained, undemanding, we always seemed to know what the other wanted. Some of our happiest times were spent wandering round the farm in the evening, although we could never be long out of the house when the children were small. Between us, we were our own shepherds - the woollies were always objects of affection for Deb - and the first lambing season after we were married was almost a repeat of the one before, although by then she was pretty pregnant. Her small hands helped a great deal in the midwifery operations, as we had already discovered. Next year Charles made it a threesome, and Deb made me howl when she said to one recalcitrant first time mother: "Look, missis, if I can do it, so can you. But I suppose I'd better help!"

She could, though, do just about any job on the farm. Excellent stockman though he was, Roger needed time off, and Deb was soon able to take her turn as No 1 relief milker, with myself and Erbie, who in the winter spent much of his time assisting with the cows, calves and beef cattle, as reserves. As with the lambs, she proved to have a natural touch with calves. We developed a poultry enterprise, and she looked after the "day-olds" as they came to us. Advisers urged us to go in for battery housing, but when we went to look at an example, Deb threw something of a wobbly when she saw the birds in cages that barely allowed them to turn round. I did not take any persuading that this was not for us and we stuck to deep litter houses where the hens were fed, and laid their eggs indoors but could go outside. It was something of a nuisance in that you had to make sure they were inside and the hatches closed by dusk, or Mr Fox would have them, but the eggs sold at a premium.

The farm finances were a struggle for many years, because we were paying off the mortgage. We determined early on that we would never go into any other debt, even to buy machinery, despite attractive-looking "finance" offers from suppliers. One or two neighbours acquired combine harvesters, balers and snazzy new tractors, but we stuck to hiring from them or from contractors, or plugging along with what we had. Only when the farm bank account would stand it did we add to our equipment, and then it was usually second hand. Five years after acquiring the farm I was still using my ancient Austin for personal transport, although we bought a rather more modern car for Deb. But as the years passed, the cash situation became easier, as the mortgage repayments grew less in comparative terms, even though we opted to increase it, ten years on, to buy a small farm adjoining ours. The purchase was almost self-funding, though, because we were lucky enough to be able to let the house, buildings and a couple of small fields to a horse-fancying couple who moved into the area, and it was certainly a good move in farming business terms. We gave up the market garden crops after about five years because although they were profitable enough and had helped us through the early days, they did not fit our farming schedule. We let off five acres of land however to a young couple who had helped us with this side of things, and they eventually developed it into a thriving nursery, Ben Arkinstall agreeing that it did not amount to a contravention of his "farming only" covenant.

By that time the dairy herd had grown to nearly 50 cows and the ewe flock to 150, all home-grown, and the extra land was needed. My father and my uncle Giles were very approving of our farming philosophy and techniques.

*****

Those happy if hard-worked days could not flow completely smoothly, though. Debra's anxieties and traumas were not to be completely over for another dozen years.

It was just about the time Charles started his secondary school. She came home from a local shopping trip, as I went in for lunch. She was almost crying with anxiety.

"Alastair, Alastair, I've just seen them - them men. At the Junction. Oh, what shall we do - they're after me. What shall we do, Alastair, what shall we do?"

I caught her in my arms. "Do you mean those men who...? It can't be, surely. They're in prison."

"It was that Jerry, certain. And that big black one. Oh, what are we goin' to do? They've come to kill me, haven't they, 'cos I made 'em go to gaol. And you, Alastair... and... oh God, the children..."

"Steady, steady, love. We'll not let them, don't worry."

"What can we do, what can we do?"

"Ssh, sweetheart. It's alright. Don't worry..."

But she continued to sob. She was very distressed.

I said: "Deb, my love, let us talk about it. We'll sort it out. Tell me where you saw them."

"It was as I was goin' into Pritchetts' (the grocer's). They got out of a car and went across to that pub, opposite, you know, the ..."

"The Plymouth Arms. Did they see you?"

"I don't know - I shouldn't think so. I'd gone through the door when I saw 'em, through the glass. But it was them alright. I'd know that Jerry anywhere. Oh man they're after me, I know. What else would 'em come here for?"

"How long ago was this? What time was it?"

"Only a few minutes ago. I come straight home. An' I put me umbrella up and held it in front o' me face." In her anxiety she had slipped back into more of her old Caribbean patois.

I said: "Let me think." And although I'd tried to dismiss her fears, memories of 10-year-old discussions with Chief Inspector Allinson came back to tell me they might not be quite so groundless.

In a few minutes, I said: "Look, I don't think it's any good going to the police just because you've seen these two. Allinson would take it seriously, but he's retired now and they'd just ask 'so what.' If the men have been released from prison they've as much right to come to Cravenbury as anywhere else. Look, I'm going to get Erbie and go down there to see what they seem to be doing. Then we'll pick the children up from school, and we'll go back to meet Charles and Roger's lad off the bus. And I'll get Roger and Mike to stop here, or round the house, until we come back. Just in case."

I picked up the phone (we'd had phones installed in the cottages, for obvious contact reasons.)

"Erbie," I said. "Could you come down to the Junction with me, right away? I'll explain when I pick you up."

I also phoned Roger and asked if he, Siobhan and Connie would go for their lunch with Deb, who would explain.

At the Junction, I parked the car and we went into the Plymouth Arms. There were half a dozen people in the bar, none of whom were the men we were looking for. I ordered a couple of halves and pork pies and asked the landlord, who I knew: "Have you had a couple of strangers in this morning, Sid? One's a black chap?"

"Yes - they're still here. In the lounge. I think they're waitin' for somebody. You, is it?"

"No, but I think I know who they are, and I'd like to make sure. Can I see them from anywhere?"

"Yes, sure, come through here."

He led me behind the bar to a spot where I could see into the lounge. Sure enough, it was the man Jerry, and I thought the black man with him was the "Jos" who had been so concerned in the assault on Debra. Back in the bar, I asked Sid quietly if they were staying with him, but he said not as far as he knew - they had not said anything about wanting accommodation.

"What's the problem - if there is one?" he asked.

"I can only tell you that if you knew them, you'd put them at the top of your 'not welcome here' list," I said.

It was not far off closing time, two o'clock, so I asked Sid if we could stay on as long as the two men were in the lounge. They left when he called time however and Erbie and I followed them out and watched where they went. They got into a big American car and, to my alarm, took the road towards the farm. We followed - by then I had a rather more modern vehicle - but we did not see them again. They must have gone straight past and up into the forest, along the dirt road which had been improved for forestry work. We stopped at home and I checked with Debra and Connie, and told them what had happened, which did little to ease Deb's anxieties. It was a wild guess, I suppose, but I thought they might themselves have been checking that nothing had gone wrong at the scene of previous villainy. Or perhaps they might have been behaving as some criminologists believed murderers often did - obeying an urge to return to the scene of the crime.

Debra though could not easily accept either of these explanations for their presence in our neighbourhood, and I could not blame her.

I determined therefore on a two-pronged course of action. I contacted the police and asked to speak to whoever had succeeded Chief Inspector Allinson in handling Shropshire's involvement in the Wolverhampton prostitution case, and after being directed down a couple of blind alleys, was put onto a Superintendent Tomlinson, who had been Allinson's junior in those days. He quickly caught on to the possible significance of the men's appearance, and said he would immediately send someone to see me.

My second decision was that we must not allow the children to cycle home from school, and must be ferried night and morning until we were sure there was no danger. Also we must not leave Deb on her own.

Tomlinson in fact came himself, with an Inspector Perks, and a sergeant, later in the afternoon. Deb and I told them exactly what had happened, about her renewed fears, and the action we were taking to protect her and the children. I said also that we knew there was still some suspicion that something had been going on in the forest at the time of her abduction and assault.

Tomlinson said: "Well, I can only say that the case has not been closed, although no new information has come to light for some time. There are forestry people working up there now, aren't there? I think we'll go up and have a word. I shall let you know if there are any significant developments. I think you are probably worrying unduly about your family's safety, but if it makes her and you feel easier, no doubt it's better you should keep up your precautions."

We heard nothing then for nearly a year, and Deb's worries subsided, although they did not go away completely. For several weeks we continued to ferry the children to and from school, but never saw or heard of the men. We did not hear from the police, either, and could only assume there had been no developments. I asked Sid at the pub whether the two had been back, but they had not. I began to think that if there was anything in their appearance in the locality, it was just down to that morbid desire to revisit the scene of a former crime.

Then one day our lane became alive with police vehicles, and an ambulance flashed by. Later, Superintendent Tomlinson came into the yard and knocked on the door. There had been a development, he told us. The forestry team had found a body.

Deb caught my hand. "Oh, Alastair," she said. And to the superintendent: "Do you think...?"

"We can't think anything until we have more information," he said. The only thing I can tell you is that our forensic people who have carried out a preliminary examination believe it is the body of a young woman, coloured they think, and it had been there for some years. It was quite close to the original track that leads on from this lane. A bulldozer unearthed it. And that's as much as I can tell you or anyone else at the moment. We shall be holding a press conference in the morning - the papers have already got wind of it."

We thanked him for telling us as much as he could. After he had gone I said: "Of course he can't say anything more, but I'll be very surprised if it doesn't turn out to be the young woman they told us couldn't be accounted for. They took her up there and buried her. Oh, God, Deb..." She clung to me. "Oh, Alastair, Alastair man," and as ever when relief came, so did the tears.

"What do you think will happen now?"

"I've no idea, love. It's more than 10 years since Allinson told Aunt Billie there were some suspicions about that gang and the missing girl, so I'm sure their inquiries are going to take a long time. They might never come to anything, even. I'm pretty sure about one thing, though. Those villains won't show their faces round here again, now this has happened."

In fact, I was wrong about the time scale. I never knew how it came about, but about three months later it was reported that three men, one of Jamaican origin, had been arrested and charged with the murder of the woman who had been found in Cravenbury Forest. I suspect there was a "squeal" somewhere. Another three months, and they were tried and convicted. It was lucky for them that the body had not been discovered a year or two sooner. The death penalty was abolished, in effect, by a Parliamentary vote to suspend it, just as their case was being heard. Still, it meant that two of them spent most of the rest of their lives behind bars, and Debra's fears, and mine, were put to rest.. Although we never knew why they had chosen a forest 30 miles away from the centre of their activities to dispose of the poor girl, who perhaps had been another naïve unfortunate like Deb.

I have never approved of capital punishment. It has seemed and does seem to me that a society that inflicts it lowers itself towards the level of the murderer it is punishing. But when I think of those evil men who treated Deb the way they did, I have to admit that such a moral stance is subjected to a degree of strain.

Nineteen

A chapter closes

My life, Deb's and the children's, continued on a relatively even tenor for many years after those events. The farm thrived, relatively. Roger O'Connell left us in 1970, as already mentioned, and was replaced by a local man, George Pryce, who while not being as highly skilled a stockman, was of a more even temperament meaning I did not have to be quite as careful not to upset him. Mike departed for retirement a few years later but was ready to lend a hand when needed, meaning that with increasing mechanisation we did not need a full time replacement.

Sooner or later, of course, we had to encounter the death of some of the folk in my parents' generation. The first was my Aunt Billie, to whom I had always been close, and to whom I had been brought even closer through the events which brought Debra to us. She was a lady of great character and a heart of gold even though she sometimes made people think she was a bit of a dragon. Her husband, my uncle Peter, lived for many years after her, longer in fact than my own father, his great friend and idol.

Dad passed away at the age of 80, leaving a massive gap in all our lives. Right up to the day he died, he was always the one I turned to for advice on practical matters, just as was my mother when emotions were the problem.

I cannot say too much in admiration and praise of my father. Coming from a background, not of aristocracy like his mother, but of a country squirearchy going back hundreds of years, he might have been expected to perpetuate the superiority complexes and prejudices of so many families of that ilk – not that the Jamesons subscribed to most of them. But he did not. He had married my mother in defiance of his own father, who while apparently a model employer and landlord in most respects, had some kind of a bee in his bonnet about maintaining society in a stratified form. He, my father that is, had very firm principles, some of which would have been held by previous generations. They were never inimical to change, though. He knew that life in general was unfair to the vast majority of people; but he was as unsympathetic to stubborn traditionalists who believed such a state of affairs was fine and should continue as he was to those who would bring it crashing down overnight. In other words, he would have liked to see a fairer society, but one that must be maintained in good order. He accepted and was paid a very good salary for running the Netherfield estate but was always ready to spend a proportion of it on those worse off than himself, through supporting a myriad of good causes. He sent us his children to expensive schools, but my mother told me he was really quite pleased when I declined his offer to do the same for mine and Deb's. She said his offer to pay for our boys to go to Shrewsbury arose from another of his basic qualities – loyalty. In this case to an establishment which had educated generations of Jamesons. As a person, I don't think he was ever disliked, even by people to whose ideas he was opposed. Uncle Peter told me the men under his command in the first war almost adored him, at a time when many other units positively hated and despised their officers. At Netherfield, he was also highly regarded, from the top by his boss, Lord Netherwood, and from below by the tenants and employees. He was quiet but never taciturn, enjoyed a chat and a joke with almost anyone, and worked hard all his life. And I think he and my mother were as deeply in love when he died as they had ever been.

Uncle Giles survived Dad by four years. When he died, his 700-acre farm, the residue of the Lyndford estate, and his other assets, passed to his wife Elizabeth in trust for his nephews and nieces, for he had no children, having only married late in life. When she passed on, less than a year later, it meant it all went to me, Peter, our sister Kathleen, and Aunt Billie's two sons. We agreed, very amicably, that they would have the cash and I the farm, subject to a modest "rent" payment for a limited period. I had the best end of the deal, without a doubt, but they were all pleased to see what remained of the Jameson acres stay in the family. And Deb and I were not in clover, by any means. We had only just raised our Forest Farm heads completely clear of the water, and taking over Lyndford meant a heavy immediate commitment. I had to abandon my resolve to pay for everything out of income, and run on a bank overdraft. It worked out well enough, however, and we were clear of debt in about five years.

Dad's death brought home to Debra, and me, that her own parents were getting on in years. We decided we could afford a trip to the West Indies. I tentatively suggested she should go on her own, but she was so reluctant that I agreed to go as well. She could not, even now, so many years later and with all the villains locked away, rid herself of the spectre of their threat, that they'd have her in a wooden box almost before she had landed.

I knew how poor the Edworths were, from what she had told me. And I readily agreed to her plea, after we were married, that she should have a little pocket money of her own – and knew what she did with it. Every month it went to Masterman Creek. As hard as we had to struggle financially, during the early years at Forest Farm, we were rich beyond compare to her father and mother. I never resented those few pounds that made such a difference to them. But I was not prepared for what I saw, even though their life and conditions had improved greatly over the twenty years she had been away.

Mr Edworth had been able to double the area of land he rented, but even so I was amazed to think that a living could be wrested from half a dozen patches, each no bigger than the old garden at Lyndford Manor, and not as big in total as one of our smaller fields. No wonder the temptation to get away, to the promised luxury of life as a servant girl in Britain, could not be resisted.

They had been able to build a new house, with four rooms instead of two, and to bring the beachcombing Auntie Mima to live in the original. Deb showed it me.

"That's where I was born, Alastair, man," she said. "Aren't I jus' the luckiest girl in all the world?"

On a hill half a mile away was a porticoed mansion, bigger than Lyndford Manor. I asked her who lived there.

"Him – he's the man who owns all the land here. He's not a nice man. Some say he bosses the gangs in Kingston." She shuddered. Her father told me the house had once been the centre of a big plantation, that a hundred and fifty years before had been worked by slaves, some of whom had been his own ancestors, he guessed.

Back home, we moved to the farmhouse at Lyndford, leaving Erbie and Connie in charge of Forest Farm. It pleased me no end to see Erbie, the little Cockney sparrow who I'd met in prison, in charge of a farm of more than 200 acres. My mother told me that if I did no other good in my life, I could take credit for that. My son Charles was too young to take that farm over, at that time. After school, he went to Harper Adams Agricultural College and joined us at Lyndford, ready to succeed eventually and become, as sections of the Press gleefully trumpeted, the first large-scale black farmer in Britain, whose father had once served a prison term for drug smuggling. None of us became worked up about it, though, and it gave me a platform from which to take the offensive and tell the media and everyone else what I thought about racialism.

Edward left school at sixteen, went on to a technical college which was what he wanted, and earned him a place at Loughborough, then thought of as Britain's top university of technology and sport. He came out of his three years there with a "first" which took him to a famous firm of aero-engineers. Deb and I were always pleased with his success, perhaps because it was so hard-earned. But the early part of his time at Derby, installed in a house with three other young engineers, brought more worry for his mother, when she and Connie paid a visit to the house where he was living with three other graduate apprentices.

"You should have seen it, Alastair. The kitchen sink was piled high with dishes. I think some of them had been there for a week - there was food still on them and it was mouldy. We had to stay and give that kitchen a proper clean, but I bet it'll be as bad in another few days. Edward's was the best of the bedrooms but that was pretty awful - you couldn't see the bed for clothes, an' books, an' everything else, an' the floor wasn't much better."

The boy appeared to survive the lack of hygiene, however, and I was rather amused than worried. But we were both a little concerned when one of his housemates introduced him to motorcycles, which led on to racing. Edward became a top class bike racer, was sponsored by a firm of importers, and could easily have been a full time professional. He steadfastly refused to go down that road, however, preferring to keep his sport as a hobby – although quite a lucrative one eventually, until he gave it up on landing a very good job with a Birmingham firm of advanced technological engineers. And soon after, becoming engaged – a development I at least did not at first welcome wholeheartedly, for reasons which may be related elsewhere.

Then - Emily Jane, who almost became a touchstone threatening the emotional tenor of my life. She was – is – a bright, popular girl, who played hockey, tennis and cricket to a high standard and announced at the age of 16 that she wanted to be a doctor, or better still a scientist working in medical research. I think it was because she had a particular friend who suffered from a rare genetically-inspired disease, and who expected to die before she was 30. Anyway, Em's A-level studies were aimed in this direction, she obtained excellent results, was accepted for London University and eventually for the medical school at St Thomas's Hospital, which led to what could have been an upset for Deb, and me.

At home on one of her breaks, when she was walking with me one day to inspect some cattle, she said: "Dad, one of our lecturers says she knows you."

My stomach turned over. It could only be Angie.

I said, as calmly as I could: "I don't think I know any university lecturers in London. What's her name?"

"It's Margerrison - Professor Margerrison. I think her Christian name's Angela. She asked to be remembered to you."

So she was married, and a professor. One bit of me said I ought to be heartbroken, but it lost out to a hope that she had found happiness. But the mention of her still brought that kick in the stomach.

"It's a long time ago - getting on for thirty years. Her name was Royston when I knew her, if it's the same person."

"She asked about you quite a lot. Wanted to know what you were doing, and who my mother was. Was there - was there anything between you, Dad?"

"There might have been, love, but we lost touch with each other. Is she good – I mean, do you find she's good for you?"

"Oh, yes, she's very good, and popular. She's head of the department I'd like to join - you know, genetics. She's the first professor. I like her."

"Good. Tell her I'm pleased to hear of her, Em, love."

And despite what it had done to my emotional equilibrium, I was pleased. Pleased to know that my sacrificial effort had not been in vain, and that she was obviously succeeding in her profession. I wondered who she had married, and if she had any children, but those thoughts did not distress me, and I did not want to pursue such matters through Emily Jane, or indeed via any other route. Nor did I tell Debra that our daughter had mentioned her.

Before she spoke about Angie to me, however, Em had told her mother, in their inevitable conversations over her work and London life, about Professor Margerrison and her work, and that she thought she had known me, years ago. When our daughter had left, she mentioned it to me.

"That was the girl you told me about before we were married, wasn't it?"

"Yes, that was her."

"Did Em tell you much about her?"

"No, except that she's a professor, and her name's Margerrison, so she must be married."

"Wouldn't you like to know a bit more? You needn't think I'd mind, Alastair. I expect Em's told her about ..... us."

I was so pleased that I'd told her, more than twenty years before, about Angie and other things from that time. It would have been terrible if it had come out through the back door. She would have been hurt, that I hadn't told her if for no other reason, and protecting Debra from hurt, helping her recover from the terrible things that had happened to her, had been my main objective, a driving force, through all our years together. It would have been grossly unfair to someone whose whole existence, I knew, revolved around me and our children, and whose life had become entwined with mine to the extent that we hardly had to speak our thoughts, often, for the other to know what they were. No woman in the world, even Angie, could have drawn me away from Deb.

This went through my mind then, but before I could say anything, she asked: "Do you still think what you did then – I mean what you decided about… Angie… was right?"

"Yes. Absolutely."

"But you didn't really want to marry me, at first, did you?"

"No, but it was not because I was still thinking of her, although I was, I suppose. Oh, my dear, it's so hard to explain. I loved you from the start, Deb. But it was more like loving a child. You were so much younger, and so helpless after … all that. I'd have done anything to protect you. Do you remember that night in the lambing shed? I think that's when I realised you could be much more to me than a child in need of looking after. Do you remember?"

"Oh, Alastair, man. I never stop thinkin' about it. It was the most wonderful day in my life - up to then, anyway. You asked me to marry you.

There's been lots of wonderful days since, though. Our weddin' day, an' when the babies came, an' - oh, millions of 'em."

As I said to Em, it was a long time ago. Angie was still there, away in my psyche, but locked away. And I was all those years older and there was so much else in my life; Debra, the children, the farm. Despite that kick in my stomach when she was mentioned, or I thought of her, she did not dominate my emotions the way she once did, and for so much of the time. And I only had to see or even think of Deb, when something like this reminded me of Angie, to get myself back on an even keel. She had been a wonderful wife and helpmate for a quarter of a century, through tears, trauma and a great deal of hard work, as well as happiness and joy.

Not long after this, the final link between the family generations was broken when my mother died, after a longish illness. She had always been remarkably healthy, but after my father's death she appeared to contact all kinds of ailments, particularly of the lungs and chest. Always small, she seemed to shrink as she was wracked with successive bouts of coughing. As we were only a couple of hundred yards from the Manor, Deb spent a great deal of time with her. They had always been very close - like Mother and my grandmother. Those were wonderful relationships, almost inexplicable if you thought of the apparent gulfs between them. My grandmother from the aristocratic background of her baronet father, and my mother her kitchen maid. Then Mother, by now more or less lady of the manor, although she would round firmly on anyone who tried to call her that, and my little Jamaican. I suppose the qualities that nutured the relationships were there in all three of them, to some extent. But dearly as I held Debra, and the memory of my grandmother, I could not help thinking that my mother was the pivotal character, almost impossible not to love.

Deb and I, and Peter, were with her when she died. Kathleen had been in America, abandoned her work when we told her we thought the end was near, but did not quite make it in time.

Apart from the effect her death had on all of us emotionally, we all benefited. Dad had not left her fabulously wealthy by any means, but there were appreciable funds, and they came in equal measure to her three children, after a few legacies to charities she felt strongly about, and had been connected with. But we had to decide what to do about Lyndford Manor. It had been the family base ever since it was built a couple of centuries earlier. It was by no means a stately home, therefore no point in offering it to the National Trust, but it was too big for us. Neither Deb nor I wanted a house with two or three maids, even if they could have been found - domestic service was by then a no-go area for young English women, and who could blame them, and in any case we could not have afforded them. My mother had got by on the loyal help of older local people, who persuaded their daughters and daughters of their friends to spend a little time as housemaids to her; plus a succession of au pairs, latterly Deb's almost constant attendance, and more or less shutting up part of the house. Not long before she died, she had expressed a hope that it might if possible be used for some good work such as a school for handicapped children, but there were practical difficulties, as so many owners of big old houses have found out.

We settled in the end for renting it to a university as a field centre, at a figure which would allow it to be kept in repair. It would mean some jobs for local people, which would have pleased my mother.

Six years after Mother died Charles, who by then was doing most of the farming, was proposing to get married, to a girl he had known from school. I thought it was a good time to retire - I was 64 - and suggested to Deb that we might enlarge and take over one of the increasing number of vacant cottages. We never made any of our staff redundant, or dismissed them for any other reason, except one chap who we found to be stealing and selling lambs, but many retired or left for non-agricultural work and were not replaced as mechanisation took over. We tentatively considered moving back to Forest Farm, but we did not want to disturb Erbie and Connie although they were now on their own there, their children having flown the nest. We did just that, then - expanded Jasmine Cottage, where Aunt Elizabeth had once lived, until it had four bedrooms, enough to cope with family or other visitors, and handed the farm over to Charles, keeping enough of a financial interest for us to live on.

I did not find retirement boring. I'd been playing the odd game of golf, often with my brother, or Charles, and I took to playing more. We went to Jamaica again, visiting Deb's brothers who had moved to Kingston and were doing well in a business they had set up there, and helping make sure their parents were as comfortable as possible in their old age. And we did a little more travelling, mostly to continental Europe. I know there's a lot of opposition in Britain to European integration, but I like to see the barriers coming down and I'm quite sure the development of the EU has been the biggest single factor in preventing European wars. My father who fought in the first of them in our lifetime, and saw goodness how many millions of English, French and German soldiers killed, and I who helped slaughter – I use the word deliberately – many thousands of women and children, always agreed on that.

And then, I discovered the project that banished any possibility of boredom. Debra prompted it.

We sometimes reminisced about all the things that had happened, and that had brought us together. One day she said: "Why don't you write it all down, Alastair man? Write a book, perhaps. Lots of people 'ud like to read it, I'm certain. There's been so much."

I scoffed, of course. I was not illiterate, but – a book. That was a bit beyond me. The seed had been sown though, and it grew. On Deb's suggestion, I put a notebook in my pocket, and when I had a few slack minutes, I started to note down recollections as they occurred to me. One memory led to another, and I started by putting down all that my mother and father, and Aunt Billie, and others in dribs and drabs had told me, that created a picture, I hope an accurate one, of their earlier lives. In only a few weeks I was finding I wanted to put them in chronological order. Deb helped. She would say as I recalled some episode: "Yes, and do you remember what (Aunt Billie, say) said? She said, didn't she...? " And the thing started to come to life. I found myself devoting hours at a time to it, and enjoying them.

Twenty

Back towards the future - *Angie*

After what had gone before, I suppose that letter from Alastair, from Lewes Prison, should not have taken me completely by surprise. Indeed it did not. But still, I was devastated. Somehow, I suppose, I had been thinking it would all work out. Loving someone like I loved Alastair could not end like that. The termination might be tragic, if he was shot down in a war or something, like Josie's Derek. But not like this. Not through a cold-blooded decision to end it all because having anything to do with him might damage my career.

I knew though that he was utterly sincere in wanting me to cast myself off from him because he thought he would be a dead weight on my future. And to be honest, I think then, in 1948, his fears had some foundation. I can just imagine what people like Miss Halloran, a hospital matron of whom more later, or the people who interviewed me for a place in the medical school would have said if they had got to know I had a sweetheart in gaol. Thank goodness we are leaving such attitudes behind. At least I hope so. (Although only the other day I heard a sister say of a young nurse, who had impressed me as a caring and competent young woman: "Keep an eye on her. She comes from a pretty dodgy area.")

I worked hard and made good progress at St Thomas's, the agony of Alastair pushed into the background as much as possible. But well on my way through basic training, I made a decision that had a big effect on the rest of my life. I had intended to specialise in coronary care, because I was interested in it from a technical point of view. But coming into contact with children - usually very young children - suffering and dying from cystic fibrosis made me change my mind and opt for genetics, only comparatively recently identified as the cause of this terrible disease, which in those days prevented most of its victims even reaching school age. I know you should not be emotionally involved, and I wasn't, but it was clear that here was a branch of medicine very much in need of doctors and scientists dedicated to trying to do something about it. My tutors and superiors agreed, and welcomed my change of plan.

I was no longer living at home. I had a little flat, just a bedsit really with a kitchenette and bathroom, only five minutes walk from St Thomas's. Dad paid the rent and with my grant and the small amount I was now paid for hospital work I managed quite well financially. Social life was sparse, though, mainly consisting of paying visits home two or three times a month.

Sometimes Josie and her husband Martin were there - they'd only recently been married. He was very good for her, solid and dependable, just what she needed. I would sometimes go with them to the theatre or cinema, or for a meal, often with some of their friends. I think Josie and my parents were hoping I'd meet someone I'd click with, as she had, and the memory of Alastair would be erased. They probably thought it had been, already, because I never talked about him. But it didn't happen. None of their young male friends, while being pleasant and mostly quite intelligent, attracted me, even if I'd been in the market. And they probably thought I was a blue stocking type, interested in nothing but my work.

Then – along came Bill. Certainly not an ordinary guy, who you'd meet on the street and never notice. He was very tall and thin, had an unfashionable beard, and wore little steel-rimmed glasses of the kind that went out of fashion before I was born, through which shone, incongruously I thought, bright blue eyes. He was quite a bit older than most of the rest of Josie's friends, not far off 40, but I immediately liked him, although there was no romantic-style click.

Josie, no doubt trying to act the matchmaker, told me a bit about him. He was Martin's boss in a small firm of research chemists, which he had set up when the big firm who'd employed him refused to allow him to take his work in the direction he wanted. Not enough prospect of profit, Josie said. So he had sold a big house left by his parents, to raise capital, and started his own company with this and a grant from a medical trust. He'd had a fiancee who however waved him goodbye when the house she'd been looking forward to queening it over disappeared, and his personal income shrank. I asked what branch of research he was interested in, and my ears pricked up when she said it was genetics.

Short conversations with Bill led to professional topics, and a few months later he asked me out, on my own. Nothing romantic about it, we simply went for a meal in a pretty ordinary restaurant and talked about our work. But it set a pattern for most of the time I was training and for some time after. He'd phone to ask if I'd like to see a certain film, or play, if I was free. I never allowed him to pay for everything, because by then I had found out how tight his finances were - he regularly had less to live on than he paid my brother-in-law Martin. We did not therefore eat "out" very often. Instead we would go to either my flat or his, which was hardly any bigger, and either cook a meal or fetch in fish and chips. We talked, about work, the film or play we'd just seen, books, current affairs, anything. Our views often coincided, although not always. But we always enjoyed the discussions. I don't know why the intimacy that grew up did not develop into something more, on my part. No that's not true. I do know. It was Alastair's psychological presence that meant there was no "click" for me. Still, Bill became an important part of my life. I found he was the only person to whom I could unburden myself when there was some problem or other nagging me about my work, and sometimes he would ask for my on-the-ground comments about what he was doing. But there was more to it for him, as I somewhat reluctantly began to realise, but which only came out in the open about four years after I'd met him, by when I was on the way to becoming a consultant specialising in genetically-based diseases, which meant, mostly, cystic fibrosis. By then also, he had sold his little firm to a more-enlightened bigger concern which was giving him the scope he wanted, and paying him a good salary.

We were having a meal at a little fish restaurant we particularly liked. I thought he was rather quieter than usual, but did not infer anything particular from it. But when we were waiting for the coffee, he said: "Angela, can I ask you something special?"

Not over all the years had he ever said anything to me that could be called romantic, but I was immediately afraid I knew what was coming. I looked straight through those funny little glasses.

He asked, softly and gently, like he said most things: "Would you consider marrying me?"

Before I could answer, the waitress brought the coffee. I spooned sugar into his, and poured cream into mine.

"I don't love you, you know. Not like that. I like you very much, and we get on very well. I think I could be happy with you. But I don't feel – like that - about you."

"I think I know that. And I know there was - someone else. And what happened to him. But I still want to marry you. I've loved you since the first time I saw you."

Just how it was with me and Alastair, 10 years ago. I sat still.

"He's still there, you know. In here, I mean" - touching my breast. "Wouldn't you be worried I was always looking over my shoulder?"

"I could live with that if I knew there was a bit of you cared for me," he said.

"You know that anyway, dear Bill. I wouldn't be here tonight if there wasn't. But - suppose he suddenly appeared, and I couldn't help... feeling like that again?"

"I'd risk it," he said.

I sat still again, for minutes.

"I'm a bit of a blue stocking."

"You're no blue stocking, Angela. You're an attractive, highly intelligent and caring woman. I wouldn't want to marry any other kind - and anyway, I've told you. I love you. I don't know why it's taken me so long to tell you so."

We sat for more minutes, looking at each other.

Finally I said: "I'm not going to give you the answer now. I must have a little time. I'm sure we'd get on together. And I know passion isn't always the be-all and end-all of a basis for marriage. But I've got to think, about what I want my life to be, Bill. I'm not going to say something silly like 'I'm wedded to my work.' But it is very important to me. You know that, don't you? Can it be reconciled with being married - even to you, my dear?"

He said, after a pause and very quietly indeed: "If you didn't want children, you know... it would be alright."

I knew it would not, though. I said: "I wouldn't marry you on those terms."

Another pause, and I told him: "The day after tomorrow. Come round the day after tomorrow, and I'll tell you then."

The next day was Saturday, and I was so busy at the hospital that I had little time to think about anything personal, even something like marriage. But on Sunday I resolved not to leave my breakfast table, or anyway the kitchen sink and the washing up, until I had made up my mind about Bill's proposal. I had to break that resolution, though. I just could not get my mind to move away from the dilemma it was presented with – work versus marriage. The two were irreconcilable. About lunchtime I went out to walk in the park, my thoughts still crashing into each other like dodgem cars at a fairground.

It was a beautiful early summer day. The park was littered with groups of people, mostly families. One caught my eye especially. There was a young mother - no more than 25, I thought, with two lively little boys, and dad and a dog playing ball with them. My mind suddenly became sharply focussed. Did I want to miss out on this? Emphatically not. Did I want to give up my work? The same answer came up, just as emphatically. But instead of leaving me with the dilemma that had plagued me all day, the two apparent opposites coagulated into the only possible answer. They would have to be reconciled. It was the only way, for me. What on earth had I been thinking of? There wasn't a problem. The two would simply have to be fitted together, like a complex joint in a piece of furniture.

Oddly, although I had not suddenly fallen in passionate love with Bill, Alastair never came into my deliberations. That evening, I told Bill I would marry him. And I wanted to.

We decided we would be married in about two months time, and live in Bill's flat until we could find a suitable house. We told my parents, and Josie and Martin. They were all delighted. I remember thinking Josie looked a bit smug.

*****

I'd always been happy at St Thomas's, but my decision to marry Bill brought the only miserable period of my time there – almost a full adult lifetime.

Miss Halloran, in charge of our section, was the only one of her kind I ever knew who came up to the fearsome reputation endowed on the genus of matron by some films, plays and books. I'm sure she had redeeming features, but she seemed to keep them well hidden, and most people, especially her victims, could be forgiven for thinking that she believed she had been put on the earth, and given her job, with a main objective of making the lives of probationer nurses as miserable as possible, and above all to make sure they stayed single.

For Miss Halloran hated married women nurses, and all female doctors. She almost seemed to hate the children, mostly suffering from cystic fibrosis, who came under her care. Married women doctors were completely beyond the pale, a disgrace to the profession and to womanhood. I started off therefore as anything but one of her favourite people, and when the news of my forthcoming nuptials reached her it was like applying a match to a touchpaper. She became almost openly antagonistic, and behind the scenes spread much poison.

Her campaign reached its apex about three weeks before my marriage, when she accused me - behind my back of course, but the venom was meant to reach me - of hastening the death of one of our young cystic fibrosis patients by one of my "new fangled" treatments. The treatment was the use of a nebuliser or inhaler, partly to help the administration of the antibiotics we were then beginning to apply with, usually, helpful results. The lad, only seven years old, was almost on the point of death, and if I had been there I would certainly not have used the technique. But the intern on the ward was told by the duty nurses that "Dr Royston always tells us to use an inhaler." It caused the poor child great distress which possibly did hasten his end, if only by a few hours, and gave Matron her opening.

I am sure she never said anything officially, certainly not to me personally, but her vituperation spread round the hospital and reached my own ears as I have no doubt was intended. I was deeply distressed, as much as anything because I felt I was in the wrong to some extent - I should not have allowed my practice to be interpreted as a blanket instruction.

When I got home that evening, I was so miserable that I could not eat anything, let alone cook it first. I was sitting on a kitchen chair with my head on the worktop when Bill came in and of course wanted to know what was the matter. And over the next few hours, I came to realise what the gentle kindness that was at the core of his character would mean in our marriage. He was wonderful. He insisted on my drinking a glass of tonic wine, then on preparing a meal - only scrambled egg and toast, but it was just what was needed. Then he talked me through what had happened, and as on more than one occasion in the years to come, guided me out of a personal trauma into a state of comparative peace and calm. It was how he was. That evening, I took him into my bed for the first time, and the gentleness showed there, too. I'd never had sex before.

We were married very quietly by a registrar, with only my family and Bill's sister and brother-in-law present. For an equally short honeymoon, we went to Derby to see Stewart, who could not get away for our wedding, were introduced to the girl he later married, and had a couple of days in the Peak District, where I had never been.

Back in London, we set about looking for a house. We could afford to be a bit choosy, we felt, for we were comfortable enough in Bill's flat, especially as we did not spend much time there.

However, three months later, when we still had not found anything, we had to revise our ideas. I discovered I was pregnant.

"Oh, my darling," Bill said. "But are you sure, so soon?".

I said: "My dear, it's a natural result of what we've been doing most nights for the last three or four months. Didn't you know?"

He laughed. "I meant, we haven't made any preparations. Oh, darling, how wonderful. But we'll have to get on with things, won't we?"

We did try to get on with things, starting there and then with stepping up our search for a house, and lowering our sights somewhat. We'd already divined that although we could afford a substantial property, our target of half an acre of garden was unrealistic. Apart from the cost, such properties just weren't around, where we needed to live. "Large garden" in the estate agents' brochures proved to mean about 30 yards square in many cases. But about 30 by 60 was what we had to settle for if we were to be installed before our little treasure appeared. We bought it however, or rather took out a mortgage to buy it, although the amount we had to borrow was relatively small because the sale of Bill's company had provided a large part of what was needed to fund it outright. And the house had the plus point of being near my work and my parents.

We also decided we would need a nanny. Finding one was no problem although making sure she came up to our expectations, and was able to fit into our timetable was not so easy, but we eventually signed up Helen, who was going to be free at the right time. Then, thinking about how it was all going to work, I realised a nanny was not going to be enough if I was going to keep up my level of work. We would need a housekeeper, or something like it. But we struck lucky, through the same agency. A recently-widowed Welsh lady was looking for a job and accommodation in London, to be near her son and daughter. We liked Mrs Davies immediately, and apparently she liked us, for she stayed with us for many years. The house was big enough to allow her a separate bedroom, sitting room and bathroom, and we immediately put the necessary work in train.

My pregnancy proceeded without any substantial problems. Even the morning sickness that makes life so miserable for some did not plague me greatly. I worked, in laboratory and ward, until a fortnight before I was "due." Goodness knows what the Halloran thought when my big tummy preceded me on my rounds, but I didn't care. I felt I was blooming, and almost wanted to say, most uncharitably I know, "Look what I've got - don't you wish!" Now I just feel sorry, deeply sorry, for women who are prevented by their prejudices, sometimes not even real, from enjoying the fulfilment of motherhood, that nine out of ten want almost above anything else. And even more sorry for those who are physically unable to enjoy it, although I'm not sure that we are always right in regarding motherhood as so all-important.

Without problems, but not completely devoid of surprises. Two weeks before I gave up work, I went to one of my paediatric colleagues for a routine examination.

"Any indications of whether it's a him or a her? " I asked.

"I can't be sure," he said. "It could be either - or rather both. It's twins, my dear." Collapse of stout party!

The news made us wonder of course whether our provisions for baby care were adequate. Would Helen the nanny-elect agree to cope with two infants at once, for a start. But we need not have worried. She had three in her present post, all of whom she had cared for since birth. Two babies would be a different kind of challenge, but one she would look forward to, she insisted. We also had back-up - my mother. In fact I had to overcome a certain amount of opposition from her to having a nanny at all.

"What d'ye think grandmothers are for?" she asked us with a degree of asperity. "I looked after the three of ye when ye were all wee babbies, and I didna have a washing machine and all these devices you have nowadays. I could manage two, nae problem - as long as ye didna ask me to suckle them. I'm a bit past that, I'm afraid." Bill blushed.

The idea was a non-starter, of course. Mum was sixty-five, and it was not just a matter of looking after the infants, but of getting them to her, or her to them, which would eat into time neither Bill nor I had. We wanted the time we would be able to spend with our children to be as free from clockwatching stress as possible. We soon found of course that such time would be in short supply. But I pointed out to Mum that back then she did not have a demanding, full time job, and that there would no doubt be plenty of scope for her to step in as relief, from time to time, and with my father's help, I succeeded in convincing her. His arguments included something like "well, you wanted her to succeed in her life, Mother - you have to accept that this is how it has to be." He was delighted with grandfatherhood, but frankly, I don't think he really wanted to have two infants on their hands, and he knew what a burden they must eventually be.

Our two girls duly made their way into the world with a minimum of fuss, I wouldn't say stress, especially for Bill, who was like a cat on hot bricks from the time we were told there were two of them. But when all was over, safe and sound, the other feline characteristic took over- he almost purred. We called them Jeanne, after my mother, and Josephine or Josie after my sister, both names at Bill's suggestion. I stayed at home for a month, a lazy month after they arrived, during which we established a routine that was more or less followed after I went back to work. I seemed to have lots of milk, so breast-fed them as long as I could, but handed over the graft of washing nappies (disposables were only just making their appearance) and other clothes to Helen. After I returned to the hospital they had to have bottle feeds part of the time, but I continued to nurse them myself when I was able, to my mother's pleasure.

From the start, our domestic arrangements worked well. Both Helen and Mrs Davies were most flexible in their working schedules, and Bill and I tried to echo the flexibility in our demands on their time. We were often tired, of course, both of us, for Bill was unstinting in his readiness to tackle any job that needed to be done, at any hour of the day or night. Our finances were now well stretched, or he might have had a part-time gardener. But as he said, plans in that direction could wait. The garden may not have been a showpiece of blossom, but the lawn was always mown on Saturday afternoons, unless it rained, so we could sit there with the babes after lunch on Sunday, weather permitting. My mother, as I knew she would, always stepped in to plug gaps in the care routine, and Dad tackled gardening and maintenance jobs. It was hard work, but we coped, and I was able to keep up my work at an enthusiastic level.

*****

Helen stayed with us until the girls had been at school for two years and more. She was married by then to a young electrician and would have carried on for longer but for having a family herself. Even then she would come and do the occasional babysit, always busying herself about the house while she was there. Like Mrs Davies, she had become a real friend, and we kept in touch with her and watched the progress of her children with interest. After she left, we, or rather Mrs Davies, had to make do with a succession of "dailies," with varying degrees of satisfaction, but Mrs D always kept the ship on course.

We sent the girls to the local primary school. Neither Bill nor I liked the idea of fee-paying education, on principal, although we had both been to private institutions ourselves, Bill through the full system of prep and public school. We knew that the twins were highly intelligent and with our help would come well out of any system, and we knew our local primary was well run and the children well taught. We did however enrol them at a nursery school for a year before they entered the mainstream, although now I'm not sure whether we should have done even that.

There were never any serious health problems with them, apart from the illnesses all children contract. In their early years, they became very close to both Helen and Mrs Davies, in whose kitchen they spent a lot of time. But it was Bill who was the centre of their world. Their eyes would follow him everywhere. When they were babies, if he picked up one or both of them when they cried, they would stop as though a switch had been flicked. There was, it seemed, some kind of telepathy connecting them, and it persisted all through his life. They loved me, still do, and we could hardly be closer emotionally. But with Bill there was something extra. They were a trio, who hardly needed speech to communicate ideas, while dear old Mum had to have them spelt out to her. No, that is exaggerating. My maternal instincts worked as well as any. But not through that something extra that Bill had. Ought I to have been jealous? Well, I certainly wasn't. I was happy in my children, and in their relationship with their father.

Some may think I married Bill on the rebound, although if I did, I must have been a mighty long elastic, for it was 12 years since I had seen or heard of Alastair. I married him in fact for three reasons, which did not include romantic love in the accepted sense. One - important as my work was to me, I did not want to become a blue-stockinged old maid; two, I wanted children and a family home; and three, Bill was a dear, kind, gentle man who I liked very much and knew I could get on with, even in as intimate close quarters as marriage.

More than one novelist, essayist, philosopher has asked if unrequited love can exist, or exist for long. I think not, completely unrequited anyway.

But although he never engendered the stomach-wrenching, heart-stopping passion of the kind that hit me the first time I set eyes on Alastair, when I was trying to nursemaid Josie, I grew to love my husband sincerely. I hated having to spend nights without him, when either of us was away on some conference or special project. He was my friend, my helpmeet, we thought alike on almost everything, we shared a delight in our children, our instincts regarding them worked in harmony.

Alastair was still there. But he had been consigned to a special mental compartment, a cupboard I had locked, and hidden the key. Was it perhaps that I daren't open the cupboard for fear of what the skeleton there would do to me? Maybe. Perhaps if Bill had ever showed anything but the love and gentle kindness that was the essential him, it might have been different. I might have thought: "Where is he? Where is my Alastair, who set a torch to my soul with every glance?" But he never did. Not once in twenty years did my husband say a harsh word to either me or our daughters, and I grew fonder of him year by year.

The girls did very well at school. The much-maligned eleven-plus was then in operation, and both flew through it to secure places at the semi-independent girls' grammar school where I had been. Their intellectual interests were in similar directions, on the practical rather than the arts side, which pleased Bill no end, although I am quite sure they would have had exactly the same encouragement and support if they had wanted to go along a route that would bring them to thinking that unmade beds or random splodges of paint on plywood could be labelled "art." Personally I'm glad they didn't. I love Picasso and adore Henry Moore, but that's as far as I go in that direction, I'm afraid. But I didn't have to worry. Jeanne achieved high grades in maths, physics and English; Josie equalled her in world history, English and biology. Both enjoyed sport, playing cricket and hockey for school elevens at various ages, and were much interested in music, playing violin and flute in the orchestra.

Twins are always supposed to have a special relationship with each other. These two were no exception. They were not identical twins, but up to adulthood they seemed to be so close it was almost worrying. For example, while they were very young, they shared a bedroom. When they started secondary school, we gave them a room each. It lasted for one night, or only part of one night. Next morning they had to be dug out of the same bed. And the first thing they did when they arrived home that evening was to take Josie's workdesk and other personal furniture into "Jeannie's room."

Both worked and played in there, and slept in the other. And that was how it stayed until they went to university, where they were of necessity separated in term time, only to take up the old habit during vacations.

I said to Bill, one time when they were in the sixth form at school: "Do you think it's natural?"

"They were pretty close when they were in your tummy, weren't they? I think it's perfectly natural. Long may it continue," that fount of much of the wisdom in my life replied. A few years later, when Bill was no longer around to keep us all so firmly in order, there was a rift. But more about that in another place.

I have no idea why we had no more children. We never took any measures to prevent it, and our sex life, satisfactory from the start despite that lack of passion on my part, never grew less so. Some may say it was mere animal lust, but I don't think so. It was quite uninhibited though, if my mother had heard the language we sometimes used she'd have been shocked. (Or would she? I sometimes think the image of the Victorian wife lying back and thinking of England was only that - an image, a myth.) I was as enthusiastic about it as Bill, although his gentle consideration showed there as everywhere. But the outcome in terms of a bigger family was nil.

It did not worry me, except that I sometimes wondered whether he would not have liked a son or sons. I asked him one Sunday afternoon, when we were watching the girls, then about six, romping round the garden with our Alsatian.

"Perhaps we'll have one, one day," he said. "But if we don't, it won't be any kind of tragedy, for me. I'm not one of those chaps who think you must have a son to carry on the name, and all that, am I? And what son could bring me any more happiness than those two, and you?"

I said nothing, and we sat for five minutes or more, watching Josie hide in the little shrubbery my father had planted, for Jeannie to find her, with Griselda, the dog, watching to see what happened.

He opened up again: "What about you? Would you like to have more? A boy, especially?"

"It's just the same with me. Alright if it happens, if it doesn't, well..."

Another pause. Then: "You know, Angela my darling, I am so terribly happy. I never thought it could be like this, for me. I do love you, you know."

I pressed his hand, but did not say anything. I suppose now I was afraid to speak of love, even the kind of love I had for Bill. I might set that skeleton free.

Twenty One

Unto the Clee Hills

I continued to be engrossed in my hospital work and the research running alongside it. And although progress was painfully slow, we did make some. When I first went to St Thomas's, in the fifties, not many of the little cystic fibrosis sufferers survived long enough to go to school. Like doctors and researchers round the world, we were desperately seeking a cure, which has still not been found, although the treatments we have developed, between us, have eased the dreadful symptoms to such an extent that the median survival age has climbed into the thirties, and is going up every year. And we are at last beginning to hope that the rapidly growing knowledge of genetics may indeed one day enable that cure to emerge.

When our daughters were about to go to university, my working career was crowned, I suppose you'd call it, and happily while my parents and Bill were all still there to see it. The university hospital instituted a chair of genetics, a professorship, and I was appointed to it. Dad and Mum were by then both over 80, but they made no attempt to hide their pride.

"Oh, ma bonnie lassie, ma bonnie lassie, how weel ye've done" she said, the tears running down her face. My father, as always, was more restrained. "Great stuff, girl. But it's only what you deserve. You've worked hard."

Bill was of course delighted. He was by then 66 and we were thinking he would soon retire and take on supervision of the house, for Mrs Davies was planning to leave us. He had been quite happy in his work and for some years had been a director, supervising the division of the company he had worked for since before we were married. In fact he would have retired at sixty-five had not a fellow director had to give up work through ill-health and Bill took on his work as well as his own.

He never seemed to be unduly stressed, even then, took it all in his lean and fit stride, apparently as calm as ever. But about a year after my appointment he collapsed at his laboratory bench, or rather the computer-laden office desk it had become. It was a massive heart attack, one of the kind that sometimes takes people who look as though heart problems are the last thing likely to affect

---

them. I was sent for, and within half an hour was at his bedside at Guys. Too late. They told me he would have died pretty well instantaneously.

Oh, Bill, my dear, good, kind husband. Why could not I have been there to tell you how happy you had made more than 20 years of my life? How empty it would have seemed, professor's chair or not, without you and our daughters. Why could you not have been there to see their achievements as well as mine, perhaps help guide your grandchildren as they started along their own paths through life?

Jeannie and Josie were devastated, dashed home from Cambridge and said they did not want to go back. I was reminded of how it was with me, years before, but I, and Mrs Davies of course told them to scrap any such ideas, and they listened. But they told me afterwards that they lost enthusiasm for work for the rest of the term. They were so very close to him.

They came through all right in the end, though. A first in physics for Jeannie, the same in philosophy for her sister. Jeannie decided to go on to a masters degree, and later a PhD in astrophysics; Josie had been edging towards creative writing and decided journalism was the route she must take, despite the comparatively low pay it offered, at least at the start. She applied for several places on newspaper training schemes, was offered more than one, including on national daily papers and in radio, but opted for a regional daily. She said she wanted to work her way up, which she did, at some speed.

The girls' successful progress helped ameliorate what must otherwise have been a terrible period for me after Bill died, although as always, my work continued to be an equal driving force in my life. But then there was another blow, the loss of my parents, and I found my enthusiasm for almost everything having to be consciously prodded to life.

Mum and Dad had become frail, indeed were soon to develop the illnesses that brought their deaths, within two months of each other. It was the old enemy, cancer, and I knew enough about it to also know that there was little hope of recovery, for them. Happily they remained in full possession of their faculties almost until the end. My brother Stewart, who had moved back to the south-east, and sister Josie and their children, bore the brunt of the care from the family end, but I put in as much time as my work would allow. It was a sad time.

On one of my last visits to him in hospital, less than a week before he died, and when talking was becoming difficult, Dad asked me: "You were happy with Bill, Angela, weren't you?"

"Oh, Dad, of course I was. You knew I was, didn't you?"

"Yes, love, I knew... only... only..."

"There were no 'onlys' or 'buts,' Dad. We were very happy."

"Yes, love, I know. It's just that..."

I think I knew what was coming, but I also knew that I must not stop my dying father – for we both knew the end was near – saying something on a matter that was clearly worrying him. I remained quiet for a few moments, just looking at him in a way that I hoped said "Yes, Dad, tell me, if you want to."

He said: "It's something that's worried me ever since ..... ever since you were at school. That chap you wrote to, in prison. I think I was very hard, Angela. I meant it for your good, but I've thought many times that I was hard, and I didn't ever want to be hard, on you."

I patted his hand, and said: "Dad, I know. You've been the most wonderful father to us all. And you weren't wrong, you know. He – Alastair, I mean – thought exactly the same as you did. He made me promise to go away and forget him, and keep up my study, and work. He was a good man, Dad."

"Do you know what happened to him, afterwards, Angela?"

"I know a bit, now. I didn't, for a long time. But there was a girl of the same name who was one of my students and it came out through her. She's his daughter - he's a farmer, in Shropshire."

I paused, then said: "Dad, there was lot I couldn't tell you back then. If I had, I know you'd have thought differently about him. I remember you telling me there was more to it than I was saying, and you were right. Could I tell you now, please, Dad?"

And I did, all I felt I could tell him without distressing him more than he had already distressed himself. About Steve Parrimore, the flights, how Alastair went to prison and "cast me off;" and his role in "rescuing" Josie, except that I only called her "a girl I was very fond of." Dad guessed who it was, though.

He asked: "That girl... it was... Josie... wasn't it? That was why you couldn't tell me."

I said: "Yes, Dad. But you won't say anything to her, will you?"

"No, of course not. I'm glad you've told me, Angela. I feel better about it now. I know it's a long time ago. Do you... think about him... at all, now?"

"Dad, he's still there. I don't think I can ever stop. But I believe he's very happy now – like I was with Bill - and I wouldn't dream of doing anything to interfere with that."

"Oh, Angela, my dear girl..."

Once again, I was made aware that I must keep that cupboard locked. But I had a great many other matters to help me do it. Dad died soon after that conversation, and blessedly Mum followed him within a few weeks. Her illness had happily brought her less physical pain, but she was almost unable to talk at all during her last days.

Her "happy release" brought anything but happiness for me. Mrs Davies – she had become a dear friend as well as our housekeeper but I never called her anything else and I was always "doctor" to her - was soon to go to help her busy son and daughter-in-law and their growing family and I would be left rattling round on my own in a big house, with only occasional visits from the twins now they both had full time jobs. Sister Josie and Stewart suggested I move back to our old home at St Johns Wood. I toyed with the idea, but shelved it as Mrs Davies's plans for leaving fell through when her own children suddenly announced they were moving away from London, to a smallholding with a farm shop attached which meant they were at home most of the time. We could both have gone to St Johns Wood but that house was let to a good tenant so we decided to stay put.

My work, her company, and visits from the girls, who stepped them up as much as possible as they saw how much I depended on them, helped keep me on an even keel for the next five years, although I still think it was emotionally the lowest point of my life, apart from that awful time when I was first parted from Alastair. But it took another knock when Mrs Davies received a frantic appeal from her daughter in Wales, whose husband had died leaving her with three small children and the need to step up her own work. I decided I must not attempt to persuade her to stay with me. And in any case my own life took another turn as I came to retirement age.

Jeannie had acquired a boy friend, Simon, as she neared the end of her PhD studies, and they decided they would be married while I was still living in London. Simon was being offered a job as a researcher into veterinary medicine near Cambridge, Jeannie was expecting to carry on working at the university. They had been living together for a few months but Simon especially wanted to make it "official."

"I want to show her, and everyone else, especially you, that I'm committed," he told me when in an old fashioned way he sought me out to tell me of their plans. He was a nice boy who reminded me of Bill in many ways and I was delighted with the prospect of having him as a son-in-law, although I was disturbed when I learned that he was marrying my daughter in defiance of his father, who was a strict orthodox Jew and objected to Simon marrying outside that faith. I also hoped that Josie would not feel out in the cold. She did not appear to, however, either before or after they were married, very quietly with only a handful of others present – my brother and sister and their families and a few of their own friends.

The turn my life took was the offer of a part-time consultancy at a big Birmingham hospital, which with my work on various national bodies would keep me well occupied and bring more than enough income for my needs. I was a Londoner born and bred, but I did not feel my roots there were so deep that the old plant would wither and die if they were dug up. Josie was by then living in the little town of Bewdley, on the River Severn in Worcestershire. I thought I could find somewhere near her, not far from Birmingham and not a million miles from Cambridge. I quickly decided to take the job.

As soon as she knew I was doing so, Josie started to look out for possible houses for me, mostly through the local papers. I waited until she had collected three or four possibilities and had a couple days off, and went to look at them. One I immediately fell for – an old mill in the Clee Hills, less than an hour's drive from the hospital and only half an hour from Josie, although she was not likely to be at Bewdley for ever. And although as I had told my father I had not the least intention of ever seeking him out, it was not far from Alastair's home country, which I think now must have come to the back of my mind. I bought The Mill, and soon settled into life there. The girls helped me move in, and find local tradesmen to do the jobs that were needed to put the property in complete living order. The upstairs was not large - three bedrooms - but downstairs was more extensive and there was a range of outbuildings that had once been the working part of the mill. The waterwheel had gone, but its shaft still protruded and there were other bits of machinery redolent of the past. If Bill had been with me he would have wanted to do some restoration - I could just see him eyeing up a rebuild of the waterwheel to get it driving something or other, except that the stream that once worked it was now a comparative trickle. I learned later that it had been diverted higher up. But he'd probably have put in some kind of sophisticated electric motor or something to drive the wheel.

My consultancy at the Birmingham hospital was limited to three days a week. I was also on the committees of three national quangos, those much-derided quasi-autonomonous non-governmental organisations which in fact often do a great deal of important work, especially in health fields, and these occupied me on average for another day a week, usually involving travel to

London or further afield. It will be seen therefore that I was not left with unlimited free time. Also, either Josie or Jeanne, and Jeannie's Simon would often come for the weekend, sometimes all together.

Now I had moved, the knowledge that I was not so far from Alastair's country made me decide to indulge myself to the extent of exploring the area and finding out a little about it, perhaps even seeing where he and his family lived. Once again I must emphasise that I had no idea of seeking him out, much less of disturbing the happy marriage that I knew of through his daughter. And it was a trifle wicked, perhaps, even to seek to find vicarious satisfaction in knowing where he was from day to day. But I was going to do it.

It was some weeks before I was able. Then one Saturday when I was on my own I got into my old Citroen Dyane - a car which sent my daughters into hysterics but which had delighted Bill when I bought it - and set off for Lyndford, having found it on the map. I stopped for lunch at Cravenbury, at the Plymouth Arms, where I was one of only two people in the bar. The landlord saw my car and started to talk about it.

"Not many of those about now," he said.

"My daughters laugh at it," I said. "But I like it. It suits me - one old crock with another, I suppose."

"I certainly wouldn't say that," he laughed. And when he brought my soup and roll, he asked: "Visiting the area?"

I was quite pleased to have an opening for conversation. I told him I'd never been in Shropshire until a few months previously when I bought a house at Clee Marton, but a girl I knew at work came from a village called Lyndford - in fact I thought she'd been born near Cravenbury.

"Oh, I wonder if I know her - be a surprise if I didn't - there aren't many I don't know."

"Her name's Jameson - Emily Jane Jameson - "

"Oh, of course I know her, at least I know her father, very well. He used to come in here for a drink and a bite when he come back round here first, oh, must be nearly 30 year ago, and he still does, sometimes. We knew his dad, as well, and his mother, like everyone did round here, after they come back from Leicestershire or somewhere. They were grand folk, they really were, everybody liked 'em."

"I met them once," I said, immediately realising I should not say too much, although I had, already.

"Do you know Em - Emily Jane - I think she's Dr Jameson now - d'you know her mother and father?"

"I knew her father, briefly, but I haven't seen him for about 40 years. So obviously I've never met his wife. But the daughter's told me quite a lot about them both. She was a student of mine. Her mother's from the West Indies, isn't she?"

"Yes, and a very nice lass she was, still is. She worked like a - I were goin' to say like a - oh, dear I was goin' to say nigger - sorry - she worked hard to help Alastair Jameson get that farm on its feet. They did very well in the end, but good luck to 'em. I don't know anybody who doesn't like 'em, either of 'em. Course, they don't live there now. They moved to Lyndford, to the big farm that used to belong to his uncle. But their son's there now - they've retired."

I enjoyed the food, with a half of shandy, and coffee afterwards. When I went to pay, the landlord asked: "Are you goin' to look them up, p'raps?"

"No, not today." Or ever, I thought. My heart had been doing high jumps all the time we were talking, but that was as far as it must go.

I drove on to Lyndford, though. I must put substance on the image I had of the place - the ancestral home manor, the farm, the wooded valley Emily Jane had described.

I was not disappointed. It was as beautiful as she said, as the surroundings of my new home, perhaps even more so. But the manor, easy as it was to recognise, gave me something of a surprise. A big sign at the gate proclaimed it to be: Lyndford Manor - Aston University Department of Agriculture Field Centre. I drove up to the entrance and went inside.

"Can I help you?" the receptionist asked.

"Sorry, I'm only being curious. I used to know of the people who owned this house. How long has it been your field centre?"

"Only about two years. Do you know the Jamesons, then?"

"Slightly. Where do they live now?

"Well, Mr Charles Jameson lives at the farm just along there - Home Farm. His mother and father live at Jasmine Cottage, a little further on. We all know them quite well, in fact the manor still belongs to them. They're very nice."

My heart or some part of me fluttering, I drove on, past Home Farm and Jasmine Cottage, an obviously expanded farm cottage and easily identified by the name on the gate. So that was where he lived. The flutter was still there, but my brain was fluctuating between hoping I would see him and dreading the possibility. I carried on half a mile or so further, as the single track road climbed towards Wales, and stopped in a gateway to take in the magnificent vista, back towards the Clees, north to Corndon, the Stiperstones and the Long Mynd.

Nearer at hand, the other side the field whose gateway I was parked in, a couple were walking, hand in hand, coming not directly towards me but at an angle that would take them back and down towards Lyndford - no doubt to another gate. Something about them stopped me taking my eyes away. As they came nearer me, at one point not more than 150 yards distant, I could see that the lady was dark; not black, but certainly brown, and she looked younger than the grey-haired white man, to whom she kept looking up and laughing. My heart, stomach, lungs, brain, every organ in my body pounded; my legs and arms turned to jelly. There could be no doubt - it was Alastair. He must be - what, 69? - but as upright and handsome as ever.

I don't know how I got home, don't remember which way I went, what I saw, how long it took me. Looking back, I suppose I was lucky to make it in one piece. When I got there, I collapsed into a chair, shut my eyes, and allowed pent-up emotion its freedom. I never cried, though, just wallowed in feelings that could not be thrust aside. There he was, as deep in me as ever, after more than 40 years, a far-from-unhappy marriage, two lovely and talented daughters, a successful career. How utterly, utterly stupid I had been to allow him to cast me off when I knew he loved me like I loved him. How stupid as well to take this trip and allow him to invade my consciousness - physically invade it this time - after all those years of keeping the skeleton locked away in its cupboard.

Then reason asserted itself again. I had the daughters; the career had helped bring positive benefits to many young people - to thousands who were leading productive lives when 40 years ago they would have reached little more than the age at which they could start to read; and Alastair and his West Indian wife had produced someone who was helping carry on that work.

Perhaps strangely, I slept like a log that night, and next day, Sunday, I and my new hiking boots were ready for a ten-mile walk with a couple of neighbours, and enjoyed it. We walked over the Brown Clee, and I revelled in the panorama stretching before me in every direction, including, to the west, the Welsh Marches. My mind's eye shaped the Clun Valley and its offshoots, only twenty miles away, where Alastair was no doubt having his farmhouse Sunday lunch, perhaps with his eldest son, and grandchildren.

Oh, my god. If I had known where he really was, or of the terrible event that day that was to dominate my life in weeks to come.

Twenty Two

Mourning and waiting

Life for me however went on fairly routinely for the next few weeks. My consultancy work continued, busily, but one of the committees in which I was involved went out of existence, not that that made much difference to my work level. I resisted the temptation to revisit Lyndford - it would only re-open the old wound. And I made a few more friends at Clee Marton. Josie visited more or less weekly, Jeannie and Simon when they could.

The old Citroen, much as I loved it, had reached the end of reliable life, I was told, meaning I had to buy a new car, which I obtained from a garage not far from the hospital. One day, I had dropped it off for a service, and was walking back to collect it after my afternoon clinic, when I met my ex-pupil, Emily Jane, with another girl and a young man who looked quite like her.

"Emily Jane - Dr Jameson," I said. "How nice to see you. Is this one of your brothers?"

"Yes, this is Edward - my younger brother. And his wife, Stella. Ed, this is Professor Margerrison, who you've heard about."

The young man held out his hand, and shook mine, and his wife did the same.

"Em's told us about you, Professor. It's very nice to meet you."

I said to her: "What are you doing in Birmingham? I thought you were still at St Thomas's."

They both looked at me, with distress, I thought, not far from their eyes.

"We're going to see my father," she said.

Once again, that heart-wrenching turmoil.

"Is he - in hospital or something?"

She looked down, and caught her brother's hand.

"Yes. He's been there for a month. He and mother had an accident. Mother... died..."

Oh my god. And I'd seen them together, looking so happy.

"Oh, my dear. I'm so sorry. And - your father...?"

"He was very badly hurt. They didn't think he'd make it. And he's been left in a coma. He doesn't seem to know anyone, even us. He's almost better now, in other ways. He had a broken leg, and a fractured skull, and some internal injuries. They're all mending, but..."

"Where is he?"

"At the Royal Birmingham. But I think they'll move him soon, to the neurological unit, as soon as they can be sure his injuries are completely repaired."

Oh, Alastair. My Alastair. He'd been in the hospital where I worked, for all that time, and I didn't know. I had a job to stop the distress showing. In fact I could not, and Emily Jane saw it, and Edward.

She said: "I knew from St. Thomas's that you were working up here somewhere, but I didn't know which hospital, until the other day. I just happened to see your name on a notice board. I was going to try to contact you."

Edward said: "Did you not know about it, Professor - the accident I mean? It was big headlines in the local papers?"

"I've only just started to take them, I'm afraid. But look - have you time to have a cup of tea with me, and tell me more about it?"

Emily Jane said, looking at her brother: "It won't make any difference to Dad. He doesn't know us anyway."

I said I had better collect my car before the garage closed, but I would meet them in a few minutes at the League of Friends tea-room.

I had recovered enough equilibrium to hide my own feelings, and with tea and scones before us I was able to ask what happened.

"They were waiting at a level crossing," Edward told me. "Someone came behind and pushed them straight into a train, an express. A big lorry. The driver was killed as well, and there were people hurt on the train. They don't know why it happened. They've put off the inquest in the hope that Dad will recover and be able to tell them something. He was a Belgian - the driver. Mother died instantly, they told us."

Oh, my Alastair. Their Alastair, of course. But my Alastair. After I'd found him again. Even though he was as far out of my reach as ever, I'd found him, seen what he looked like, could see that he was happy. And then not to know he was in "my" hospital.

The brother and sister told me more of the background to the accident. I think by then they were finding it good to talk to me. Edward had recently started an important job with a highly thought of Birmingham firm of advanced technological engineers, where Stella also worked. The new job meant giving up his hobby of motorcycle racing, which had taken him to the verge of full time professionalism. The Derby-based club to which he had brought many honours was holding a presentation lunch to mark them, and his mother and father, who had watched him race many times, were invited. They were on their way when it happened.

"Professor Margerrison knew Dad at one time," Emily Jane told her brother and sister-in-law.

"When I was very young - still at school," I said. I did not want to go any further. "But your sister has told me a lot about you all, and I felt I knew you. I am terribly sorry."

"Would you like to see him?" she asked. "He wouldn't know you, but if you'd like to..."

"He wouldn't know me anyway. It was a very long time ago - 40 years...but yes, if it's alright, I would like to see him."

Oh yes, please, I must see him. I must say goodbye. And I think my voice must have given something away, for the boy again looked at me searchingly, I thought.

He was in a small room off a general care ward. Emily Jane introduced me to the ward sister, who was quite deferential, although I'd not met her before.

He was apparently asleep, looked quite well though, and forty years or not I'd have known him anywhere for the man who set my soul on fire. All that had happened in those four intervening decades vanished with little more than a glance. I had to summon all my mental resources to stop my features betraying the emotion that surged again.

I wanted to stroke the near-white hair, hold the uninjured left hand, stay there for ever, or until he left me, again. But I knew that these two young people had a greater call on him. They were his flesh and blood. I turned and left the room, sat down outside where the sister came to me and asked: "Can I get you anything, Professor? A cup of tea?"

"You're very kind. But no thank you - I've just had one. I'll be alright."

She stayed close, and I asked: "What can you tell me?"

"Not very much, I'm afraid. He seems quite normal, bodily, except that he has to be fed intravenously, and so on. But he seems to be completely unconscious. Did you... have you... known Mr Jameson well?"

"Quite well, but a long time ago."

She looked at me a little as Edward had. "Would you like to see Dr Richardson? He'll be along in a few minutes, but I daresay I can get you a word with him if I tell him who you are."

I thought that might be unfair on the Jameson family, but I was desperate to know all I could.

The sister picked up a phone and a minute or two later she said: "I'll take you along, Professor."

Richardson was a middle-aged, rather brusque individual who was however quite forthcoming about Alastair - no doubt because I was a fellow professional with, I suppose, some kind of reputation. I told him I had known him years ago but that I knew the family well, as indeed I felt I did.

He explained that he was an orthopaedic surgeon, told me the details of Alastair's broken limbs, thought the internal bruising was not too serious, but it was the brain injury that was now the most worrying aspect of the case, clearly.

"The x-rays don't show any great damage," he said. "But the tests my neurological colleagues have carried out have shown no response to the normal stimulae. There seems to be no intellectual activity. "

"Do they... think there is any chance he will recover?" I asked.

"They just don't know. There have been cases like this where the patient has come out of this apparent unconscious state quite spontaneously. On the other hand, there have been many that have gone the other way."

I thanked him and made my way back to the Jamesons. I told them what Dr Richardson had said. And I added: "I'm in the hospital two or three days a week. Can I help you keep an eye on him?"

Emily Jane said: "Oh, yes please. But what do you think?"

"It's not my field. You're probably more up to date with this kind of thing than I am. I think we can only go on what the experts say. But I know one thing - we must never give up hope."

I could not keep my feelings completely out of my voice, and again I caught Edward looking at me as though wondering what it was about.

I said goodbye to them, and left for home. But I couldn't go there, yet. Still ten miles away, I parked up and let the tears flow.

*****

Even now, weeks after the disaster, Alastair's sons and daughter spent every possible moment with him, but they all had their own lives to live, work to do. Emily Jane, already beginning to be well thought of in genetic fields, where there was much more activity than when I was her age, was following a path almost parallel to my own. Edward had a very responsible job where he was spearheading some advanced technological development. Charles could not take unlimited time away from his farms, and he and his wife Maria had a young family.

For me, it was different. My work, and travelling, still occupied much of my time, but most of it took me near him, and I spent many hours at his bedside, mostly when I thought the family were not likely to be there. They seemed to welcome my interest, although at that stage none of them knew what drove it. I think the hospital people almost came to look on me as one of the family. Certainly they talked as frankly to me as to Edward, Emily Jane and Charles. No doubt also the fact that I was "one of them" had a bearing on how they regarded me.

When no-one else was there, I talked to him. I would say: "Hello, Alastair, my darling. It's me, Angie. I'm here. I'll always be here, my love. I'll never leave you. But come back to me, and the children, please." And sometimes I would talk for longer, telling him how I'd kept my promise, and tried to do some good in the world. I told him about how I'd married, and about my daughters, and how I'd helped Emily Jane become a fine doctor herself, and how much I liked Edward, and Charles. And about my new home, and was looking forward to the day I could take him there, and help him get better. And, again and again, how I loved him.

Was I being disloyal to Bill, who had loved and cherished me through twenty years of marriage, and more? I don't think so. I had been so happy with him, I knew how good he was, how almost everything he did was with my well-being and happiness in mind, and the well-being and happiness of our daughters. In spite of the warning I had felt I must give him, when he asked me to marry him, I quickly came to know that if Alastair had suddenly re-appeared, physically, I would not have deserted Bill. If the thunderbolt, the lightning flash that hit me when I saw him on that hillside field had come before Bill died I would have been rocked as I was a month ago, but I would not have let it divert me from the steady course on which I knew I should continue, of caring for my husband and daughters. At least I trust so. I trust I would have remembered the sacrifice Alastair himself had made when he ordered me to go away and forget him. And that I'd have been able to stick to the principles I'd been brought up in, that made me detest the thought of hopping in and out of relationships, often on not much more than a whim, as it seems so many do today.

Now though it was so different. That was another world. Bill had been gone for years. Alastair had also been left alone, in the most tragic circumstances. As

I wanted to remember Bill, I felt he would always remember Debra, and love her. But I hoped that within his apparently unresponsive mind, that feeling for me, of something even deeper than love, was still there, as mine was for him, and that one day it would come into the open again. So I continued to tell him how much I loved him, day after day.

Eventually, though, I was unmasked, one day when I had spent best part of two hours with him. That time, if I had been a different sort of person you would have said I was praying. So I was, although not to God, or Jesus, or the Virgin Mary. I was praying to every entity that might work to bring him back to his children, and grandchildren, and me. Finally I got up to leave, and, not for the first time, I kissed his forehead. Just as Edward came in, alone.

I couldn't help it. I started to cry. He caught my hand, and held it. After a moment he said: "You... loved him, didn't you?"

"Yes" I whispered.

"All those years ago?"

"Yes. Edward, please..."

"You still do. I can tell."

"Oh, Edward, I'm sorry, I can't help it... I'm sorry... your mother..."

"It's alright. It doesn't matter. Dad and Mum were very happy."

He was quiet, but he still held my hand.

"Do you want to tell me about it? It was before he knew my mother, wasn't it?"

"Yes. I was seventeen."

"I really would like you to tell me about it. It won't hurt my mother, or me. Come and have a cup of tea."

I didn't really want to talk. But I could see the boy was quite desperate to know. And I liked him, very much. It surely could not do any harm.

Seated, with the tea, he said: "You see, there's quite a lot we don't know about Dad's early life. Perhaps Charles and Em don't mind, but I do. We know he was in the air force, in the war, and that's about it, except how he came to marry Mum. We know about that – most of it, anyway. Was he in the air force when you knew him?"

"No, it was just afterwards."

"You don't want to tell me it all, do you? Did you... were you... lovers?"

"Not in that sense. We loved each other, but we never..."

"What happened?"

"Edward, if he hasn't told you, I don't think I should."

"Was it something bad?"

"It was something unfortunate."

"Please tell me, Professor. I won't even tell Charles and Em. I don't think they worry about it like I do."

"Call me Angela, Edward, please."

"Please tell me, then - Angela."

"I think you'll wish I hadn't."

"If you don't, I shall worry about it even more. I knew there was something, you see."

"You mean, something in your father's past that he was not telling anyone about?"

"Well, that he wasn't telling us about, anyway. And since we've met you, I've had the idea, somehow, that it was to do with you."

"Yes, some of it was. I suppose I'd better tell you." And I did, how I had met him, and we fell in love, and he "rescued" my sister, then had been arrested and sent to prison because he had helped smuggle drugs and arms into Britain - although he didn't know drugs were involved - and how he had made me promise to have nothing more to do with him because it would damage my career.

Edward listened to it all, only asking one or two questions to make sure he'd got the chronology right, and bringing out things like my own father's reaction.

At the end, I told him: "You must not think he was bad, Edward. He was just young, and a little reckless, and he was looking for excitement - the police, and the judge at the trial, and prison governors all accepted that. But he had to be punished, to show that society wouldn't stand for that kind of thing, the judge said."

"What did you think about it?"

I looked at my teacup. I couldn't look at Edward. But by now I wanted to talk to him.

"You were right, Edward. I loved him. I loved him more than I can say. I've never stopped loving him. I love him now. But he made me promise to 'cast myself off from him' as he put it, and I really believe he'd have been distressed if I hadn't."

"But you married someone else?"

"Yes, more than ten years later. Bill. I didn't love him, in the way I loved your father, but I didn't want to be just a blue-stocking-type old maid.

He was a dear, kind man, Edward, and he knew about your father. I have no regrets – we were very happy. He died eight years ago, but I have two lovely daughters, twins, about your age."

He said no more, but he caught my hand again, and gave it a little squeeze.

"You didn't know any of this?" I asked.

"No. I don't know whether Mum knew. I expect she did. She had a very rough time before they were married, you know."

"What kind of a rough time?"

"Well, we don't know all the details, but it was obvious that it was absolutely terrible – horrible. It seems she was brought over here from Jamaica by a gang who were recruiting young girls as prostitutes, pretending they were bringing them over for domestic work. When she found out what they really wanted, and she refused to do it, they assaulted her, hurt her very badly. She nearly died, would have done, I expect, if Dad hadn't found her in the road, near his house, and took her in and looked after her."

"And then he married her?"

"When she left hospital she went to stay with my grandmother, apparently, and helped Dad on the farm quite a lot – it was just when he was getting it started. From what you've told me, it must have been quite soon after... prison. They were very fond of each other – Mum and my grandmother, I mean. She talked about her a lot, after Gran died. And before that, Gran told us how good she was with animals, on the farm, and lots more about those times."

It brought back what the landlord at the Cravenbury pub told me. But I did not tell Edward how I had been to Lyndford and seen his mother and father. It was too heart-numbingly close and precious.

We were quiet for a few moments. I said: "Your grandfather and grandmother knew about your father and me, you know."

"Really! How do you know that?"

"They came to see me after Alast – your father – was arrested. I thought they were wonderful. Your grandmother tried to persuade him not to break off so completely with me. She said love was more important than any career."

"Do you think she was right?"

"It had been for her, you know, and your grandfather. But lately, since I've come to know more about all of you, I've made myself look at what might not have happened if he had listened to her. You wouldn't have been born, your father would probably not have become a successful farmer, I might not have helped do worthwhile work for people with terrible diseases, and I wouldn't have had my daughters. And he wouldn't have saved your mother from those awful people, would he?

"Our lives are full of 'what if's', Edward, aren't they? Your father thought that what he was doing, when he said I must have nothing more to do with him, was right. I think we should just accept it."

We were both quiet for another few minutes.

"Do you want to tell your brother and sister? About me, and your father, I mean."

He thought for a while.

"No, I don't think so. Perhaps you'll tell them, sometime. I think that would be better."

I left him to go back to his own commune with his father. I was pleased to have told someone in the family about Alastair and me, and Edward was the right one. There was a little shared something between us, something in common that I did not quite have with the others, even Emily Jane. There could be no question of telling my own two, I did not quite know why, but it did not matter, then. Their own father was more important to them. Perhaps some day.

*****

Over the next week and a half, I continued to see him most days. It was easy to avoid the family, because I could go outside visiting hours. But I met his brother and sister-in-law, and his sister Kathleen, and his son Charles' wife Maria. And a little cockney who said he was Erbie and worked for "Ally" - "the best bloke I ever knew."

"I 'spect yer know 'ow I come to meet 'im, Perfessor" – like my mother and her Scots, he had never lost a London accent you could cut with a knife. "But I can tell yer that if yer searched frew every church and chapel congergation in the country – yerse, and frew the parsons, as well, yew'd never find a more honester man, or a kinder one. E'd no need whatever to offer me a job an' bring me up 'ere – I wuz just a dahn an' aht, in clink. Me an' Connie – that's my wife – we fink 'e's the best chap to work for yew could ever find. An' 'e's more'n that – 'e's a real friend. I mean the sort as'll never let yer dahn, an' never leave yer needin' 'elp."

Kathleen was already known to me and millions of readers through her work as a campaigning and investigative journalist in the field of equal rights and pay for women. She was married to a former MP, Michael Housman, who had lost the seat he had held for many years when he switched from the Labour

Party to the Social Democrats. Their son and his wife were currently working as anthropologists in Bangladesh and Kathleen and Michael were looking after one of their grandchildren while the parents were away. Although I had seen her once or twice on television, and heard her on the radio, Kathleen surprised me when I saw her in the flesh. She was a matronly 67-year-old, much quieter than I would have expected from her feisty reputation. Not surprisingly, bearing in mind their Aunt Billie's activities in her youth, she and their aunt had been great friends.

Peter and his wife Aelwen – she was Welsh – I met early on. He was thinking of retiring from the estate agent and surveying business he had run ever since he left the air force after the war. One of his two daughters, who I did not meet, was going to take it over.

I did not know, at that stage, quite what to make of Maria. She talked a great deal, might almost have been called "mouthy." But I later found that much of it was masking a nervousness she felt in the company of people she thought, usually wrongly, were her intellectual superiors. At home, she was a good mother and farmer's wife, doing all her husband Charles' secretarial work and sometimes helping with physical work outside.

Then of course there was Stella, Edward's wife of less than a year.

She was an assured, confident, competent and attractive young woman who, I was to learn later, had pulled herself up by her own efforts from a humble and poverty-ridden childhood in Manchester to become, at the age of 25, personal assistant to Edward's managing director. I thought she was rather hard, and could not quite understand how he had come to marry her. He was such a warm and understanding boy, also with a little something extra, to my mind, as he had shown when we talked about his father. But there was no sign that they were anything but happy.

They made a fine family, though. Surveying them in my mind took me back to that evening, almost 40 years before, when I met their grandparents, after Alastair's arrest. How I loved them, at first sight, and wished now that they were still around.

Getting to know them, talk to most of them, led me to reveal what only Edward knew up to now. In fact Stella, the apparent hard one, was the first.

It was one day when there were rather a lot of us seeing Alastair and she suggested she and I should go for a cup of tea. To my great surprise, she broached the subject.

"I hope you don't mind, but Edward has told me about you and his father, when you were young," she said in her modulated voice with only a trace of northern accent. "I thought I must tell you I knew."

"It's alright, my dear. He rather wormed it out of me, but I was happy to tell him in the end. It was a secret I'd been carrying myself for a very long time. But I'm glad he's told you. I like Edward very much – as I like all of you. Husbands and wives shouldn't have secrets from each other, should they? Not big ones, anyway."

"Did your husband know about it?"

"Yes, he knew before we were married."

"Edward says you still care for him."

"My husband – Bill – you mean?"

"Well, him as well. But I meant Edward's father – Alastair."

I had to think. Was it right to unburden my soul to this comparative stranger, tied to me though she was in a way she probably could not begin to understand? Had she some ulterior motive in wanting to dig it all out of me?

She saw my hesitation and said, quite softly: "It's alright if you don't want to tell me any more. He hasn't told any of the others. It's just that – oh, I know Edward thinks a lot about it, but he doesn't say much. And as you said, we shouldn't have secrets."

I said: "I think the time has come to tell all of you about it, perhaps. I wouldn't be surprised if Emily Jane has guessed some of it, anyway.

"Yes, I still care for him, Stella. I've never stopped caring, in more than 40 years. And I hope that if he comes out of – this – he'll care for me again. My husband and I were very happy, and I know Alastair and Debra were, too. But he and I had something different, very special. I couldn't get rid of it, even though he told me I must, and I feel somehow it was the same with him.

"I shall tell Edward, when I get the opportunity, that he can tell Emily Jane and Charles about it. Or you can tell him, if you like. Or I'll tell the others, if you and Ed want me to. Whatever."

She reached over and touched my hand. "Thanks, Angela – if I may call you that. I'll ask him what he wants to do. "

Was she after all as hard as I'd thought? Somehow, it didn't look quite like it. I hoped not, for Edward's sake.

He did tell them, at least Charles and Emily Jane. And they took me off into the tea shop and told me they knew, and said it would be wonderful if one day I became even more part of the family. "We think of you as one of us, now," Emily Jane said.

But just as I was beginning to hope, really hope, that my prayers would be answered, and he would come back to me and us all, I found myself besieged by more distress, some of which, or consequences arising from it, has never gone away, and never can.

It was about one of my daughters, but I'm not going to relate it all here. Perhaps in another place, when it's a little further in the past. For now I was just keeping close to Alastair.

Twenty Three

Awakenings

He was moved to the neurological unit adjoining the main hospital, mainly to free bed space. Visiting times were rather limited, but I was able to pull a string or two and see him more or less when I wanted to. And I made a point of getting to know the consultant neurologist, Dr Merrickson.

One day, when I had gone in after my afternoon clinic, I found him there, talking to the ward sister.

He said: "Ah, Professor, I'm glad you've come in. I don't want to raise false optimism, but I think we may be seeing a development. We have detected signs of something stirring in the brain. He appears to respond to changing light, and we think he can feel pain. One of the nurses thinks she saw his eyes open, flicker at least. I'm telling you because you're the first of his regular visitors since this happened. I shall tell his family of course."

I went back to his bedside, sat down and caught his good hand. Was it the fancy of a super-optimist, or did it squeeze mine, ever so slightly? I waited for two hours, until Edward came. I told him what the doctor had said, and about the signs I thought I had detected.

"Oh, Angela..."

I was there again next morning. As I walked in, I was sure his eyes opened and he looked at me. But they closed again, and there was nothing more until I had to go for my clinic. Afterwards I went in again. Sister was there and said: "He seems restless - he's moving about. We've sent for the doctor."

Merrickson came, examined him carefully, told the nurses to watch him closely. "I think something may be happening," he said.

I went away for my clinic. Later Sister said: "He came round, Professor. He actually spoke. We think he said 'Deb.' That was his wife's name, wasn't it?"

I stayed until quite late. All the family came, and Merrickson, who told them what he thought was happening. "There is definitely some brain activity there," he said. "But we can't say yet what it will lead to."

Next morning, I went in before my clinic. Edward, Charles and Emily Jane had been there all night, sleeping in turn in a little room kept for the purpose. The doctors thought they ought to be there in case he recovered complete consciousness and had to be told about their mother. They said he had spoken several times, but to himself, incoherently although distinctly enough.

I went in again at lunchtime. The boys were still there and said he had shown more signs of returning consciousness. The doctors asked them to be patient, but to stay, if they could. If he came round completely, it would be best if he saw his family's faces.   Later, they told me what happened.

He did indeed recover consciousness, about three-o'clock, spoke both their names, and asked : "Is Mum here?"

Edward, having to choose between a lie and the awful truth, could only say: "No, Dad, she can't be here."

Alastair, apparently exhausted by his effort so far, sank back into stupor. In another few minutes however, he woke again, and asked: "Where's Mum? And Em. I want to see them."

By this time, both sons were distraught. They did not know what to tell him. Charles said: "Em will be here just now, Dad," which sadly implied that their mother would not.

Alastair looked at them, and asked: "What's happened? This is a hospital, isn't it?"

"Yes, Dad. You've had an accident."

"Is Mum here as well?"

Again they did not know what to say, and hesitated.

Alastair said: "Has she been hurt?" And when the answer was again silence, he said: "She's - died, hasn't she?"

Their continued silence was enough. But he persisted: "Hasn't she?"

"Oh, Dad," Edward sobbed. And Charles' silence confirmed his brother's answer.

Alastair gave a huge sigh, but said no more. The doctors had appeared by this time, examined him carefully, ushered the boys out and asked them and Sister, who had been present throughout, exactly what had just transpired.

When I joined them, two hours later, he was still apparently unconscious, although emitting that sigh from time to time. Clearly the shock of hearing about Debra had brought a halt to his apparent progress.

Nothing happened over the next few days. I went in to him every time I was in the hospital, often two or three times during the day, but there was no sign of any change. Charles, Edward and Emily Jane were beginning to despair again. As was I, with a succession of near sleepless nights. In the end, I resorted to tablets.

The days turned into weeks. It was nearly three months since the accident. The family were again finding it difficult to see him so often. I offered to make sure I was there every day – I would have liked to have done so earlier but I did not want them to think I was butting in – and they accepted the offer. I spent so much time with him that the hospital staff, I think, came to look on me as more of a relative than his own children. And because of my professional position, there was never any problem about seeing him at any time of the day, or night. I was usually there by ten o'clock in the morning. I kept closely in touch with Charles, Emily Jane and Edward, as well, and tried to make a point of seeing them whenever they were there. None of us ever gave up hope. He was not on life support, except for feeding, because all his organs were functioning, and the doctors continued to say they could see no reason why he should not recover, in time. They had known similar cases where this had happened but the time stretched on to near the end of September.

It was one day in late September. The staff nurse who was going off duty said: "Oh, Professor, there's very good news. He seemed to come round properly, late last night. He wanted to know how long he'd been there, and he asked after the family, and you. And he wanted something to eat. We've phoned Charles. They'll be here soon."

"Are you sure he meant me? Not his wife?"

"Your name's Angela, isn't it? He said: 'Where's Angie? I thought she was here.' "

My heart skipped about a hundred beats, but I managed to say: "Alright if I go in?"

"I think he's asleep now. But it seems to be ordinary sleep, Dr Merrickson says. Of course it's alright."

He appeared to be fast asleep, as Staff said. I sat and watched him for half an hour and more. No young girl in the throes of her first romance could feel more than I felt just then. I was trembling from head to foot.

"Oh, my Alastair, please come back again," I whispered. And after a time I stood up, bent over, put my lips to his forehead.

He awoke, just as though it was the end of an ordinary night, the start of a new day. He looked at me, not in surprise, but with a smile all over his face.

"Angie... I've been dreaming about you. Where've you been?"

"Nowhere that matters, my love. Nowhere that matters. Not now."